TORQUERE PRESS NOVELS

Achilles' Other Heel by Tulsa Brown • Bareback by Chris Owen
Blasphemy edited by M. Rode • Broken Sword by Emily Veinglory
Bus Stories and Other Tales by Sean Michael
Caged by Sean Michael • Catching a Second Wind by Sean Michael
The Center of Earth and Sky by Sean Michael
Chance Encounters edited by M. Rode
Cowboy Up edited by Rob Knight • Date Night by Kathleen Dale
Don't Ask, Don't Tell by Sean Michael
Dust and Violets by Mike Shade
Farr Anderson Lane by Kathleen Dale
Fine as Frog Hair by Sean Michael
Fresh Starts edited by Rob Knight • Gemini by Chris Owen
A Gentleman of Substance by Julia Talbot
Gods and Monsters by Sean Michael
The Happy Campers by Gale Chester Whittington
Honor Bound by Wheeler Scott • In the Strangest Places by Willa Okati
Jumping Into Things by Julia Talbot • Lassoed by BA Tortuga
Latigo by BA Tortuga • The Long Road Home by BA Tortuga Manners and Means by Julia Talbot • Monsters edited by Rob Knight Mysterious Ways by Julia Talbot • Myths edited by Rob Knight Naughty edited by M. Rode • Need by Sean Michael
Night's Kiss by Catherine Lundoff
One Degree of Separation by Fiona Glass
Out of the Closet by Sean Michael
The Peacock and the Firebird by Julia Talbot • Perfect by Julia Talbot
Playing with Fire by Sean Michael • Post Obsession by Julia Talbot
Rain and Whiskey by BA Tortuga • Second Sight by Sean Michael
Shifting and Shifting Too edited by Rob Knight
The Sound of Your Voice by David Sullivan
The Stallion and the Rabbit by Mike Shade
Stress Relief by BA Tortuga • Tempering by Sean Michael
Three Day Passes by Sean Michael • Tripwire by Sean Michael Wheel of Fortune by Julia Talbot
Where Flows the Water by Sean Michael
Winning Hand by Sean Michael

Out of the Closet

Sean Michael

Torquere Press

This is a work of fiction. Names, characters, places, and incidents either are the product of the author's imagination or are used fictitiously. Any resemblance to actual events, locales, organizations, or persons, living or dead, is entirely coincidental and beyond the intent of either the author or the publisher.

TOP SHELF
An imprint of Torquere Press Publishers
PO Box 4351
Grand Junction, Colorado 81502

Cover illustration by Jessamy Falcon
Published with permission
ISBN: 1-933389-41-9
www.torquerepress.com

First Torquere Press Printing: December 2005
Printed in the USA

Chapter One

Retired Gunnary Sergeant Jim "Rock" South put on the right turn signal and turned off the highway. He rubbed his hand over his high and tight -- unlike Dick, there was no way he was letting his hair grow long just because he was out of the service. Twenty years was long enough that a man made habits he was happy with. He glanced into the side mirror, making sure Dick was still behind them in the truck. It wasn't going to be long now. Fuck he was tired.

He'd had to wake Rig about an hour ago to navigate. The blond curls had been resting against his shoulder, Rig's skinny body leaning against him. Maybe not the safest way to drive, but damn it made the time pass more pleasantly. He didn't mind driving, but they'd been pushing it, trying to get to the new house on the coast in good time. Rig wasn't sleeping anyway. It made sense to just press on as hard as possible, him and the kid trading off the extra vehicle with Rig taking catnaps in between. First thing they were going to do was set up the bed and then he was going to fuck Rig until the man fell asleep.

The scenery had changed as they drove in and he swore he could smell the ocean now, the air salty and cool. And greasy. Oh, Jack in the Box.

"Give the kid a call, tell him we're picking up take out at the drive through coming up." They could fuck after they ate.

"Hmm?" Rig blinked over, grey eyes red-rimmed and exhausted, then grabbed the cell. "Oh. Right. Food. You want him to get it while we wait?" Rig didn't wait for his nod, just dialed. "Pretty. Rock wants Jack in the Crack. Get him his favorite -- ultimate cheeseburger -- no lettuce or onions, double fries, chocolate shake."

He grunted and nodded. "Make sure you get Rig something, too," he called out. Not that the kid wouldn't, but Rig needed to know they weren't going to let him continue to live on coffee and cigarettes and oh yeah, he'd noticed the fucking cigarettes were back.

He heard the kid's laugh, saw Rig roll those eyes. Then the phone was turned off, Rig leaning back against him. "I can smell the ocean."

"Yeah. It's going to be weird having it right out the back door. How long you think we have 'til we get there?" he asked as he pulled off, waiting for Dick to go through the drive through.

"This is the north side of town, the house is south. Fifteen, twenty minutes?" Rig gave him a grin. "It doesn't seem real."

He returned Rig's grin, putting his arm around his lover. "No? The drive has seemed real enough."

"God, yes. I'm glad we decided not to stop and see Momma. We'd still be there and have two days of drive ahead of us."

He nodded. "Moving's not a good time to be visiting family." He would have popped Bobby for sure, Rig's asshole brother always a sore point. Tired and ready to get settled as he was? Rock knew he'd have barely managed polite and Rig's Momma deserved better than that.

"You got that shit right, Blue." Rig nodded, shifted restlessly. "I just want things put to rights, you know? Want to see our place, make it good."

They'd only seen the little house on the beach once, when they'd come out to have Rig interview with the Johnson Clinic. They'd made an offer on it and on a bigger place that needed less work about three miles off the coast. None of them had been disappointed when the beachhouse contract stuck, even if it meant fixing things.

"Make it ours." He winked over at his Rabbit. "Fuck our brains out all over the place."

He got a low, sexy chuckle, those grey eyes shining. "Oh, they let retired marines fuck still? You sure?"

He growled softly. "I'd like to see them try to stop me."

There was a honk from behind them, Dick back with the truck and, presumably, their food. His stomach growled just at the thought of it. "All right, let's get this parade in the garage."

Rig nodded, grabbed the little notebook with the printed directions. "Head down through town and then right on Desau. We're the eighth house on the right."

He followed the directions, checking after every turn to make sure the kid was still with them. The houses were far apart, far enough they were going to have their privacy. No more nosy old ladies watching them and complaining about this or that.

"This one here it?" he asked, slowing and putting on the blinkers.

"1293? Yeah. Yeah, Blue. That's ours." The house was white, a little porch on the front, a good-sized carport along the side. He left the Uhaul on the street, figuring it would be easier to not have to back the trailer out again. Dick pulled the truck up and around into the carport as he and Rig got out.

He put his arm around Rig's shoulders, other arm out for Dick as the kid joined them. "Well here we are."

Rig took some of the food bags from Dick so the kid could encourage the dogs into the yard, then he had his men on either side, warm and wide-eyed, all of them looking. "Can you believe it?"

Dick shook his head. "No. But I'm still amazed I get to go to bed with you two every night."

Rig chuckled. "Kid learns slow. Only been doing it for five years."

"He just knows not everyone gets a stud and a slut like us." He gave Rig a wink and nodded. "Well come on, I can't carry anyone over the threshold if we don't get there."

"I hope the utilities are all on." He hid his snort as the kid chuckled. As if Rig hadn't called and checked and fussed and worried for the last month over every little detail.

"We'll manage. There was a fireplace, wasn't there? And a grill out back." They headed up the front steps.

Rig unlocked the door, hit the light switch and the lights came on in the little entryway, the wallpaper faded except for a huge rectangle where a mirror had hung. "Bedrooms to the right, everything else to the left. We're going to like being able to go to the beach from the kitchen."

He nodded and wrapped an arm around each waist and lifted them through the door. "There. It's official."

"Yeah." Rig turned, body pressing against his. "Kiss me. Y'all kiss me and we'll go eat."

Oh, now there was something he could get in line for. The three of them came together, lips open, tongues all tangling together. Three on three. Fucking sweet. He heard one of the bags hit the floor, Rig reaching up and holding on, diving into the kiss.

Yeah. Fucking before eating and then more fucking. He wasn't a stick in the mud, he could change the plan. Dick just moaned, pressed against them, porno noises starting up right on cue. Two hard cocks drilled against him, bodies rubbing and rocking, getting off.

He rubbed back, hands sliding between them to undo zippers and get their pricks all rubbing together. Rig's fingers worked his jeans open, so quick, so hungry, a little cry pushing into his lips. This was what it was all about. This was why they were here. So they could live and love and be together, fucking and kissing and coming. He flicked his thumb across the top of their cocks, the kid going first with a jerk and a cry.

"Blue..." Rig's hand tightened, entire body jerking, pushing into his touch. He waited until both his men came before he let himself go, roaring out his pleasure in them as he came.

"Fuck." Rig leaned, panting, breath hot on his throat.

He purred. "Now there's a welcome fucking home I can live with."

Rig hummed, nodded. "Yeah. Yeah, Blue. Welcome home."

Dick just grinned and gave them both kisses. "Food and then something to sleep on and the coffee maker, yeah? The rest of it can stay put until tomorrow." It was cute, the way the kid was growing up, taking care of them.

"Towels, too. There's a box in the very back of the UHaul with the shower curtain, towels, coffee, that stuff." Of course, Dick had good training with their Rigger.

"All right. We'll eat on the deck. I want to see if I remember it right, if we really can see the ocean right *there*."

Rig nodded, stripping off his t-shirt to clean them all off before they headed back. The kitchen was one of the good things about the house, big and bright, the back door leading out to a little deck that ended on the sand, the ocean huge and blue and there. Rig stopped, blinked. "Wow."

"Fuck, it's closer than I remember. Awesome."

It was. Big and huge and right in their own fucking backyard. And it put a smile a mile wide on his boys' faces.

The sun was setting and Rig settled on the end of the deck, toes digging into the sand, just staring at the water, watching.

He and Dick opened the bags and he got his own meal out, passing Rig's over to Dick. "He needs to eat."

"He will," Dick answered softly. Dick went over, rubbed Rig's shoulders for a minute, coaxing their skinny redneck into digging in, before Dick devoured his own burger.

He nodded, grunted and made short work of his own food. Yeah. They were home and things would be back to fucking normal in no time. Or at least something that passed for normal.

He watched the sun setting in Rig and Dick's eyes as he finished his fries and his shake.

Retirement maybe wasn't going to suck.

***

Rig woke up with the sun, checking on Grimmy and Lucy, then starting the coffee, staring out the kitchen window at the birds, the boats in the distance, the water.

Fucking cool.

He found himself a pair of cutoffs and a shirt from the suitcase Rock had brought in and his sneakers from beside the door, and headed out to the truck. The sun was still low, so it was cool and a little misty. They had a nice little set up -- a slip of private beach with two empty lots on either side so the next neighbor was a ways away. They'd be busy for the next little while, but they had time. He didn't start at the clinic until August and Rock and Dick...

Well, they needed to figure out what all they were wanting to do.

He started unloading boxes, propping the doors open so the air blew through, pouring himself more coffee as he worked, Alan Jackson on the truck radio, loud enough to hear. The house was a little bigger than the one he'd sold in Fayetteville -- they had two bathrooms now.

The bedroom he was going to use as an office was good-sized and their bedroom was huge, but the third bedroom was damned near all closet and they were going to have to build a workshop or a garage or something for his tools, and in pretty short order...

Dick was the first one up, wandering naked into the kitchen, yawning. "Rig? Wow, how long have you been up?"

He leaned over, took a kiss. "Since five or so. Sleep good?"

"I did. It was good to be in our bed instead of smushed up in a hotel double or in the truck." Dick leaned in and gave him another kiss. "Did you sleep?"

"Yeah, some." He brushed their lips together, just sort of enjoying the warmth, the pleasure in Dick's eyes.

"Rock's going to sit on you soon, make sure it's more than just some," Dick noted, licking at his lips.

"His bark's worse than his bite." He leaned a little harder, starting to get a little derailed from the boxes.

"Oh, there's nothing wrong with his bite," murmured Dick, giving him a wink, one hand sliding under his shirt.

"Mmm..." He nodded, belly muscles rippling, loving Dick's touch. "You're trying to distract me."

"No I'm not! I just want to make love."

He laughed softly, arms sliding over Dick's shoulders. "I'm all sweaty and dusty."

He got an unrepentant and so not worried about it grin. "You'll be even more sweaty when we're done."

"Mmm... promise?" The boxes could wait. Their lips met, the kiss sweet and slow for a heartbeat, maybe two, before it got wild, sharp-edged, hungry.

Oh. Oh, yeah.

Dick moaned, pushing him back until his ass hit the counter and then pushing their hips together. "I promise."

He hopped up, sitting on the edge, legs wrapping around Dick's waist. "Mmm... Pretty."

"Oh, I like this setup." Dick's fingers worked his clothes off, sliding warm along his skin.

"Yeah..." It felt amazing -- the doors open, the sun on him, Dick's hands making him hard.

Dick got his shorts off and rubbed against him, their pricks pressing, sliding. The kisses just got hotter, harder, Dick making his own personal fucking porno soundtrack. It made him ache, made him need and Dick just gave it to him. Dick's hand wrapped around their cocks, stroking them together.

"Oh. Yeah, Pretty. Just like that." He let his head fall back, hips moving furiously.

Dick's hand moved faster, mouth latching onto his neck, working up a mark. Just the idea that they could, that he could wear their marks, pushed him right over the edge, spunk spraying.

"Oh, Rig." Dick moaned and came, shuddering.

"So fucking good, Pretty." He leaned forward, nuzzling Dick's shoulder.

"Uh-huh." Dick's hands slid along his back. "We should go back and wake up Rock properly. Then we can get the unloading happening." He was given another kiss. "I'll fuck you while you suck him."

"Mmm... sounds perfect."

Sounded just like home.

***

Dick grabbed three beers and followed his lovers out onto the deck. There were chairs out there now and he sat in one gratefully after handing out the brews.

Everything was in the house, Rock having returned the UHaul and trailer to the local rental office late in the afternoon. He'd followed with the truck, the two of them picking up tacos on the way home for supper. Between the three of them they had all the furniture set out and the bedroom and kitchen organized. Dick realised that boxes against the back wall of the kitchen wasn't quite good enough for Rig, but they had the basics for eating and cooking and he was going to take Rig on a grocery run after sunset. It was pretty damned good for the first day and god knew they'd only gotten as far as they had because Rig wouldn't stop working until it was all done.

Tomorrow was Saturday and Rock had already made 'I'm watching fucking sports' noises and Dick figured they'd pretty much lost him for anymore unpacking. All the heavy stuff had been shifted and the boxes were in their proper rooms though and the man hated the fiddely stuff, so it was all good. He'd help Rig with the rest. If Rig actually went to bed instead of getting it all finished overnight.

"Nice sunset," he commented.

"Hell, yes." Rig stripped off his tshirt and leaned back, swigging his beer, one hand petting Grimmy's heavy fur.

Dick held himself back from reaching out to touch Rig and then remembered that not only were their closest neighbors too far to see, but they didn't have to hide here. Smiling, he leaned forward and ran his hand along Rig's belly.

Rig's eyes went wide, then Rig relaxed, moving toward the touch. "Gonna take a while to get used to that."

"I know." His hand slipped up and he traced the mark he'd left on Rig's neck. "But it's a nice thing to have to get used to."

"Sluts," accused Rock and Dick grinned at him.

"Like you aren't going to leave any marks on him or keep from touching him under the sky."

"You're still sluts."

"Yep." Rig didn't look the slightest bit worried about that, either, all grin and shining eyes.

Rock chuckled and shifted, putting a leg on either side of Rig and snugging up against the lean back. Dick grinned and watched them, stroking Rock's side as well as Rig's belly. Sexy motherfuckers. Rig looked happy, stretched out, thighs snugged up to Rock's, head leaned back. He shifted himself and leaned forward, bending to take the ringed nipple in his mouth.

"Oh..." Rig moaned, near empty beer bottle clattering to the deck.

Rock purred, hand on the back of his head, keeping him where he was. Rock needen't have worried, he wasn't going to stop, not with Rig writhing beneath him. Rig's hips started rocking, rubbing back into Rock, soft little sounds escaping. Dick pushed his hand into Rig's jeans, grinning around the nipple in his mouth as he met Rock's hand, the thick fingers working open Rig's zipper.

"Y'all..." Rig arched, moaning low. "Damn..."

He hummed happily and Rock purred, the sound low and sexy. Dick shifted, letting the hot little ring slide from his mouth with Rig's nipple and then moved down, licking his way to Rig's belly. Rock tilted Rig's head up, took that talented mouth, Rig arching between their lips.

He smiled as Rig's cock nudged his chin and he turned his head, sucking the tip in between his lips. Even muffled in Rock's kiss, he could hear Rig's little cry. Rock's hands were sliding on Rig's chest, teasing as he sucked at Rig's cock, taking his time before he deep throated the hard flesh. Rig was sweet, hot on his tongue, hard and stroking, pushing. One hand fell on his head, petting him.

He hummed happily, getting louder as one of Rock's hands slid over his head as well, petting. He pushed his hand into Rig's jeans to get to Rig's balls, cupping and holding them.

"Oh. Oh, damn. Pretty." Rig moved a little faster, fingers tightening in his hair.

He opened wide and let Rig take his mouth, lips still working the suction, dragging against Rig's cock every time his lover pulled out.

"Oh, fuck..." Rig started humping, bucking, pushing back into Rock.

"That's it, kid. You've almost got him." Rock's voice was gravelly, hungry.

"A...almost. Oh. Oh, fuck. I..." He glanced up, seeing Rig's grey eyes wide, happy. It made him suck harder, finger pushing back behind Rig's balls to tap at his hole. Rig jerked, cock pulsing, spunk pouring over his tongue. He swallowed it down, that flavor familiar and right and good, making him know he was home even if everything else around him was unfamiliar. Their own personal redneck leaned back into Rock, eyes closing. "Damn."

He grinned and leaned up to share the taste of Rig with Rock, moaning at the way Rock's tongue swept hungrily through his mouth. Rig's hand wrapped around his waist, fingers drawing little designs in the small of his back. He shivered and pressed against Rig's belly; it felt damn good.

"Yeah..." Rig's mouth slid over his shoulder, teeth just teasing.

"Oh, fuck, I need." He rubbed against Rig's belly, Rock's lips taking his again, devouring him. Rig's mouth and hands sent electric shocks to his spine and down to his cock.

Rig rocked back and forth between them, giving them both something to rub against. Rock's moan pushed into his mouth and it made him jerk and hump harder, close. Rock's fingers met Rig's on his back and then slid up his spine, teasing and warm. "Come on, Pretty. Give it up. You know you want it."

He cried out, rippling against Rig as he filled his jeans.

"Mmm..." Rig's hum mingled with Rock's smug chuckle, just like that.

"You're next," he warned Rock.

"You say that like it's a bad thing, kid." Rig chuckled, hips rubbing, teasing Rock.

Rock purred. "You gonna show me what that mouth can do, Rig?"

"I could show you what my mouth can do, Rock."

"I'll take you both on." Rock was still looking damned smug.

Rig purred, sliding down Rock's body, fingers pushing the sweatpants down. "Greedy. You already got one blow today..."

Dick hid his grin as Rock answered. "You got a point, Rig?"

Rig licked the tip of Rock's prick, tilting his head. "Hmm..."

He did chuckle this time, pushing Rock's legs further apart so he could settle in next to Rig and do some licking of his own. Rig licked at his lips, at Rock's prick, humming low the whole time. He met the licks with his tongue and pressed Rig's lips for a kiss, trapping Rock's cock between.

"Oh, Fuck, yes!" Rock was enthusiastic about that.

Rig was happy, laughing, he could see it in those eyes, feel it in the vibrating kisses. He licked Rig's lips one more time and made his way down Rock's massive cock to lick at Rock's balls, taking one in his mouth. Rig shifted, head bobbing, taking Rock in deep, pulling hard enough the thin cheeks hollowed.

Rock was groaning and moaning, those big hands dropping to his and Rig's heads, hips starting to pump. They both knew exactly how to give Rock what he needed and they did it, pulling and sucking and humming. It wasn't long at all before Rock was roaring, giving it up to Rig's mouth.

Rig cuddled against Rock's belly, eyes closing, hand stroking that stunning six-pack. Smilling, he looked up at Rock, those blue eyes smiling down at him fondly. Rock petted his belly beside Rig's head and Dick took the hint, lying nose to nose with Rig against the warm muscles.

Very nice sunset indeed.

***

Third day in a row since they got here Rig was up past midnight. The man would work through the night if he could get away with it. Well not on Rock's watch.

Rock got out of his shower, swatted the kid, who was brushing his teeth, on the ass and headed for the kitchen, which was where the cowboy music was coming from. "Bedtime, Rabbit."

Tired, tired grey eyes met his, but he got a slow, warm smile. "I'll be in in a bit, Blue Eyes. I'm just puttering."

"No, I think you'll be in now. The kid's brushing his teeth, we're both naked. All that's missing's our skinny redneck."

"I'm not skinny." Rig winked and turned to wash the newsprint ink off his hands.

He snorted. Compared to him and the kid, Rig was a stick. "Does that mean if I tell you to get your skinny ass over here so I can fuck it, you won't come?"

"Blue, if you're fucking my ass, you'll drill me until I come, I guarantee it."

"Exactly, so why aren't you over here, encouraging that to happen?" He spread his arms out, showing how they were empty. Rig was half-way across the room before Rock figured his Rabbit even started thinking. Chuckling, he wrapped his arms around Rig. "Took you long enough," he grumped good-naturedly.

"Oh, you feel good..." That sharp chin lifted, begging a kiss. He gave it willingly, tongue splitting Rig's lips and pushing in. His Rig just melted against him, moaning for him, opening up. There. No more thinking about the fucking boxes.

He grabbed that sweet ass up and headed down the hallway, hoping like fuck he took the right turn into their bedroom. Rig wrapped those long legs around him, holding on.

Dick came out of the door he turned into. "Oh, you've got him, good. Bedtime."

They headed down one more door and into the bedroom and he didn't let go of that sweet mouth the entire time. Rig was humming, all happy octopus Texan, tongue sliding against his own. The bedroom was full of boxes, but the big, big bed was there, made, their pillows piled up for them.

He put Rig down, following, rubbing against too fucking many clothes. He could always trust the kid to be on top of something like that though, Dick was already working on buttons. Rig never let him go, stealing his breath, kisses deep and lazy and hot. Dick's hands slid over him, over Rig, leaving shivery sensations behind. Rig moaned, arching up into him.

"Lube, kid," he muttered.

"Yeah, I'm with you." Dick's fingers slid between them, slick and sliding toward's Rig's balls, pushing beyond them.

It was telling how tired his Rabbit was, the slow, easy way Rig moved, eyes closed, mouth sliding over his throat, his jaw. Should make fucking him into oblivion pretty fucking easy. Not that it was ever a *chore* to fuck Rig. No, that was necessary like breathing.

"Mmm... my Blue..." Rig licked the hollow of his ear, moaning low.

"Nope, that's the kid's fingers in you." The tease would have been more effective if he hadn't been moaning.

"Yeah... gonna be you. Gonna be your cock..." A soft gasp tickled his ear.

"You know it." He was going to fuck his Rabbit, good and hard and right.

"Yeah..." Rig's leg wrapped around his waist, one hand reaching for the kid.

He nudged at Dick's fingers and they slid away, wrapping around Rig's cock as he slid into that sweet, tight ass.

"Oh." A man could live a whole lifetime on a sound like that. A whole fucking life.

Dick moaned softly. "Fucking sexy, the pair of you. Want you, Rock."

He nodded as he started to move. "Take what you need, kid."

Rig was giving up noises and cries, fingers sliding over his head, bringing their lips together. He sank into the kiss, tongue plundering Rig's mouth, filling himself with the taste. Dick's long fingers slid into him. First one and then another, letting his own movements pull them in deep.

Rig's body pulled him in, rippled around his cock, so fucking hot. He groaned, buried deep inside Rig, stilling for Dick. Rig panted as Dick pushed in, filling Rock, stretching him with that long cock. Rock groaned, placing long kisses over Rig's face and then they were moving again, like a three headed animal, smooth and wanton.

"Oh... Oh, sweet fuck, Blue."

"Yeah, that's what we're doing, Rig. Sweet fucking." He groaned as the kid nailed his gland. "Fuck, Dick. Right fucking there."

Rig moaned, eyes blinking open to watch them. "So fucking fine. My men."

He moaned and bent to kiss Rig, his own cock shifting inside the tight body and making Rig jerk. Rig groaned, moving faster, riding his prick. Dick fucked him and he fucked Rig and it was fucking perfect, just like it ought to be.

Lips brushed his, Rig panting, needing, squeezing his cock. "Blue..."

He worked a hand between them, wrapping it around Rig's hot prick. "Yeah, Rabbit. Show me how good it is. Come on my cock."

Fuck, he loved that cry, the look in those eyes, shocked and needy and happy and it was all his fault. Rig's ass went tight tight around his cock and he groaned, moving hard for a few more thrusts, roaring as his ass squeezed around Dick's cock, his own pushing spunk deep into Rig. Rig's hands held him close, eyes closing.

He held most of his weight off his Rabbit, Dick lying against him for a few moments before slipping out and curling up next to Rig. He came out himself and collapsed on the other side of Rig, sandwiching the man good and tight between him and the kid.

Rig snuggled into his chest, fingers twined with Dick's, holding them all together. "I ought to finish the..." The words were interrupted by a yawn, Rig cuddling in deeper.

"Sleep," he grunted, one leg going over Rig's.

"Yeah, sleep," agreed Dick, one of his legs sliding over Rig, too.

"Mmm..." Rig settled, soft little snores starting almost immediately.

He grinned and met Dick's eyes. "That'll do him for awhile."

Dick chuckled. "At least an hour or two."

"Well then we'll just have to fuck him again."

Such a hardship. Dick's soft laughter was the last sound he heard before he drifted off

***

It took him a full week to get rid of all the boxes. Would have been less, but his men kept distracting him.

Cocks.

Lips.

Bellies.

Asses.

Shining eyes.

"Want you, Rabbit."

"My turn, Rig."

What was a guy supposed to do?

He'd gotten up bright and early and taken the dogs down to the beach, walking and walking, planning his day, most of which involved putting a brisket in the oven, making a chocolate pie and deciding whether they wanted a garage or a workshop and whether to build that or fix the deck first.

He finally turned back and as he approached the house, he could see his ex-marines on the beach, tossing a football back and forth, Rock making Dick run all over the place for it. Rig whistled, applauding and admiring. "Lookin' good, boys!"

Rock flexed for him, muscles nicely outlined in his wifebeater. Dick grinned and ran toward him, as if he was going to do a full on tackle, making the dogs start barking and running. He chuckled and took off. He might be skinny, but he was fast. Well that got Rock into it of course and his men worked together, Dick coming around from one side and forcing him right into Rock's path. His Blue tackled him, managing to twist so that solid body went down beneath his.

"Oof." He laughed, landing hard, his body settling right into Rock's. "Mornin', Blue."

"Good morning, Rig. Fancy meeting you here."

Dick threw himself down beside them, panting, the dogs trying to lick his face.

"Took myself walking. Pretty view." He made a show of looking at his men. "Not near as pretty as here..."

Rock rumbled for him, chest vibrating beneath him. "Flattery will get you nailed in the sand."

"That would chafe, you sexy motherfucker." Rig winked and licked Rock's lips. "What would the fact that I have brisket and a chocolate pie planned for supper get me?"

"Chocolate pie -- shit, I'll let you fuck me for chocolate pie."

Dick laughed. "Oh man, we're going to have chocolate pie for days and days."

Rig got tickled, started cackling, face snuggled into Rock's throat. Fuck, this was nice, touching and shit, the sun on him. The dogs started barking again, trying to lick and Rock sat up, bringing him with. "That's mine to lick, Grim. Get your own."

That sent Dick into gales of laughter, his Pretty rolling in the sand.

Rig admired Dick for a long moment, then smiled up at Rock. "The beach suits him."

Rock smiled back, eyes speaking volumes. "Suits you, too. This was a good choice."

He nodded, reaching up to cup Rock's jaw. "Yeah, Blue. We earned this."

Rock grunted. "You got that right."

He leaned, licking Rock's lips, their bellies rubbing together. Rock purred for him, hands going to his waist.

"Mmm... morning Blue." He reached out for Dick, drawing his Pretty into the kiss. The three-way kiss was sweet and lingering. Dick's hands sliding with Rock's on his back. They ended all leaned together, breathing together. "You derailed me. I had a little list."

"I've got a list of my own," Rock told him.

Dick chuckled. "Morning blow job. Fuck the kid. Fuck Rig. Watch the kid and Rig fuck."

Rock whapped him. "Smartass."

"What? Did I get it in the wrong order?"

Rig laughed. "Mine was whether we were going to build a garage or a workshop."

"I like mine better." Rock grinned at him and took a hard kiss before standing, hauling him along.

He stumbled behind, feet barely on the sand. "Neanderthal!"

"I still don't know what that means, Rig. Though I'm guessing sexy assed fucker." Rock slowed a little, giving him a wink as Dick brought up the rear, chuckling.

Rig rolled his eyes, finding his spot under Rock's arm and snuggling in. "My sexy assed fucker."

"You got that right."

Dick grabbed both their asses, giving them a pinch. "And both these sexy asses are mine!"

He squeaked and Rock tackled and the dogs started barking and fuck. Fuck, it was fine. Happy. Right. Rock and Dick rolled around in the sand until Dick called "Uncle!" and Rock helped him up and then he had two sand covered lovers headed straight for him.

He sprinted for the hose, getting it turned on in time to spray them both. Lucky, because that bought him enough time to run for the house and get himself locked in the bathroom. When pounding on the door earned them no results he could hear Rock suggest they go take the window off from the outside.

"No way, use your imagination!"

"What're you talking about, kid?"

Dick chuckled and then the sound was muffled, as if by a kiss. There was a thump against the door, but it wasn't a fist pounding.

"Oh, man. No fair!" He washed his hands, his feet, listening.

Dick's sweet porno noises started up, followed by a low moan from Rock.

Oh, bastards.

Beautiful bastards.

He unlocked the door, stripping first. The door opened, revealing his lovers, buck naked and humping together.

"Pervs." He reached out, hands sliding over them.

They broke off their kiss, Dick going for Rock's neck, Rock giving him a wide grin. "We're just trying to get into the bathroom."

"Uh-huh. Sure you were." He shook his head, one hand on each ass.

"It worked didn't it?" Rock asked as Dick rubbed back into his hand.

"You're not in the bathroom..." He pressed closer, face lifting for their kiss.

Rock let Dick kiss him, his Blue manhandling them into the bathroom. "We are now."

"Mmm..." They'd already talked about putting in a bigger shower, one with a seat and a detachable shower head and... "Yeah."

"And we'd better get in the shower if you don't want your nooks and crannies full of the sand I'm sporting."

Dick laughed softly, moving to turn on the shower.

"I have nooks and crannies? Is that a medical term?"

"I don't know if it's medical or not, but I am very familiar with your nook and your cranny."

He started chuckling, hands reaching up to hug his Blue.

Dick was giggling, pushing them into the shower. "Damn this is smaller than the one back home. Oh -- that's going to take some getting used to."

"We've got enough saved back to make some improvements, Pretty, if we do it ourselves."

"Hey if we do it ourselves, we don't have to explain why we want certain things!"

Rock snorted. "You been playing on the internet again, kid?"

"You say that like it's a bad thing." He leaned back into Dick's arms.

Rock chuckled. "Not bad. Just hard on my credit card."

He grabbed the soap, rubbing Rock down. "So you want a garage or a workshop, Rocketman?"

"You're only making the one or the other?" Rock purred for him, arching under his touches.

"Well, if we do both, I won't have the money to extend the deck and build the brick grill until next spring." He was happier than a pig in shit -- Rock's body under his hands, Dick's body supporting him, the water falling around them.

"Woah, slow down, Rabbit. We've only been here a week."

Dick was chuckling, hands sliding on him like his were sliding on Rock.

"I know, but I only have seven weeks of vacation left and I'll be busy once I have clients..." He circled Rock's nipples, tugging a little. Rock just groaned in reply, body moving toward him.

"Mmm... " He tugged harder, thumbs sliding over the tips. Rock growled softly, legs spreading a little, going into parade rest, cock going from interested to wanting. "Oh. So fucking fine..." He licked his lips, admiring, wanting, eyes trailing over that fat cock.

"Fuck, the two of you look good together." Dick was purring, rubbing up against him.

"As if anyone could look fine between you two." He soaped up Rock's dark pubes, fingers weighing those heavy balls. "I'm the luckiest fucking redneck on earth."

"You're both lucky," Rock told them with a grin. He nodded, started to pump that hard cock. Rock groaned for him, nice and low and sexy. He hummed, licking and lapping at whatever skin he could reach. Dick was returning the favor, mouth on his back, sucking along his spine.

"Mmm..." He rippled, mouth open, gasping a little. Rock chuckled, fingers teasing his nipples, tugging on the little ring. He shuddered, eyes flashing up into pure blue.

Rock smiled down at him, tugged a little harder. "Gonna make you fly."

"Yeah? Promise?"

"Have we ever let you down?" Rock asked, Dick chuckling against his spine.

"Never once." He grinned, stretched. "Was made for this."

Rock chuckled. "Not sure your Momma would agree with that..." He was given a wink, Dick spluttering behind him.

"Isn't there some law against mentioning Momma when we're fucking?"

Rock's hand circled his prick, pumped. "Doesn't seem to have done you any harm."

He laughed, shaking his head and grinning. "Just when I think I'm immune to the Rocketman wit..."

"Impossible," Rock informed him tartly.

Poor Dick was choking on his laughter, leaning against his back.

"Damned straight, Blue. Im-fucking-possible."

"Nothing straight in here," murmured Rock with another wink.

"Oh, Fuck," gasped Dick. "Kiss him before he says anything else."

He chuckled, fucking in love with the shine in Blue's eyes. "No, sir. Not a single fucking thing."

Rig brought their lips together. Rock was ready for him, tongue pushing in deep, purr filling his mouth. He stepped closer, arms wrapping around Rock's neck. Hello. Those big hands slid around his waist, tugging him even closer, Dick following along like his Pretty was glued to his back. Oh, yeah. He moaned, so fucking happy, so hot.

"Gonna fuck his ass, kid? Get it good and ready for me?" Dick hummed at Rock's words, fingers sliding along his ass. Rig spread, leaning against Rock, a low moan leaving him. Rock's hands slid over his hips, moving slowly, heading straight for his hole. As soon as one of Dick's fingers pushed into his ass, two of Rock's joined it. That made Dick moan, the sweet porno noises starting up.

"Oh..." He arched, entire body rippling, spreading, pulling those fingers in.

"Sweet slut," purred Rock.

Dick nodded, mouth on his neck, another finger pushing into him. Rock and Dick's fingers moved, but not together, keeping the pressure against his gland almost constant, the stimulation incredible. He was caught, blinking, gasping, panting, tongue sliding over Rock's skin. Dick pushed in another finger, making it five he was riding, both Rock and Dick groaning, holding him tight between them.

"Oh. Oh, fuck. I... Fuck." He couldn't hold his eyes open, couldn't catch his breath.

Rock grunted. "Get the lube, kid."

Dick's fingers slid away and Rock slid two more in, keeping him stretched, open. He kept moving, quick little jerks, entire body focused on the pleasure. Then Dick was back, slicking up Rock's fingers, making them glide easily in and out of his body. Dick started adding his fingers in again, one at a time.

"I..." Oh, sweet lord in heaven. He lost track of how many fingers were in him, but he was soon fuller than he could ever remember being, one finger after another stroking across his gland, sliding along his hole.

"You're something else," murmured Dick.

He met Blue's eyes, words lost, good sense gone, trusting in his men to hold him, guide him.

"Yeah, kid's right. Something else," murmured Rock, eyes holding his.

Yours. Yours. Please. Oh, fuck. So much. So full. All that escaped him was a low groan, the sound broken and needy.

"Cock," growled Rock, dropping carefully to his knees. Fingers still holding him open as Dick's disappeared again, Rock's mouth took his cock in. A moment later Dick's cock pushed in with Rock's fingers, spreading him. He keened, nerves overwhelmed, entire body shaking as he came, shooting into Rock's mouth.

Rock kept sucking him, taking every last drop he had to give as Dick filled him over and over again with that long prick, sharing the tight passage with Rock's figners. He didn't think he even got soft, pleasure just ratcheting up and up and up until he shorted out, nothing more than cock and ass and need. Dick's mouth was hot on his neck, breath loud in his ear. Rock's was hot, burning around his cock. His fingers were sliding on the tile, trembling, gasping for air. Rock hummed around his flesh as Dick moved harder, faster, one hand coming up to find the ring in his nipple and tugging, twisting.

"Oh!" His body jerked, tightening.

Rock pulled harder, fingers spreading him wider. He was open and filled, surrounded, taken by them. His groan was meant to be a scream, but he didn't have the breath for it, not and come, too.

Rock swallowed him down again as Dick's cock throbbed and filled him deep with heat. Soft whimpers sounded as Dick collapsed against his back, cock sliding away along with Rock's fingers.

His knees buckled, unable to hold him up. Rock caught him, standing and supporting him and Dick both.

"I'm supposed to be the old man here," Rock pointed out, fingers warm on his skin.

"Never be too old to catch me." He believed that with all he was.

Rock chuckled. "That's because you want to be caught."

He nodded, snuggling right in. Hell, yeah.

The water fell around them, curtaining them in warmth as they rested against each other, home and happy and together.

Chapter Two

Rock pulled up into the carport, put the truck in park and slammed the door behind him. He didn't care if the kid was following or not. He needed a fucking beer. He let the front door slam behind him, too. Sometimes it just felt good to make a little fucking noise. He grabbed a longneck out of the fridge, the twistcap giving way easily and drank half of it down before heading out to stand at the railing of the deck and watch the waves.

He had to admit, it was a nice view. He supposed it was a good thing he thought so as he was obviously going to be seeing an awful fucking lot of it.

He heard the kid come out, his empty bottle was taken, a full one put in its place and then Dick sat on the stairs, looking out, too. It didn't take too long before he heard Rig's steps, hands falling on his shoulders. "Bad news?"

"No loan. No gym. We aren't interested in lending you the money." He took another swig of beer, bristling.

"That's not exactly what they said, Rock."

"It's pretty fucking close, kid."

Dick sighed.

"What exactly did they say, Pretty?" Rig's hands started massaging.

He could feel Dick's eyes on him as the kid started to speak. "They said that it was a risky venture -- we'd need to renovate, build a clientele, neither of us had any experience running a gym and the only way they'd --"

"They weren't going to give an old fart like me and a young kid a loan without collateral," he put in before the kid could say it.

"Not without --"

"Collateral."

He could feel Dick's eyes on him, but he wouldn't look at the kid. Or at Rig. Over forty fucking years old, twenty years in the marines and he wasn't good enough to risk a loan on.

"So, we'll put Grampa's land up against it. That's three hundred acres. It's worth a pretty penny." Rig's hands kept working. Rig and his brother and sister had inherited that land years ago -- right after he and Rig had met -- and Rig had bought Sissy and Bobby out, keeping the land in the family.

Dick nodded. "That's what they said. We needed a co-signee who had collateral."

He glared at the kid, but Dick just stared back, unfazed. "You don't have to take on that kind of debtload for me, Rig. We'll find another way." He could hire himself out as a bodyguard. When his old CO'd heard he was headed for California, he'd been given a couple of numbers, told it was decent money. He and the kid could work a few years, add to the downpayment, prove themselves in the community. The mere idea that he needed to prove himself after his years in the service made him bristle all over again.

He'd paid his fucking dues.

"Well, let me grab the paperwork and we'll head back." Rig's lips brushed his shoulder. "I didn't hitch my wagon to yours only for the simple stuff, Jim. You deserve this."

He shook his head, back straight. "The house at the base was yours. This one is yours. I think I live off you enough, Rig, without adding this."

"So we make him a silent partner," murmured Dick. "And we pay out shares three ways once we're making a profit. Fifty percent for him, forty precent for you, ten for me -- whatever the numbers add up to. He's not offering you charity, Rock. He's offering a business deal."

"This house is ours, you stubborn bastard." Rig nudged his shoulder with that chin. "And we're putting y'all on the deed today, too. I'm tired of you going on about living off me. You've never not carried your weight and we both know it. This isn't about money, Blue, it's about our future and shit."

"A man has his pride."

Dick nodded. "Rig's got a point though. Money in or not, wills or not, if our names aren't all on paperwork? It could be a problem. The bank will give us that loan in a minute with the kind of collateral Rig's talking about and you know it. And you know we're going to make a go of it -- you're too stubborn not to."

He shook his head and turned to look Rig in the eyes. "Stubborn as I am, you do know there's a chance this gym thing isn't going to fly, right? You could lose that land. You thought about that?"

"Yep." Those grey eyes were sure as shit, not even a little bit of doubt.

"Rig, I'm serious. I can swallow my pride long enough to admit the bank's got a point about it being a gamble, building a business from scratch."

"So it's a gamble. God knows I never make those." One white eyebrow lifted. "Never picked up a marine in a bar. Never followed his ass across country. Never threw myself out of a bird. I'm not a child, Rock. I wouldn't make the offer if I didn't want to."

"Oh, don't look at me like that. You want to risk your grandfather's land; I'm not going to stop you. But we're going to do like the kid said and draw up a partnership agreement and we'll pay the bank back as soon as we can so that land stays off the auction block."

Dick was watching them with an amused look.

"What?" he growled.

"Oh, nothing. You'd need a knife to cut the pride on this deck, it's so thick."

"Nothing wrong with a little pride, kid."

"Not saying there is."

"Nothing wrong with pride at all." Rig's hand slid around his neck, pulled him into a hard kiss. "Come on, let's go make those bastards at the bank squirm."

"We could show them the deed to the land and then go across the street to their competition." He'd like to rub that kid's nose in it.

"Fuck, yeah. Let me put my good jeans on and you can take me out to eat after to celebrate."

"The tight ones." He nodded. Yeah. All right, things were definitely taking a turn for the better.

Dick gave him a grin and he punched the kid in the arm. "What are you grinning about?"

"I'm just happy."

"Uh-huh."

Dick nodded. "Uh-huh."

He grabbed the kid around the neck and gave him a noogie, letting Dick up to kiss the soft lips. "Come on. Let's get this done."

***

Dick followed Rock and Rig into the surf and turf restaurant, grinning at the swagger in Rock's walk. They'd gone to the notary first and Rock hadn't grumbled once, letting Rig have their names put on the house and land deeds. Dick didn't have the same pride issues Rock did. Not that he wasn't proud, but it wasn't one of the pillars of his character, it had been beaten out of him as a kid and only the marines and Rock and Rig had helped give it back to him.

He also knew if Rig died and their names weren't on the deeds? Someone in Rig's family could make trouble. And while Momma and Sissy and any of the kids wouldn't dream of it? He'd bet a pretty hefty sum that Bobby'd be more than pleased to kick up a whole lot of trouble over it. Rig's no-good brother hated all three of them just because they were gay, Rock maybe most because those big fists had done a number on Bobby a few Christmasses back.

The notarizing had gone without a hitch and the expression on Charlie Ribbon's face when he'd seen the deeds, and then again when they'd walked out, had been priceless, putting Rock in an excellent mood through the rest of the day. The competition across the street had treated them like royalty and before the day was out they'd secured a loan to buy and renovate a building and start up the business. He and Rock were going to own a gym. It was a good thing he didn't have the same pride issues as his lovers or he would be feeling guilty for continuing to ride on their coattails.

They sat out on the back porch of the restaurant, the sun setting spectacularly for them. It was still a huge treat, being able to watch the sun go down over the waves. Rock ordered steak and shrimp and beer all around, charming the pants off the waitress.

Rig looked satisfied as hell, leaned back in the chair, watching Rock. The man was wearing a black tshirt and skin-tight jeans, black boots tapping along with the music. "Did you see the look on that pissy little loan manager's face at the bank? And when we told him we'd be moving all of our business across the street?"

Rock chuckled. "Was almost better than pounding him into the dirt would have been."

Dick just watched them both, hard as nails and about as in love as a guy could be.

"Oh, with critters like him, you gotta hit 'em where it hurts. He'll remember losing the money, mark my words."

Rock nodded. "And I've been doing my research -- a gay-friendly gym will do well in this town. Especially if we make the ladies feel welcome as well. There's a studs only place down the road apiece that's the only immediate competition."

Dick hid his smile. Rock's research had consisted of poking him until he'd done it.

"You gonna have classes and machines and shit?" Rig's leg reached out, toe rubbing his ankle."

"We haven't decided on the classes yet, but the kid and I'll act as personal trainers 'til we're doing well enough to hire out help. And yeah, machines, weights."

"Whirpools," he added to Rock's list, smiling at Rig.

"Ooh! That sounds fun." Rig winked, downed half his beer.

"The kid and I have discussed it at length. We've got a business plan and everything. We didn't just walk into that bank with some pipe dreams."

"No, Rock, we didn't. And now we've got the loan and we can get started. Did you see the sheets on the properties Marlene pulled out for us? There's a couple of good potentials there." Marlene had found them the house and they were sticking with her for the purchase of the gym. They could have rented, but that made renovations more expensive and in the long run, this would keep their costs down.

He leaned back in his chair so he could run his own foot along Rig's leg, rubbing the man's calf.

"The beaches," answered Rock, eyes on Rig, voice low. "That's where the trendy stores are and stuff, lots of them have rainbows in their windows." Rock rolled his eyes, but Dick knew that would play a part in the success of the gym.

Rig nodded. "Nothing wrong with that, Rocketman. I think y'all will do fine."

"Gonna make you proud, Rigger -- wait and see." Their waitress brought their salads, Rock making a face. "I didn't order this, ma'am."

"It comes with the meal, hon."

"Well that's a good way to ruin a nice piece of meat."

She laughed. "Shall I take it away, sir?"

"Thank you."

Dick was biting his lip hard to keep from laughing.

"Hell, I'll take it." Rig's eyebrows appeared over the glasses. "I'll share my potato with him to make up for it."

Dick chuckled.

"It's a deal," Rock said, smiling wide. Oh, their Rocketman was feeling all cock of the walk. He and Rig were going to be well-fucked by morning.

Rig split Rock's salad between the two of them, the action natural and easy, no thought to it, Rig keeping the green peppers because he didn't like them. Rock held court until the meat came and then the serious business of eating began.

In the end, Rock ended up with half Rig's steak and he got a huge chunk of potato because Rig wanted blackberry cobbler. With ice cream.

Rock was teasing him. "Well we'll have at least one customer."

Dick was back to watching, loving the interplay between them, the ease over a decade of loving brought. Rig rolled his eyes, hands pressing against that flat-flat belly. "I'm thinking I'll keep my figure for a week or two."

"We've got alternative ways of working off any excess calories anyway," Dick suggested with a grin and a wink.

Rock laughed. "You're right. I'll have a piece of chocolate pie."

"Won't be as good as mine." Rig winked at the waitress. "And I'll need coffee, too, please ma'am."

"Maybe not, but it's still chocolate pie." Rock patted his belly. "I suppose you want to go dancing after this."

Rig tilted his head, cheeks just pinking. "I hear there's a friendly bar off the highway. Plays a little cowboy music..."

Rock groaned and rolled his eyes. "It's supposed to be a celebration."

Dick smiled at what, for Rock, was an easy acquiescence.

Rig leaned over, just brushing Rock's thigh with one hand. "There's pool for you and the kid, Rocketman. I'm not too old to find a cowboy to swing me around the floor."

Rock grumbled. "The kid and I'll fill your dance card for the slow songs."

Dick smiled. "And I can two-step a song or two with you."

Rig smiled, looking happy and peaceful. "Y'all spoil me."

"That's what we're here for, isn't it?" Dick asked.

"That and morning blow jobs," added Rock.

Rig chuckled. "And the chocolate pie."

"You know it." Rock nodded and then winked. "Not to mention the looking studly."

Rig gave Rock one of those looks -- and he knew all about it because it got turned on him next, hot and admiring and happy. "Yeah buddy."

He smiled at Rig, lost in that look; he was never going to survive the dancing.

It looked like Rock was thinking the same thing. "You sure you want to check this friendly bar out tonight? It'll still be there on Friday."

"Mmm... stretch the celebrating out? I can handle that." Rig licked those lips, smiling.

Rock nodded. "I can give you a reason to head straight home."

"Yeah?" Rig's drawl was in full force, cheeks flushed, eyes shining.

"Two reasons," Dick added.

"Kid's right." Rock gave him a wink and put some bills on the table. "What do you say, Rabbit -- home?"

"I'm right behind you, Blue Eyes." Rig beamed at Rock and stood. "Enjoying the view the whole damned way."

Dick giggled as Rock got up and actually swaggered out of the restaurant, Rig right on his ass. Damn, the view was even better from his vantage point behind them both. And it was all his.

Happy as a clam, Dick followed their lead.

***

Fuck, but he was having a good time. Blue and the kid had gone out to look at property for the gym early and he'd grabbed Rock's truck keys and gone to the lumberyard to get the stuff to keep working on his workshop. They'd all gotten the frame up and Dick had helped with the walls. Now Rig was up on his belly on the roof, laying shingles and singing. He was thinking he'd have to put a good sized fan in the wall, so that he didn't suffocate in August.

Alan Jackson was on the radio, the sun was beating down, the wind off the ocean enough to cool him off. The nail gun was banging. Damn, he wished Daddy was here. They'd have a ball together.

He heard the truck pull up and soon enough his men's footsteps announced their arrival.

"Fuck, Rig. What are you doing up there on your own?" Rock's growl was unhappy.

"I got Alan Jackson on the radio and the cell on me. I'm good." He grinned down, knowing he looked a fright, dirty and sweaty and probably a touch pink, wearing nothing but tennies and cutoffs. "Did y'all find a place?"

"You shouldn't be up there when no one else is home." Rock didn't look like he was planning on letting it drop.

Dick rolled his eyes. "We were coming home, we'd have found him eventually."

"And if he'd broken his neck?"

"We'd have known he was dead right away. Let it go, Rock, he's a grown man." Dick turned back up to the roof, shading his eyes. "Looking sexy, Rig. And yeah, we found a place. We'll drive you by tonight when we go to make the offer."

"Yeah? Where is it? You get the location y'all wanted?" Damn, he hated pissing Rock off, but the man was going to have to relax on the worrying, it was going to give him an aneurism.

"You planning on coming down?" Rock asked, arms folded across his chest.

"Or we could go up and help him finish. Many hands and all that." Dick nudged Rock, kissed the side of that stubbornly set mouth, and started up the ladder. "Man, it's hot up here."

"Yeah? I've been up a while, so it sorta just grew on me." He made his way over, moving careful, to get a kiss. "Looking fine, Pretty."

"No making out on the fucking roof," Rock informed them tartly, making Dick roll his eyes. "I'm going to go get beer and not watch you both attempt to break your necks."

Dick watched Rock go and shook his head. "The place is in a good location, great even. Two floors, but kind of split level so it's sort of like four, you know? But it's going to take more renovating than we'd planned on. And the weight systems Rock wanted to go with are a fucking fortune, so we're either going to have to go with a lower end company or hold back on some of the other stuff.

"It's a lot of stuff to think about, to learn, and he's not used to not being a hundred percent on top of his game. Once everything's up and running and he's the guy everyone comes to for advice on how to get the world's most amazing six pack like he's got? He'll be less growly about things."

He nodded, wiped his face with his handkerchief. "He worked his whole life in the marines and now he doesn't know right where he stands."

Dick nodded. "He'll find his place." His Pretty grinned at him. "And in the meantime, fussing over you makes him feel like he's taking care of business."

Rig grinned, nodding back. "You reckon I should go down and get growled at a little?"

Dick looked at the roof. "I can finish this up myself if you want -- won't take long. You're getting kind of red anyway -- should probably take a break, have a beer. A fuck." Dick gave him a wink and a soft kiss.

"You don't want to come with?"

"You don't want some time alone with him?" Dick asked softly.

He tilted his head, they'd been three for so long he didn't worry on any one-on-one time. Still, with none of them working, there hadn't been a lot. "You think he'd like that?"

"Yeah, I do. I get you first thing in the morning and sometimes in the middle of the night. Me and him, we've spent a lot of time lately with the gym business. Neither of you would ever say anything, but..." Dick shrugged and gave him a quiet knowing smile. "I'll be at least a half hour finishing this up. Maybe an hour."

"Don't work too hard, Pretty." He took one more kiss before sliding down the ladder and heading in to love on the growliest, sexiest, finest retired marine on earth. Dick's soft chuckle followed him in.

Rock was at the fridge, growling something about where was the pie when you wanted a slice of something sweet. He leaned over and licked up along Rock's spine. "It's there in the foil, Blue."

Then he went to wash his hands.

Rock grunted and grabbed the pie plate, taking off the foil and leaning against the counter as he started to eat. "So you came down off that roof after all."

"I did." He looked over, let his eyes drag over Rock. "Something was in here calling my name."

"Me, too." Rock held up the pie plate, winking. "Chocolate pie and a beer."

He grinned, rinsed the soap off his arms and ducked down to rinse his face off. "The afternoon snack of champions."

"You're washing all the good stuff off," Rock groused.

"You want a taste of it, Blue Eyes?" He turned, leaned against the counter, stretching, tempting.

"Somebody needs to make sure you didn't injure anything important." Those blue eyes were hot, watching him, pie abandoned half eaten on the counter.

"No, somebody doesn't." He spread a little, holding that gaze. "You do."

"You got that right." Growling, Rock stalked over to him, hands sliding on his skin.

He pushed into the touch, moaning, letting his Blue know how much he needed. Rock growled again, mouth closing on his, tasting of beer and chocolate and his Blue. He gave it all up, taking Blue's worry and the frustration and the fear and the shit and leaving need behind. That big body pressed against him, Rock's chest hot as it rubbed his own, those big hands circling his waist and holding on.

Yeah. Yeah, Blue. Need this. Need you.

Soft growls filled his mouth, vibrated where their skin met. One of Rock's hands slid back to push into his cutoffs, grabbing his ass possessively. He spread, pushing back into the touch, eyes just rolling. Rock's mouth left his, sliding along his jaw to his neck, tongue licking away.

"Mmm... Blue. Made for this." He wrapped his hands around Rock's head, fingers massaging.

"You know it." Rock licked and sucked and left little marks, going back to them time and again to lick and examine, it was still so new that they could do that. He kept humming and touching, head back and encouraging. Rock finally moved down to his titties, taking in one and then the other, pulling on the ring with his teeth.

"Oh. Oh, fuck. Rock..." He jerked, watching. "So fucking hot. So sexy."

Those blue eyes turned up to him, shinning and hot. Thick fingers pulled apart the top button and then his zipper and one hand wrapped around his prick. He groaned, fucking that hard hand.

"You want this, Rig? Want to go flying?" Rock's voice was husky with need.

"Always. Always, Blue. Fucking follow you to the ends of the earth."

Rock grunted with satisfaction and the next thing he knew, he was turned around and bent over the sink, cutoffs pulled down around his knees.

"Oh..." He tilted his hips, a blatant offer. Rock growled, bent and licked at his hole, wetting him with that hot tongue. "Oh. Oh, fuck. Blue." He raised up on his toes, thighs shivering.

Rock didn't spend a lot of time fucking his ass with that hot tongue. "Just a spit and polish to get you ready."

Then sweet hot thick heat pushed into him.

His cry split the air, his eyes going wide. "Yes..."

Rock's growl held satisfaction in it, that fat prick sliding into him again and again. He didn't hold anything back, riding that heavy prick like it was the first time, letting his lover know how fucking much he needed this. Rock's hands settled on his hips, tugging him back into each thrust, just giving it to him with everything his Blue had.

"Blue!" He knew Dick could hear them, knew that he was being loud and needing and damn. Damn, it was good.

"Come for me, Rabbit. Come on my cock."

Fuck. Fuck yes. Yes...

He jerked, cock throbbing as he shot. Rock roared, the sound possessive and sexy as hell. Heat filled him as Rock came. "Oh. Oh, fuck. That's still so fucking hot, Rock. Still moves my fucking world."

Rock's hands slapped his ass as that fat prick slid out. "I know how to keep my men happy."

"You do." He nodded, looked back over his shoulder. "Always have."

Rock grunted and tugged him up, turning him for a kiss. "Come on, kid's gonna want a beer if you left him up on that roof in the sun all on his own."

He started to complain, then just nodded. "Yeah. He will. I'm thinking we might need a window unit in there. What do you think?"

Rock gave him a grin and a wink. "Thought you liked the heat."

"Yeah, but I got two lovers who worry on me and the ventilation is a good thing."

Rock nodded. "You're going to want a window onto the beach, too. I was thinking. Maybe one of those whole wall windows. We put a couch in there and a little fridge stocked with beer?" Rock shrugged. "Not that the view of your ass isn't fine on its own."

"Oh, that sounds just fine. Just fine." He got cleaned up and grabbed a couple bottles. "Let's go rescue our kid."

"Yes, sir." Rock scooped up the last of the chocolate pie and followed him out, looking a lot happier now.

The sun shone in his eyes for a second and he grinned, whistling up at his Pretty. Fuck, but he was having a good time.

Chapter Three

In two days Rig was off to work. Rock thought it was a shame, he was starting to like their easy schedule. He and the kid worked on business a few hours a day and checked out the progress the contractors were making while Rig worked on his house additions and then they did stuff together. Fucking, sight-seeing, walking on the beach, hell he'd even let himself get dragged out onto the dance floor a time or two.

All things came to an end though and while this had been nice, they were all itching to be doing more than waiting for work to start. Still. They had a couple more days before Rig was due to report at the clinic and he and Dick hid all of Rig's tools. It was playtime.

To that end he was wearing the skimpiest pair of leather shorts that hugged his body like a lover. He felt like a fucking idiot, but the kid had assured him Rig was gonna take one look at him and flip right out.

He made his way to the kitchen. If Dick was wrong, the kid was going to be singing soprano.

Of course, given the way Rig's spoon hit the floor, those grey eyes wide? The kid's balls were so safe. Rig just stepped right over the mess, too, heading toward him.

"I take it the plan of not working today has been approved?" he asked, preening for Rig, playing to that look.

Dick whistled. "I'd say you can ask for pretty much any damn thing you want and we'll just nod and say yes and what else do you want, stud."

Rig nodded. "Yes. What do you want, stud?"

"I want to fuck and then fuck and then fuck some more. No more building shit 'til next weekend." He gave Rig a warm smile. "I'll take a blow job to start though." Rig groaned, sliding down his body, mouth open, slipping down his belly. He spread his legs to find his balance, moaning as that talented mouth started to get to work. "You just gonna watch, kid?"

"Fuck, no, I'm just admiring that fantastic body in all its studliness. The shorts really look amazing, Rock."

"Uh-huh..." Rig started licking, nuzzling his cock through the leather, moaning low.

His eyes rolled a little and he moaned. Fuck, that felt nice. Different, but nice.

Dick joined them, pulling off his t-shirt before rubbing up against Rock's back. "Sexy."

"Yes." Rig whimpered, opening the waistband of his shorts.

Okay. He'd pay the kid for the shorts.

He dropped one hand down to Rig's head, fingers playing through the almost white blond curls. He reached back with his other hand, squeezing Dick's ass. Rig's moan was low, desperate, tongue sliding as the zipper slid down, fingers protecting his cock. He purred, head dropping forward as Dick licked and nibbled at his neck. Rig's lips wrapped around his cock, tugging nice and slow, eyes fastened on him. He stared right back, rumbling out his pleasure, hand twisting through Rig's curls, not guiding, just letting his Rabbit know he was there. Rig was hungry, head leaning towards his hand, lips sliding over his shaft. That mouth made magic, still, after all these years. The day Rig couldn't get him up with that mouth was the day he was ready to die.

He rumbled and purred. Dick's hands came around, stroked Rig's cheeks, and Rig moaned, throat working. Too fucking good, the three of them like one being, all wrapped up in each other. Rig's hand reached around, moving, Dick moaning low. He nodded, that was it. His own hand squeezed Dick's ass, the kid rubbing against him while Rig's mouth worked his prick like it was the best thing ever. The scent of sex and male mixed with the leather, making his balls tight, aching. Rig swallowed around the tip of his cock again and then roared at the sudden shot of lightning going up his spine, coming hard.

Rig didn't lose a drop, kept sucking as the aftershocks rocked him. He purred, fingers sliding through Rig's hair, along the warm cheeks. "Fucking awesome, Rabbit."

Rig licked his fingers, his shaft. "So fine, Blue..."

"I try." Not that it was a hardship, Rig made him feel like a fucking god.

"Oh yeah," murmured Dick. "You succeed."

Rig nodded. "Fucking beautiful and all ours."

"Good thing there's enough of me to go around."

"Hell, yeah." Rig kissed the tip of his cock.

He groaned and tugged Rig up. Taking a kiss. Reaching back, he pulled Dick around and made it a threeway. Yeah. Never let it be said he didn't know how to fill their days.

***

They'd fucked for two days straight and now Rock was snoring away, sleeping the sleep of the physically exhausted. Dick would have been asleep himself, but he could feel Rig in his arms, knew the man wasn't anywhere near sleep.

He kissed a warm shoulder. "You nervous about tomorrow?" he asked softly.

"No. Yeah. Kind of." Rig chuckled. "Yeah. I haven't ever been a PA before."

He stroked Rig's stomach. "You're going to be great. You care about people and they're going to respond to that."

"You think? I keep worrying, what if I fuck up? What if I get sued?"

"Well you have malpractice insurance, right? So if you get sued, it'll be okay. And you're not going to fuck up on purpose or from lack of caring or trying. I mean, sometimes people die no matter how hard you try and even if you do all the right things, right? You just have to do the best you can. And I know you, Rig. Your best is amazing."

"Yeah?" Rig leaned in, kissed him. "I'm going to have my own nurse." There was a bit of wonder in those words.

He chuckled. "No more bedpans for you."

"No. And I'll know how to treat one, too. Know how to be a good boss."

"Like you would have treated a nurse any way but with respect even if you didn't have experience being one." He kept stroking Rig's belly, nuzzling the warm corner where Rig's neck and shoulder met. The man smelled so good, like him and Rock and sex and Rig himself.

"Oh..." Rig hummed, moaning softly. "God, Pretty, you make me feel like I could do anything."

"That's because you can. Smart, capable, funny, sexy... Fuck, do you know how lucky me and Rock are? And we know it, too."

Those thin cheeks went dark. "Oh, Pretty... You and him. My whole fucking world."

He hugged Rig tight. "I guess that makes us all pretty fucking lucky."

He turned Rig's face and took a kiss, tongue sliding in between the thin lips. Rig sucked his tongue in, humming, loving on him. His hand slid from Rig's belly to his hip, curling around the bone and drawing Rig toward him. That got him a moan, Rig snuggling, eyes fastened onto his. The grey shone in the moonlight, pupils so large he could see his own reflection in them.

His fingers petted Rig slowly, enjoying the warm skin as their tongues slid together. Rig dove into the kiss, hands sliding down his spine, playing in the small of his back. He gasped, those light touches sending sparks through his body, making his need hard.

"Wanna? Again?" Rig nuzzled his ear, lips so soft. "Gonna make me fly?"

"Fuck, yes. Please." He pushed against Rig, feeling like a kid, so eager and wanting.

"Yeah. Yeah." Rig laughed, the sound sexy and happy, so free, something that belonged to them alone. He brought their mouths together again, licking inside Rig's mouth and moaning as those fingers splayed across the small of his back. Rig knew every inch of him, knew how to make him need, knew how to drive him crazy. Of course the reverse was also true and they were both soon writhing, bodies moving urgently together.

"Yeah. Yeah, Pretty." Rig's eyes were wide, tongue sliding over his lips.

He slid his hand along Rig's ass, fingers pushng into Rig's crease, searching for the sweet, hungry hole. Rig raised one leg, spreading wide for him. He moaned, finger pushing into the tight heat. Rig nodded, riding him immediately, eager, gasps filling the air.

"Want you." He wanted to feel that heat sliding on his cock.

"Yeah. Yeah. Yours."

"Ride me?" he asked, hand reaching for the lube they kept under the pillows. He pulled out the battered tube, handing it over to Rig. Rig nodded, took the lube and slicked up his cock, hands warm, sure. His head went back and he kept working that sweet hole, pushing a second finger in to open Rig up.

"Mmm... Want that long cock in me deep, Pretty, so deep."

He nodded, letting his fingers slide away, helping Rig straddle him and line up. "Oh fuck. So good."

"Yes. Yes, Pretty." Rig arched, sliding down on him, ass settling on his thighs. He moaned and whimpered, hands sliding on Rig's thighs, fingertips brushing his lover's hard prick. "Mmm... yeah. Touch me." Rig started moving, sliding slow and easy.

He could do that. He reached for Rig's ass cheeks, squeezing them and then wrapped one hand around Rig's cock, the other one sliding up toward the sensitive nipples. Rig purred, sliding and shifting, riding his prick. He dug his heels into the mattress, pushing up into Rig, making soft noises.

"Mmm... sexy. So sexy. Feel you so deep." Rig's eyes were burning. He cried out, pushing up hard. Rock grumbled and muttered, turning onto his side, one hand reaching out to pet gently. Rig moaned, looking so happy, so horny. "Close, Pretty."

He whimpered, nodding and pulling harder on Rig's cock, his fingers twisting the small ring imbedded in Rig's nipple. That was all it took, Rig arching, coming with a shudder. And he didn't need more than that tight heat rippling around him, holding his cock tight, milking it. He bucked up, pleasure zapping through him and making him come.

Rig slowly settled down on him, nuzzling, licking his jaw. "So good."

He nodded. "Yeah. Damn." Turning his face, he caught Rig's mouth, their kiss long and slow. "Get some sleep, Rig. You've got to wear your Doctor pants tomorrow."

"Mmm... yeah."

They chuckled as Rock reached out, hand tugging Rig into that heat. He turned and spooned up behind Rig, holding their lover safe and warm between them. Rock's hand settled on his hip, familiar and right and he slid his own over to touch Rock's hot thigh.

There they all were. Perfect.

***

His first day was filled filling out paperwork and getting lectured. He was a junior partner, he was just a PA, not an MD. Here are the laws, don't overstep your bounds. Here were the nurses, here were the rules, here was the complicated damned computer system. By the time four o'clock rolled around, Rig was desperate for a smoke and a beer. He settled on the cigarette, sitting in the little alcove, reading through a binder of codes and insurance rules. Helen, the sweet little red-headed gal from Abilene, who was going to be working with him, came out and sat.

"They slam the hell out of the new guys." She gave him a grin. "It's not as bad as it seems."

"No? Because I'm thinking maybe I ought to go back to hospital work." He took a deep drag, offered her one and lit it for her when she nodded. "I was an RN for damn near fourteen years, you know?"

He got a grin, those dark red curls escaping from their pins. "Yeah. We all heard. I have senority, so I got to work with you."

Oh. Oh, that made him feel a little better. "Why'd you leave Abliene?"

"My husband's stationed out here. Coast Guard. We love it. The people are a little odd..."

He nodded, chuckled. "Well, not everybody can be Texan."

"You got that right. My man? Oklahoma, but I love him anyway." She winked, chuckled. "You got family here?"

He opened his mouth to say roommates, then stopped himself. No. Not anymore. No lying. "Yeah, I live with my partners -- two ex-marines. I'm sure you'll meet them sooner than later."

Her eyes went wide. "Marines! So you'll sympathize when my man's riding the waves and I'm weepy."

Something hard and sour inside him that had been building all day dissolved and he laughed, nodding. "Hell, yes. I'll even buy us both a beer. Y'all have babies?"

"Not yet. We're working on it."

"Yeah? Cool. I have six nieces and three nephews and I tell you what, they're something else."

"Good sized brood that one." Helen looked over, eyes suddenly sharp. "So, what do we nurses call you then? Doctor Roberts?"

Oh, well now, there's why she really came out to chat. "I'm thinking Rigger is just fine, Helen, unless that makes y'all uncomfortable."

He must have given the right answer, because he got a real smile, a nod. "Rigger works. Doc Rigger -- it's got a ring."

"Yeah? Cool." He finished his cigarette. "So, be honest, can you get decent barbeque in this town?"

They sat, visiting, the rest of the nurses coming out as the clinic closed to visit, to introduce themselves, to invite him out for a couple of beers at the local watering hole. Maybe he could do this.

He followed the ones that could go, calling up to the house to invite his boys down. They could have a couple and then go find food. There were about six of them, drinking and swapping stories, the second beer making him lightheaded, reminding him he hadn't eaten in fourteen hours, making him glad he'd called the boys.

One of the younger nurses, Linda, suddenly got wide-eyed. "Oh, my, look at the new meat."

They all turned and there were his marines, Dick laughing at something Rock had said and pointing to their table. Damn, they did look fine, both in jeans, Rock with a white t-shirt that hugged him like a second skin, Dick in a blue t-shirt from the gym he'd worked at back in North Carolina.

"Yeah, now. Y'all be nice. Those two? *So* taken." He waved, catching their attention. "Evenin' y'all. You found me."

There were collective gasps from around the table, a couple of 'some guys have all the luck's and at least one 'why are all the cute ones, gay?'

Rock pretended not to notice, giving the table a nod and pulling up a chair next to his. "Get us a couple of brews, kid, I think we have some catching up to do."

"Hi there." Dick gave the group a warm smile, bent to kiss him. "No telling about your first day 'til I get back. I want to hear everything."

"It's a deal." He was pink and nervous and pleased and... Damn, it was nice to not be lying. "Rock, this is Helen, Linda, Greg, Lisa and Suzie. Y'all, this is Rock and that's Dick up at the bar."

"Nice to meet you," Rock said, giving them another nod. "So you're the nurses who make the doctors at the clinic look good?"

"Ah, Doc Rigger's told y'all all about us already!" Helen laughed, lit a smoke and offered him one, which he almost reached for until Rock's hand settled on the small of his back.

"Well he said he was at a bar with a bunch of nurses and anyone who knows doctors and nurses knows which ones to butter up." Rock gave her a wink, those thick fingers stroking his back gently.

Dick came back about then with a couple of bottles from the local brewery. "We're talking about buttering people up already? Damn, it's fast out here."

They all laughed, Rig's belly warming nice and slow at Rock's touch.

"So, what do y'all do?" Helen chuckled. "Were y'all medics in the service?"

Rock shook his head. "Gunnery sergeant."

"Grunt," put in Dick. "We're going to open a gym here. Down on Palm street."

"Oooh! Cool! Boys only or can desperately out-of-shape nurses come too?"

Greg snorted. "Hey! Not all of us have tits!"

"Thank god," murmured Rock under his breath, giving Rig a wink.

He chuckled as Pretty assured the girls they could come work out and passed out business cards. "Oh, he's good."

"We're open for suggestions on how to make the place more friendly to newcomers, too. It can be intimidating walking into a place full of guys built like Rock here."

"Oh, because you're *such* a ninety-pound weakling." Helen chuckled, shook her head, grinned. "I'd go to watch guys built like y'all."

Rig tipped his beer to her. "Amen, sister."

Dick blushed and hid his face behind his beer, Rock, though, was eating it up. "So you're saying if I sold tickets I could turn my work out into a moneymaker."

"Hell, yes." The girls went to hooting and hollering and the damn bar cracked up at the noise.

"Damn, Doc. You're a lucky man." Suze was giving Dick a soft, sloe-eyed look.

Rock's arm went around his shoulders. "He's not the only one. Takes good care of us, he does."

Dick grinned, blush still fairly high. "Anyone else hungry? The bar snacks are starting to look pretty good."

"No, I gotta get home. Mack's bringing pizza."

"Yeah, I have to pick my girls up at the mall."

One by one, the group dispersed, leaving him with the dregs of beer four in front of him. "Man, what a day."

"They seemed nice, if a little giggly," noted Rock.

"How did your first day go?" Dick asked, settling in a chair on the other side of him.

"The first part? Seriously sucked. The doctors are a little snooty and there's thirty-zillion rules and shit. But the afternoon? Gives me hip. Hope. Hope. Gives me hope."

Rock chuckled and Dick grinned. "Bit of a freudian slip there."

"You can have all the hip you want when we get home." Rock squeezed his shoulder and nodded at the kid. "I thought that one gal was going to eat the kid up with a spoon."

"No shit and no way. Mine. My marines." He chuckled. "Shit, I've had a couple too many on no food. Somebody's going to have to drive the Jeep."

"I'll do it -- you can ride with Rock in the truck. And I'm starving. We should grab a bite. We haven't tried the place a few blocks over yet -- and they deliver so you'd know if you liked them for lunches and stuff, seeing as they're close to work."

"Oh, that sounds good. The little Italian place?"

Dick nodded and Rock made a face.

"If they don't have meat, I'll grill you a steak when we get home," Dick promised.

"They ought to have chicken parmesan and meatball subs, Blue." He tilted his head. "Or there's a little bitty steakhouse I passed this morning. We could try that."

Dick rolled his eyes, but Rock's face just lit right up and that was that.

"There's nothing wrong with pasta," Dick informed Rock. "In fact it makes a nice change from steak now and then.

"I'm not looking for a change," Rock pointed out.

"I'll come take you for lunch one day this week," Dick promised as they headed out.

"I'd like that." He wrapped his fingers with Dick's, nodding. "We haven't been to one of our lunches together since Fayetteville."

Dick nodded and smiled. "Yeah. I know we've all been kind of in each other's pockets as we've settled in, but I still miss them."

"Yeah." He rubbed a little, happy and humming, heading Rock's direction. "We'll meet you there, yeah?"

"I'll be right behind you."

"Crawling up our asses is more like it," Rock put in, winking.

Dick laughed. "No where else in the world I'd rather be."

Rig chuckled, slid into the truck and right up against his Blue. "Mmm. Feels damn good."

"Uh-huh." Rock got the truck started and headed out, following his directions, and then that arm went around his shoulders. "So they treated you all right there today? Nobody gave you any real trouble?"

"Just the first day -- here are the rules, don't forget you used to just be a nurse, we deserve your respect thing. The computer system is damned complicated and the insurance and stuff. I imagine it'll get better when I'm working-working, not pushing paper."

"When do they let you start actually doctoring?"

"My first appointment's next Monday. I have to play shadow with the other doctors tomorrow and Wednesday and then a day of insurance training and Friday's are rotating free clinic days. So I'll get three out of four off."

"Yeah? Cool. They aren't making you take the clinic your first week?" He could see Rock already filling his Friday with fucking.

"Nope. My turn's in three weeks. You free Friday?" He grinned over, hand on Rock's belly, drawing circles.

"We'll have to drop by the gym, make sure things are progressing as they should. But we could do that on our way out somewhere." Rock shrugged casually. "Go up the coast or something."

"Oh, I'd like that. Do some exploring." He leaned in, humming with the radio. "You happy here, Blue?"

Rock grunted. "I'm ready for the work at the gym to start, but yeah. I can live with this."

"Good. Y'all have a grand opening date planned yet?"

Rock nodded. "October first. Kid's got some back to school and fall advertising tie-in thing all worked out."

"He's damned good at the marketing stuff, isn't he? Pretty keeps thinking he's stupid, but damn."

"He knows people, understands them. It's why he fits so well here, yeah? Knows what we need." Rock chuckled. "Well that and he's hot."

He laughed, nodded. "He's ours, sure enough and I wouldn't give for him."

"Wouldn't give what?" Rock asked with another wink.

"Anything." He grinned, squeezed Rock's leg.

Rock chuckled and pulled ito the parking lot. "Not a chain. This place looks like it's been here awhile. Could be a new favorite."

"If they've got salad for me and potatoes for the kid, we're gold."

Rock chuckled. "There's nothing wrong with a meal made up solely of meat."

"Only if you're talking morning blowjobs."

"Now you're talking about stuff that's sacred."

"You mean you're not tired of my mouth after all these years?" He grinned, pleased and warm and more than a touch horny.

"Tired? Of that mouth? Don't you even think it." Rock growled, eyes hot.

"Mmm..." He leaned, rubbing his cheek against Rock's arm, humming low.

Rock chuckled. "We're here. And the kid's headed over wondering why the hell we aren't out of the truck yet. You up to this?"

"The kid's known us long enough to know why we aren't out of the truck, Blue. He's coming over to tease."

"Well if I'm getting teased it's going to be *for* something." Rock's mouth came down on his, hot and pushy. Oh. He moaned, opening wide, hands jittering on Rock's chest.

Dick knocked on the window, but Rock took his time breaking the kiss, a smug look on his Blue's face.

"Keep it in your pants," teased Dick as Rock opened his door.

He blinked over, grinning like a damn fool. "Y'all need to feed me."

Dick's mouth twitched. "Substantial as Rock is, you need something more than his spunk, which means you're going to need to get out of the truck."

"Do you kiss my momma with that mouth?" He giggled -- oh, shit, if he was giggling, he was in serious trouble with his boys.

Dick's twitching lips turned into outright laughter and Rock rolled his eyes. "Don't make me carry you in there, Rigger. I don't need my caveman reputation started quite that spectacularly."

"I'm comin'. I'm comin'." He slid out of the truck, frowned. "Did I leave my hat in the Jeep, Pretty?"

"I didn't notice it, Rig. But you didn't have it at the bar, so you must have."

"Cool." He nodded. He was probably okay without it from the truck to the restaurant. Dick chuckled and for some reason, flanked him on the other side from Rock. He didn't mind it, though. They were his and he was liking it. Course it was sorta like being famous. Dr. Rigger, Blowjobs to the Stars, or some such shit. He wondered idly if you got benefits from a gig like that.

They went into the little restaurant that couldn't have had more than twenty tables, more than half of which were full. Rock took the lead, getting them their table, talking steak with the waitress who happened to be the owner's daughter. He didn't bother to look at the menu -- Rock was in his element. Hell, if the world was covered in one steakhouse after another? His Blue would be happy as a pig in shit.

They had Cokes all around, which came with his and Dick's salads and a plate of battered mushrooms. "There you go, Rig -- you can stop badgering me for the week -- I'm eating vegetables."

"Mushrooms aren't veggies, Rock." Still, they were tasty and he stole one. "Mmm... good."

"Well they're not meat." Rock grinned at him and popped another one in his mouth, forstalling any comeback.

He chewed, the couple of bites reminding him how hungry he was. "The girls looked interested in y'all's gym."

"You don't think they were just being polite?" Dick asked.

"No, that one gal wanted a look at your tail in shorts and a t-shirt, kid."

Dick stuck his tongue out at Rock, colouring just a little.

"You think it would only take a little Latina to make him switch teams?" Rig winked, chuckled.

"I'm not switching anything," assured Dick. "I'm happy where I am."

Rock chuckled. "You sure, kid?"

"One hundred percent."

Rig winked. "No one else will let him pick the peppers off the pizza and feed them to the dogs."

"How come you let him do that -- aren't those vegetables? I actually eat those. We've got a double standard going here." Rock dipped his battered mushroom in the ranch sauce and ate it.

"Okay, new rule. You pick off the peppers and feed them to the Rocketman, kid."

"Hey!" Rock fixed him with a glare, Dick giggling madly beside him.

He gave Rock a butter-wouldn't-melt-in-his-mouth smile. "We can't have double standards, Blue."

"The double standard is him getting to pick off vegetables without a fuss and me getting one every time I don't eat them." Rock looked toward the kitchen door. "Where's our steaks?"

"What did you get me, Rocketman?" He took a sip of his Coke, stealing a green pepper from Dick's salad.

"Stir fry. The kid's having the New York strip and I'm having a porterhouse."

"Mmm... sounds good." He nodded, stomach rumbling loud. "Real good."

"Patty was telling me her mother makes a chocolate cake that makes angels weep. We're taking a whole one home."

"Yeah? We have vanilla ice cream in the freezer? I like a little to cut the sweetness."

"We can pick some up on the way -- can't have too much ice-cream." Meat and sweets, and sex, that's what his Rock was all about.

"Cool. I need some supplies for my office, too. Maybe some snacks or something, in case I miss lunch."

The food came, fresh and heaped on the plate and Rock actually moaned as he dug in.

"Shit, this is good, like homemade." Dick was eating enthusiastically. "Man, I bet that cake's amazing."

It was well done, nice and spicy and he ate, surprisingly hungry, the three of them quiet. As they finished up their meal, two different feet started playing footsie with him. He chuckled, shook his head, grinning ear to ear. "Y'all..."

"You want us to stop?" Rock asked, one eyebrow going up.

"Never." He gave into the temptation to touch Rock's cheek, the action making him hard. Those blue eyes got darker, Rock purring for him. Fuck, it was sexy being able to touch them in public without worrying about being seen. "So fucking fine." His throat was dry and he swallowed hard. "Take me home."

"As fast as I can," murmured Rock.

Dick grinned. "Go ahead, I'll get the bill and the cake and follow in the Jeep. Just make sure there's some of that left for me."

"Always, Pretty. Thanks." His eyes were burning in his head.

Dick kissed his cheek and rubbed Rock's belly. Rock's arm went around his shoulders, his Blue's chest puffed up; his Blue obviously proud to be seen with him.

"Home, Blue. Remind me why I left Texas." He was damn near purring.

"Every chance I get, Rabbit."

"Thank God for favors large and small."

"I'm a large favor," Rock told him. Oh, his Blue was on a roll.

"Hell, yeah." He grinned, let Rock direct him to the truck. "My favorite kind."

Rock chuckled. "Flattery will get you fucked through the mattress."

"Mmm... have I called you a stud yet today?" He winked. "Oh, wait, when I finished sucking that fat cock this morning..."

"Is that what you said? I couldn't quite hear for the ringing in my ears."

He leaned over, nuzzled Rock's ear. "I said, I called you my stud, after you fucked my mouth with your fine fucking prick."

"Fucking Christ, Rig. Get in the truck before I forget how to be decent and fuck you right here in the parking lot."

"Whatever you say, Blue." He hopped in, all hot and bothered.

"I say I think you need to suck my fucking fine prick again. As soon as we get home."

"Mmm... dessert." He licked his lips, nodding. "Home, Blue. Now."

"Fast as I can go and not get stopped by highway patrol."

"Amen."

He grinned, stretched out along the seat.

Yeah. A-fucking-men.

Chapter Four

There were times when Dick wished he'd taken up smoking. Or that he at least liked it enough he could steal a few from Rig's secret stash and smoke them. But, while he wasn't as fanatical about it as Rock was, he disliked the smell and the taste of it in Rig's mouth and wasn't about to pick up the habit himself. Not even for something like this.

Instead he headed out along the beach, barefoot so he could feel the wet sand between his toes, so he could let the waves slide over his feet and occasionally kiss his ankles or shins. The letter was still in his hand, clutched in his fist. He didn't think he could open his hand right now to read it, but he didn't have to. He'd read it a half dozen times already, waiting for it to sink in, looking for the part where it said 'april fools' or 'smile -- you're on candid camera'.

His father was dead.

That wasn't why he was so upset though. Not that that in and of itself wasn't upsetting, but the thing that was twisting his guts was that his father had died almost a month ago and it had taken his mother three fucking weeks to sit down and send him a letter -- a fucking *letter* -- to let him know.

He'd walked until he'd fallen and then he'd cried. He hadn't seen them in years, but they were still his parents and now one was dead and the other might as well be and it hurt. It hurt that his father was dead and it hurt that he wasn't wanted or loved, no matter how good his chosen family was; it still hurt that his mother didn't love him.

Then he rubbed his face and turned around and went home. By the time he climbed the little deck stairs, he was feeling pretty numb and the most beautiful sunset was filling the sky with colour.

Rig was sitting on the deck, watching the sunset, waiting for him. "Hey, Pretty."

He was handed a bottle of cold water and a clean towel.

"Hey." He drank down half the water and put the towel around his shoulders, sitting down with a sigh.

They just sat for a long time, Rig quiet and relaxed. Then Rig shifted to kneel behind him, removing the towel and beginning to work the tension out of his neck and shoulders. Ah, fuck he was going to start crying again if Rig was nice to him. Letting his head drop forward, he soaked up Rig's care and bit his lip -- he'd cried enough fucking tears down on the beach. Lips brushed the nape of his neck, fingers sliding and pushing and refusing to let the tension build again. He reached back to touch Rig, needing the connection. He slid his hand along Rig's leg, stroking as far as he could reach.

"Can I help?" Rig settled closer, legs bracketing his, holding him. Long fingers still moved over his skin.

He sighed and shrugged, something inside him easing. "Got a letter from my mother."

"Yeah? What did she want?" Rig's voice was flat; Rig quite possibly liked his family less than anyone on earth. Still those hands were gentle, keeping him close.

"She wrote to inform me that my father was dead." He laughed, no humour in the sound. "She *wrote* to tell me that. And do you want to know what the punchline is?"

"What's that, Pretty?" Rig's cheek rested against his shouldblade, arms circling his waist.

"He's been dead almost a month."

"Oh, fuck." Rig shook his head. "That's just not right, Dick. Not at all."

He nodded his head. He knew it. No chance to go to the funeral, to say goodbye, he wasn't sure he'd have wanted to, but the choice should have been his to make. "She sat down three fucking weeks after he died and wrote me a fucking letter like I was some old aquaintance that needed to be told when she felt up to taking care of it."

"She's a thoughtless bitch who never deserved you." The soft kisses started again, brushing over his shoulders, his back.

Dick gave a half laugh and sighed, leaning back into Rig. "Not that you're biased or anything."

"Not in the least." Rig started stroking, licking his skin now, just a little.

He murmured and let Rig touch him, lick him, make him feel good. After a bit he asked, really softly. "Rig? Can I ask you a question? I mean, I know I can, but I want you to promise me you'll answer truthfully and not what you think I want to hear."

"You have my word, Dick. Ask away."

"Is it... is it wrong that I'm more upset about the way and when she told me than I am upset that he's dead?"

Rig tilted his head, shaking his head. "Y'all weren't close, so there's not a huge hurt, more an ache on that front, yeah? But your momma? She's done wrong by you and done it with thought. Your daddy didn't choose to pass on. The old bitch chose to be evil."

He nodded. "All it would have taken was a phonecall, you know? 'Your father's dead, please don't come to the funeral.' End of story."

He sighed, leaning back heavier into Rig. "I don't know why I expected better of her, or why I care. She made it clear a long time ago she had no love to waste on me."

"Stupid woman." Rig's rumble made him smile. "Doesn't know a beautiful man when he's put in front of her."

He tilted his head back, wanting a kiss, *needing* it. He got it immediately, hungry and perfect and warm and echoing all the way down to his knees. And more soothing than walking a thousand miles or crying a million tears. He turned his torso, one hand sliding up and wrapping around Rig's neck, holding his lover lightly. Rig licked and nuzzled, pulled gently at his lips. The sun had set, the stars coming out, the sounds of the waves soothing his nerves. Those grey eyes were dark, easy. Just a little concerned. "Hate when you're unhappy, Pretty."

"You always know how to make me feel better though." He managed a small smile for Rig. "You and Rock..." He shook his head. "Best thing that ever happened to me."

"That's how it's supposed to be. Wouldn't be love otherwise." Rig kissed the side of his mouth, lips tickling. "It is love, you know. Has been for a long, long time."

He closed his eyes and whimpered, burying his face in Rig's neck. Oh, he knew that Rig and Rock both loved him, but... well it was one thing to know and another to *know*.

Rig just held him, hands moving him until they were settled together, his legs wrapped around Rig's waist. It should have been silly, him sitting like that, being held like that, but it wasn't. It was Rig and it was him and it felt good. The letter was taken from his hand, folded, and stuck in his back pocket.

"I love you, too," he whispered, hands holding tight to Rig. "I have for a long time, I just never know how to say it."

"Oh, Pretty..." Rig's chuckle was soft, tickling his ear. "Christ. Nobody shows it like you do. Nobody."

"Are you accusing me of wearing my heart on my sleeve?" He didn't know whether to be horrified or pleased.

"Nope. We're not sharing that, so it has to be deeper than that." The tease made him chuckle; the tongue sliding over his ear made him gasp.

"Want you," he murmured, lips finding the skin of Rig's neck. "Want you to make me forget everything and then make me scream."

"You've got me, Pretty, and it would be my pleasure." Rig's voice was soft, liquid, fingers finding the ring in his nipple and stroking. The little moan Rig gave was fucking sweet in his ear. "I like these rings so much -- knowing how good it feels, knowing I have one, Blue has one, knowing how the skin and metal taste together..."

He shuddered. "Yeah, I know what you mean. 's so fucking hot."

"Mm... yeah." Rig's hands cupped his ass, drew him closer. "Wanna go inside, Pretty? Somewhere soft where there's lube and a big old grouch who's worried about you?"

"Rock's back?" He chuckled. "Staying out of the sticky emotional stuff, that's our Rock."

Rig nodded. "Sometimes fucking doesn't fix things." Those fingers tickled his ass again. "Right at first."

He chuckled. "But eventually..."

Rig pushed him over, twisting until he was straddled by lean thighs. "What do I always tell you, Pretty? Fucking's better than talking any day of the week."

Then his lips were taken in a hard, straightforward, I'm-gonna-make-you-come-Pretty kiss. He made a noise, pressing it up into Rig's mouth, hips moving restlessly beneath Rig's as the kiss made his cock hard just like that. Nodding, Rig slid his hands down to start tearing away clothes, the kiss growing deeper, hungrier. They weren't making it inside. Not this time. He helped with the getting naked, moaning at the slide of flesh on flesh.

"Yeah. Fuck, yeah." Rig started moving, rocking into him, their cocks sliding together in long pulls. "Wanna fuck you, Pretty. Closest lube?" The closest lube was too fucking far away. He grabbed Rig's hand, pulling two fingers into his mouth and sucking hard, meeting the grey eyes. Rig groaned, nodding again. "So fucking sexy. Hurry, Pretty. Want to feel you all around my cock."

He bucked up, letting Rig's fingers slip from his mouth. "Fuck, yeah."

Rig's fingers pushed deep without hestiation, stretching him for that sweet cock. "Yeah."

He moaned and moved with Rig. "More. You."

"Fuck, yes." Rig's fingers disappeared and he was filled with hot, thick cock. Rig watched him close, grey eyes warm. "Oh, fuck. So fucking hot."

He pushed up, wanting still more, wanting Rig to fuck him. His lips were taken in a hard kiss, Rig's cock beginning to move in hard, steady strokes, Rig's hands hard on his hips. He whimpered, meeting the thrusts, feeling Rig inside him.

Rig ripped their lips apart, panting as he raised up on straining arms, angle shifting. "C'mon, Pretty. Wanna hear you. Wanna *know* you fucking feel me."

"I feel you." He gasped, moaning as Rig nailed his gland. "Oh fuck -- I feel you!"

"Good." Rig pegged him again and again, not letting up, encouraging his cries and need with every ounce of that long body. He whimpered and moaned and shouted and begged, writhing and bucking beneath Rig. So good. So fucking good. Nothing else mattered but the next thrust and then the next, each one putting him closer to soaring.

Rigger bent close, fucking him hard, and bit at his earlobe. "I love you, Pretty. Now, Dick. Come on my cock. Let me feel you."

He screamed, coming hard, body squeezing Rig's cock.

When the aftershocks faded, Rig was resting against his chest, breathing quick, tongue lapping at his skin. He wrapped his arms around the skinny redneck and held tight, hugging Rig. "Thank you."

"Anytime. Anytime at all." Rig kissed him, hips bumping against his. "And I'm not just being polite, either."

He chuckled and stole another kiss. "No, I don't expect you were."

He ran his hands down along Rig's body, cock stirring as his palms cupped that fine ass. "I think it's time for something soft and grouchy, don't you?"

"I do." Rig nuzzled his jaw. "If we're lucky, we can have hard and horny, too."

That made him laugh outright. "Oh, I don't think luck has anything to do with it."

Rig grinned and stood, wiping himself off before holding a hand out for Dick. "C'mon. Someone's waiting to give you what you need."

Dick stood and grabbed Rig's hand, heading inside to find their other half. Or third. Whatever.

They'd find Rock and he'd ask if everything was okay and Dick would tell him it wasn't, but it soon would be and then they'd fuck like nobody's business and it *would* be okay, because they loved him.

And that was all he needed.

Chapter Five

The gym was coming together. Actually *looking* like a gym. They had interviews set up for the following week for staff. A secretary, a couple of equipment managers, training assistants. He and Dick would do a lot of that themselves, but they couldn't do it all alone. They needed back up. Most of the equipment was coming in next week as well. It was starting to feel real instead of like they were just playing at it.

They had their last three day weekend coming up, as soon as Rig got home from work.

The kid had a nice meal on and everything, but Rig was late. Week three of actually seeing patients and the man had been late every single night. His Rabbit always had worked too hard, cared too much. It was what made him fucking good at his job. Of course if he had something to actually do, he probably wouldn't even have noticed -- being a retired stay at home man? Was not for him. Next week was set to get better.

Meanwhile there was roast chicken to eat and men to fuck, and where the hell was his Rabbit?

It was almost an hour later, after they'd eaten and shit, that the Jeep pulled up, Rig coming through the front door with a huge box of papers. "Hey. Smells good. I'm going to put this stuff in the office and see if anyone called my voicemail. Dr. Johnson left the clinic today -- just left -- and I'm picking up his patients and then Holly is on call, but had theatre tickets, so I had to work after-hours clinic."

"You could have called," he growled after Rig's retreating back. Dick glared at him. "What?"

"He's tired, you've got all day tomorrow to be an asshole."

"Fuck off, kid."

The door to Rig's office closed, maybe a little harder than not.

Dick glared at him. "Nice fucking going, Rock."

"Where are you going?"

"In there to talk to him. He worked his ass off and all you could do is tell him off for not calling?"

He rolled his eyes. "I'll go."

"You're just going to make it worse."

"Well then you can be the even bigger hero and mop up after me."

"Watch out, Rock, you're on a fucking roll." Dick stalked off, the bathroom door closing loudly.

Jesus fucking Christ he just wanted to eat his fucking chicken and fuck his men, when did he become the bad guy? Grunting, he got up and headed for Rig's office, knocking.

"Come on in. It's not locked." Rig was sitting at his desk, hand rubbing the back of his neck, shirt open. "Hey there, Blue Eyes. Sorry I was late. You pissed at me?"

"I've been happier." He hoped the kid appreciated him making an effort here.

"Yeah." Those grey eyes looked up at him, tired and still. "You can take it out of my ass, if you want, but I didn't set out to piss you off."

He nodded. "Your ass is part of the problem. Been used to seeing a lot more of it."

"Yeah. Yeah." Rig shook his head. "I don't know if I can do this, Rock. I just gained thirty patients today. One's pregnant. There's kids, babies. Old folks that're dying..."

"You, not able to take care of people who need you? That's not the Rigger I know." He moved around to the back of Rig's chair and started massaging the tight shoulders. "Of course the Rig I know would've called."

"Yeah. And if I'd not been a fool and left my cell at home today?" Rig sighed, relaxing for him. "Truth be told? I'm getting tired of being the shit, new guy already. I went through forty-five patients today, all told. Forty-fucking-five. I was too damned pissed to call."

He kept working on Rig's shoulders. "Well if this Johnson guy left, you won't be the shit new guy for long, right?"

Rig chuckled, head falling forward. "You got a point, Blue."

"Yeah, well I've been looking forward to fucking you all day, leaves a man a little pointy."

"I could so handle that. I'm real ready to stop being Doc Rigger for an hour or twelve and just be y'all's."

"Oh, I've got you down for an honest to fuck three day pass, Rig." Three whole days to fuck their brains out. Just like the old days.

"Yeah?" The paperwork got put aside, Rig standing to push into his arms, bodies touching knee to shoulder. "Hey, Blue Eyes."

He purred. Now this was more like it. "Hey."

"Mmm..." Those arms wrapped around his neck, lips warm and eager against his, tongue sliding. He met Rig's tongue, hands grabbing that perfect ass. "Oh..." Fuck, there wasn't much like that sound to make a man feel like a god, like the fucking center of the world.

It soothed away the last of his bad mood and he bent Rig back over his desk, intent on making sure Rig was having a good time, too. Rig went easy, trusting him, holding on and opening wide. It brought their groins nicely together and he rubbed, that one hand on Rig's ass making sure his Rabbit was getting full benefit.

"Mmm... We haven't fucked on the desk yet..." He got a grin, that tongue licking and lapping his lips.

"Well then it's about time we did." He reached past Rig and then stopped before sweeping everything to the floor. "Anything gonna break?"

And how was that for sensafuckingtive?

Rig rescued a little plant in a holder and put the box of files on the desk chair. "Nope."

Grinning, he pushed the rest of the stuff off with one sweep of his arm and pointed to the desk. "Plant it, Rigger."

"Ah, romance..." Rig stripped off his shirt, worked the dark brown slacks open and off.

"I'm fucking you on the desk -- sounds plenty romantic to me." He stripped his own jeans and t-shirt off. "Though I'm betting there's no lube in here yet."

"You'll have to improvise." That sweet little ass was bared for him, settling on the desk. He just growled and bent, getting his mouth right where it was needed. Fuck, Rig tasted strong and male and so fucking familiar, it made him hard just like that.

"Sweet fuck! Blue!" Rig's hands stuttered on the wood of the desk, cry echoing. He purred. Oh yeah. He kept licking, wetting Rig, tongue pushing in a little.

"Well that's more like it," murmured Dick from the door. The kid was wearing a towel, hair still damp.

"H...hey Pretty. Oh, fuck. Hey. Rock. Fuck me."

Rock chuckled. "Working on it, Rig."

Dick grinned, hand going to his towel. "Can I join the party?"

"Mmm..." Rig licked his lips, eyes hungry, wanting, like they should be. Dick's towel dropped, revealing the long cock already hard and leaking at the tip. "Oh... Isn't that pretty..." Rig ripped, humming. "Is it for me?"

"Uh-huh." Dick slid his cock along Rig's cheek and Rock figured it was about time he reminded Rig of the other cock in the house. Standing, he rubbed the tip of his prick along Rig's hole.

"Yeah..." Rig spread, body and mouth begging for it. He purred, watching his own prick slide into that tight little hole, watching Rig take Dick's cock deep. Their own personal slut took them both, flushing and shifting and fucking humming for all he was worth. He watched the kid across the desk as they both started to fuck Rig, his own pleasure evident there.

Rig had one hand stroking his belly, the other draped around the kid's thigh, ass sliding on the polished wood. He looked like the slut he was, fucking decadent and sexier than just about anything Rock had ever seen.

He pushed harder, faster, one hand pulling Rig back onto his cock, the other wrapping around that fine prick. Rig groaned, entire body jerking, ass tight and hot around his cock. "Gonna come on my cock, Rabbit?"

Dick moaned at the question, body moving faster. Rig's hand slid over his, the touch light, sweet. He purred. This was worth fucking living for. His fucking men.

The kid cried out, sounding fucking close and he sped his own movements, pushing Rig hard and fast. Rig clenched down, thighs shaking hard, cock jerking and spraying spunk in his hand. Oh, fuck, that was all he needed and with a roar he came, filling Rig deep.

Rig was swallowing around Dick's prick, humming low, fucking purring. He slid his hands along the smooth skin, loving the way Rig felt beneath him. Rig relaxed, rippling and quiet, peaceful.

He leaned in and kissed the kid and then kissed his Rabbit. It was late. Time to put his men to bed, maybe fuck them to sleep. "Bed. Now."

Rig nodded, reaching up to wrap those long arms around his neck. "Yeah. Now."

He grunted, hands going to Rig's ass, pulling that skinny body up close and tight. His Rabbit curled around him, lips on his throat, legs around his waist, counting on his strength. He hadn't let Rig down yet, he wasn't planning on starting now.

He headed down the hall, Dick's hand stroking his ass as the kid followed them.

***

"Blue?" Rig sat up with a frown, nerves jangling. "Dick? Did y'all hear that?"

He listened again, something was on the fucking porch, he could hear Grim and Lucy growling. He crawled out from between them, frowning, grabbing a baseball bat on the way to the front door. He moved through the front room, Grim and Lucy snarling, all puffed up and fuzzy. Fucking wild dogs, people ought to keep care of their critters...

The sight of eyes peeking in through the fucking window startled the *fuck* out of him.

"Goddamnit! Get off my property!" Rig hit the door, Grimmy and Lucy barking furiously. The guy ran like a bat out of hell, heading for the road as fast as his legs would take him.

"You want me to chase him?" growled Rock from behind him.

He jumped, damned near dropped the bat. "Damnit! Oh! Shit. No."

Rock's arms slid around him, his Blue still growling. "You sure?"

He nodded, leaned back into Rock's arms. "Damn, that scared me. I thought it was critters."

Dick had his jeans and a pair of sandals on. "I'm just going to go around the house a time or two with the dogs. They aren't going to calm down until they can see for themselves that everything's fine."

He frowned. "Be careful, Pretty, 'kay?"

"Grim and Lucy won't let anything happen to me."

Rock grunted. "Let me get my piece."

Dick shook his head. "We saw the guy take off, remember? These two are enough to scare anyone off once they get going. I'll be back before the bed cools."

"Okay. Just... hurry." Rig wandered to the kitchen, fretting, messing with the coffee maker, opening the dishwasher to unload it, nerves just jangling, hands shaking.

"What the hell time is it anyway?" Rock asked, grabbing his hands and pulling him to sit on Blue's lap in one of the kitchen chairs.

"Huh? Oh..." He squinted. "I can't tell without my glasses, Blue. 2:15?"

"Right. Soon as the kid gets back in, we're going back to bed. No dishes, no coffee, no cleaning. Bed. Maybe a bit of kissing and some fucking."

"Pushy bastard." He blushed dark, his Blue knew him so well. He was itching to move, to *do*, and he wasn't sure he could sleep. Not now.

"Hey, you got me up at O dark thirty, the least you can do is indulge in a little action."

The front door opened and slammed closed again, the dogs coming into the kitchen followed closely by Dick.

"It's all clear outside. The ground near the front window has some footprints, but that's it." Dick looked over at Rock. "You still have the card for the guy who put in the security at the gym? He mentioned he did residential as well."

Rock nodded. "Yeah, at the office. I'll call him in the morning."

Grimmy whined, coming over to be petted and loved on, praised. "Such a good boy, protecting our house. Good boy." He was shivering, unnerved. "I don't think I can go back to sleep, y'all. I'm *awake*."

Dick nodded. "Yeah, me too."

"Well that's fine by me. You two can come on back to bed with me and I'll nail you both to the mattress."

The sure, definite tone of Rock's voice made him grin, made him chuckle. "You sure you're up to the two of us, old man?"

Rock snorted. "Have I ever not been?"

"Nope. Never. You're a stud." He nodded, not even teasing. His Blue was a stunning piece of work. Rock grunted and nodded, getting up and herding them all toward the bedroom.

He helped Dick get naked, then Rock eased them both into the mattress. Rock kissed them each in turn, feeding from both him and Dick. He moaned, both from the sensation of his Blue's kiss and the sight of his lovers, so pretty, so good together.

"Who wants a piece of me first?" Rock asked, hand stroking that sweet cock.

Rig chuckled. "Pretty, first, Rocketman." That way, if he couldn't get back to sleep, he'd be sure they both would.

Dick grinned and gave him a quick kiss. "You gonna suck me while Rock fucks me?"

"Greedy," noted Rock.

"Hell, yes. Need my men." He leaned down to nuzzle Dick's belly, breathing in the scent of sex and need.

"I just know what I like," Dick told Rock. Then his Pretty's mouth was busy again, Rock kissing Dick as he searched for the lube. Rig found a comfortable spot, tongue teasing, just sliding over the tip of Dick's cock. His Pretty moaned, the sound muffled by Rock's mouth.

That made him chuckle and he started relaxing, forgetting the world and focusing on his Pretty, his Blue, their need. Rock's hand stroked across his face, fingers sliding tenderly before moving down to disappear behind Dick's balls. Rig closed his eyes, mouth surrounding Dick's cock, the suction gentle and slow, matching Rock's motions.

Dick rocked between his mouth and Rock's hand, making those sweet noises he'd never get tired of hearing. Rock was purring, making happy noises of his own. Rig reached out, hand petting Rock's thigh, that hard belly.

"You're like magic," Rock growled.

"Oh fuck yeah," added Dick, pushing up into his mouth with a gasp.

Oh. He moaned, blinking up at his Blue, tongue working his Pretty for all he was worth. Rock settled between Dick's spread legs, guiding that fat prick in as Dick's moans got louder.

He found Dick's hand, brought it to his head. Loved it when they touched him, when they let him know how good it was. Dick whimpered softly, hand sliding through his hair and clutching at his shoulder. He moved in time with Rock, head bobbing. His cheek brushed Dick's soft curls wtih every downward motion, the sensation warming him deep inside, making his cock throb. Dick's other hand came up, sliding over his back with long, restless strokes. His Pretty's hips were rolling, meeting Rock's thrusts and pushing into his mouth.

He buried his face into those curls, deep-throating his lover, pulling in counterpoint to the motion of those hips. Dick wailed.

"That's it, kid, come on my cock."

With a shout, Dick did just that, spunk splashing down the back of his throat as his Pretty came. Rig swallowed every drop, easing the suction, drawing out the pleasure. Rock was purring, Dick gasping and panting, hands sliding over him.

"Mmm..." He dropped soft kisses over Dick's belly. "Fucking sweet."

Dick murmured, the sounds sweet and full of love. Rock slid out of Dick, solid hand stroking the ridged belly. He worked his way up his Pretty, licking and kissing until their mouths met. Dick's lips wrapped around his tongue, pulling lazily as Rock's hands moved from Dick's skin to his. His moan pushed right into Dick's mouth, body responding immediately to his men.

"Come lie on top of me," Dick murmured, tugging at him. Rock helped, getting him spread out over Dick's warm body.

"Feel so good, Pretty." He smiled at Dick, licking and lapping at those open lips, cuddling close.

Dick's hands slid over his skin, mouth taking his in a long, lazy kiss. There was nothing lazy about the fingers sliding into his ass though, Rock was all business. Whimpering, he parted his thighs wide, wanting now, need beginning to bloom inside him.

"He's ready for you, Rock. Loose and wanting."

Rock grunted and that fat prick slid against him.

"Blue..." His back rippled, hips canting, begging.

"You know it." And then just like that his Blue was pushing in, stretching him wide, filling him.

"Oh... Oh, yes." He groaned, licking at Dick's lips, almost purring. Dick's hands slid slowly up and down his sides, Rock's fingers playing his spine. He let Dick take his weight, started rubbing against the strong muscles, against smooth skin, cock hard and wet-tipped. Dick kissed and caressed him, held him as Rock's prick thrust deep.

Oh, fuck, he was happy. He was so lucky, so fucking lucky.

Dick's hand slid down and found his cock, circling it, giving him something to move into as Rock fucked him. Oh, yes. He bucked up into Rock's strength, then settled in, hips moving faster, the rhythm familiar and addictive and perfect.

"You guys look so perfect together. I thought so the first day I watched you make love and I've thought so every day since." He moaned, words lost. He reached out, cupped his Pretty's jaw, trying to tell his lover how much they had needed, even when they hadn't known it. Dick turned and kissed his hand, eyes warm and intense. "I love you," Dick murmured. "I love you both."

Rock thrust harder, a moan coming from his Blue. Rig came with a cry, completely lost, completely overwhelmed. His Blue's roar followed his, heat filling him as Rock collapsed on him.

He was cradled between them. They were hot and solid and his.

He reached out, fingers twining with Dick's, his Blue's joining them. "My men."

Rock growled and kissed the back of his neck, Dick giving him a soft smile. He opened his mouth again, but instead of words, he yawned, the sex and heat and pleasure making him boneless. Dick chuckled and Rock slid away to the side, pulling him along so he was still in between them. Rig thought about getting up, but Dick pushed up against him and Blue's arm wrapped around him, the 'stay' weighing heavy in the air.

Dick's hand squeezed his and a soft kiss met his neck, two sets of lips sliding over his skin and each other.

"Night," whispered Dick.

"Mm... night." Held close, he let Rock's steady heartbeat and Dick's soft sounds lull him to sleep.

***

Dick was exhausted. Just plain tired out. Opening day had been a resounding hit. Tons of people showing up and a whole lot of them signing up, too, which was really cool.

But he and Rock had been up since... well earlier than he'd been up yet since leaving the corps. He'd shook more hands and given the spiel about the gym and the facilities so much he could do it in his sleep, hell probably if he was dead. Rock pulled up at the house and he grabbed one of the bags of take-out and made his way in without a word. Rock was right behind him, just as quiet.

He opened the front door, blinking at the sight of the low table in the front room covered in a cloth, three plates with steaks and potatoes waiting, a huge ass chocolate cake in the center. There was a tin tub full of beer and ice, too. Rig came out of the kitchen, drying off his hands. "Well, did you survive?"

He beamed at Rig, feeling almost perky. "Yeah. Just."

Rock grunted and tossed his bag of take-out at the garbage can under the desk. "You, Jeremy Alexander Roberts? Are a fucking star."

"Come on in and sit and eat." Rig puttered idly, getting them both settled, beers in hand. "I drove by at two; y'all were rocking."

Dick nodded, watching a moment as Rock dug in like a man starving. Come to think of it, they hadn't had lunch -- they were both starving. "We didn't have a dull moment. Four of us welcoming people and we could barely keep up. I think we did good."

Rock nodded. "We did, kid."

"Cool." Rig started working Rock's shirt off, rubbing the thick neck, giving him a smile. "You're next, Pretty."

"You should eat, too," murmured Rock. The big guy groaned though and leaned his head forward to give Rig room to work.

"I'm not going to say no, but Rock's right -- your steak's gonna get cold."

"I can warm it up." Rig grinned as Rock finished his. "Assuming there's any left after y'all finish. Go on, eat."

"You sure?" Rock asked, fork spearing Rig's meat.

"Yep." Rig nodded, fingers working hard, digging into Rock's shoulders. Rock groaned, stopping for a moment to just enjoy the massage.

Dick grinned and worked on his meat and potatoes, taking a bite of salad now and then. "Folks really liked that the mirrored stuff was all up on the top floor, so they could avoid it if they wanted. And having the juice bar? That was a stroke of genius, Rig. We owe you one."

Rig nodded, grinned over. "I'm glad it was worth getting the license for."

Then the lanky Texan slid across the floor, took his shirt off, and those fingers digging in. "Mmm... oh, I'll take another dozen days like today if this is how it's going to end."

Rock nodded. "Yeah. There dessert?"

Rig grinned. "No, Blue. The big chocolate cake that says 'Congratulations'? Just for show."

"Oh fuck, I didn't even see it." Rock shook his head and Dick chuckled.

"You must be tired if you're not seeing chocolate cake, Rock."

"Y'all had a long damned day." Rig winked, reaching out to brush a finger along Rock's cheek. "Besides, he was blinded by the steak."

Dick laughed. "Me-e-eat."

Rock swatted him, but the blue eyes were twinkling. "Brat."

"I try."

Rig chuckled. "Congratulations, marines. Y'all rock."

"We didn't do too badly at all. Thanks, Rig." Rock looked happy, proud and it made Dick smile. It was a good look on the big guy and he was thrilled to be a part of it.

"Yeah, thanks. We couldn't have done it without your support."

Rig chuckled. "Sure you could, but you don't have to. Cut the cake, Pretty."

"Just not the cheese, kid." Rock gave him a wink and they all groaned.

Rig chuckled. "Oh, man... And he's got dozens of customers to work his act out on now..."

"They were eating him up with a spoon." He grinned, cutting the cake. "Derek, Melanie and I? We'd do if the big hunk was going to be more than a half hour's wait."

Rig's eyes were fond, warm. "He's a beautiful man, right enough."

"Yep. And all ours." He grinned. More than one guy and gal had been disappointed to find out Rock was very much off the market.

"Hell, yeah." Rig nodded, fingers sliding down to tweak his nipple ring. "My marines."

He squeaked, pushing back against Rig.

"That's right." Rig nuzzled, lips soft and warm on his jaw."Mine."

"I can think of worse things to be."

Rock nodded. "You got that right, kid."

Rig's cheek heated against his, hands and body close and touching and warm. He cut them each a piece of cake, distracted enough by Rig that Rock's was a little on the small side. The big guy shook his head and cut himself another slice to go with the first.

Rig chuckled. "He found the cake, Pretty."

He giggled. "He usually does."

Rock just grunted at them, happily eating cake.

Rig's tongue slid over his neck, fingers petting his belly. He moaned, picking up a bite of cake and passing it back to Rig with his fingers. Rig hummed, licking and nibbling the cake from his hand. He moaned softly, leaning in to lick the chocolate taste from Rig's mouth.

"Only you two could make eating chocolate cake obscene."

"Jealous..." Rig pushed into his lap, the kiss going deep and hungry. Rock might have answered, but he was too busy kissing Rig, too busy touching that warm skin. Rig tugged off his own shirt, rubbing them together, belly-to-belly. He whimpered, fingers sliding, searching for the spot near Rig's right rib and the one on Rig's belly and those two sensitive little nubs of flesh that would make Rig go wild. He got a low, hungry moan, Rig's tongue fucking his lips, fingers massaging his temples. He found Rig's nipple ring and tugged it gently, twisting it a bit to vary the stimulation.

"Oh..." Rig pushed closer, eyes wide.

"Save some for me," growled Rock, cutting himself another piece of cake and stealing the last bites of his steak.

"Mmm... You gonna save some, Pretty?" Rig chuckled, rubbing hard, moaning low.

"Oh, I bet we'll be able to get it up again for him." He popped open Rig's top button, fingers sliding in to tease the tip of Rig's cock.

"Oh...More, Pretty. More." He got the zipper down and gave Rig what they both wanted, his fingers tracing the hard cock, searching out the veins and following them. Rig moaned, leaned back, hips rocking.

"Wanna taste you, Rig." He pushed Rig back, bending double to lick away the liquid from the tip of Rig's cock.

Rig stretched. "You're not careful, I'll tump over the table."

"Mmm, sounds like fun." He grinned, lapping some more, taking the head into his mouth and sucking.

"Oh. Oh, it's good." Rig's hands stuttered over his head.

Moaning, he took more of Rig in. The awkward position they were in eased suddenly, Rock shifting the table and kneeling behind Rig, supporting the skinny body. Rig hummed, mouth lifting, searching for Rock's. He watched, eyes looking up that long body as their mouths joined. It made him moan again, made him suck harder on Rig's prick.

Rig rocked, cock sliding on his tongue, parting his lips. He opened his mouth wide and wrapped his hands around Rig's hips, encouraging the movements. Rig was jerking, moaning low, pushing into him. Needing. Rock's hands slid around his, helping Rig move. Faster and faster that hot prick slid into his mouth, bumping the back of his throat.

"Gonna... Oh, sweet fuck, Pretty. Feels so good..." Rig pushed deep, crying out as his mouth was filled with spunk. He swallowed it down, loving the taste of Rig in his mouth.

"Oh. Oh. I... I was gonna celebrate y'all..." Rig moaned low, licked his lips.

"We're not celebrating?" he asked.

"Feels like celebrating to me," noted Rock.

Rig grinned. "Y'all are the *best* celebrators."

Rock purred. "Come on, let's get horizontal. I'm gonna celebrate all over your ass."

"Oh, yeah. Yeah, Blue. I'm all about that."

"I know you are."

Dick laughed and kissed Rig's belly. "You could do me while Rock's doing you."

"Mmm." Rig nodded, grinning, eyes twinkling. "I could."

He beamed up at Rig and kissed that belly again. "Thanks for making this special, Rig."

"Well, y'all deserve it." He got a wink, a grin. "Come on, y'all. Bed."

"Best thing I've heard all day."

Rock nodded and stood, pulling Rig up with him. Dick followed them, watching a great pair of asses . Fuck, he was a lucky man.

Chapter Six

The house looked nice with the lights all on, the workshop finished and drywalled and painted. The flowers were all faded back for the night and the late autumn, but hell, as chilly as the wind could be, it wasn't cold. Rock's truck was parked beside Dick's new car -- he and Rock had both blinked and sputtered when Dick decided to get it. A car of all things. Still, Rig had to admit it was comfortable and they could all fit in it together. Had a kick-ass stereo system too.

He sighed, grinned at himself. Man, he was tired if he was spending time admiring the cars instead of hauling his butt in and seeing if someone had saved him a plate.

He slid out of the Jeep, grabbing his paperwork. Grimmy came ambling over, limping just a little. "Hey, pretty boy. That glucosamine helping your arthritis? You're looking good."

He stopped to pet and chat, first with Grim, then Miss Lucy, throwing the ball a couple times before heading up the stairs. "Hey, y'all."

Rock and Dick looked up from their take-out burgers. Rock gave him a grunt and Dick a warm smile.

"Hey. We brought you supper -- didn't beat you home by much either." Dick nodded to a third bag sitting on the coffeetable.

"Long day?" He sort of asked the question as he headed back to his office to unload his files and check his messages.

"When aren't they?" Rock asked around a mouthful.

"Yeah." He could hear Dick agree through the open door. "Man, sometimes it feels like we never see each other anymore. I mean Sunday's the only day we're all guaranteed off and fuck, it's half taken up by sleeping."

"Yeah, that and erranding and laundry and shit. It's hell being a grownup." He checked his messages, then headed into the bedroom to change. "Did y'all feed the dogs?"

"Are they in here trying to get the burgers out of our mouths?" Rock called.

Rig chuckled, pulled on a pair of sweats and one of Rock's sweaters before heading in to grab his sandwich. "Thanks for supper, y'all."

"Sorry it's not something decent, but I was so not up to cooking, even just throwing something on the grill." Dick gave him an apologetic smile.

"We're all too fucking busy," grunted Rock.

He nodded. "I'll start putting something in the crock-pot before I leave some mornings."

"Only on your nights." Rock sounded very sure.

Dick chuckled. "You just don't want beans more than a couple times a week."

"I like Rig's beans well enough, but he's as busy as you and I are."

"I know." Dick sighed. "I'm not sure I can even remember the last time we all just snuggled together after fucking. It's hard to believe we see less of each other now than we did when we were in the corps."

Rock nodded, grunted. "I don't fucking like it."

"It'll get better, eventually, and I can make other stuff in the crockpot..." He finished his burger and his soda, wrapping everything up before going to figure out whose lap to snuggle into.

Rock solved that for him by tugging him in hard. Those big hands started wandering right away, almost as if Rock was assuring himself that Rig was okay.

"We need a night just for us," muttered Rock. "A no excuses, I have to get home unless I'm fucking dying standing date."

He pushed closer, rubbing and humming, just enjoying those hands. Then what Rock said hit him. A date. For all of them. His Blue must be really missing them. "I'd like that."

"Oh yeah, me too." Dick was nodding, cleaning up his and Rock's garbage and pushing onto the sofa next to them. "And if it were on a Saturday night it wouldn't matter how late it went, because we all still have Sunday off."

Rock grunted, the sound pleased. "Exactly."

Rig hummed as Dick's warmth settled against his back. "Mmm... good food, good sex, it sounds perfect."

"It does. We'll start tomorrow," Rock informed them in a voice that brooked no arguments.

Dick chuckled, hands sliding on him, on Rock. "I think we need to practice the good sex part. Just to make sure we're up to speed for tomorrow."

"I do like the way you think, kid."

"Ah... A little practice-run fucking." He chuckled, lifted his face for Rock's kiss. Rock gave it to him, mouth hard and sure, tongue invading and taking the taste right out of his mouth. Dick moaned softly and whispered 'yeah' and rubbed against his back. He arched, rubbing nice and slow, steady, moans pushing into Blue's lips.

Dick's hands worked on undressing them, pulling off his and Rock's shirts and then starting on their pants. Rock's hands were busy, too, stroking his skin. His hands were on Rock's face, stroking and touching, admiring. Rock purred for him, Dick's sweet noises starting, sliding along his spine as Dick's mouth found his skin.

"Oh. Oh, y'all..." He moaned, sliding and moaning, rubbing between them.

Rock growled, fingers finding his ass and squeezing as one of Dick's hands slid around his hip and circled his cock. They kissed over his shoulder, the sounds wet and hot in his ear.

He fastened onto Rock's throat, licking and sucking, lapping the salt off the hot skin. A shudder moved through Rock and Dick gasped as the kiss ended. "It still fucking turns me on that we can do that and not have to worry."

"Mm-hmm... Mine. My men." He was hard now, wanting, needing maybe.

"That's my line," growled Rock, taking his mouth again, really letting him feel the kiss. His cry pushed right into Rock's mouth, hips rubbing against that hard belly.

Dick's thumb pressed against his hole, Rock's fingers spreading him wide as the muscled body moved with him. He groaned, eyes fastening onto Rock's, suddenly close, balls tight, needing. Rock pushed a moan into his mouth and Dick's tongue pushed unexpectedly into his hole. He shot with a cry, eyes rolling, heat flooding his skin.

Dick's tongue kept working him, Rock purring, those blue eyes burning, hot. His hand found Rock's prick, pumped it nice and slow, entire body rocking with the motions of Dick's tongue.

Rock purred for him. "Gonna suck me, Rabbit?"

"Oh. Oh, fuck. Yeah, Blue. Yeah..." He dipped his head, licked Rock's nipple.

Rock groaned and spread his legs wide, offering him that fine prick. Dick just moved with him, tongue busy, fingers sliding on his belly, his hips, his cock. He took Rock in, moaning at the heat, the salt, the flavor. Christ, he needed this, needed to make Rock feel this. Those big hands slid through his hair, petting his head, solid and warm and Rock. Humming, he took more and more, swallowing, hips moving in time, cock filling again.

Dick was still making sweet noises, the sounds making his whole ass vibrate as that tongue parted him again and again. He lifted his head for a second, groaning. "Fuck me. Come on, Pretty. Need you."

"Oh, fuck. Yes." Dick licked his ass one more time and shifted, prick hot and hard as it slowly pushed in.

Fuck, yeah. That was it. Caught between heaven and sheer perfection. Rig groaned and started moving, fucking himself between them. They moved with him, Rock's low moans and Dick's sweet porno noises mingling together as their hands slid on his skin, their cocks pushing into his body over and over.

His hands slid around Rock's waist, holding on, nose buried in the soft pubes. Rock's groans got louder, cock throbbing on his tongue. He swallowed hard, tightening around both cocks, fucking his men.

"Rig!" Dick went first, crying out and filling him with heat.

He nodded, throat closing around the tip of Rock's prick. That earned him his roar, Rock pushing deep as he shot. He took everything Rock had to give, cuddling in and cleaning that heavy prick with his tongue.

Dick's cock slipped from his ass, his Pretty's warm hands sliding on his skin as Dick settled against him.

"Mmm... " He relaxed, cheek on Rock's belly, happy as a clam.

Rock stretched a little and settled as well, rumbling happily. "Not bad, not bad at all. Might want to practice a bit more before tomorrow night though."

Dick chuckled. "And he calls us the sluts."

"Mmm... Yeah." He nodded, licking Rock's belly, grinning wide.

Rock grunted. "That would be because you are."

"Takes one to know one," suggested Rig with a grin.

Dick's laughter was soft, happy. "Yeah, I guess it does at that."

"Yep." He scooted up a little, grabbed the remote and found something painless on the tube, Pretty draping the quilt around them.

Rock was soon snoring softly, Dick's fingers sliding on his skin in a gentle, soothing caress, his men holding him between them, surrounding him.

Damn, it felt fine to be home. Just fine.

***

Thanksgiving and Rock was sitting on the couch watching the start of the game, wearing proper Thanksgiving attire -- his loosest sweats. The place smelled amazing. Fuck only knew when Rig had gotten up to start the turkey and everything, but that smell sure put him in a happy place.

He was gonna eat until he busted, starting with game munchies, which he hoped were going to put in an appearance soon. If Rig and Dick hadn't decided to munch on each other in the kitchen...

He heard a soft moan, a chuckle, another quiet laugh, the sounds floating in from the kitchen.

"Hey! Where's my munchies?" If they were going to make out, the least they could do was do it where he could see and bring munchies for him to enjoy while watching. It was Thanksgiving after all, not some random Thursday.

"Get your butt in here and get some, if you're hungry." Rig's voice was husky, happy, horny.

"Excuse me?" He hadn't heard that. No fucking way.

Dick's soft laughter said that yes, he had.

"I said, get your butt in here and get some. There's food."

"What if it's not munchies I want?" If they made him get up he was going to have to do something to retaliate and goddamnit he was comfortable where he was.

Rig's face appeared in the doorway, lips swollen, cheeks flushed, looking like a man who'd just been on his knees. "Are you being lazy, old man?"

"It's Thanksgiving, Rig. It's my god-given right to be lazy, to have the game on TV, munchies in my hand and that mouth wrapped around *my* prick." Damn, that was a sweet look. Made him fucking hard.

Those eyes just danced for him, Rig happy and smiling at him, playing right along. "I thought that was your god-given right on Veteran's Day, Blue."

He nodded. Yeah, he could handle that. "That, too."

"You're spoiled." Rig licked his lips.

"Yep, and too long in the tooth for you to stop spoiling me now."

Rig laughed, pushing into his arms, straddling his thighs. "I reckon you're right."

Dick came out with Rig's homemade salsa, guacamole and chips along with something else that smelled divine.

He purred, hands sliding up Rig's back. "Oh, now I'm a happy Rocketman."

Rig chuckled, kissed him nice and slow, the flavor of Dick on the sweet lips. Oh, yes. Definitely a happy Rocketman. He pushed his hands into the back of Rig's jeans, cupping that sweet ass, chuckling into Rig's mouth as he realised his slut was going comando. Rig wiggled that pretty ass for him, making Dick laugh and stroke the skin between Rig's jeans and t-shirt.

"You're going to make me forget all about my stomach," he told Rig with a wink. Damn if that didn't make the kid laugh that much louder.

Rig grinned, hands pushing down to slide against his belly. "This stomach?"

"Oh, see now I'm thinking of it again." He chuckled, muscles moving beneath Rig's fingers.

"Mmm... You are one beautiful son of a bitch, Blue Eyes..."

Yeah, he knew he was. He worked hard to be. And that look in Rig's eyes and the soft moan that Dick gave, fingers stroking his side? That made it all worth it. Rig leaned in, kissed him good and hard, that mouth working hard to make the room spin. Damn if it didn't work, too, Rig just sending him flying, making him want good and hard.

"Too many clothes," muttered Dick and his chuckles filled Rig's mouth. He could always count on the kid to make sure naked happened.

Those eyes were watching him, grey as a winter sky, but warm, happy, focused on him. The kid worked their clothes off, sharing kisses on their skin. Fuck it was hot, sexy. They both were. He growled, hands starting to wander Rig's body.

"Mmm... love that sound." Rig drew the kid around, making the kiss a three-way.

Oh, fuck, yeah. Three way kisses were hot and sweet and made his cock fucking throb happily. Rig moaned, rocking and rubbing, holding Dick close. He fed one soft growl after another into the kiss, knowing it would make Rig wild, that that would make Dick wild.

It worked just like he'd thought, those grey eyes flashing dark, kiss harder.

Dick's sweet noises started up, muted by their mouths. "Is this the traditional Thanksgiving sex? Isn't it supposed to happen after we eat?"

"We're out now, we can fuck before and after we eat."

"Fucking A, Blue." Rigger laughed, pushed back into the kisses.

"No, you're fucking me." He winked and Dick groaned. That got him an eye roll, another kiss, all full of laughter.

He kissed back, feeling happy right down to his balls. This was what the holidays were supposed to be about. He knew Rig was a little disappointed they weren't going back to visit his Momma, but they were all so busy, they needed to take this time for themselves.

And it felt good, their house, their home, their bodies.

He got their asses in his hands, fingers teasing along their creases. Both so fucking hot and eager for him.

"Damn, Blue. Feels good. Fucking fine."

"You know it." He pushed his fingers in, Dick moaning loudly.

Rig chuckled. "He got sucked off and he's still begging for it."

"Sluts. The pair of you." Fuck, he wouldn't do without them.

Two fingers in Dick, two in Rig and they were both writhing. All he needed was two pricks. Rig's hand was working his cock, pumping in time. Soft pants brushed his lips, his cheek. "Who wants to get fucked first?"

"Oh, you're feeling full of piss and vinegar today." Rig chuckled, pumped a little harder.

"It's Thanksgiving. I've got to make sure my men remember what they're grateful for."

"Oh, I don't think I'm gonna forget," Dick murmured, kissing him and then Rig.

"Not a fucking chance." Rig grinned, sliding behind Dick, searching for the lube.

He worked the kid's ass. "Looks like Rig's letting you go first."

"I'm so good to him." Rig slicked up those long hands, one going to his cock, the other disappearing behind Dick.

He groaned as Rig's figners slid into Dick's ass next to his own. "Fucking sexy, the pair of you."

The kid was panting, wanting, eyes hot as Rig worked his ass.

"Want a piece of the Rocketman, kid?"

"You know it, Rock. Fuck."

"Yep, that's the idea."

Rig chuckled, shifting the kid up a little. "Come on , Pretty, he's hard for you."

Dick moaned and let Rig guide him. Rock pushed up into that tight heat, purring as Dick sat down on him. Yeah. Yeah, the kid was hot, tight, eager. Rig's hand slipped down, started stroking his balls. He moaned, Dick's hands tight on his shoulders as the kid bounced up and down on his prick.

"So pretty." Rig kept touching, kept humming low. He growled, taking Dick's mouth, starting to pull the kid down hard onto his prick. He could feel the tight ass start to ripple around him, Dick close. Rig's hand reached around, pumping Dick's cock, good and hard. "Come on, Pretty. I know you want to."

Dick cried out, squeezing him hard as he shot.

"That's it..." Rig sounded as satisfied as if he'd been the one fucking the kid's ass.

Rock chuckled and licked at Dick's lips, happy blue eyes looking into his own. "Good one, kid?"

"They're all good, Rock. You're a stud."

He puffed up a little and gave the kid another kiss.

Rig chuckled, eyes shining over the kid's shoulder. "There enough of you for me, Blue?"

"Isn't there always?"

"You know it."

He patted his thighs. "Saddle up, Cowboy."

"Hooboy." Rig nudged the kid out of the way, thighs spreading. He purred, hand sliding on Dick's belly before turning his attention to Rig. Dick's hand slicked him up again for Rig's ass. Rig was grinning, rocking slow, tempting. "Gonna make me fly, Blue?"

"You know it, Rabbit." He met those grey eyes and smiled, let the kid get them set up and fit together, hand in glove, cock in ass. Rig nodded, sank down and took him in deep, fucking tight and hot. He moaned, eyes rolling.

"Mmm... Yeah. Yeah, Blue. Fucking hot." Rig started moving, riding him nice and slow. He spread, got his footing good and solid and started meeting Rig's body, thrusting up into that perfect heat. Rig stretched, head thrown back, stomach rippling, riding him like a pro.

His hands started to wander, sliding on Rig's slim belly, up to tug on the pretty little ring in Rig's nipple. Those eyes went wide. "Oh..."

"You like that, Rig?" As if he didn't know. As if he couldn't tell by the way Rig's ass went tight around his prick.

"No. Not sensitive at all..." Rig's eyes rolled.

He laughed and tugged again. "Give me a hand here, kid. Rig thinks he's not sensitive."

Dick grinned and kissed Rig, hands starting to move over the fine skin. Rig opened right up, leaning back into Dick, one hand wrapping around Dick's neck. He pushed up harder, faster, tugging on that little ring. Rig's belly flushed, long throat working, cock jerking hard.

"That's it, Rigger. Come for your old man."

"Yeah. Yeah, Blue." Rig panted, all done playing, eyes rolling.

"Uh-huh." He shifted slightly, nailing Rig's gland hard on the next thrust.

Spunk sprayed over him, Rig jerking, groaning low. That sweet ass held him so tight and he waited a moment, until Rig loosened just a little and then he thrust up, grunting as he jerked hard into Rig's body. Dick's fingers slid across his chest, found his nipple ring and tugged him right into shooting. He roared, filling Rig.

Rig moaned, leaning down to rest against his chest. "Mmm... Oh, yeah. I'm thankful."

Dick chuckled. "Fuck, yeah."

Rock nodded, grinned, feeling lazy and good. Not to mention he'd gotten his munchies and his men without having to leave the couch.

Life? Was fucking good to him.

***

Dick finished up the dishes, singing along to some country song or another on the radio. He couldn't tell you who was singing or what the name of the song was, but he knew more lyrics than he'd maybe admit, thanks to this being Rig's radio station of choice. He supposed he could change it to find something else when he was in the kitchen, but he didn't mind the music that much and it made him think of Rig, which was never a bad thing.

He was stuffed to the gills, Rig's Thanksgiving Dinner a real winner this year. Not that it wasn't always, but this one had been extra special. Maybe it was just getting a little older, living life a little more openly. Ah, maybe he was just turning into as big a pig as Rock when it came to good food.

And stuffed as he was, that didn't stop him from filling a tray with three coffee cups, the pecan pie, a can of whipped cream spray, forks and the plate of brownies and cookies. Damn, he was going to have to do some extra working out next week.

He took the tray into the living room, grinning at the site of Rig curled up next to Rock on the couch, the big guy snoring lightly as the game played on the television.

"Should we wake him for pie?" he asked quietly.

"No, Pretty. Let him sleep. He'll get some later." Rig gave him a sweet, slow grin. "How're you doing?"

He smiled back, but Rock spoke up before he could answer. "He'll have some now *and* later. I can sleep once the pie is gone."

Dick chuckled passing out plates and cutting big pieces of pie for them all.

Rig blinked and shook his head. "Y'all going to help me finish this?"

"Lightweight," accused Rock.

Dick just grinned. "I'm betting we won't let it go to waste, Rig."

Rig stretched, patted that thin belly. "I'm going to gain thirty pounds today alone."

Rock snorted and Dick grinned. "You can join the gym. We'll make up a personal training regimen for you."

"So long as that means soaking in the hot tub? I'm so there." Rig grinned, winked.

He laughed, but Rock snorted again. "Be good for you, Rig. To work out. Work off some of the stress from work."

"Right." Rig gave Rock a wide-eyed look. "Have you *seen* the boys that work out at y'all's gym? Good Lord, it's hard enough to hold my own with the two of you, much less an entire gym full. Shit, no."

Rock shook his head. "No fucking way. We set that place up so people wouldn't feel like that at all. Spread the work out stuff out so the housewives and spare tire guys wouldn't feel bad. The pretty boys all work out on the third floor with the mirrors."

Dick nodded. "The second floor has all the same equipment, no mirrors and the shape of the clientelle varies. Plus there's the private rooms."

Rig's cheeks went a dull red, their redneck reaching for a coffee cup, pie plate taking its place. "Did I remember to feed the dogs?"

"Yeah, they're curled up together in the kitchen." Grim liked the warmth when they had the oven on, he wasn't getting around as much as he had been and Lucy was settling with him, keeping him company a lot.

Rock grunted. "You want to be a muscle man, Rig? The kid and I can get you there, but that's not why I want you at the gym. You work fucking hard, you can't forget your body needs to be kept in shape is all I'm saying."

Dick had to hide his grin. Rock needed to take his own advice and eat the vegetables Rig put in front of him. They were old arguments.

"I'll stick to getting my exercise hauling my ass up and down the hospital stairs and dancefloor, thanks."

Dick slid a hand along Rig's leg, offering quiet support. No one could honestly accuse Rig of being fat or out of shape, not even Rig himself. Rock just grunted again.

"Are y'all closing for the week of Christmas?" Rig finished his coffee, stood and stretched. "I need another. Y'all both good?"

"No, just the 24th through the 26th." Rock tugged on Rig's jeans. "Sit down, the kid'll get your refill."

Grinning, Dick stood. "Yeah, I will."

He gave them each a kiss and grabbed all three mugs. Rig chuckled, shook his head, but settled back into Rock's arms, humming softly. When he came back with the coffee it was to find Rock making it up to Rig with long, deep kisses, Rig's head tilted back, held in one big hand. Fuck, they looked good together and he could live to be a few hundred years old and he was sure it would still make him happy just to be a part of them, to know he belonged with them.

Rig was all stretched out, snuggled into Rock, tension and unhappy loved right out of him. Dick put the coffee cups on the table and settled on the other side of Rock, pushing into the warm kisses, moaning softly as room was made for him, just like that. Rig's hand reached out, wrapped around his neck, holding on.

He moaned, rubbing against Rock's side, hand sliding along Rig's back, around to stroke the skinny belly. Rig pressed into the touch, moaning low. He whimpered and moaned, noises just leaving him like they always did when they touched.

Rock's rumbles underlaid everything and he knew they were all present and horny and feeling good.

Feeling at home.

***

He put the guys' presents in the workshop and locked the door, then went back to the Jeep for the lights and shit for the house. Rig checked his watch. Five thirty. Damn, it was later than he'd thought. The lights could wait until tomorrow. It was half an hour 'til date night. He checked the chili in the crockpot, put the onions and cheese and fritos on the table. The boys would bring home dessert and beer. Then the puppers were fed, Grimmy given his pills. At 5:55, the truck pulled in the drive and Rig turned off the phones and the pager.

They came in laughing, Rock with Dick in a headlock, fingers running through the getting long hair, giving Dick a hard time about it. He chuckled. "Evening, y'all. You leave that boy alone, now. Hell, I didn't even know his hair was dark 'til last month..."

Dick laughed. "I keep threatening to let it grow down my back."

Rock snorted. "And I keep threatening to feed him his teeth if that happens."

He tilted his head, looked. "I don't know, Pretty. It'd get in the way of fucking, I think."

Dick's eyes widened comically. "Go get the clippers, Rock!"

Rock gave him a pleased, smug look.

He laughed, winked. "What's dessert? I made chili."

"Oh!" Dick turned and high tailed it back outside while Rock chuckled.

"We got distracted."

He chuckled and wandered over for his kiss, happy all through. "Y'all have a good day, Blue?"

"Yeah, we did. Lots of folks are signing up, taking advantage of the Christmas specials. And the kid promises me that New Year's is the boom time for gyms. I hope so, we're not seeing anything near a profit yet." Rock visibly pushed the worry away, bringing their mouths together in a long kiss.

"Hey, no getting started without me -- I was rescuing the cheesecake."

Rig grinned, deepened the kiss, teasing the kid a little. There was a thump and then Dick was pushing against their sides into their arms and into their kiss.

Rock broke it off after a moment or two. "Tell me you didn't drop the cheesecake."

"I can, but it wouldn't be the truth." Dick looked unrepentant.

"It is white chocolate raspberry or chocolate-chocolate?"

"It's half and half, though there might be chocolate chocolate on the white chocolate raspberry now." Dick laughed and kissed them both, earning a glare from Rock. "Come on, big guy -- the worst that happened is it's a little smushed."

"There better not be any raspberries on my chocolate."

"You can feed them to me, Blue. I love raspberries." Rig pressed closer, rubbing a little. "I'll lick them off your cock."

"And here I thought there was nothing that could make a fruit or vegetable a good thing."

Dick started laughing, eyes dancing happily. "Fuck, I love date night."

"Come on, I got the new shoot-em-up at the video store while I was out. We can eat and watch."

"Cool. Supper smells good?"

"It does," Rock nodded, breathing in deep. "Corn bread?"

"Would I make you eat chili without cornbread, Blue?"

Rock shrugged. "You've been busy as we have, Rig. I didn't want to presume."

He looked at Rock, blinked, and then pushed into those warm arms. "The day I can't take ten minutes to make you cornbread, Blue, is the day I cut my hours back."

Rock grunted something non-commital, hands sliding on his back, but Dick was grinning at them like a fool, eyes soft. He was willing to bet Pretty was just barely holding out on teasing Rock for his concern.

"I'll go get supper, you two sit and get the movie set up." Still grinning at them, Dick headed for the kitchen, taking the box of cheesecake with him.

"You know he just stole the cheesecake, don't you?"

"S'okay. I've got the best treat in the house."

"Flattery will get you laid, Rocketman." He pressed closer, licking Rock's lips. "Happy Saturday."

"That is the plan." Rock grinned wide, hands cupping his ass and tugging him in close. "This was a good idea, wasn't it? It's working well."

“It was." He nodded. "When shit is bad at work, it's good to know I only have to wait 'til Saturday to set it down."

Rock frowned. "Things still bad, Rabbit? I thought you were mostly just busy."

"Oh, you know -- some little kid really sick, that sort of thing. I had to send a wee thing to Children's this week. Leukemia. It's hard to lay that sort of thing down, but I gotta or it'll eat me up."

"Oh, that's different from always drawing the short straw." Rock nodded and tugged him toward the couch, laying him down and starting up a massage.

"Oh..." He groaned low, entire body melting into the sofa, eyes rolling. "Fuck..."

"Nope. It's a massage. But I know I'm good, so I understand how you might get it confused..."

"Uh-huh. Don't stop."

Rock chuckled. "Not planning to."

Dick brought out bowls of steaming chili, giving them a grin. "Oh, that looks nice." Then he went to get beer and the cornbread, bringing them out along with utensils.

Rig's eyes closed and he stretched, more than willing to forgo food for a minute for those hands. Hell, he'd forgo breathing.

Rock's fingers worked their way down his spine and then back up again and then patted his ass. "Supper's on."

"You can keep going," murmured Dick, "the chili's pretty hot still."

"I'm hungry," growled Rock. "Rig wants more when we're done he can have it."

Rig chuckled. "Go on and eat, Blue."

Dick dug into his chili, Rock only a half step behind. "'s good, Rig."

He let his eyes fall shut again, grinning. "Course it is."

"Aren't you going to eat?" Dick asked.

"In a minute. I'm comfy." Dick laughed and Rock made a smug sound, hand patting his ass. He dozed off, listening to Dick and Rock chatter, laughing about this or that. He was woken by those hands on his shoulders again, digging in and insisting on taking any tension he had left. The smell of coffee was strong, and beneath it was the far subtler scent of chocolate and raspberries.

"Mmm... feels good." He hummed, head pillowed on his hands.

"Of course it does."

Dick's soft laughter followed Rock's words and a spoonful of white chocolate raspberry cheesecake was brought close. "Have some dessert, Rig."

He opened his mouth, the sweet rich and tart and cool.

Rock's hands continued to make him melt, stopping only to strip him down to skin, and Dick continued to feed him, one sweet bite after another. It was slow and lazy and relaxing as fuck.

"Y'all are good to this old boy." He moaned as Rock's fingers found a tender spot.

"You take good care of us," Dick pointed out.

"Couldn't do without my morning wake up call." Rock's fingers gentled, worked the spot for a long time.

"Oh..." Magic. Oh, he hadn't even known he'd hurt there...

"You tell me next time -- before you get like this," growled Rock. "I don't mind giving you a massage now and then."

"Didn't know I needed one."

"Then I'll declare it date and massage night."

"Oh, does that mean I get one, too?" Dick asked.

"Sure, kid. When Rig says he's done."

Dick laughed. "You mean when pigs fly?"

"Hey, I'm not... It just feels so good..." He stretched, back popping.

Dick's laughter got louder and he got a kiss. "Hey, if it was me, no way I'd tell Rock I was ever done. Feels too good, having those big, strong hands on your skin..."

He grinned, nodded. "Almost better than sex."

Rock's hands stilled. "What?"

Dick bit his bottom lip, eyes just dancing. "I think Rig said it was better than sex."

"Bitch. I said almost." He shook his head, grinned.

Dick's laughter sounded again and he got another kiss as Rock patted his ass again. "I think it's time to fuck. Just to make sure you remember what's better."

"You melt me and then you want me to move?" He winked at Dick, thighs spreading a little.

"You don't need to move for me to be able to fuck you, Rabbit. He really has forgotten, kid. This calls for drastic measures."

His Pretty looked like he was going to choke he was laughing so hard. Rig hid his grin. "Oooh... Drastic measures! That sounds fun!"

Rock snorted. "Making fun of me doesn't get you fucked, Rabbit."

"I wasn't making fun, Blue. I was encouraging drastic measures."

"Well that's all right then." The strong hands moved down to his ass, spread his cheeks, thumbs pressing. He clenched a little, then spread further, moaning low, happy deep down. Dick moaned softly and kissed him, mouth warm and eager. Oh. Sweet. He pushed into the kiss, groaning low.

Dick's mouth opened wide, tongue dancing with his as Rock's thumbs pushed into his ass. He arched, hips tilted, cock sliding on the sofa. Rock groaned, mouth finding his spine as those thumbs fucked him.

"Oh..." He shifted. "Oh, that's good."

"Yeah? He pushing those thick thumbs into you?" Dick asked. "Spreading you wide?"

His eyes went wide, fastening onto Dick's pretty eyes. "Listen to you." Fuck, that was hot.

Dick's eyes went dark. "You like that?" His Pretty's voice had gone all husky now, too. "You like it when he gets you ready? Stretches you out with his hot, thick fingers, making sure you can take that wide cock?"

His hips jerked, not sleepy at all now. Sweet fuck, no. Now he needed. "Yes..."

"Yeah? What're you going to do to him next, Rock?"

"Gonna fuck him hard, kid."

"You hear that, Rig? Rock's going to slick up that huge cock and push it into you, hit your gland and make you fly."

"Shit, Pretty..." His cheeks were hot, flushed dark, heart pounding.

"Want me to stop?" Dick asked, just as Rock's thumbs slid away.

"No. No, don't..." He brought their lips together, hips rocking, begging Rock for more. Rock purred, hands returning to his ass to hold his cheeks apart, that slick, fat cock nudging at his hole.

"Oh, let him in, Rig. Let that fat cock slide inside, split you wide and fill you right up. Fuck, it feels so good when he does that. So good when that hot cock plunges in again and again." Dick was whispering now, hand moving slowly on his own cock.

He was whimpering, eyes fastened to his Pretty's, heat filling him. "Fuck. Oh. Oh, Pretty..."

"Yeah, Rock's fucking you now. I can see his cock going into you and coming out again. And again. Oh, fuck, I hope he's got some left for me when he's done you. I know what it feels like, that cock like a hot rod inside you, hitting your gland and setting you on fire."

Rig jerked, starting to ride hard, panting hard. "More. Shit. Shit. I need."

"Harder Rock," Dick ordered. "And take his cock in your hand. Stroke him. Run your thumb over the top, press into his slit, you know he likes that." Rock started moving harder, faster, hand sliding beneath him to follow Dick's quiet instructions. "Oh, that's it, is that better Rig? Can you feel that fat prick sliding against your gland now?"

"I..." His eyes rolled, throat working hard, entire body shuddering as he came.

"Fuck, you two are sexy," murmured Dick, hand still working his prick.

"Save that for me, kid," muttered Rock, still moving in him, softly, gently pushing in and out.

He just moaned, aftershocks making him shudder. Dick kissed him again, tongue sliding eagerly into his mouth as Rock's prick disappeared.

His ass and legs were covered by a blanket and then Rock was pushing the coffee table away and kneeling behind Dick. "Hands and knees, kid."

Rig just kept kissing, loving his Pretty the best way he knew. Dick shifted but didn't let their lips part and a soft moan was pushed into him. He held that gaze, so fucking happy, so at home, so fucking in love it hurt. He could tell as Dick got close, the pleasure glazing the pretty eyes, Dick's kisses growing sloppy, needy.

Rock was groaning, the sound of skin slapping on skin loud. He reached out, hands sliding against Rock's hand, Dick's back. Dick shuddered as his fingers teased the small of his Pretty's back and a sharp sound filled his mouth, those eyes going wide.

"Yeah, Dick. Fuck." Rock's words were hoarse and he moved faster, jerking and then growing still, collapsing against Dick's back a moment later.

He licked at Dick's lips. "Y'all are... something else."

Rock chuckled. "That's why you keep us around."

Dick just smiled at him, eyes soft now, sated.

"Mmm..." He scooted back, gave them room to settle in with him. They did, all three squished together on the wide couch, Dick in the middle, Rock taking the outside.

"We never got around to watching your movie." The way Rock said it they weren't going to take the time now.

"We got tomorrow." He relaxed, fingers stroking whatever skin he could find.

"Yeah," agreed Dick. "That's the best thing about these date nights. They're only the beginning."

Rock chuckled. "I'm a smart, smart man."

"Yes, sir. Fucking brilliant."

Dick chuckled and Rock must have pinched his Pretty's ass or something because that laugh turned into a yelp, which made Rock chuckle.

Lucky. Sweet fuck he was lucky. Home. Happy.

***

Rock wrapped the fully loaded toolbox for Rig and manhandled it under the tree.

That was the last of them.

Rig and Dick hadn't put their gifts under yet and who knew where Rig had hidden the big box that came from Momma, full of her gifts for them, but even with just his stuff, it looked like Santa was being generous this year. He was fucking proud of himself. Not one gift had he gone in with the kid or Rig on. And he hadn't asked either of them what he should get the other either. It was all him.

The kid was bringing home the stuff they'd gotten at the gym, boxes of chocolate, bottles of wine, from clients and from vendors they dealt with, even some stuff from vendors who were trying to get in with them. They'd given out protein bars and energy drinks for free all week along with candy canes. He'd insisted that gym or no, it wasn't Christmas without candy canes.

He picked up the living room to Rig standards and then went and fed the dogs and checked on supper.

Rig was doing Christmas dinner, of course. All his favorites, so in a flash of inspiration he was now regretting, Rock had decided to make supper for Christmas Eve. And not steak and potatoes, no, that was his kind of food, not Rig's. He'd talked to Lesley, his secretary, and she'd walked him through a beef stir fry over noodles. With fucking vegetables and everything.

But he'd made the noodles already and they were starting to get soggy, so he'd dumped them out of the water and into a glass bowl, shoving them in the microwave. He'd heat them up when they were ready to eat.

The beef had been marinating and he'd cut up a thousand fucking vegetables into lopsided, funny shaped pieces. All he needed was Rig and Dick to be home and it would take five minutes to all cook up. In theory. It had taken him all fucking afternoon to cut up the vegetables though -- was it any wonder he didn't like them? Work intensive little time-wasters.

He wandered back out of the kitchen, restless. If he sat down and found a game to watch, he wouldn't want to budge and he hadn't cut up those little green buggers for nothing.

He went to the front window, relieved to see Rig's jeep pulling up and that the kid was right behind him. Rig had a huge bakery box in his hands, looking fine and happy in a bright red sweater, a black hat.

He hoped whatever it was would keep because he'd also made rum-soaked trifle, courtesy of Lesley. He figured it wouldn't matter if he'd screwed it up, anything that contained a half bottle of rum was going to be edible. He chuckled when Dick came around to give Rig a kiss, a bakery box in his hands too. Maybe he shouldn't have told them both the other one was cooking, but he'd wanted it to be a surprise.

Making sure they were coming in, he headed for the kitchen and turned on the wok, put the oil in the bottom of it. Lesley had assured him no Californian household should be without one, so it wouldn't be a wasted purchase even if he never made another stir-fry in his life. Of course he didn't want to be encouraging Rig to make stuff with a ton of vegetables on a regular basis either.

He heard the door open and close as he put the meat on, the thin slices starting to sizzle.

"Oooh... something smells good. Blue? Where are you? I brought a chocolate mousse cake and Dick's got a... what is that, kid?"

"Sweet rolls of various types for breakfast tomorrow. Whoa. Rock's cooking." The kid took in the set table and him throwing vegetables into the wok, making it hiss and scream. "I thought you said Rig was taking care of supper."

"I said it was taken care of -- you assumed that meant Rig was doing it. You wanna turn the microwave on for a couple minutes for me?" He glared a little, daring either of them to make a comment about domesticity.

"Oh, wow..." Rig was all smiles, stealing a piece of red pepper and munching. "This looks great, Rocketman."

Dick turned on the microwave and nodded. "What do you want us to do?"

"There's wine in the fridge. You can open it and sit down. This is almost ready." I think, he added under his breath. What the hell did he know from cooked vegetables?

Rig's hands slid around his waist, hugging him tight. "Thank you, sir. This is grand."

"Thought you shouldn't have to cook on Christmas Eve, seeing as how you take care of the good stuff for tomorrow." His voice was rough.

He got a soft warm kiss pressed to the back of his neck. "Thank you."

"You're welcome," he grumbled. The microwave beeped and he dumped the stif fry into a bowl. "Come on then, this is ready."

Rig settled at the table, all grins and pink cheeks and warm eyes, all for him. It was almost worth chopping vegetables.

To his surprise the food was good. He liked the beef and the noodles and the mushrooms. The sauce was pretty good, too, and he'd made enough he wasn't feeling hungry after, which he'd worried about.

The kid ate well, but the best was his Rabbit, who finished one plate and then took seconds, laughing and joking, telling about his afternoon playing Santa at the children's hospital.

When they were done, the kid cleared while he put on the coffee and brought the dessert out of the fridge and then put Rig's mousse alongside it. "Just in case it didn't turn out." Or they were like him and were planing on a bowlful of both.

"Dessert, too? Oooh... rum. I want that one. I can have chocolate anytime."

He beamed at Rig and then at Dick as the kid helped himself to a heap of his trifle as well. "Lesley gave me the recipe."

That made Dick laugh. "If that's the case, is there anything but booze in here?"

He chuckled. "Just a bit of cake and pudding."

Rig tucked in, red-cheeked and chuckling by the bottom of the bowl. "Damn, that's a good flavor."

He was stuffed after his own large helpings of each and he leaned back, patting his belly. "Not bad at all, if I do say so myself."

"Really good," Dick told him, starting to clear up and put the dishes into the dishwasher. "If you're not careful, we're going to expect you to start coming up with dishes like this every time it's your night to cook."

He snorted. "Don't push your luck, kid."

Rig stood up, swaying just a little, chuckling. "Man, rum goes right to my head."

He grinned. "Yeah? Come here."

He reached out and tugged on one of Rig's belt loops. He got a soft noise -- almost a giggle -- and Rig settled in his lap. "Hey, Blue."

He chuckled. Fuck, Rig was sweet like this. "Hey, Rabbit. You ready to have a good holiday?"

"I am. I love seeing Momma and shit, but there's something fine about Christmas morning with just us. Something good."

He nodded, glad that Rig was seeing the good. It had been an easy enough decision not to go, none of them really had the time to spare and he wasn't willing to have Rig go on his own. Not even for Rig's Momma. He slid his fingers along Rig's ribs, enjoying the easy laughter. Dick was laughing too, watching as he finished loading up the dishwasher.

Those long fingers were sliding over his head, those eyes happy and young and for the first time Rock knew, just knew they'd done the right thing, coming here. He bent and took Rig's mouth, kissing his Rabbit hard before the emotion became too much. Rig hummed, opening right up, tongue sliding against his, fingers holding them together.

He fell into the kiss, into Rig. Shit, for that look, for this? He'd chop vegetables every fucking night.

Dick's hands slid over them for a moment and then the water in the sink came on, the kid quickly washing up the stuff that had to be done by hand.

Rig was warm and relaxed against him, tongue sliding and hot, those eyes offering up everything, making fucking promises that neither of them had to say out loud. He just kept kissing, taking everything Rig had to give and giving it all back.

When the water turned off and Dick's hands slid over his shoulders, smoothed across Rig's, he groaned, everything just about as fucking perfect as he could want. His chair creaked. Well, except for maybe the setting.

Their lips parted and Rig panted, eyes warm. "Bed? Sofa? Somewhere we can touch?"

He nodded. "Bed." They fit better there, more comfortably.

Maybe he was just getting old.

"Cool." Rig stood, stripped off the red sweater, giving them a nice long look at that tight little ass in jeans. Maybe he was just smarter than the average bear.

He gave that ass a happy swat and slid an arm around around each of his men's waists. Maybe he was just the luckiest man in the world.

***

Dick woke Christmas morning to the smells of the turkey starting to cook, along with coffee and baking. Rig was up, had probably been up since five or so, getting their feast going. Stretching, Dick got up and went to put on his sweats.

"Don't, kid. Bring him back here."

He grinned over at Rock. "Okay."

"Coffee and those buns you got wouldn't hurt either. It's Christmas, he'll let us eat in bed."

Chuckling, he headed for the kitchen, with a quick detour to empty his bladder.

Rigger was dancing, humming along with the Christmas carols, kitchen filling up with food.

"Merry Christmas, Rig." He grinned and crossed over to wrap his arms around Rig.

"Oh, good mornin', Pretty." Rig leaned back against him, all smiles. "You sleep good?"

"Yeah, I did." He kissed Rig's neck. "Rock's asking for you. Suggested coffee and breakfast in bed, too, for after."

"Oh, that sounds good, Pretty. The turkey's got hours left and there's nothing pressing in here." Rig stretched, offered him more skin.

"Cool. We'll go and you can give the big guy his blow job." He kept nuzzling and licking. "I could give you one while you're doing it."

"Mmm... merry Christmas to me..." Rig poured the coffee into a carafe and grabbed three mugs. "Get the rolls?"

He nodded and grabbed the box, thinking they'd be better warmed. But then they would just get cold again while the three of them played their favourite game of wake up, so he didn't bother.

Rig was still whistling as he headed back for the bedroom, grinning wide at the sight of Rock stretched out on the bed. "Merry Christmas. Have you been a very good boy?"

Rock pulled back the covers with a grin, his cock hard and curving toward his belly. "Come and see for yourself."

"Mmm..." Dick grinned at that sound, low and wanton, Rig setting the coffee aside, already focused on that cock.

He put down his box of breakfast rolls and climbed onto the bed on the other side of Rock. "Get undressed first, Rig."

"Hmm?" Rig blinked over, licking those parted lips.

"Get naked, Rabbit. We're gonna fuck before we go open presents."

Dick grinned and rolled his eyes at Rock, but nodded to Rig. "Yeah, I'm doing you while you do Rock, remember?"

"Hell, it's Christmas, we might as well make a chain," put in Rock. His cock throbbed and he swallowed. Rock didn't suck all that much, making it a huge treat when he did. Rig shimmied out of sweats and jeans, pulling the blanket around his back as he stretched over Rock's thighs, nuzzling the heavy balls.

Rock grunted and then moaned happily, shifting slightly as Dick stretched out with his head in Rig's lap. He licked at Rig's cock, taking the head in to suck at the very tip. When Rock's mouth circled his own prick, he cried out, hips jerking. Rig's chuckle was low, warm, fingers reaching down to pet his head. He purred around the cock in his mouth, his own fingers sliding along Rig's balls, pushing teasingly beyond them.

Rock's mouth just sucked him steadily, the pressure good, making pleasure throb through him. Rig was hummng, rocking, hard and happy, sliding into his lips. He found the rhythm with his own hips, careful not to push too hard, but Rock's hands grabbed his ass and he was encouraged to move faster, so he just let go, moaning as he slid deep.

It felt good, the three of them, together and wanting, motions sure and steady. Their movements sped together and as Rock sucked harder, so did he, tongue working the silky flesh as his balls started to draw up. He hummed urgently, letting Rock know he was close.

Rig moaned low, thighs going tight and hard under his cheek. He cried out around Rig's cock, hips jerking uncontrollably as he shot down Rock's throat. Heat filled his mouth as the big guy roared, the sound muffled by his cock. He swallowed Rig down, taking his time to clean and love the softening prick, just like Rig had taught him.

Rig hummed, the sound low, sweet. "Mmm... mornin'."

"Merry Christmas." He was grinning, happy and sated, feeling good and lazy and happy that Rock had suggested the breakfast rolls and coffee be right there for them.

Rock chuckled and tugged until he and Rig shifted up so they were all at kissing height. Rig settled, arms and legs wrapping around them, lips joining into their kiss.

"Merry fucking Christmas to us," murmured Rock, purring.

"Mm-hmm. Yeah." Rig nuzzled, lips trailing over Rock's jaw.

He nodded his agreement, snuggling in. Food and presents could wait. This was more important.

***

Rick's was a little bar close to the house -- quiet, pool table, dance floor, beer, cute bartender, the whole package. Rig and his men met there once or twice a week -- shot some pool, drank a couple of beers, normal stuff. Easy. Quiet.

Made the invitation for the New Year's Eve party there especially cool. New Year's Eve. Out. Real kisses at midnight.

He moseyed up to the bar to order another round for his marines battling at the pool table. The cute bartender served up his bottles and gave him a warm smile. "You busy at midnight, Cowboy?"

He blushed, tipped his hat. "I reckon, unless they press together and leave me in the cold."

"Well if you're by the bar, you won't be kissless." Chris winked and looked him up and down.

"I'll keep that in mind." He took the beers back towards the pool table, feeling young and good and sexy. Rock looked up and gave him a warm smile before going back and taking his shot. Dick reached for one of the beers, hand sliding on his arm. "Hey, Pretty. How's it going?" He leaned in, resting against Dick's heat.

"The old man is trouncing me." Dick didn't sound particularly upset about it, one arm going around his waist.

"Yeah? He's had a lot of practice." He started swaying with the music.

"Yeah, you keep distracting me with this dancing thing." Dick turned and looped both arms around his waist, moving with him.

"Mmm..." He pushed into those arms, hips moving, arms draping around Dick's neck.

Dick's hands settled on his ass. "I could forfeit the game."

"You don't need to forfeit, kid. I'm about to wrap it all up."

He raised his face, grinned into riverstone eyes. "I'm a good consolation prize."

Dick grinned back. "The kind of prize that would make a man lose on purpose."

"But you didn't," growled Rock. "I beat you fair and square."

"What's making you rumble, Rocketman? I didn't promise to kiss the pretty bartender at midnight, even though he asked nice."

Rock's rumbling got worse and Dick hid a smile against his neck. "The bartender wants a kiss at midnight?"

"Mm-hmm, but I told him I was busy." He looked over at Rock, admiring, playing. "I am going to be busy, right Blue?"

"You better believe it. Anyone but the kid and I come near those lips and they're going to have to answer to me." Rock puffed up and glared around the bar before taking his last shot and sinking the eight-ball right where he called it.

"Our stud," chuckled Dick.

"Hell, yeah." He winked. "We're lucky men, Pretty."

Dick nodded, smile encompassing both him and Rock. "Yeah, we are."

Rig nodded, "Am I playing the winner or are we dancing?"

"We're dancing," murmured Dick.

"Yeah, go ahead and dance -- I'll take the next buckle polisher." Rock waved his beer at them and handed his cue over to a group of guys waiting to play.

"Mmm..." He led Dick to the dance floor, fitting right in those strong arms like they were made for it. Oh, yeah. Dick's cheek rested against his as they moved around the floor, his Pretty's hands warm and sure on him. One song flowed into another and Dick and Rock traded him back and forth, the two of them even dancing together for one song, laughing as they tripped over each other's feet, both trying to lead.

God, this was fun. Perfect. Normal.

As midnight got closer, Rock got them all champagne and they stood together, counting down the year with the rest of the bar.

For the first time ever, as the New Year was rung in, he kissed his men, all three of them together, in front of God and everyone else at the bar, not caring who saw.

Chapter Seven

Rigger pulled into the driveway, half laughing, half groaning. He *loved* the one day a week he spent at the low-income clinic. *Loved* it. Honest. Rock, on the other hand... Well, Rig was fairly sure Rock lived in fear of the Zavala Clinic days.

Now, not *all* of the things brought in lieu of money or as gifts were horrible. Rigger always received loaves of bread, tortillas, Mrs. Pecina brought pink cake almost every week and Sr. Llaves brought garlic and dried peppers. Of course, there was the goat incident. And the week of fish. And that man who had carved him a set of wooden false teeth.

Rigger stopped the jeep and looked back -- a good-sized brisket, pink cake, peppers, two little puppies, a nice bagful of woodchips, a used tire, a bicycle to fix for Lucia Ramirez, and an afghan done in the ugliest shade of orange he'd ever seen. Yep. Rock was gonna shit a brick. He'd best improvise.

"Dick? You busy? Come help me unload?"

The kid came out, wearing nothing more than a pair of cut-offs and a smile. "You're back! Got some good stuff?" The kid loved clinic day. The weirder the stuff the better, as far as Dick was concerned. Dick opened the back gate and peered in. One of the puppies whined and the other one bounced up to lick his face. Dick started to laugh. "What, were they having a two for one sale?"

"No." He shook his head. "I'd stopped in to give the chickens that I'd got today to that sweet older lady – the one with the sick husband? -- at the vets. Well, Dr. Thomas was going to have to put them down and they're not sick and have their shots and she said she'd throw in neutering on both of them if I'd take them and I couldn't just leave them there, Pretty, and Rock's going to *kill* me."

Dick was still chuckling. "Yeah, he is."

"Now, Dick. I'm *counting* on you, here." He sighed. What the *fuck* was he thinking? There was a *reason* Rock never let him take Grimmy in to Dr. Thomas' by himself... "I'm really too fucking young to die, you know?"

Dick was still fucking laughing. "Yeah, and if you're dead and Rock's in jail for killing you, who am I gonna fuck?"

"My point exactly! Now, *help*! What the fuck am I gonna do?"

"Take 'em back. Find a home elsewhere for 'em. Hope Rock goes blind in the next five minutes. And deaf. And stupid."

Despite his laughter and asinine suggestions, Rig knew it was going to be all right. Dick was making googly faces at the puppies, who were licking all over him. When Dick reached in and picked one up, he knew Rock was as good as convinced.

"I can't take them back. They were gonna *kill* them!" He heard the back door slam again and winced. "Don't let him beat me too hard, Dick? I didn't *ask* for them!" And they were as cute as little dark brown buttons -- all ears and paws and waggling butts.

Dick gave him a grin. "We'll figure something out," the kid said with a wink.

"Figure what out?" asked Rock.

The kid turned right around and handed Rock the first puppy and then reached in and gave him the second. "Happy Birthday, Rock!"

Rig just stood there, staring at Dick, then Rock, then the puppies. Well, that was one way to do it. It would've worked better if it wasn't fucking weeks 'til Rock's birthday and if one of those pups wasn't nipping Rock's chin and the other one wasn't peeing down the front of...

He was fucking going to die.

"I'll put the brisket in the freezer." Him? A coward? In the face of two hundred eighty pounds of testosterone-driven sprung-steel? Fuck, yes.

"Hold it right the fuck there," growled Rock.

He kept moving and Rock followed him. He could hear Dick trotting along behind, sealing the deal. "I know we're like, really, really early -- but they're yours so they're going to need names and collars and I'll help you walk 'em."

"I don't want the fucking dogs."

"All right," said Dick. "You can take 'em to the pound -- best do it today before you get too attached."

Rock stopped moving, dogs still in his arms. "I can *what*?"

"Take 'em to the pound -- can't just let them go to fend for themselves. They're cute enough, hopefully someone'll take 'em home before their week's grace period is up." Rig looked at Dick, stunned. The kid was either fucking crazy or fucking brilliant and either way he owed him a blowjob or three.

One of the puppies was licking Rock happily, the other gnawing on his fingers like he'd just been given to the world's greatest chewtoy. "I don't want a dog."

Dick nodded, looking perfectly happy. "You haven't got a dog."

"Dick," Rock growled.

"You don't -- you have two dogs. Not even dogs -- puppies. You've got to admit they're cute, even if one of them did pee on you -- that's a sign of endearment and affection you know."

Rock didn't look happy, but he still hadn't put the puppies down.

"Want me to get you a blanket and a clean shirt while you come up with a couple of names?" Dick asked.

"Don't push it too far, kid," Rig whispered, handing the kid the brisket, the cake and the peppers. "Clean shirt and a towel and Lucy's old puppy basket ought to work for them, Dick." Then he turned to Rock, not offering to take the pups. The longer the big guy held on, the better their chances. "They've got their shots and they're healthy and they're seven weeks old and brothers."

"Rig..." Rock shook his head, blue eyes begging. Dick quietly put away the food and headed down the hall.

"Dr. Thomas was gonna kill them, Blue. They're all full at the pound and just putting them down one after the other. I couldn't just let them die." He looked at the pups, one of which was now sleeping, head propped up on Rock's chest. "'sides, they're yours now. Dick said. You don't want 'em, then let's go take them in now, before Grimmy and Lucy meet them."

Rock looked down at the puppies in his arms, the one that was awake reaching up and licking him across the face. "Aw... fuck."Rock glared at him. "I'm not naming them though. They're nothing but mutt and trouble to me."

Dick came in and put Lucy's basket on the ground by the door.

"Not there," growled Rock. "Too cold. Put them in the living room next to the fireplace."

Rig nodded, forcing himself not to so much as crack a smile. Looked like Blue just inherited himself some dogs. Who'd have thought? "Mutt and Trouble work for me. There's some of that good puppy food and collars in the jeep, along with bowls and stuff. Dr. Thomas was plumb pleased."

He watched Rock walk holding those puppies and damned near keeled over with lust and pride and sheer pleasure. The man looked good happy, even when he was faking pissed.

Dick gave him a grin and tossed him the shirt and a wet washcloth. "I'll grab the rest of the stuff out of the jeep -- you go make sure he doesn't put the pups *in* the fire."

Rig grinned and mouthed a silent 'thank you' before going to help Rock. The problem was, the puppies really didn't want to get down into the basket. They wanted Rock and everytime Rig put one in, it immediately started whimpering.

Rock gave him a helpless look. "I'm not holding them all night, Rig. I'm *not*."

"No. Hold on, let me grab the towel you used this morning." He ran down the hall and grabbed it, putting it in the basket and putting both puppies in, sighing as they both settled, comforted by Rock's scent. He knew the feeling. "They're just little and scared, Rock. They'll settle in." Rock just gave him a look that said they'd better and peeled off his wet t-shirt. He took the t-shirt and handed Rock the washrag without a word, then handed over the clean shirt. "I'm gonna go get changed myself. Long ass day. Zavala Clinic, you kn... yeah, you know."

Rock looked over at the puppies. "They'll be all right on their own, right?"

Rig looked down at them, both sound asleep, tails over noses. "Yeah, we'll put the grate over the fire and shut the door, they'll be fine."

Rock did as he'd suggested and then followed him. "I deserve something special for this, Rig."

"Anything." He pulled off his workshirt, shaking his head. "I just stopped in to give the desk lady some chickens. Her husband's got pluerisy and they've been struggling and Dr. Thomas, the evil bitch, she saw the jeep pull in..."

"I don't want to hear your excuses, Rig. I just want to know how you're going to make it up to me. I expect I'll be coming from now until Christmas."

"Someone's gonna have to walk those pups between now and then," Dick said, joining them in the hall.

"That's why you're here, kid."

"Whatever you want, Rock." Rig took off his slacks, put them in the dry cleaning pile and just grabbed the hamper and kept on going to the laundry room, throwing in his undershirt and drawers. Might as well start a load now. He found a load in the dryer, grabbed it and put on some sweatpants and a sweatshirt, stopped in the bathroom for some aspirin and to wash his hands, remembering that he needed to write up a few charts over the weekend for Sally, 'cause she was out this week. He headed back to put the laundry away and ran smack dab into his naked lovers, both of them giving him the "work's *over*, Dr. Roberts" look.

"Oh, hey." He felt his cheeks heat and grinned.

"Bedroom," said Rock. "Now."

Dick just grinned at him.

"Yes, sir." He rolled his eyes at Dick, headed towards the bedroom. "You can take the man out of the Corps..."

"Oh, I don't think you're in a position to be making accusations about how a man conducts himself, Rig." Rock pushed him down onto the bed where Dick proceded to strip him. Once he was naked, Rock came down on top of him. "You owe me, Rig. I want kisses and I want blow jobs and I want to fuck that sweet ass of yours and then I want to do it all over again and when those puppies are grown and stop peeing all over me, maybe by then you'll have paid your debt. Pound or no pound."

He grinned and wrapped his arms around his Blue's neck, smiling into eyes bluer than Sinatra's. "Christ, I hope not."

He leaned up and took a long, deep kiss, leaving Dr. and puppy and clinic and everything behind for a while except for him and his men. Dick was laughing, the sound sweet and arousing. When the kiss ended, Rock smiled down at him and started another, body hard and moving slowly against him.

He pulled Rock close, legs parting. One hand reached out to pull Dick close, humming into Rock's mouth as Dick's cock slid against his hip in time with Rock's on his belly. Dick's mouth attached to his and Rock's, the kiss opening to three as easy as breathing.

Dick's hair was long enough to dig his fingers into now, thick and beautiful and so fucking soft. He loved it -- enough that he'd spent a week or so badgering Rock to grow his before turning the fight back to five servings of fruits and veggies a day -- and his fingers slid deep, moaning and licking, lost in the kiss.

Dick and Rock each had one arm around each other and one hand playing with him. He wrapped one leg around Rock's hip, shivering as the angle of their cocks changed, bumping the head of his cock against that muscled belly. Rock moved harder against him, Dick quickly matching the rhythm, the three of them moving together, slick and easy and beautiful.

He came first, crying out as his nipples brushed Rock's chest, eyes full of riverstones and blue. Rock and Dick came almost together, their faces beautiful in pleasure.

He sighed happily, nibbling on Rock's bottom lip, warm and relaxed. Happy. Really fucking happy.

Rock chuckled and rubbed against him a little. "No falling asleep, I'm not done with you yet."

"No? Promise?" He nipped again and then stretched out, getting a good grip on the headboard and using it to leverage himself against Rock's weight.

Rock groaned and pushed back. "I promise, Rig. Not even close to done yet."

"Good." He shivered, digging his feet in and rubbing against Rock, spreading their spunk between them, Dick's chuckles sliding around them both. Rock rumbled, lips covering his for a kiss as Rock shifted, raised and lowered his hips, cock suddenly at his opening, nudging against him. Dick murmured and slid two slick fingers inside him, opening him up for Rock. He gasped and pushed back against the instrusion, horny and ready as ever. "Yeah."

Dick gave him a kiss and then those long fingers disappeared, Rock's cock once again pressing against him. He tilted, body searching for the stretch and weight and heat of his Blue, deep and hard and right.

"Yeah, just like that." And just like that Rock was pushing into him, filling him.

"Oh, fuck. Yes." He rocked into the first thrust, the feeling of their hips pushing together welcome and perfect.

"Yeah," Rock agreed again, moving with him.

Rig looked over at Dick and smiled. "You're too far away."

Dick grinned at him. "I'm just where I need to be to get Rock ready for me."

"Mm... Rocketman sandwich." He leaned up and licked the corner of Rock's mouth. "A delicacy."

Rock chuckled, tongue touching his, tangling with it. "Rare but delicious?"

"Fuck, yes. Served oiled and hot as fuck." Rock's eyes were beautiful -- part amused, but mostly aroused. They made his belly tighten, made him groan. "My sexy old man."

Rock growled at him. "I'll show you old."

Bending, Rock took the skin of his shoulder into that hot mouth and bit down before starting to suck. Meanwhile Dick shifted, finding his place behind Rock, making his Blue moan and push in deeper.

"Oh, fuck! Easy, you're going make me shoot before we're near over!" He reached up for Dick, gasping, body clenching Rock's prick.

"God, you are such a slut," said Dick, tone fond.

"What's your point?" He took deep, even breaths, forcing himself to relax, to go easy.

"His point is -- if you come now, you can come again, so let's just fuck already." Dick laughed at Rock and shifted, making Rock moan.

"Some of us aren't sixteen anymore, jackass." He grinned, backed far enough away from the edge to make jokes, winking at his Blue.

"He was hoping you hadn't noticed," teased Dick, the kid's voice was thick now, full of need and arousal.

"He fucking noticed, kid -- you don't even look sixteen anymore."

"You both are still the hottest fuckers I've ever seen." He leaned up, fastened his lips to Rock's, groaning as Rock pushed deep.

"Ditto," said Dick, pushing Rock even deeper as the kid thrust into Blue.

Rock just made a noise into his mouth, part growl, part purr, all sex. He swallowed it, answered it with one whimper after another of his own, rocking and moving with his men. Dick drove their rhythm, keeping it slow and easy.

Rock's eyes never left his, just grew darker and hotter the longer they were at it. Rig threw himself into the kiss, tongue sliding and tasting and licking each of those places that made Blue shudder and cry out and ache.

Dick was providing their fucking soundtrack, moans and groans and whimpers and gasps and sometimes he thought a man could come just from those sounds alone. He reached down, pumped his cock in time with their thrusts, floating with them. Needing.

Dick seemed to know just when things were about to become too much and the kid pushed them all faster, harder, driving into Rock, driving Rock into him. It was hard and fast and deep and so fucking good. He grabbed Rock's tongue, sucking hard, demanding his Blue's pleasure, wanting to see it, up close.

His Blue was stubborn though and he could see it set in Rock's eyes, his Blue determined to make him come first. Just then Dick shifted and drove in hard, Rock's eyes going wide, losing their focus. A loud, strong cry pushed into his mouth, as Rock came with a roar.

He whimpered, eyes full. His hips snapped as he came, entire world pleasure-filled blue. The kid was still working it, Rock's cock pushing across his gland each time Dick jerked into his Blue, sending little aftershocks dancing along his spine. Then the kid moaned loudly and went still.

He reached up, stroking Dick's hair, Dick's face, feeling the aftershocks of his Pretty's orgasm in his fingers. Dick turned, mouth finding his fingers and sucking them in. Rig purred into Rock's lips, knowing Dick could hear, that Dick would know.

Dick pulled harder and then let his fingers go, making soft noises of his own. Rock pulled out and rolled to the side, bringing Dick with him. Two hands slid over his belly.

He stroked his hands over the top of theirs, eyes closed, breath easing. His family. Their family.

One of the pups whined and Rock grunted. "You still owe me, Rig."

"Until the end of your days, Rock."

Rock's hand squeezed his just a little. "You better believe it."

"He does," said Dick, voice sleepy.

He nodded. Yeah, he did. He rested for a minute, trying to hear whether Mutt and Trouble were going to get up or settle back down. Forever, thank God for small favors.

Chapter Eight

They hadn't been at the beach house even a year when they went through their first earthquake. Rock was barbequing and Rig directing him in that long drawl he liked to put on when they were doing something he felt was particularly in his bailiwick as the resident Texan. Dick was rocking on the hammock, drinking his beer and staying out of it. Eventually there would be food and then there'd be sex and it was a good, good life.

Then the ground started shaking.

"What the fuck?" Rig blinked and grabbed Rock's waistband, hauling the big guy away from the grill and down the porch stairs, then started for the dogs' collars. Dick got Lucy and Mutt himself and joined them as Rig caught Grim and Trouble.

It felt like it was going on for fucking ever, but it couldn't have been that long, the steaks were still medium-rare when they took them off the grill.

"Holy fuck."

"Yeah." Rig headed toward the house, face set as he headed back up the stairs. "Gonna grab the radio and the phone."

Rock's hand wrapped around his waist. "I don't think so."

Dick nodded. "I'll go get them. Anything else? I'm not doing this run more than once."

"Bullshit. I need my bag, need to find out if I'm needed at the hospital. I'll be fine." An aftershock rocked the ground, set the dogs to barking.

Rock's arms circled Rig, holding him in place and Dick nodded. "Okay, your bag, the phone, the radio."

He went and collected the things, grabbing a case of beer as he got the phone from the kitchen. He thought maybe they'd need it. He got back outside without anymore shakes happening. He handed Rig his bag and the phone, Rock only then letting him go.

Rig rumbled, dialing the phone and heading around the side of the house, hands running through his hair.

"He's going to be pissed at you."

Rock nodded. "Don't care, wasn't risking him going in."

He nodded, heading after Rig, Rock right there with him.

"Yeah, Sheila, you know it." Rig shook his head, chuckled. "Nah, it's the first. Gimme a tornado any day. Okay, y'all need me, you holler. Sure enough. Evenin', lady." Rig hung up, shooting Rock a glare. "Just a baby one. No sweat. Girls thought I was cute for worrying."

"Just a baby one?" Dick shook his head. "Fuck. If that was a baby one..."

"Yeah." Rig walked back to the porch and grabbed a beer, surrounded by the nervous dogs as soon as he sat down. "Sh... sh... 'sokay pups. Y'all are fine."

Rock went over and sat next to him, chugging back a beer of his own.

"It's not beer *I* want," he told them.

"The steaks are done, Pretty, so's the salad. Eat." Rig was still pissed, he could hear it, flat and threatening full-out anger.

"I don't want food. I want to fucking touch the two of you and know you aren't dead."

"Nobody's dead." Rig stood up, shaking his head, moving close enough that he could smell coconut oil and sweat. "Just a baby one, yeah? We're fine."

He nodded and slid his hands around Rig's waist, leaning his forhead against his lover's. Rig reached up, arms twining around his neck, grey eyes unsettled, unnerved, but right there. He pressed their mouths together, gentle for a moment and then he groaned, the kiss growing hard, needy.

Rig opened to him, tongue sliding against his, body plastered to him. He grabbed onto Rig's ass with one hand, pulling him closer, reaching for Rock with his other hand. It was taken, Rock coming to stand next to them, wrapping them both in the thick arms.

"Still pissed at you." Rig grumbled, then pulled Rock into their kiss, one hand sliding around Rock's neck.

The kiss went on and on and then he pulled back and nipped at Rig's bottom lip. "You can be as pissed at me as at him -- there was no way I was letting you go in either."

"And why the hell not? I'm just a capable as you yahoos." Rig's eyes flashed, temper flaring again.

"We were trained marines, Rig."

Dick winced, pretty sure that wasn't going to make Rig feel any happier.

Rig stiffened, mouth going hard. "And I was what? Some pussy nurse, right? You both fuck off."

"It's not like that." Dick sighed and swatted Rock.

"What did I say?" complained Rock.

"We were marines, way to go."

"We were!"

He rolled his eyes and grabbed Rig around the waist, holding him close. "Don't listen to Rock -- that had nothing to do with it."

"Right. Fine. What the fuck ever. I'll go heat up the rolls and the steaks." Rig pulled away with a frown, heading toward the house. "I swear to fuck, Rock, the kid never saw me in action, but *you*? I should fucking have your respect."

"Ah fuck!" Dick stomped up the stairs after Rig, grabbing him and turning him around. "It's got nothing to do with who could do what, it's got to do with you being the center of us. Come on, Rig -- something happens to you and your two big tough ex-marines turn into scared little kids. If one of us gets hurt, you'd be able to handle it, to make it right."

Rig opened his mouth, gasping sort of like a fish and then just knocked him to the ground, mouth covering his. He guessed he'd explained it right and hell, as Rig said, kissing was always better than talking, so he just went with it, opening to Rig's mouth. Rig kissed him with a focused desperation, tilting his head and taking his mouth hard. Then, just as suddenly as it had begun, Rig's mouth was gone. Panting and flushed, Rig looked hot, needy, beautiful with his grey eyes flashing up at Rock. "Get your ass over here, marine."

Rock grunted, moving quickly and without saying a word. Dick grinned; good man. Rig pressed up for Rock's kiss, thighs and belly trembling as they stretched, arched and tight. Rock slowly sank down to join them in the sand, hands firm on him and Rig, moving slowly, methodically over them. Rig's hands were cupping Rock's jaw, sliding over his belly, eyes dark as the kisses grew longer, harder.

His own body was hard and the need pushed at him from his gut, from his heart and the base of his skull. This wasn't just physical -- he *needed* his lovers. Totally and absolutely and immediately. Needed them alive and well and fucking.

Someone got his shorts pushed down and then Rig was straddling him, Rock's hand guiding his prick into that fucking tight, hot hole. "Fuck me, Pretty. Need you."

Moaning, he pushed up, hands finding Rig's hips and pulling him down onto his cock. Rig's groan was wild, sweet, the sound stolen by Rock's mouth as Rig's ass landed in the cradle of his hips. He reached out with one hand, sliding it over Rock's skin. Needed them both, all three of them touching. He started to move, hips bucking, cock sliding out and in again.

Rock's fingers were hot on his balls, Rig's sliding over his nipple ring as they fucked, proved their need, that they were all okay and here and hot and fuck it was hot. There was an edge to it, made it more, made it in his face and *real* and so fucking good to be touching and fucking.

"Wanna suck you, Rock. Wanna come with you both filling me up." Rig was fucking dancing on his cock, moving with a fierce passion.

He groaned almost as loud as Rock. He didn't stop fucking though, just watched as Rock stripped out of his shorts and moved to stand over him, thick cock pressing at Rig's lips. Rig's arms wrapped around Rock's ass, body rippling around his cock as the sounds of lips and tongue against cock started to fall around him.

"Oh, fuck." He groaned and moved faster, sliding his hand up to cup Rock's balls. Rig's moan was sweet, fingers white-knuckled against Rock's ass.

It felt so good. So fucking good and necessary.

He just kept bucking up, fucking Rig hard. Rig started jerking, sobbing around Rock's cock, hands opening and closing convulsively. He grabbed Rig's cock, stroking hard. It was the best way he knew how to say it was going to be okay. Rig clenched tight around him, tight enough to make him buck and jerk as spunk sprayed over his hand and chest.

"Fuck!" He bucked up hard and shot deep into Rig's spasming body, the sweet ass milking him. Rock's roar wasn't far behind him, Rig's jaw working to take it all in.

Rig slumped against Rock's hips, breathing hard and heavy, shuddering. He reached out to pet each of them, one hand along Rock's leg, the other along Rig's belly. Rig's eyes were closed, cheek pillowed against Rock, one hand sliding down the thick leg to touch Dick's jaw, stroke his cheek.

He nuzzled into the touch, watched as Rock's hand slid along Rig's cheek, gentle and full of everything Rock couldn't actually say. Rig relaxed, letting him and Rock hold him, support him, resting on their strength. He turned and licked Rock's leg, letting the big guy know it wasn't just Rig who was glad, who needed and loved and was happy they were all okay.

Rock grunted.

"Come shower with me. We'll salvage supper later." Rig shifted, pulled off him, standing on unsteady legs.

"Not that hungry, but I could use a shower," admitted Rock and Dick nodded as he stood up, grabbing them both around the waist.

Rig caught Rock's gaze, then a soft, sweet kiss was pressed against the crow's feet lining Rock's eyes. Another brushed Rock's cheek, his jaw, the strong, square chin, Finally Rig kissed Rock's mouth, the actions rich with 'I'm sorry' and 'all's forgiven' and just simple love.

He stroked their backs, content just to watch, to know he was a part of them, a part of *this*. It was good to be alive.

***

Rock watched the puppies falling all over themselves in the sand, Lucy rounding them up anytime they went too near the water. Grimmy sat on the deck, watching with the resigned patience of an old man. He knew how the old dog felt, two young pups playing around while he sat and watched.

It wasn't so bad.

He gave the old boy a pat on the head and Mutt, or Trouble, came bounding up, pushing jealously against his hand, demanding attention. Damn his two human pups for forcing these two doggie pups on him. There was no heat in the thought though, how could there be with that tongue licking at his face?

Rig's hands fell on his shoulders, rubbing nice and slow, a soft chuckle sounding. "Hey pup, you loving on my old man?"

"He heard you owe me big and is trying to get on my good side." He looked up, giving Rig a bit of a grin. "Don't think I don't know you and the kid orchestrated that whole thing."

Rig grinned down, winked. "I couldn't turn them down, Blue. I just couldn't."

"You're too soft, Rig." And if anyone -- anyone -- said anything about him letting the pups stay being soft, he would put them in his truck and take them to the pound like a shot.

"Yeah, and you're too good to me." Rig kissed his temple.

He grunted. "And don't you forget it."

He grabbed Rig's arm and tugged him down to sit at the top of the stairs with him, watching as the puppy went back to Lucy and his brother, Dick throwing things for them to catch.

Rig leaned against him, Grimmy crawling over to rest against Rig. "Hey, pretty boy. What do you think about those pups?"

Grimmy's tail wagged, once, slapping on the deck.

Rock chuckled. "He's got about as much enthusiasm for them as I do."

Trouble came up this time, running into his arms and demanding petting and damn it all how was he supposed to play it like he was aggravated if the damn pups were going to keep coming over and demanding loving?

Rig chuckled, reached out and skritched the base of Trouble's tail. "He sure thinks you hung the moon."

"He's a smart dog." He turned a wink on Rig and played with Trouble's ears. Just like Rig, they knew the way to his heart.

"Well, hell, those hands loving on him? You can't blame the pup."

Oh, Rig was laying it on thick. He purred softly. He wasn't above taking advantage of the situation. "You know about that, do you?"

"I do. I could learn more about it, though, any fucking time." Rig scooted closer, humming a little, flirting.

"You could, could you? What do I get out of it?" Never let it be said he didn't know how to flirt with his men.

"Hmmm..." Those eyes smiled up. "Chocolate pie? Undying gratitude?"

"That's a good start. Of course the words I was thinking of start with a b and a j."

Rig chuckled, head tilting. "Uh... boating and jumping jacks?"

He whacked Rig on the arm. "No."

"Beans and jalapenos?"

Two could play the teasing game. "Looks like the puppies get to keep the date with my hands."

"Oh, now, that's no fair. Those puppies can't give you what I can."

"And what's that, Rabbit?" he nudged Rig's shoulder with his own. Rig shifted, tongue sliding up the side of his throat, ending at his ear. He bit back his purr. "Oh, they lick me all the time, Rig. All the fucking time."

"Yeah, but they can't suck start a leaf blower..." Rig sucked his earlobe in, soft and easy, tickling.

He did groan at that. "You offering to suck start mine?"

"Anytime, Blue Eyes."

"Go for it." And if his voice was fucking husky, well who could blame him?

"You hard already? Wanting?" Rig hummed, fingers sliding his zipper down.

"I am unless you've lost your touch."

"Not a fucking chance, you beautiful son of a bitch."

He chuckled, spreading his legs as Rig let his cock out and sliding his hand through Rig's curls.

"Mmm... all for me?" Rig leaned down, lips brushing over the tip of his cock, tongue sliding over the slit.

"Not for the fucking dogs, that's for sure." He spread his legs further, burying his other hand with the first in those sexy blond curls. Rig moaned, fingers cupping his balls, head bobbing nice and slow, giving him just what he liked.

"Sweet..." he murmured, hands dropping down to trace Rig's cheeks, his jaw and neck.

"Mmm." Rig moaned, throat working, lips sliding up and down his prick, suction sweet and steady. There was nothing on this earth like Rig's mouth and he said as much, fingers moving to Rig's shoulders. Rig pinked, eyes closing and he focused on the up and down of that mouth driving him bat-shit crazy.

He stopped trying to do anything but feel, Rig's mouth just making him insane. Up and down, those curls were bobbing, heat flooding him, Rig working his cock. It was a beautiful thing and he held on as long as he could, wanting it to never end. Rig's fingers stroked his balls, tongue tapping the slit on every upward stroke.

"Fuck. Fuck." He groaned, balls tightening up. A hum and swallow answered him, Rig's throat vibrating.

"Fuck!" He shouted it this time, hips pumping up as he shot down Rig's throat. His Rabbit didn't miss a drop, swallowing him down, petting him.

His shout must have allerted the kid, Dick coming up from the beach. "Woo! No one told me it was playtime."

He chuckled. "You usually sniff it out faster than that, kid."

Rig grinned. "You were busy."

"I'm never that busy!"

He laughed, hands sliding on Rig. "You can help me get our slut off. I promised him up close and personal with my hands for the right payoff."

Dick's eyes went wide. "You're going to fist him?"

Oh, trust the kid to think of that. He raised an eyebrow at Rig. Rig's eyebrows went up. "Not on the deck."

Oh, they had a game on.

"Bed's made, lots of lube in there, too." Dick bounced a little.

"Perv." Rig winked at Dick, stood, heading for the house. "Come get me."

Dick bounced and took off after Rig. He followed a little slower, tucking himself in and getting the dogs into the house -- he didn't want to be disturbed.

Rig and Dick were stopped in the hall, sharing a deep, hot kiss, Rig rubbing nice and lazy. And wasn't that fine looking? There was nothing wrong with eager puppies. Nothing at all.

Rig's eyes met his, warm, shining. "You come to play, Blue?"

"Just admiring the view."

"Oh, it's not much of a view yet," Dick told him. "Just wait 'til we're naked."

Rig chuckled. "Kid's *all* about the naked."

"Kid's pretty bright." He grinned, hand sliding over Rig's ass.

Rig wiggled, rubbed. "He is. Smart. Pretty. Hung. Damn, we're good."

He laughed. "Well we've got him down to single word sentences, we must be doing something right, kid."

Dick laughed, hands working on Rig's clothes.

"Neanderthal." Rig winked, arms up so the kid could strip him.

"That's still only one word, Rig." He grinned, starting stripping his own clothes off.

"My neanderthal."

He laughed. "Get your ass in the bathroom, Rig. Unless you want to forgo the full treatment."

"Man, you are a pushy old bastard." He got a wink, a wiggle.

"Yep. Gonna push my hand right inside you." He held his hand out for Rig to see. "This one right here that I believe you were admiring oh, one blow job ago."

Rig reached out, fingers sliding over his. "It doesn't seem possible, looking like this."

He purred, turning his hand to curl their fingers together. "Won't be the first time."

"No." Rig stepped up, cuddling into him, eyes dark and focused. "Kiss me."

He purred. "I can do that."

Bending, he brought their lips together. Rig opened for him, body plastered to his, warm and lean, cock already full, eager. He slid his tongue into Rig's mouth, slowly walking Rig into the bathroom. His Rabbit moved easily, let him guide them.

Dick had the stuff they needed out on the counter, warming up the water.

Rig sucked his tongue, arms draped around his shoulders, holding on. He just kept kissing as Dick spread Rig's legs and bent him a little. Rig took a deep breath, but kept kissing, kept looking and holding on.

"Just my fingers to start, Rig," murmured Dick.

"Mmm..." Rig kissed the corner of his mouth. "My Blue..."

"Not yet, Rabbit." Dick laughed softly at his answer, smiling over at him. Rig chuckled.

"No. Now it's my Pretty... sweet touch..."

"Yeah." Dick sounded sappy. Rock supposed there was no better time to be sappy. Rig nodded, hips riding Dick's fingers, cock rubbing his belly.

"Get him ready, kid." Rig was good and relaxed, hard. It was time.

Rig leaned into him when the tubing went in, skin sheened with sweat, breath panting.

He licked at Rig's lips, hands soothing down the long back. "I've got you."

"Always." Rig moaned low.

"You know it."

"Filling it now, Rig," murmured Dick.

He purred, sliding his hand around to rub Rig's belly. Rig closed his eyes, lips soft on his throat, moving so easy. He could feel Rig start to tense up a little and massaged harder.

"Oh..." Rig nodded. "Yeah."

"Won't be long, Rabbit. And then it'll be my hand."

"Done now," murmured Dick. "I'll take the tubing out and get the shower ready.

"'kay. 'kay, Pretty." Rig was panting faster now, harder.

Rock licked at Rig's lips. "Easy, Rig. You know the routine."

"Yeah. I know. I'm with you."

He purred. "I know you are. Need some help getting to the pot?"

"No, I got it.'" Rig made it, sitting hard, cheeks a little pale. That pallor faded once he got his Rabbit in the shower with Dick, the hot water warming the gold skin right up.

They fooled around, not taking it too far, keeping it light, but by the time they were back in the bedroom, Rig all spread out, him and Dick on either side, they were all pretty fucking hard. Rig was moving between them, sliding, taking long, sweet kisses. He and the kid started slowly, sharing the task of opening Rig up. One finger each, and then two, stretching, kissing Rig, each other, fingers always moving.

Rig took it, driving nice and slow, hips sliding, happy moans in the air. Rock added more lube and was about to slide in a third finger, but Dick shook his head and reached for Rig's hand, tugging it down to Rig's ass. He groaned. Fuck, the kid had some amazing ideas. Rig shuddered, fingers sliding with theirs, one joining them."Oh..."

"Fucking shit, that's..." Fuck, he didn't have the words for what that was, all three of them inside Rigger together. He made a noise and just watched.

Rig moved in slow ripples, breath panting against his chest. Dick, as always, provided them with their soundtrack, noises fucking sexy and a little desperate. They just stayed like that for awhile, all moving together, breathless, more than halfway to the sky.

Rig got a long kiss from the kid, then turned to him, eyes wide, dark, lips swollen. "Blue..."

"I know, Rabbit. It's time." Their fingers all slipped away and he bent, bringing his and Rig's lips together, kissing hard and deep as Dick spread more lube on his fingers, on his hand. Settling back on his haunches between Rig's legs, he curled his thumb into his palm and pressed his fingers against Rig's hole.

It didn't seem possible, even though he'd seen it before, done it before. Rig spread for him, stretched, soft little cries painting the air. Dick took care of kissing Rig, of petting the thin belly and stroking, licking the long cock. Rock held onto one thigh, carefully working his hand inside Rig, just pushing, slowly, inexorably, listening carefully for any kind of distress.

They reached the widest part of his hand and Rig groaned as he pushed, body suddenly pulling him in, seeming to tug his hand.

"Oh, fuck, Rig." A moan was pulled from him as Rig's body sucked him right in, ring of flesh hard and tight around his wrist.

"Oh. Oh, fuck. Blue. Pretty. I..." Rig arched, swallowing hard, so hard, so fucking fine.

He purred. "Fuck, yeah." He knew exactly what Rig meant.

The air was filled with the sounds coming from Dick as he took Rig's prick into his mouth, and with the sound of men panting -- he was almost as breathless as Rig was, his hand making tiny movements inside Rig's body. Those eyes fastened on him, wide, so clear. "You have me."

"I do, Rabbit. Holding you in my hand. Mine." His throat was tight, emotion swelling inside him.

Rig nodded, giving him a slow, sweet smile. "Yes. Yes, Blue."

"Keep sucking, kid, I'm going to start moving more." Dick hummed around Rig's cock, head starting to bob, eyes on his hand, where it disappeared into Rig's body. He pushed forward, his knuckles rubbing against Rig's gland.

"Oh..." Rig jerked, hands twisting in the sheets. "Again!" Oh yeah, he could do that again. So he did. Again and again, making Rig twist and jerk, riding his hand like it belonged there. Rig's shoulders left the mattress, entire body going tight. "Fuck!"

"That's right. Fucking you with my hand." He growled the words, pushing Rig back onto the bed, fingers sliding down to stroke the flat belly. "Just relax and let it happen, Rabbit."

Rig keened, nodding. "So fucking full..."

"That's right. There's nowhere to go, Rig. Just you and me and the kid. Everywhere." Rig always made him feel like a fucking god, but that went double with those noises coming from him.

"Just us. Oh, sweet fuck." Lips and eyes and body open, flushed and panting, holding him -- his Rabbit looked like every man's wet dream. Dick's sucking got stronger as Rig's ass started to ripple around his hand and he moved a little faster, still careful, making sure there was nothing but pleasure in those grey eyes. "Close. Fuck, Blue. So fucking close."

"Do it, Rig. Come for us." He moved his fist. "Come on my hand."

"Yes..." Rig tensed, entire body rippling, Dick swallowing hard. He groaned as Rig's body went tight around his hand, a flush working from Rig's balls up. Fucking beautiful.

He met Rig's eyes, moaning softly as he came. Rig reached for him, fingers brushing his jaw. He nuzzled into the touch, keeping his hand still. Dick pulled off Rig's cock, pressing kisses along Rig's belly.

"Y'all's." The word was soft, whispered.

He nodded. Yeah, theirs. "Time to come out, Rig."

Dick nodded and slid so he was lying next to Rig, cuddled up close, hands distracting. Rig's body fought him for a moment, holding him tight, squeezing. He leaned in and kissed Rig's inner thigh. "Come on, Rabbit. Gotta let me go."

Rig nodded, relaxing, breathing deep.

"That's it." He lubed his wrist up, sliding it in a tiny bit further and then starting the slow, tight pull out. Rig stretched, body reluctantly letting him go, stretching again.

"One of us is going to have to take a piss sooner or later," he teased, hand stroking Rig's thigh. Rig chuckled, the motion helping him out, letting his hand free. He groaned, hand cold now that it was no longer buried inside Rig. Bending, he kissed Rig's hole.

Rig moaned, the sound deep, low, body shivering. He licked and kissed again before lying down next to Rig, kissing his Rabbit hard. Rig curled into him, rubbing and purring.

The kid tucked right in behind Rig, keeping him safe, warm, close.

He smiled, happy, at peace. He might be the old dog with these young pups, but he still knew the best tricks.

***

Dick woke a few hours after they'd fisted Rig, feeling loose and easy and happy. Fuck, he loved living here. Loved the sun and the sand and the surf. And Rig and Rock, but that went without saying.

He got up and took a piss and went to let the dogs out the back, make sure their food and water were topped up. Rock's puppies were all barks and wags and sheer puppy energy, Lucy herding them off from Grim, protective of her old man. It was cute.

Kind of reminded him of Rig and Rock a bit.

Not that he'd ever tell either of them that. And of course that would make him the puppies and he wasn't sure he wanted to be the dogs who peed all over the place. He chuckled and got some coffee going, looking for something rollish and sweet to go with it.

He heard movement, Rig appearing in short order, wearing a pair of sweats, looking half-dazed, still well-fucked.

"Siren call of the coffee?" He held open his arms.

"Mmm... heard you wandering." Rig cuddled in.

"Oh, siren call of me. I like that." He kissed Rig softly, loving the relaxed, cuddly well-fucked feel of his lover. Rig hummed, open and easy, wrapping around him and snuggling in. "Having a good Sunday?"

"Uh-huh." Rig smiled, blinking slow. "All melty still."

"It's a good look on you. Hot." He stroked Rig's back, fingers of one hand finding Rig's curls and stroking through them.

"Oh. Oh, that's good, Pretty." Rig stretched a little, all lazy and sensual.

"Yeah? You like that." He grinned -- Rig always made him feel studly.

"I do. Love how you touch me."

"Love touching you, Rig. I live for it." He pushed his lips against Rig's, sharing another kiss.

Rig draped long arms around his neck, rubbing nice and slow, eyes warm and happy, shining. He moaned softly, cock getting hard, just like that. "Mmm... sweet sound."

He moaned again, not even having to fake it to offer the sound. Rig chuckled, licking at his lips, leaning close. He chased Rig's tongue with his own, just loving the easy play between them.

"Mmm... you feel so good..."

"Ditto." He rolled his hips against Rig. He shouldn't have put his sweats on. Rig slid his hands down, pushing his sweats over his ass.

"Good thinking," he murmured, happily rubbing his prick against Rig's belly.

Rig chuckled, nodded. "I learned from the master of naked."

He laughed. "Rock?" he asked with a wink, knowing darn well he was the one with the reputation for keeping getting naked a high priority.

"Nope, the other beautiful fucking stud I live with."

"You live with two beautiful studs? Imagine that -- so do I."

Rig snorted. "My ass. You live with a stud and a cowboy."

"I live with a damn sexy cowboy. Don't you be selling my lover short."

Those thin cheeks pinked, Rig grinning. "Shit, Pretty. I got eyes. I see the guys that y'all see everyday..."

"And yet, I'm here with you, hoping I'm going to get lucky again." Rig wouldn't let him sell himself short, no way he was going to let Rig turn around and do the same to himself.

"Hell, yes. I am a lucky fucking redneck." Rig pushed close, brought their mouths together. He groaned and grabbed Rig's ass, tugging them in tighter. The moan Rig fed him was sweet, fine, wanting.

"Wanna go back to bed or just get it on over the kitchen table?"

God, Rig's laugh felt good. "Bed. Somebody's there waiting on us."

"You mean sleeping." He grinned and licked Rig's lips. "Not that he ever objects to getting woken up, as long as you do it just right."

"Hell, he doesn't mind just being there and holding after, so long as we're quiet."

"Yeah. He'd never admit it, but he's damn good at cuddling." He grabbed Rig's hand and headed back down to the bedroom. There were lots of things Rock was good at that he wouldn't necessarily admit to.

Rig nodded, licking his shoulder. "He is, but I can't sleep right without you there. You keep my dreams sweet."

He made a soft noise and stopped Rig, giving his lover a tight hug. "My pleasure."

Rig pressed close, taking a low, slow kiss. "My pretty lover..."

He felt his cheeks heat and buried his face in Rig's neck, lips and tongue tasting the salt there.

Rig purred, nuzzling him. "I need this, you know, need my Pretty, my lover, my friend."

"I know. If you didn't, I wouldn't be here with the two of you."

Rig nodded, kissed his jaw, his ear, rubbing them together. He whimpered and pressed Rig against the wall, suddenly needing now. Rig's leg slid up along the outside of his thigh. "Yes..."

He nodded, whimpering again, pushing against Rig over and over, making their cocks slide. Rig's fingers tangled in his hair, holding their mouths together. Bracing himself with his hands on either side of Rig's head, he just went with it, the feelings coursing through him. Rig rocked nice and slow, cries pushing into his mouth. He cried out as he came, heat splashing between them. Rig was behind him, panting, hands gripping tight.

"Oh... fuck, it's good." He leaned against Rig, hands sliding down along Rig's sides.

Rig nodded, breathing hard. "Fucking amazing."

"Uh-huh." He licked at Rig's lips, tugging the sweet lower lip into his mouth. Rig moaned, leaning against him.

"Be even more fucking amazing if it happened in here." The words were growled, but not heated.

Rig chuckled, licking his lips. "Someone's wanting."

"We'd better not keep him waiting."

"Hell, no. He deserves some loving." Rig rubbed their noses together.

"Always." He linked his hand with Rig's again and made it the rest of the way to the bed where Rock waited for them.

Life was most definitely good.

Chapter Nine

Rock was working late, dealing with a mountain of paperwork. He'd sent Dick home, said there was no reason they both had to be tied up -- one of them ought to be spending the evening with Rig. Dick had offered to flip a coin or something, but Rock had just smiled and tossed him a flyer from a dance club that had just opened in the area. Tuesday night was cowboy night.

"Hey Rig," he called out when he got in.

"In the kitchen, Pretty. Want a beer?" Rig sounded good, happy, relaxed.

He made his way to the kitchen, leaning casually against the doorframe. Rig looked good, too. Already changed out of his scrubs and wearing jeans and a real nice blue shirt.

"I was thinking about getting one at that new club on Saleto Street. Gotta support the new businesses, yeah? Wanna come with?"

"Oh?" Rig nodded, looking pleased. Long fingers ran through white-blond curls, those grey eyes deep and dark as they reflected the shirt. "Sure. Sounds good. Let me leave a note under Rock's beer and put on my boots."

"Yeah, I'll just go put on my new jeans and a clean shirt. Rock's dealing with the fucking paperwork. My turn next month." He went and gave Rig a kiss first, just a soft hello, all lips and tongue. Then he was off to change. He wanted to wear something nice, but had to be careful -- too nice and Rig would know something was up.

In no time at all they were on the road, chatting about their day as they drove, Rig insisting on taking the jeep. They found a spot in the lot next to the club and headed in, Dick hiding his grin and waiting for Rig's reaction as they passed the chalkboard pronouncing Tuesday's Cowboy Night "Beer for a buck and all the two stepping you can handle".

"Dick?" His favorite redneck gave him a grin and a look, cheeks flushed. "Cowboy night? Yeah?"

He nodded, grin getting loose. "Yeah. I thought you might like to show these west coasters a thing or two about how cowboys dance."

"I..." One shoulder nudged his, Rig's grin spreading ear-to-ear. "Damn, Pretty. You just made my day."

He beamed over at Rig, that smile making his heart sing. "Rock helped."

The sweet blush deepened and those eyes just shone. Fuck, but their Rig looked good happy.

They paid their cover and ordered a couple of beers before they found a little table at the edge of the dance floor. Rig was singing along to whatever was playing on the jukebox, swaying slightly as he drank.

"You let me know when you want to go up and I'll do my best to keep up with you."

"You asking me to dance, young man?" He got a wink and a grin, the flirting warm and easy as breathing.

"I do think I am." He smiled back, feeling good and happy. "What do you think? Wanna polish some belt-buckles?"

"There's precious little I'd like more." Rig finished his beer, knee bumping his gently. "Ready when you are."

He got up and held his hand out to Rig. "May I have this dance?"

Rig met his eyes, nodded, and stood, sliding that long hand into his. "As many as you want, Pretty."

He chuckled as he pulled Rig close. "I'm feeling pretty greedy, Rig. You may just be dancing all night."

"Sounds like fucking heaven." Rig moved right into his arms, joining the other men on the dance floor and moving together. Rig's hips snuggled in with his, thin belly warm as they danced, Rig singing along, voice soft and low. It felt good, moving slowly, intimately, with Rig, bodies swaying together. Felt even better knowing how much Rig enjoyed this.

Rig moved like he was made to shuffle around a dance floor, motions easy and flawless, almost drawled. When the songs changed to something faster, they got to laugh and flirt. He got to chase those hips across the floor. When the song was slow, his arms were filled, cheek resting against his, his own personal cowboy singing soft and low, just for him. They stopped only long enough to grab a quick bite and another beer and then they were back on the dance floor again, two-stepping the night away.

Dick was beginning to see why Rig loved this so much. He was warm and loose, holding his lover. They got to laugh and flirt, talk about their day, share long, slow kisses during the slow songs. The whole time, Rig's eyes never left him, never once let him slip from being the center of the fucking universe.

He could have danced all fucking night, but the place closed down around two in the morning and he let Rig go with great reluctance.

Rig leaned up, licked his lips as they stepped off the dance floor. "Let's go home, Pretty. We can finish making love there."

Oh... yeah. That's what they'd been doing.

He captured Rig's mouth, taking a long, deep kiss. "I love you," he whispered softly.

One hand stroked his cheek, those grey eyes warm and bright. "You never let me even doubt that, Dick. Take me home."

He grabbed Rig's hand and led him back out to the parking lot, Rig's jeep the only vehicle left there. The temptation was strong to suggest they make out in the jeep, but instead he slipped into the passenger seat, letting the anticipation build.

Rigger drove, hand resting on his knee, humming along with the radio. When they pulled up to the driveway, his lover looked over, gave him the slowest, sweetest smile. "Thank you."

He covered Rig's hand with his own. "It was my pleasure."

And he meant every word.

Chapter Ten

He sat out on the back porch, stroking Grimmy's muzzle, listening to the old boy breathe, watching him sleep. Just petting.

He wouldn't have many more mornings with Grim, the vet said time was catching up with the big old heart, that Grim wouldn't make the month. Rig had nodded, brought his boy home. So long as Grim wasn't hurting, Rig figure'd he'd give him as many dawns as he wanted to watch. Trouble and Mutt were chasing crabs, Miss Lucy nipping their little butts when they wandered too far off. Rig grinned as he watched, drinking his coffee, watching the sun on the water.

The screen door slid open. It was going to need oiling again. Bare feet came across the porch. He was expecting his Pretty, he got Blue.

"Mornin' sunshine. You're up early." He offered Blue a smile and a sip of his coffee, they all drank it the same, made it easier.

He got a shake of the head and a grumble, Rock's eyes half closed against the growing light. "Thought you could use some company."

"Always." He wrapped one hand around his coffee cup, the other running over Grimm's head. "Just sitting with the pups and watching the sun."

Rock grunted and sat, warm and still beside him.

He leaned against that strength, drinking it in, letting it ease his soul. "He's been with me longer than you have, you know? Living in a crate on the balcony of that tiny little apartment in San Antone."

"I know."

"Little shit was sick the entire drive to fucking North Carolina, wasn't sure he'd ever get used to the motion." He took another drink, swallowing hard. "He sure remembered you, though, didn't he? Little butt going ninety to nothing, slobbering on your jungle boots."

"Had fucking dog smell on those things for weeks." That made him laugh, made Grim snort and snuffle, harrumphing at Blue, managing somehow to look offended. "Dog hair in my beer and on my sheets. Hell, it wouldn't be home anymore without it. Crazy old mutt."

Rock reached past him, hand sliding along Grim's nose, scratching behind his ears.

"Gonna break my heart to lose him." He sighed, shaking his head and swallowing his coffee, watching as Mutt, or was it Trouble, he couldn't tell from this distance, noticed Rock was up and out and started bounding towards the house, barking and wagging and boucing.

Rock's hand slid slowly along his back, fingers moving over his shoulders. A kiss was dropped onto his head and then Rock went and got a chew toy, tossing it across the beach and sending Trouble back off in the other direction after it.

Then Rock was back, hand on his knee, just sitting with him. Eventually he reached out, twined their fingers together and held on for all he was worth.

The sun was pretty much up when his coffee cup was taken from his hand, replaced with a fresh one. Dick crouched behind them, a hand on each of their backs. "I called us all in sick."

He couldn't answer, couldn't speak past the lump in his throat to say thank you. So he just nodded and lifted his face for a kiss. Dick's lips were soft and warm, tongue sliding into his mouth. He opened to the kiss, keening softly as his Pretty loved on him, one hand lifting to cup that morning-stubbled jaw.

Someone -- Rock -- took the coffee cup out of his hand and Dick's fingers slid along his spine, moving slowly up and down. He reached out, drawing his Blue close, adding the flavor of strength to the comfort of the kiss. Rock's hands slid along his thighs, thumbs stroking along his prick.

Between them they laid him out, legs still on the stairs, Rock between them. He let them ease his soul, let the flavor of Dick's mouth mingle with the sea salt in the air. Rock's hands smoothed open his shorts, his Blue's breath warm and gentle against his cock, his balls.

Oh... so good, so sweet. No one had ever been loved like he was; he fucking owed somebody upstairs big. Rig moaned into Dick's mouth, looking into those eyes that knew him so well, knew his fucking heart.

They loved him as surely as the lips that moved against his own, the hands that slid over his belly, his nipples, the mouth that was taking his cock in deep. When he came, the sun was in his eyes, sparkling and bright, wavering in the sky as Dick swallowed his sobs.

They lay on either side of him, his Blue and his Pretty, bodies warm, hands stroking gently, loving him, holding him, comforting him.

Supporting him as they lost one of their own.

***

Rock stood on deck, watching Rig wandering along the shoreline, looking out at the ocean. Grim'd been gone a couple weeks, creamated, ashes scattered on the beach Rig was walking on now, so the beast would always be with them. Like any of them could ever forget

Grimmy with his drool and his shedding and his deep and abiding love for all three of them.

Lucy was wandering around, half-heartedly keeping the pups in line, missing the old man. Kind of lost. Kind of like Rig.

Dick had spent a lot of time with Rig, talking, remembering. Rock wasn't so good at that kind of thing. He spoke with his hands, with his cock. Luckily for him it was a language Rig understood.

When it was clear Rig wasn't coming back in anytime soon, he headed on out. Rig looked up, gave him a smile. "Hey, Blue. How's it hanging?"

He grunted. "Not bad. You?"

"Tired, kinda, but okay."

He put his arm around Rig's shoulders, just walking with his Rabbit. "You've been working pretty hard the last couple weeks."

"Yeah." Rig slid one arm around his waist, leaning just a little. "How's things at the gym? I haven't been by in a while."

"Not too bad. We're interviewing to hire on two new trainers. Not that it's going to free us up any, just ease the workload a little. Kid keeps saying in a couple months we can ease off and let the place tick along on its own. We'll see."

"Yeah? Cool. You think maybe we can get away around October? That gives us all a few months to plan."

"It would have to be after the anniversary of the opening -- kid's got all sorts of promotional crap planned. You got something in mind?" A vacation. It'd been too long since they'd had one.

"Wine country. Vegas. Mountains. Key West. I'm easy." Rig gave him a grin. "I just want to get away."

"Oh, now, you and easy just go hand in hand." He winked and squeezed Rig's shoulders. "Yeah, getting away sounds nice. We should do something close though. There's lots of country out here we haven't seen."

"Yeah. Yeah, Blue. I'd like that." Rig nodded, took a deep breath. "Do you think I'm stupid? Missing a dog?"

"Nope. There's a whole lot stupider things folks mourn over. Grim was good to you -- always there to drool on you, say hey when you got home. Never yelled at you, stood by your side when I did. Only ate food that got left out uncovered." He shook his head. "He was a good beast."

"Yeah." Rig grinned, nodded, resting against him. "He was."

They walked in silence for awhile, watching the waves on the shore, the breeze picking up as the sun started to set.

"I want you to kiss me." Simple, sure -- just needing him like his Rabbit always had.

"Anytime." He stopped and turned Rig, hands sliding through the soft curls, tilting Rig's head. He looked into those grey eyes, just looked, for the longest time, and then he leaned in and brought their mouths together. Rig opened, easy, quiet, eyes clinging to his. He could see it, when Rig stopped thinking, stopped worrying and just felt. He let his tongue slip in between Rig's lips, deepening the kiss, taking what he wanted and leaving what Rig needed.

Rig stepped closer, relaxing in his hands, against his body. He purred into Rig's mouth, hands sliding down Rig's back. Rig held on, moaning, rocking into him, not heated, just nice and warm.

He could do this all fucking day or night, and he just went with it, moving, kissing, loving on his Rabbit. Rig's fingers slid against his head, petting, stroking, sliding. It felt so good, his Rabbit's touch on him, those lips. He was even enjoying the sound of the fucking waves. Of course, that could be because Rig was moving with them, rubbing against him.

He chuckled as he realised it. "You wanna move this inside, Rig? Somewhere less sandy?"

"Yeah. There's places that don't need abrading."

He laughed heartily at that. "You got places that do need abrading, Rabbit?"

Rig gave him a grin, cheeks heating. "Yeah. Yeah, I might just at that, Blue. You willing?"

"For you? Anything." Grinning, he turned them, heading for the house.

"Mmm... so good to me." Rig chuckled as he saw the pups, ears flapping, trying to reach them. "Now y'all! Get on back to the house, you know better."

"Face it, Rig -- everyone wants a piece of you."

"Uh... Rock? They're coming for you."

He snorted, surprised as the dogs leapt at him and not Rig. He guessed he'd just sort of assumed they'd gravitate toward Rig, especially with the old boy gone now. Rig chuckled, smile a little melancholy, but not much, more pleased. He petted the dogs and then sent them back up to the deck. "Go on."

He had a lover to fuck.

Rig chuckled as they turned the puppy eyes on him, Trouble (or Mutt) whimpered, tail wagging. He put his arm back around Rig's shoulders. "Inside, Rig. We've got a date with a flat surface."

"Oh, wow. I won over puppy eyes." Rig went up the porch steps, tight little cowboy butt wiggling.

He snorted. "You'll always trump the damn dogs, Rig. You'll trump whatever you stick in front of me and if you don't know that, I obviously need to fuck you harder."

"Oh, I'm all for a good, hard fucking, Rocketman." Rig turned to kiss him, cuddling in.

He purred. Yeah, Rig always was. Just one of the things he loved about his Rabbit. "Come on, the kid's no doubt got the lights off and the bed turned down in the bedroom already, just waiting to strip us down."

Rig's fingers twined with his and they opened the door. "He's good that way, our Pretty."

Rock chuckled. "He sure is."

Sweet and eager and theirs.

Rig led him down the hall, down to where the light shone from under the bedroom door. The kid was already naked, waiting in bed with a book, trying to look casual, but that eager grin shone at them as soon as they went in.

"Hey Pretty." Rig stepped out of his shoes, grinned. "Whatcha reading?"

"Something not nearly as interesting as the two of you." Dick put aside the book. "You guys need help getting naked?"

Rock chuckled. "We got it covered, kid."

"You can just watch. Admire Rock's beautiful bod."

Dick made one of his porno noises, hand sliding down to his filling cock. "I'll admire you both."

"You tell him, kid."

Rigger chuckled, stripping off the tight t-shirt before reaching for his buttons. He slid his hand along the slim body, slowly working Rig's jeans open as Rig undressed him.

"Mmm..." Rig's belly rippled, sucking in to give him room.

"Sexy motherfucker," he murmured, bending to bring their mouths together.

Dick moaned and he could hear the kid start to pull on his cock. Rig moaned, opening up, thighs parting as they rocked together. Their jeans were pushed away and his moan joined theirs as skin met skin. Rig's hand slid around his waist, down to cup his ass. He cupped Rig's ass in return, pulling their hips together hard.

"Oh. Oh, fuck. Blue." Rig groaned, tongue fucking his lips.

"Yeah." He pushed Rig back toward the bed. Rig moved easily, trusting him, focused on the kiss. The kid was right there, helping Rig lie back onto the bed and he climbed up after, sliding their bodies together. One long leg curled around him, holding him tight, fingers sliding over his shoulders.

He purred, letting Rig have his weight, pushing his hips into Rig's, sliding their cocks together. Fuck, it was good. The kid's hands and mouth slid on him, on Rig, warm and sure and making his cock drip. Rig's mouth covered his, tongue pressing in deep, a soft cry sounding.

Yeah, this was what he loved, the three of them moving together, leaving everything else outside the door. Dick's slick fingers circled his cock, teased his skin and his groan filled Rig's mouth. One of Rig's hands joined Dick's, pumping and petting, stroking him right off.

"I want Rig to do me while you do him," murmured Dick, fingers going away and coming back slick.

"Mmmm... all of us together." Rig nodded. "I can handle that, Pretty."

"Sounds like a plan, kid."

And it looked like Dick was ready to do all the work of preparations as well, the kid's other hand sliding along Rig's prick and then down beyond to push into Rig's hole.

"Oh..." Rig arched up against him, rubbing.

"He likes that, kid."

Dick chuckled. "I know. I can feel it."

"Uh-huh. Do it again."

Dick laughed happily and Rig bucked again and then again.

"Oh. Oh, fuck. That's... yeah." Rig panted, eyes rolling a little.

"Yeah, I want some of that myself." Dick's hand slicked his fingers up and tugged his hand to the kid's hole. Rig's mouth slid over his throat, breath hot and sweet. He pushed two fingers into Dick's body, letting them slide deep, making Dick jerk and cry out. Bingo. Again and again, he hit the spot, making Dick dance as much as Rig had.

Rig moaned low, "I need. Come on, now. Enough playing."

He chuckled as Dick moaned and whispered "fuck yes."

"On your knees then, kid. Let's get this train set up."

"Choo choo." Rig grinned, looking horny and happy. All his.

He swatted that beautiful ass as it was turned and gave one to Dick for good measure.

"Oh, baby, hit me again," giggled the kid.

Rig stretched out along Dick's back, rubbing. "But I wanted to fuck you."

Dick giggled and nodded, pretty ass wiggling. "Yeah, please."

He watched, waiting for Rig to get settled so he could fuck his Rabbit. Rig rubbed, lined up and pushed in, both of them moaning low. He didn't waste any time following suit, pushing into Rig's tight little hole, groaning as his cock was squeezed and pulled in.

"Oh. Fuck. Yeah." Rig nodded, taking a deep breath before beginning to move.

He let Rig set the pace, pushing into Rig everytime Rig pulled out of Dick. That pushed Rig back into the kid and they'd start the circle over again as he pulled out. The sounds of all of them together were sweet, sexy, driving them harder and faster. Flesh slapping on flesh, groans, panting, it was all there, all them. The scent of male was strong, familiar, good.

"Fuck this is sweet, hot." Rig groaned, head dipping, mouth on Dick's shoulder.

Dick whimpered and nodded, pushing back into each thrust. He grunted his own agreement, hands on Rig's shoulder and hip, loving the way the skinny body fit in his hands. It was intense and fucking awesome, felt good deep in his balls.

Rig reached around, pumping Dick, hips moving faster, harder. He could feel Rig's ass starting to ripple around his cock, knew it wouldn't be long. "Come on, kid. Let us feel it."

"Mmm... yeah. Come for us, Pretty." Rig was breathless, panting, shivering. Dick shifted slightly and cried out, body going still and shuddering as the scent of spunk filled the air. Rig groaned, shivered. "Sweet fuck."

"Your turn, Rabbit."

"Fuck, yes..." Rig nodded, panting. He thrust hard, nailing Rig's gland and Dick almost buckled beneath them. "Oh! Again!"

He did and the kid must have braced his arms, because Dick held them up, so he drove in again and again, pegging Rig's gland each time. "Give it to me, Rig."

"Yeah. Fuck. Yeah. Blue..." Rig arched, crying out, body milking his cock. He roared as his own orgasm was pulled out of him, the pleasure flooding his body as he flooded Rig with his come.

He collapsed onto Rig who collapsed onto Dick who collapsed onto the bed, groaning, but not complaining about the weight of them. Rig hummed, snuggling between them. "Feels good."

He purred, petting Rig, Dick, whatever skin he could reach. Dick murmured an agreement, hand reaching out. Rig's hand slid into Dick's hand, twining them together. Purring, he covered them with his own.

His men.

His.

Chapter Eleven

Dick was kicking butt on the playstation.

"Hoo Yah!" He pumped the air as he took out the big bad at the end of level twelve. Only one more level to go. He still had it.

"Dick? Pretty? That you?" Rigger's voice floated in from the front door. "Can you give me a hand?"

He put down the control and glared at the dogs. "Do not touch the game."

Lucy barked.

"Uh-huh." He gave them all another glare and headed for the front door. "Coming, Rig."

Rigger tottered on the front porch, bags in one hand, briefcase and boot in the other, crutches under both arms. The man's right ankle was wrapped and held up, cheeks bright red. "Don't ask. I'm fine. Tell me Rock's not home and take the groceries before I drop them."

"Christ on a cruch, Rock is going to kill you." He grabbed the groceries and Rig's boot, backing up and keeping the door open with one foot, while he kept the dogs away with his free arm. "Go in and sit down before they topple you."

"Yeah, thanks." Rig wandered into the front room, collapsing on the couch. "What a long fucking day."

He dumped the groceries in the kitchen and grabbed a couple of beers. He sat next to Rig. "You allowed one of these?"

"Fuck yes." Rig grabbed it and guzzled the brew down, slumping against him. "Hey, Pretty. How goes it?"

He wrapped his arms around Rig, settling his lover against him. "Tell me what happened."

"You remember little Lacy Gordon? Today was immunization day. Helen let go of her, she took off running out the back. I followed and went right past two of three steps. That old thigh just isn't ever going to be what it once one. Nothing's broken, just a nasty sprain." Rig blushed. "Fucking embarrassing. I headed to do my chores and shit before coming home."

He shook his head. "You should have called." Stubborn old cowboy.

"Hush, now. I'm fine." Rig rested his head against Dick's shoulder. "You think Rock'll notice?"

He snorted. "That man would notice if you had a splinter, Rig."

Rig groaned. "We could take the wrap off... When's he coming home?"

"He'll be home in a couple of hours -- Donna called in sick so he's closing down tonight. And you are not taking the wrap off -- you need crutches for the love of Pete!" He shook his head. Stubborn, prideful, old cowboy. And Rock was just as bad, that overprotective streak was going to go into overdrive. He leaned down and gave Rig a kiss. "Of course if you were already in bed when he got home..."

"Oh *excellent* idea, Pretty." Rig reached up, wrapped long arms around his neck. "Gonna join me and make me forget my troubles?"

"Yeah, that was kind of the plan." He brought their lips together again, moaning softly at the sweet taste of Rig. Rig's lips parted, tongue sliding into his mouth and licking at him. He stroked Rig's hip, sucking and licking and just enjoying that talented as fuck mouth. There was nothing like Rig's kisses. Rigger cuddled closer, loose and lazy in his arms. Those grey eyes shone at him, glittering and familiar and fucking beautiful.

"Let's get you to bed before we get too busy right here," he suggested, nibbling at Rig's bottom lip. If they made love here, they'd probably still be dozing on the couch by the time Rock got back.

"Mm... yeah. Help me, Pretty?" The words were soft, whispered against his neck, low enough that they could both pretend they hadn't been said. Bull-headed, stubborn, prideful, sexy cowboy.

He kissed Rig again, hard enough to leave the man breathless and then he stood and picked Rig up, one hand under the thin shoulders, the other at Rig's knees, and carried Rig into the bedroom.

Rig's tongue slid over his neck, soft kisses tickling him, teasing him. He chuckled and tilted his neck back, just enough to give Rig more room to play; he wasn't going to risk dropping Rig.

"Mm... yummy." The purr vibrated all the way down to his balls, gave him goosebumps.

He got Rig into the bedroom and onto the bed, all thoughts of going back to get the crutches disappearing under the onslaught of that tongue. He followed Rig down, being careful to stay off Rig's legs, attacking that sweet mouth with his own. Rig opened wide for him, just as hungry and needy as he was. That hot tongue pressed deep, fingers tugging his t-shirt up and off.

He moaned at the sweet sensation of those fingers on his skin, sucking on Rig's tongue. He returned the favor, too, pulling Rig's t-shirt off and getting to work on the scrubs. Rig's mouth fastened on his shoulder, sucking up one mark after another, fingers untying the waistband of his shorts, sliding in to stroke his cock.

"Oh, fuck..." Dick groaned and moved into that touch, fingers fumbling for a moment before finishing the task of getting Rig's scrubs off. He pushed his shorts right off as well, moaning again as Rig's thumb slid across the tip of his cock.

"So fucking hot, Pretty." Rig was working him hard, teeth on his shoulder, hand on his prick, body rocking beneath him.

"You're not so bad yourself, Rig." He buried his face in Rig's neck, licking the sweet-salty skin and then sucking, pulling up a mark of his own. He found Rig's cock, working on returning the favor.

It didn't take much before Rig was bucking beneath him, all hot, liquid sex. His cock was pulled and stroked, thumb sliding over the tip again and again. He shifted and pushed and pulled and wriggled until their cocks were together, two hands stroking two pricks.

"So friggin' good, Pretty. Make me feel so *good.*" Rig was moaning, breath hitching as they moved.

"Yeah, me too." He gasped and moaned again, the pleasure settling in his balls, in the base of his spine, getting him ready to fly. He found Rig's mouth again, kissing Rig with everything he was.

Rig cried out, jerking hard beneath him, heat splashing on his hand. He moaned softly, loving the feel and scent of Rig's pleasure. He jerked his own hips hard, pushing his cock through the tunnel of their fingers, the way slick with Rig's come. A gasp left him as he came.

Rig moaned against his chest for a few minutes, then cuddled close, making those snuffling, sleepy, Rig noises.

He lay there, holding his lover, softly stroking the warm skin, dropping occasional kisses on Rig's head. He'd wait until Rig was asleep and then he'd go put the groceries away, fetch the crutches in and put them under the bed and put Rig's briefcase in his office.

Then there was a game to beat before Rock came home.

With any luck, they could keep Rig in bed with sex instead of having to tie him down. His cock jerked and he grinned, giving Rig another soft kiss. Of course that didn't sound half bad either.

***

Something woke him at dawn. Rock grumbled and turned over, wanting nothing more than to go back to sleep. Only the bed felt a little empty and that fucking octopus wasn't wrapped around him. He sat up, blinking in the half-light. Rig wasn't in the fucking bed.

He was going to kill that fucking stubborn, prideful, mule-headed cowboy. Dick had told him what had happened. Or what he figured was a light and happy version. It didn't matter though. What did was that that skinny, stubborn, prideful...

He growled and got out of bed. When he found Rig he was going to... to... carry him back to bed and fucking tie him there if he had to. After he got his morning blow job. If the man was well enough to be up at dawn doing god-fucking-knew what, then he was well enough to be lying in bed sucking cock.

He found Rig floating in the bathtub, neck-deep in water, sound asleep, hurt leg dangling over the side.

"God fucking damn it! Are you trying to kill yourself or waiting for me to do it?"

Stupid, stubborn, skinny, mule-headed, prideful jackass was going to get himself drowned. Rock pulled the plug and grabbed a towel.

"What? Shit! Sorry, man. I must have dozed off. I woke up sweaty and itching like anything and figured the bath was safer." Grey eyes blinked up at him. "Hey, Blue. How did closing go last night?"

He growled. "Closing went fucking fine. Unlike your day." He grabbed Rig up and hauled him carefully out of the tub, mindful of that ankle. "You should have woken me or the kid."

"You and Pretty looked sound asleep, Blue." Rig moved into his arms nice and easy, head burrowing onto his shoulder. "Smell good."

Skiny, stubborn, prideful, sexy asshole. "Which is why I said you should have *woken* one of us," he complained, gently drying Rig off.

"Mm-hmm. Yeah, Blue." That hot tongue was sliding over his collarbone, hand stroking his hip. "I was dreaming about you, Rock. About riding your cock in the sunshine. Was good."

His prick started to fill. "You're trying to distract me," he growled, though he was having trouble putting any weight behind the sound.

"Mmm..." It was really difficult to be irritated with a snuggly, warm, purring cowboy whose fingers and tongue kept touching all your hot spots.

"I'm taking you back to bed." He stood, Rig in his arms and carried that skinny, sexy motherfucker back to their bedroom.

"You're gonna hurt yourself one day, carrying me." The complaint was soft, purred, familiar.

"Not unless you start eating more." He put Rig on the bed next to Dick and stared down at the pair of them. He was one lucky fucker.

Rig held out those long, thin arms. "'mere, Blue. Need you."

He purred, sliding in on the other side of Rig and leaning over to take a long, easy kiss. His Rabbit snuggled close, all hums and touches and lazy need. Fingers stroked his spine, those white eyelashes brushed at his cheek -- pure sex, his cowboy. Pure fucking sex. He curled his arm around Rig's back, pulling that skinny body in close, rubbing them together. So fucking good.

"Mmm... Blue..." Rig's cock slid against his hip, hot and stiff. "'s good."

"Yeah, fucking good." He took another kiss and then another and another, pulling Rig's murmurs and purrs into him. Rig was warm and pliant in his arms, focused on nothing but his mouth, his touch, those eyes just clinging to him. He rolled onto his back, bringing Rig with him, settling his cowboy on top of him and moving them both. Their cocks slid together, hot and silk and just right.

"My Blue." The words were whispered into his lips, hot and hungry. "My Blue."

He growled his agreement, hands on that sweet ass, guiding their movements. They didn't hurry, didn't rush, just kept pushing and rocking and sliding until Rig whimpered into his lips, shivering. He slid one finger between Rig's asscheeks, finding that tight hot little hole and pressing against it as he nipped at Rig's bottom lip.

"Blue!" Rig shot over his belly, hole jerking under his finger. Fucking perfect. That smell was one of his absolute favorites. He let himself go, his own spunk sliding between their bodies.

Rig settled down against him, eyes already closed, just snuggling and still. He rumbled and pulled the covers up over them. Now that everyone was where they were supposed to be he could get back to sleep.

Chapter Twelve

Dick wasn't looking for a replacement for Grim. He knew that if Rig had wanted one, he'd have gone out to the pound himself. Hell, they had three dogs now as it was, even if his Lucy was the old lady of the bunch, she had some good years left in her yet.

So he wasn't looking at all. Still, when he'd gone in to open up on Saturday morning and two big eyes had looked up at him from the sorriest looking mutt he'd ever seen... well sometimes things were taken out of your hands.

The back door wasn't used except by staff, so he put out a bowl of water and went across to the grocers for some dog food to put out as well. The little beast needed a good bath, so he wouldn't bring it in. Besides, this would give it most of the day to wander off again after its belly was full. He and Rock had started trading off Saturdays now and given it was his Saturday and not Rock's, he was unsurprised when he went out at two and the little guy was still there. Even less surprised when the pup followed him to his car without even a word from him.

He opened his bag and pulled out a t-shirt, laying it out on the floor in the back seat. "I don't want to see you on the seats or all bets are off, okay?" The dog gave him a bark and climbed in, settling on the shirt. "Rock's gonna kill me. Hell, Rig might, too."

Grumbling to himself, he got in and started on the way home. There wasn't a sound from the puppy the entire way and he almost expected to have imagined the whole thing, but when he got out and opened the back door, the pup climbed out and headed for the stairs as if it knew it was home. Shaking his head, he tossed the t-shirt back in his bag and shouldered it, following the pup.

Rig was whistling as he walked around the side of the house, wearing nothing but old jeans. "Hey, Pretty. I've got steaks on the... Hello, who's this?"

"You tell me. He insisted on following me home and it looks to me like he knows where he's going." He grinned as the pup's tail started to wag, whole back end just going nuts.

"Following you home?" Rig got down on his knees, the pup moving right over, tail beating the air. "Good Lord, you're filthy.

Probably hungry too, yeah? Where'd you come from, baby?" Rig gathered the ugly, matted little grey dog up, murmuring quietly, heading toward the backyard.

He followed happily, grinning, not even caring if Rock was going to be pissed, it would be worth it. "He was hanging out around outside the back of the gym this morning. I thought a bit of water and a bite of food would have him heading back out to whereever he came from, but he followed me right to the car without a word from me. Seemed to know where he belonged."

Rock looked up from the paper. "What's that?"

"A little..." Rig lifted the pup's tail. "Girl puppy. That needs a bath."

Rock glared. "We have puppies. We're full up of puppies. There's no room at the inn." He went back to his paper.

Dick just grinned. "Want me to get the pool?"

"Yeah, Pretty. And the flea dip." Rig nodded, looking in her ears, nudging the other pups away as they came to investigate.

Dick picked up a couple of chew toys and sent them sailing away down the beach before going over to pull the kiddie pool they washed the dogs in out from under the deck.

Then he went in for the flea dip, Rock growling at him as he came out. "You bring that thing home?"

"It followed me. Figured she belonged to Rig."

Rock looked over the top of his paper, grunted, nodded, and went back to reading. Grinning, he made his way back to Rig. Rig was already washing, singing quietly, long fingers moving over the skinny body, untangling the fur, which was slowly going from grey to white.

"Oh, man, look at that, she's gonna clean up nice."

"She's a sweetie. Did she have a collar?"

"Not that I could see." He hunkered down and smiled at the pup, reaching over to let her smell his hand.

She licked his fingers, then turned to Rig, barking brightly, tail wagging hard enough the water flew. "Did Pretty give you the love, pup? It's a wonderful thing, yes, ma'am."

He chuckled, warmth filling his belly and he gave Rig a kiss. "She got a name yet?"

"Huh? No. No... I mean, Rock's right. I don't need another dog..." Rig washed out her ears, so careful, so gentle.

"Right." He wondered if it would be worth taking bets with Rock as to whether Rig had her named before or after dinner.

"Come on, Miss Thing, let's get those nasty fleas off you. I ought to see if we've got any dewormer in there from when we brought the twins home..."

"You think she's full grown? We've never had a small dog." He hid his grin.

"She's not a baby-baby, I don't think." Rig stroked her head, looked at her teeth. "She's not full-grown, though. I imagine she'll be less than knee-high, maybe twenty pounds."

"Bet she'll lead Mutt and Trouble around by their noses. She'll certainly give them someone to horse around with, let Miss Lucy be the grand dame she wants to be."

Fuck, Rig looked at least halfway to in love already. It was a good look on him. Rig chuckled, lifting the puppy up, drying her in a big towel. When the pup appeared from the towel? She was pure white and fluffy, little black button eyes, tail wagging furiously. "Oh, look at her!"

"Aw, man, Rig, she's the cutest thing. Rock, you've got to come see."

"No, I don't."

Rig looked over at Rock, smile fading a little. "Let's get the camera, Dick. We'll take pictures and I'll call the paper, put an ad in."

Rock's paper rustled and Dick shot him a glare. Rock glared back. "You know fucking well you're keeping the dog, Rig. I don't need to see it to know that. Don't be making me out to be the bad guy here. There is no fucking bad guy."

Rig flushed a deep dark red, ducked his head and put the puppy down. "Yeah. You want to start the grill up, Rock? I'll get the steaks from the marinade."

Rock sighed and got up, stopping Rig when he would have gone in. "Keep the dog, Rig."

The little white pup had followed Rig and was looking at up at him, whining softly.

Rig leaned into Rock for a second, closing his eyes, relaxing, arms wrapping around Rock's waist. Rock's hands wrapped around Rig's head, holding him in place as Rock kissed him. Dick ducked his head, watching. Fuck, they looked good together. Rock kissed until Rig's flush was back, crawling up the long spine, the last of the man's tension dissolving.

Then Rock's hands slid along Rig's spine and settled on his ass, their mouths slowly breaking apart. "Give your dog a name, Rig and then come fuck your old man."

"Hey, what about me?"

"You can fuck me, too, kid."

"Suzie-Q. Her name's Suzie." Rig grinned against Rock's lips. "Dick found me a puppy."

"Yeah. Trust the kid to find her."

He just grinned. "Aw, come on, she's cute as a button and you're going to look adorable walking her on a leash."

"She's a sweetie. I'll take her to the vet tomorrow." Rig grinned down at her. "Get her a collar, shots."

Rock rolled his eyes and Dick just grinned. "It was meant to be, man. You can't fight fate."

The pup looked up at Rock, vibrating, baring her teeth, growling, trying to protect Rig. Rock chuckled and went down onto his haunches. "You growlin' at me?"

She backed up a step, looked at Rig, and then shivered, standing up to Rock.

"Oh, you are. Brave little thing aren't you? I like that."

Rig knelt down too, hand sliding along her back. "You defending your claim, pup?"

Suzy turned, wagging again, pushing into Rig's touch.

Dick grinned. "Looks like she got the pick of the litter."

"She's a brave girl. Lord, Rock's twenty times her size..."

"She is brave, but you can tell her she can turn it elsewhere. I don't want to get growled at everytime I try to fuck you."

"So long as she doesn't nip at your balls..." Rig chuckled, scooped the pup up and carried her in, Trouble, Mutt and Lucy following behind, wagging and curious.

"Oh man, this dog is getting carried? Rig? We were gonna head to the bedroom?"

Dick followed Rig and Rock, chuckling. He hadn't seen that particular grin on Rig since Grimmy'd died.

"I'm coming, Blue. Let me get her settled and safe in a bed. Lucy won't let the twins hurt her..."

"Hey. You're supposed to tell her I'm one of the good guys, remember? Rig? Rig?"

Rig's chuckle sounded and he heard Rig's voice. "...and you can't growl at Blue because he's mine. Pretty, either. But anybody else comes? You let us know, Suzy-Q."

The dog barked happily and he grabbed Rock around the waist. "She's just a little pup, Rock, not going to be a big old slobbery thing like *your* dogs."

"Shut up, kid."

He chuckled, slapping Rock's ass before high-tailing it after Rig.

***

"Doc?" Helen's face peered into his office, flushed as hell. "I have your morning appointments all ready."

Rig grinned over, nodded toward the coffee pot. "Yeah, what do I have?"

She shook her head to the coffee. "Mrs. Johnson's here to have her stitches out. Diabetes followup for Mr. Galen. Then a load of basketball team physicals." He groaned and she chuckled. "But, the good news? Angie Harrison's bringing her twins by for their six-week checkup."

"Oh, that's a pleasure." He loved those babies, had been pleased as punch that Angie hadn't found a pediatrician for them. "And you okay? I never saw you turn down coffee, miss."

Helen grinned wide, cheeks going bright red. "I can't. Doctor's orders?"

"Oh? Oh!" It hit him what she meant, all of a sudden. She and her man had been trying to have a baby for months. "I take it we're not having smoke breaks anymore either?"

She shook her head. "No. No more smoke breaks. Well... not until April, anyway..."

Rig stood, gave her a hug, grinning ear to ear. "Damn, girl! Congratulations!"

"Thanks, Doc." She hugged tight, then stepped back. "So, if I said I needed May, June and July off work?"

"Then I'd say we'll put a call into that nurse temp service and find somebody to keep your space warm." Like he'd fire her. Good Lord, she was the first one to be good to him here.

Helen's eyes filled up with tears, hands fluttering. "Yeah? Honest? 'Cause we're buying a house. Rich's getting out and going civilian and I need this job and..."

"Hey. Hey, now. You've got a place here so long as you want it, hon. I couldn't work without you." He hugged her tight, then stepped back with a grin. "Have you got a crib? Dick's been curious about learning about woodwork and that would be a great project for us."

"Oh... Oh, Doc. That's too cool." She got teary again and fanned her face. "Okay. It's eight o'clock. Time to heal the sick, old man."

"Old? I'm not old." He nodded, grabbed his coffee. "I'm right behind you, girl. Let's get to work. Oh, Dick's taking me to lunch today, so make sure you don't schedule me walk-ins from noon to two, 'kay?"

"You got it. Where are y'all going?"

"There's a little Italian place down the road. Rock's not fond of it, so we go there when it's just us."

"Yeah? Vinnie's? That's a nice place. Quiet." She grinned. "Okay, we're in Rooms 2, 3 and 4 today. Get to work."

Work was right. The entire damned basketball team needed physicals and the twins needed a long appointment so everyone could see them and their momma needed some iron pills because she was trying to get anemic. By the time his last patient was gone, it was ten 'til noon and he was right on schedule. He went back to his office to do some paperwork, wait for Dick to show, relaxed and easy in his skin.

There was a knock on his door and then Dick grinned at him. "Hey, Rig, you about ready for lunch?"

"Hey, Pretty." He grinned up, nodding. "I'm ready. I've got until two."

"Cool." Dick gave him a kiss and a warm hug as he came over to the door. "I hope you don't mind -- I have to drop back in at the gym. I promised Rock I'd have some forms signed by lunch and they're still sitting on my desk."

"Oh, because you know I dread having to give the Rocketman a mid-day kiss." He chuckled, shook his head. "I don't mind at all, Pretty."

Dick grinned and nipped at his nose, opening his car door for Rig. Rig slid in, stretching out. He did like this car -- not enough to consider buying one, of course, but it was comfortable.

Dick gave him a knowing grin and headed them toward the gym. "How's your day?"

"Busier than a one-armed paper hanger, but good. Oh! Pretty! Helen's going to have a baby." He grinned over. "She wants us to make her a crib."

"Us? As in you and me? Cool!" Dick beamed at him. "How much time do we have?"

"She's due in May, so we've got time. We can search for patterns online, start planning."

"Oh, cool. It's going to be fun." Dick looked excited about the prospect, still beaming like crazy as he pulled into the gym's parking lot.

"I think so. Hey, if you want, we can grab food closer, instead of heading back across town to Vinnie's." He unbuckled his belt. No reason to wait in the car when he could get a kiss from Rock while Dick ran to sign the papers.

"Sure. There's that little mom and pop Mexican place that just opened up around the corner." Dick held the door to the gym open for him.

"Oh, yum. That sounds good." He wandered in, grinning back at Dick. "Enchiladas."

Dick nodded. "I think enchiladas can be arranged."

"Cool." He nodded to the little gal at the front desk, "Afternoon, Julie."

"Hey, Doc, you looking for the Boss? He's on the second floor."

"Go on up," Dick told him. "I'll come get you as soon as I've put my John Hancock on those forms."

"Okay. I'll be hunting the Rocketman." He headed up, whistling, nodding to the people he knew.

He thought he heard Rock's voice from one of the rooms where aerobics and shit were taught, so he peeked his head around only to have just about everyone from the clinic and lots of others besides yell out "surprise!" His eyes went wide, mouth dropping open. "What on earth?"

"Happy one year of working as Doc Roberts," Dick said, coming up behind him and giving him a big hug.

There was music playing and a long table against one wall full of food.

"Well... I'll be." He blinked, shaking his head and grinning wide. "Y'all... Thank you."

Then he turned, hugged Dick hard. "You're good to me, Pretty."

Dick hugged him back. "Rock and I are proud of you, Rig. We wanted to share that."

He just beamed, pleased as punch, and surprised as hell. He hadn't even remembered. "Thank you."

He turned, looking for his Blue, wanting to thank Rock, too. Rock was talking to Helen, smiling and nodding pleasantly, but those magnificent eyes turned, searching him out. He smiled, caught like he'd been damned near fifteen years ago. Fascinated. Rock smiled back and then turned and said something to Helen, patted her arm and then his Blue was striding toward him. He met Rock halfway. "Thank you. It's fabulous."

Rock grinned and gave him a wink. "Food's good." Leaning in, Rock kissed him. "You still happy being a doc?"

"I am. It's one of two things I was made for." He winked, grinned.

Rock laughed. "You'll have to wait for the other one until we get home. I told the kid this should be just the three of us."

He laughed good and hard. "So? Show me the buffet, Rocketman. What goodies do we have? Oh, and did Helen tell you her news?"

"Yeah, I was congratulating her while we were waiting for you." Rock put an arm around his waist, tugging him close like he wasn't planning on staying right there for the duration.

"I was surpised. Y'all did good." He smiled up. "Real good."

Rock just beamed down at him. There were good munchies -- nachos and taquitos and flautas and little quiches. He filled a plate, mingling as best he could, as he leaned against Rock's side, or Dick's when he was close enough. Everyone from work managed to drop by, even if only for a few minutes, including the doctors. There were friends from their local watering hole and a few of the neighbors, the gym staff.

But most of all there was Rock and Dick, his men looking so proud and happy.

He shook his head, smiled. "Man, it's going to be hard to do my afternoon appointments now. I'm full and here with y'all."

"The kid'll take you back, we've both got stuff to do, too. But we're home at four today. So as soon as you're done you hightail it home for a proper celebration."

Dick chuckled, but was nodding. "I'm picking up beer on my way home and we'll bring the leftovers from here. And I put clean sheets on the bed this morning."

"Cool. So no cooking, just snacking and mattress dancing?" Fuck, he was a lucky man.

Dick nodded, grinning at him. It was Rock who purred and kissed him.

He just beamed. "This is great, y'all. Thank you."

"You're welcome," Dick said softly.

"You can show us how great you think it is once we're home this evening." Rock squeezed his hip.

"You can count on it, Blue Eyes."

"I do. Every damned day."

He nodded, leaning into Rock's hand one more time before going. "Yeah. Yeah, me too."

Him too.

***

The anniversary of the opening of the gym seemed to follow right on the heels of the little celebration they'd had for Rig's first year mark as a physician's assistant.

Dick had come up with a bunch of great promotions to mark the anniversary and draw new people in. So it was less a celebration and more an exercise in being busier than a one-armed paper hanger.

The kid had been right though, they'd signed up a ton of new members, added to their visibility in the community. It looked like they were going to have to hire new staff soon and he and the kid were even considering cutting back their hours some. They were making a fucking go of it.

And he was going to be fucking late to his own date night if he didn't get out of this fucking traffic. He'd been late heading home, the customers all wanting a piece of him on the last day of their week-long 'celebration'. It amazed him how hard it was to get them all together in the same spot on Saturday nights. There were a thousand different things pulling at them. The holiday they were going on at the end of the month was looking damned good.

Rock pulled into his spot behind the kid's car with minutes to spare. He was showing up empty handed, but at least he was showing up on time.

He opened the door, little Suzie barking like crazy until Mutt and Trouble barelled past her to launch themselves at him. Lucy pushed past them like a grand dame, deigning to let him pet her before returning to her bed near the fireplace.

"I'm home!" he called out. As if they couldn't tell from all the ruckus.

"Hey, you made it!" Rig grinned as he walked into the kitchen, chocolate icing on that talented mouth.

"I wouldn't disappoint my men." He went over to Rig and took a taste of that chocolate icing. Rig moaned, opened right up. The man tasted of chocolate and whipped cream and sex. "You and the kid started early."

"Mmm... I was home today and he came home at four. I warmed him up."

"Lucky, kid. Gonna warm me up, now?"

"You know it." Those grey eyes just shone for him. "Gonna make you hot, Blue."

He purred, already feeling the heat. Rig knelt, sliding down his body, fingers working his pants open and down. Oh, fuck, yeah. He slid one hand through Rig's curls, cock hard just from this, body know what was coming.

Rig nuzzled in, inhaling, breathing him in, lips soft as silk against his balls. He purred, stroking Rig's soft hair, eyes half closed as he enjoyed the amazing sensations.

"Hey, you made it!" Dick came up behind him, pressing against his back. He grinned, turning his head to give the kid a kiss, chuckling as he tasted Rig in the warm mouth.

"Of course he did..." Rig's tongue slid up his shaft, hot as fuck.

"You didn't see what it was like at the gym, Rig. Scary. And they all wanted a taste of the big stud."

He chuckled. "Flattery will get you fucked, kid."

"Mmm... I want a taste of the big stud. It's been hours." That tongue slid over his slit, pressing.

"I'm all yours, Rig." His voice was shaky, that fucking amazing mouth making him ache, making him need.

"Yeah..." Rig's eyes met his as those lips dropped slow and sweet over his cock. He groaned, watching, feeling, leaning back into the kid and letting them take him where he needed to go. Rig's mouth worked, tight and sweet on the way up, hot as hell on the drop down.

"Fucking awesome, Rabbit," he murmured, balls pulling up, aching. Rig's response was to take him deep, nose buried in his pubes, sucking hard. He roared, hands tightening on Rig's head as he started to fuck that perfect mouth. His Rabbit took everything he was, hands sliding up under his t-shirt, eyes burning.

He let it go, giving Rig everything he had as he spilled down Rig's throat. Rig took it all, then started nuzzling and drawing out the aftershocks, making him jerk. It was a good thing he had the kid propping him up, Rig was just blowing his fucking mind. Rig's fingers cupped his balls, stroking nice and slow, lips circling the tip of his cock, sucking so gentle. "You're something else, Rig."

That tongue slid, slow and easy. "Y'all's."

"You got that right." He purred, relaxed and easy between the two of them. Rig's tongue on his cock was conspiring with Dick's on his neck to make him hard again. Fucking A. Rig worked his pants the rest of the way off while Dick got the top half of him naked, both men focused on him, on making him feel good. He realised as they got him naked that the kid was already there. "Rig's needing a little defrocking, kid."

Dick chuckled. "What am I - minister of naked?"

"Vice-president in charge of nudism." Rig winked up.

He chuckled as the kid started laughing, but not so hard he couldn't go around and start pulling Rig's clothes off, too.

Dick tossed Rig's t-shirt across the kitchen. "There. Now we're all even."

Rig nuzzled against his thighs, lips brushing his abs.

"Don't suppose you can drag the mattress in?" He sure as hell didn't want to move. Wasn't sure he could stand all that much longer either though, not with his Rabbit fucking melting him.

"The sofa's only a few steps away..." Another kiss, a little lick.

"Not sure I can make it, Rabbit. You got me all... flummoxed." His voice was growly and rough, his hands on Rig's shoulders, steadying his knees. Rig hummed, nuzzling right in, hands warm and sliding around his knees. Dick came and stood behind him again, solid and warm against his back and fuck, weren't they good to this old man?

He closed his eyes and purred, just enjoyed the touches and care.

Chapter Thirteen

The smell of coffee woke Dick and he raised his head, blinking at the clock radio. Not quite five am. Rig was up earlier than usual.

Then he remembered that today was his birthday -- making him twenty-five -- and he grinned. He could go get himself a happy birthday blow job, give a thank you one in return. Hell, maybe they could make it a 69. Now that sounded like a good start to a year. He gave Rock a soft kiss without waking the big guy and then padded out in search of Rig. There was no need to put on any clothes -- he'd just have to take them all off again anyway.

Rig was in one of Rock's dark blue, heavy sweaters and nothing else, humming along with the radio and icing what looked like homemade sweet rolls, bare butt peeking out every few hip swivels.

Fuck, that was sexy. He whistled and then said as much. "Damn, you make half dressed look good."

Rig turned, blushing dark and grinning. "He left the sweater in here last night and I got chilly."

He could just make out the bottom of Rig's balls and the tip of his cock, hanging beneath the sweater as Rig moved and he moaned softly. "Sexy."

"You want some coffee, Birthday Boy?" Rig looked pleased, motions growing smoother, slower.

"I was kind of hoping for a little something else first," he admitted, sliding his arms around Rig's chest, letting his prick snug right up against Rig's ass.

"Mmm..." Rig leaned back, rubbing. "Anything for my Pretty."

He rubbed back, moans and whimpers coming from him at the contact. "I was thinking, when I woke up, that we could suck each other off. That that would be a really awesome way to start my birthday."

"I could handle that..." Rig bent a little, ass sliding on his cock.

"Oh, fuck..." His hands slid to Rig's hips and he rolled his own. "Or we could just... do it like this."

"Yeah..." Oh, Rig was warm and eager, rocking against him.

With another whimper, he reached over to the cupboard, grabbing the lube off the second shelf where it was hiding behind the extra coffee mugs. Then he was slicking up his fingers and sliding one into Rig's heat.

"Pretty..." Rig's thighs spread, his lover rocking, the sweater framing the tight ass.

"You are," he murmured, letting Rig ride his finger, just nice and easy.

"Feels good. Damn, Pretty. So good." Rig arched, humming low. He nodded, his own noises soft and constant as he pushed another finger in beside the first. It gave him more room to reach with and he found Rig's gland, sliding his fingers across it. "Oh..." Rig pushed into his touch. "Again..."

He did it again. And again and again, loving the way Rig's movements became more urgent, his own cock throbbing along.

"In me. Need you now. Deep." Rig's voice was rough, husky. Moaning, he let his fingers slide away and coated his prick with lube. Then he was sliding into Rig, moaning again at the tightness, the heat and tug around his cock.

"Yeah..." Rig stretched, thighs hot against his, hands braced against the windowsill above the sink. He wrapped his hand around Rig's hips again and started to move, sliding in deep over and over again. They shifted and pushed, Rig rocking and riding him, squeezing him tight. It felt so good and he wrapped his hand around Rig's prick, tugging in time, not wanting to be the only one coming.

"Pretty!" The cry was sharp, sure, Rig's ass clenching and rippling around him. He moaned as heat splashed over his hand, his own orgasm sweet, hot, making him see stars as Rig's ass held him tight.

"Oh. Oh, shit that's sweet." Rig was panting, rocking slow.

He nodded, rubbing his cheek against Rock's sweater. "Yeah. Really nice."

"Happy birthday, Dick. You happy?" Every so often, Rig asked, just checking.

"So happy I expect the happy police to show up and tax me or something." He grinned, sliding out of Rig with a groan.

"Happy police?" Rig chuckled. "Nut."

He laughed and turned Rig, bringing their mouths together. Rig's kiss was sweet, hot, happy, tongue sliding against his own. His arms slipped around Rig's waist and he cupped the sweet ass, rubbing them together, enjoying the slide of skin and scratch of sweater.

"Mmm... shower, now? Then breakfast in bed?"

"Oh, happy birthday to me." He smiled and rubbed their noses together, feeling good to be alive.

"Yes." Rig nodded, then led him down the hall, that pretty ass swaying. Yeah. Happy birthday to him.

Chapter Fourteen

Rig rushed up the porch and kicked the door, drycleaning in one hand, briefcase in the other, the rain spitting down, soaking him.

"Come on, y'all. Lemme in!" Man, he was *so* ready for their vacation. They'd all been working like demons, trying to get ready. Six days in the mountains. A cabin. No phone. No computer. No work. Just them. "Open the fucking door. My hands are full."

"Damn, someone's cranky."

Dick's laughter followed Rock's comment, his Pretty opening the door for him. "Hey, you're all wet."

The dry cleaning was taken from him, Dick half dressed, hair tousled.

"It's raining." He rumbled, tired and stressed out and grumpy as fuck.

"Yeah, but you're on vacation." Dick hung the clean laundry in the hall closet and grabbed his briefcase from his other hand, tugging him in. "Come on, grumpy butt -- go take a ride on the Rocketman. That'll cheer you up."

"Grumpy butt?" He looked at Rock, eyebrow arched. "Did you hear that?"

"I did. Better haul it over here so I can inspect for myself. Come on, front and center, Rigger." Rock's jeans were open, t-shirt rucked up so that magnificent belly was showing. His former marines had obviously been playing when he got home. He was already moving, fingers reaching to pet before he even thought. Those blue eyes watched him, happy and horny, warm and soothing, almost like a touch. Rock's hands reached out and grabbed his ass, squeezing. "We can't have any grumpy butts on vacation, Rig."

"We haven't fucked in days, Blue. We've just worked." He was pouting, rubbing against those hands and wanting, but pouting.

Rock nodded. "I know. I've almost got a grumpy cock."

Dick burst out laughing, his Pretty's hands warm as they worked off his tie and started in on the buttons of his shirt.

Rig grinned against his will. "Almost? Your cock gonna cure all my ills?"

"It's almost as good at curing what ails you as your mouth." Rock gave him a wink, hands reaching for his titties as Dick bared them.

"Mmm..." He pressed into Rock's hands, moving to straddle those strong thighs as soon as Dick pushed his slacks down and off.

Rock purred. "Check out his ass, kid, see if it's less grumpy yet."

Laughing softly, Dick's hands pushed apart his cheeks and then that laughter pushed against his skin in soft brushes of air, his only warning before Dick's tongue slid along his crease.

"Oh!" He pushed up against Rock, their bellies sliding together. Rock's hands slid along his spine, big and hot, stroking his skin as his mouth was taken in a hard, heads-on Rock kiss. He forgot about all the bullshit, just like that, eyes wide, body caught between those two mouths. Rock's tongue fucked his mouth hard, while Dick's fucked his ass, soft and hot and wet and almost delicate. Rig moaned, sliding, rocking, wanting it bad, right where he belonged.

Eventually Dick's hands pushed between them, making Rock's prick all slippery and then his Pretty's tongue slid away, Dick's hands lifting his ass, guiding Rock's cock to it.

"Oh..." His head fell back, and he groaned. "Yeah..."

"Yeah, now we've got your ass happy," murmured Rock, hips pushing up, sliding that fat prick deep. Dick stood behind him, pressing in close, cock hard and wet-tipped as it slid along his back, Dick's fingers finding his nipples and playing.

"Been needing..." He leaned back against Dick, moving.

"All work and no play makes Rig a grumpy cowboy," murmured Dick, bending to kiss him. Rock's mouth slid along his throat, down to wrap around one of his nipples, tongue playing with the ring.

"Uh-huh..." He nodded, jerking, bucking harder. Rock's hands were solid bands on his hips, tugging him down onto that sweet prick over and over. Oh. Oh, fuck. Yes. There was nothing like this, like the heat and pleasure and pressure. One of Dick's hands slid around to pump his cock, his Pretty's prick like a brand against his spine. His body rippled, his balls just giving it up, spunk spraying. "Yes!"

Rock roared, pulling him down several more times before that fat prick throbbed inside him, filling him deep with spunk.

"You now, Pretty. Come on. All of us."

"Oh." It was a breath of air, surprised, wanton and then heat splashed along his back.

"Mmm..." He smiled, leaning down to cuddle against Rock, Dick warm on his spine. "Better."

Rock chuckled. "Slut."

He blew a raspberry against Rock's neck. "Y'all's."

Rock's chuckles turned to laughter, one warm thumb teasing long his ribs.

Dick rubbed against his back. "We're all packed and ready, Rig. We can leave first thing in the morning."

He blushed a little, grinned. "I told the clinic we were leaving tonight, so I wouldn't get paged."

Dick laughed and Rock just grinned at him. "We gonna screw the night away?"

"Fuck, yes, kid."

"I'm so there." He nodded, settling in for the duration.

***

The mountains were nice. They could spend all day hiking and being rugged, studly men and then return to the cabin, which was the fucking lap of luxury. Rock was impressed. The kid had spent days researching to find them the perfect spot and he'd succeeded. He brought in a last armful of wood, stacking it near the fireplace and then wandered into the little kitchen for a beer and, if he was lucky, a taste of supper. Of course if he was really lucky he'd also get a taste of the cook.

Rig was stirring a pot of stew, cornbread already made, looking relaxed and cozy in sweats and sweater.

"Kid wanted one last look at the trees. He's convinced there's deer out behind the cabin." He wrapped his arms around Rig from behind, burying his face in Rig's neck. "You took a shower."

"I did." Rig made a soft, happy sound, leaning back against him. "Feels good."

"You should have waited until I had a chance to lick you clean first," he murmured. He did love a good, sweaty man.

"Mmm..." Rig stretched, swallowed. "You make me want, Blue."

"Yeah? I notice you made stew." Food would still be good if they let it sit awhile. He let his hands wander, sliding over Rig.

"Yeah... Cheesecake in the fridge... Oh..." Rig moaned, head falling back against his shoulder.

"Chocolate?" he asked, one hand sliding beneath the sweatshirt to play with Rig's belly.

"Yeah. Love your hands."

"Love your chocolate." He grinned, snaking his other hand beneath Rig's sweatshirt as well. Come to think of it, the sweatshirt looked like Dick's. Rig chuckled, rocking a little for him, rubbing against his cock with that tight little ass. "We should take this to that big bear rug in front of the fire, make sure the kid can find us when he comes in."

He started to slowly back up.

"I'd hate Dick to think we've been snatched by Bigfoot..." Rig came easy, leaning against him.

He chuckled, kept moving, kept touching. "He might get jealous, especially if what they say about big feet is true..."

Fuck, but that little laugh was the sexiest fucking thing in the whole world. He managed to get them all the way into the main room with its big comfy couches and its fireplace and bear rug. Then he turned his Rabbit right around, taking that talented mouth with his own. Rig opened right up, eager and hungry and willing as ever.

The kid found them like that, lip-locked and rubbing slowly together.

Rig reached out, drew Dick in, making the kiss a three-way. The kid tasted fresh and outdoorsy and like cinnamon. He purred, hands sliding along two spines. Rig was humming, relaxed, those eyes shining and clear.

He chuckled as the kid started to work on their clothes.

"What? Someone has to do it." Dick gave him an unrepentant grin.

"Mmm... don't throw them in the fire, Pretty."

"Why not? If you didn't have clothes, you'd have to be naked all the time." Rock had to admit the kid had a point.

"I'd freeze."

"We'd keep you warm." The kid nodded in agreement with him.

Rig chuckled, leaning in for another kiss, this one slow and deep, stealing his breath. He purred, hands stuttering on Rig's back as the kid pulled off Rig's sweatshirt. Rig cuddled into him. "Keep me warm, Blue."

"Is there any doubt that I will?" He tugged Rig right in, only giving the kid enough room to slide the rest of their clothes off. Then Dick was pressing up against Rig from the other side.

"Not even a little." Those grey eyes smiled at him, making him the center of the fucking universe.

"You got that right." He puffed up some, Rig just bringing it out in him; he could do anything for that look.

Rig just hummed, snuggling right up, arms sliding around his neck. With the kid plastered up against Rig's back, he had a whole armful of men. He kissed Rig, trusting Dick to push in and join them, which the kid did, after licking at their lips for a few moments, the sensation maddening and sensual.

They finally made it to the fur, close together, rubbing. And fuck that was nice against the skin. If they had one of those at home, he'd not be so averse to winding up on the floor over the couch or bed. His cock was hard, leaking against Rig's belly as the rug rubbed along with them. Rig's fingers slid over the tip, then his Rabbit sucked them clean, moaning low. He shuddered, moaning himself. "Still sexy as fuck, Rigger."

"Uh-huh." The kid was breathless, rubbing against Rig's ass.

"Got great fucking incentives." Rig leaned in, took a hard kiss.

He was grinning wide by the time it was done, hard and happy. "You hear that, kid? We're incentives."

"I heard, Rock."

"You sure, kid? I'm not the only one getting older."

Dick laughed. "I'm sure, old man. Rig speaks, I listen."

Rig laughed, rolling on top of him, straddling his waist, tweaking his nipple ring. He bucked, part surprise part pleasure.

"Ooh! Ride 'em cowboy!" Rig chuckled, did it again. Snorting, he bucked, just for his Rig. Dick was laughing next to them, eager hands moving on both of them. Rig threw his head back, laughing and happy, the sound ringing. Well then, he just had to do it again and again, giving his Rabbit a real bronco ride.

But then Rig slipped and his cock got snuggled right up against that hot crease, Rig rubbing hard and the laughs turned into moans. "Get the slick stuff, kid."

"I'm way ahead of you," murmured Dick, fingers sliding on his cock, Rig's ass. Rig moaned, leaned down to snuggle into him. Purring, he held Rig's ass open, giving Dick room to work that sweet little hole open for him.

"Fuck..." Rig's mouth worked his jaw, his throat.

"That's the idea, Rig. Can't put anything past you."

Dick chuckled, fingers squeezing his prick as they spread lube over him.

"You both going to have me?" The question was soft, quiet, but it made Dick moan.

His voice was rough when he answered. "You want us both here or the kid in your mouth?"

Rig's eyes were dark, all focused on him. "Want you both together filling me up."

He purred as Dick whimpered. "We can do that."

Rig nodded, relaxing against him. He kept Rig's ass open, letting Dick do the work of opening their lover up, fingers sliding in and out, one and then two and then three and then four. Rig panted, moaning against his throat. "Oh. Oh, fuck. Blue..."

"Gonna stretch you so wide, Rabbit. Fill you with us."

"Yes... My men. My lovers..." Rig nodded, tongue sliding out to taste his skin.

"You first, Rock," murmured Dick, fingers sliding away. He felt the kid slick him up again, making his prick good and wet with lube. Rig slid down on him, taking him in one smooth, sweet motion.

He groaned. "Fuck, yes." His hands found Rig's waist, eyes holding grey.

"Yes..." Rig shifted, slid, riding him nice and slow.

"Oh yeah," murmured Dick in a soft, needy whisper.

He almost bucked when one of the kid's fingers slid in with his prick. Rig moaned, snuggling in. "Oh..."

"So fucking tight," moaned Dick, the kid's sweet sounds hitting overtime as he pushed another finger in. Rig's thighs parted, motions slowing a little. "You gotta relax, Rig. Let me in."

Rock forced himself to let go of Rig's waist, hands sliding along the tense back, soothing, running into Dick's cheek rubbing along Rig's spine. Rig moaned, tension easing, relaxing for them.

"That's it," murmured Dick. The kid's fingers disappeared, the way easing for his cock for a moment, but then he could feel Dick's prick against his, wanting in. Rig took a deep breath, shivering, then let go and let Dick inside.

"Oh fuck!" Dick's voice was tight, full of awe.

Rock groaned, one hand sliding along Rig's spine, the other coming forward to tweak that shiny little ring. Rig groaned, the sound pushed out of him. "Oh... Y'all's..."

"Ours." He and Dick spoke at the same time, bodies melding all together inside Rig. They moved, finding a rhythm, Dick pushing in while he slid out. Back and forth, slowly, taking their time. Rig was resting against him, panting, cock hard and hot as fire on his belly,

"Fucking sexy, Rabbit. Sexiest fucking man I know." He spoke the words quietly against the top of Rig's head. Rig moaned, body rippling around them, squeezing them together.

He could feel the kid shudder, felt the ripples in his own body. "Fucking shit." It was something else.

The kid's noises were constant, little moans and whimpers, loud catches of breath, familiar but more.

"So full." Rig lifted his head, eyes rolling, lips parted. He found Rig's mouth with his own, short circuting a little as their tongues slid together. It was a good thing they had the kid there, keeping things moving, making sure that circuit just kept shorting. Rig's hands cradled his head, holding them together, the motion stretching the thin body farther, making Rig groan.

Dick worked a hand between them, fingers sliding against his belly as they wrapped around Rig's prick.

"Close," murmured Dick with a half-sob. "Fucking close."

Rig jerked, nodded, whispered 'please' against his lips. He purred into Rig's mouth and squeezed Dick's arm. The kid got the message, started working Rig's prick hard as they sped up their movements. Jesus fuck, he could feel it in his toes. Rig was keening, the sounds constant, steady, desperate.

"Come on, Rig. Give it to us. Come on our cocks. *Ou*r cocks, Rabbit. Me and the kid, both of us inside you together. All three of us in one place."

Rig sobbed, entire body shuddering, tightening, milking them as spunk poured out over Dick's fingers, onto his belly. The kid wasn't even seconds behind Rig, crying out, heat spreading all around Rock's cock and he roared, letting them pull him along, the pleasure like a fucking freight train, knocking the wind from his lungs.

Rig was heavy and still against him, eyes closed, panting softly.

"You okay, Rig?" he asked after clearing his throat a few times.

Rig nodded. "Uh-huh. Good."

"Kid?"

"Fuck, yeah, Rock. The best." Dick's prick slid out, leaving him in Rig, and the weight on him doubled. "Let me just rest a minute," Dick murmured.

"You're good." The day he couldn't hold the weight of both his lovers on him was a long way off.

Rig was asleep in seconds, worn out, sighing against his chest. He purred, halfway there himself. The kid roused long enough to get a blanket, tucking it around them and settling against him.

It occured to him as he drifted off that the setting really didn't matter. Just the two men sleeping with him.

Chapter Fifteen

Rig came home Halloween night with a pizza and four more bags of candy, bunny ears and tail that Dick had found still in place. Helen had dressed as a nun, one of the other girls as an angel, and all the kids had gotten a kick out of them in costume. Now he was ready for a shower and bite to eat and maybe even a nap. "Boo. I'm home."

Rock gave a shout and put his hand on his heart. "Help! Kid! There's a man-eating bunny in the house!"

He snorted and grinned and threw the bags of candy over, thwacking Rock in the chest. "Here, sugar. I need a bath. I brought pizza."

"Oh, pizza, cool!" Dick came down the hall, wearing jeans, cowboy boots and one of his hats, otherwise naked from the waist up.

"Mmm..." He stuttered a little, derailed.

"You're still in your bunny costume, cool. Later I want you to model it without the clothes." Dick came up and tilted the hat back to kiss him. "Rock's not dressed yet, you can help me talk him into something sexy. That old gladiator skirt's gathering dust."

"Oh, he'd look fine..." He walked up, hands sliding up Dick's belly. "I haven't had a cowboy in a long, long time."

Dick blushed and pressed a little closer. "You like my costume?"

"Uh-huh." He leaned in, licking and lapping at Dick's skin. "Wanna dance?"

"Oh. Yeah. I do." Dick's arms went around him, a soft sigh sounding.

"What about the pizza?" Rock grumped.

"It's all yours." He tugged the rabbit ears off, sent them flying and they started moving, nice and slow. Rock grunted and sat back on the couch, but his attention was caught by riverstone eyes looking down into his face as he and Dick swayed together.

Oh, now... This was an old fantasy, dancing in some cowboy's arms, moving nice and easy. Rock had the news on, but Dick was humming softly, fingers stroking his waist. He moaned low, eyes caught in Dick's gaze. "Hey."

Dick smiled slowly, keeping him warm with those eyes alone. "Hey yourself."

Their mouths brushed, slow, sweet. "This is... Damn, Pretty."

"And now that I know all I need to do to get that look on your face is take off my shirt and put on a cowboy hat? Get ready to wear it a lot."

"Mmm... you look fine." He petted Dick's spine, moaning, rocking their hips together. Dick shivered as his fingers stroked that sensitive lower back. He grinned, brushed against his lover, hips grinding a little.

"Oh, Rig... I do like the way you dance." Dick's voice was rough, dragging on the last word.

"Yeah." He closed his eyes, lips sliding along Dick's jaw, up toward that ear. "Love this." Dick nodded and whimpered, hands drawing him closer, one settling on his ass. Fucking sweet. He blew in Dick's ear, whispering low. "Love you."

"Rig." Dick's whisper was barely a breath, a shudder moving through his Pretty, the scent of Dick's spunk suddenly filling the air.

Oh, now, that made him feel sexy as hell, hot and fine. "Yeah..."

Dick's face buried in his neck, his Pretty holding him close, tight, their hips still moving slowly to the music they heard in their heads. His hand stroked the nape of Dick's neck, holding on, so fucking happy he hurt.

"Could do this the rest of my life," murmured Dick.

"Okay." He nodded, grinning. "Works for me."

Dick chuckled and licked at his neck, tongue sliding on his skin.

Rock snorted. "You know you still got that tail on your ass, Rig?"

He grinned. "Thanks, Blue. I'd plumb forgot."

Dick kept laughing, lips moving on his skin, hand sliding to grab the tail and play with it.

"Obscene, kid."

"I try, Rock."

"Y'all are buttheads. Mine, but buttheads, nonetheless." He winked at Dick, grinning wide.

Dick laughed, muscles in the sweet belly tightening. "You gonna go get sexy in that gladiator outfit, Rock?"

"You want me to hand out candy wearing that little bit of leather?"

"Only if you're handing it out to me." He grinned, eyes dragging over Rock's bod.

"You'll have to wait your turn." Rock gave him a grin as the doorbell rang. "Kids don't wait for dancing." His Blue winked and gave the candy to Dick. "I'm going to go get my costume on."

He took the bowl. "I'll get it. You're... half-naked."

"Yeah, and I need to change my jeans." Dick gave him a grin, eyes hot.

"Yeah." He chuckled. "I still got it, huh, Pretty?"

"Fuck yes." The doorbell rang again and Dick laughed. "Go pay the pipers, Rig, before Rock comes and growls."

"Yes, sir. I'll hop to it." He laughed at himself, going to feed the kiddos some chocolate.

As he was closing the door he was goosed and when he turned he found Rock, dressed in his BDUs, blood down one side of his face, one hand looking like hamburger, a big, wet blood stain on his belly. "Oh, that's gross. Well-done, but gross."

Rock grinned wide. "Gonna scare the shit out of the kids."

His Blue couldn't fool him though; Rock loved Halloween, loved handing out the candy and scaring the kids.

"You are. Stud." He handed the bowl over, leaned up for a careful kiss. "Any pizza left?"

"I wouldn't let you and the kid go hungry." Rock grinned again. "You made him cream his jeans. It's no wonder he's the king of naked." He got a wink from Rock and then the bell rang and Rock grabbed the bowl from him, limping and moaning as he opened the door. The kids gasped and squeaked and he got himself settled in, watching the show. Sexy fucker.

Dick returned, still shirtless, clean pair of jeans on, looking splendid in his cowboy hat. He was given a piece of pizza as his Pretty settled in next to him. "He's gonna give the little ones nightmares for weeks."

"Yep. He's having a ball." He leaned closer. "And the first one that cries will get a soft voice and Uncle Jimmy all over the place."

"I know. It's his best kept secret, that soft center." Dick was watching Rock, fond look in his eyes.

Rig nodded, cuddled in, smiling. "And we won't tell a soul, will we, Pretty?"

Dick gave him a wide-eyed, innocent look. "Tell who what?"

He chuckled, finger brushing Dick's nose. "What's my best kept secret?"

Dick caught his finger and sucked on it a moment before letting it go again. That innocent look hadn't changed for a moment. "You? Secrets?"

It felt good to laugh, to lean into that warm skin. "You stopped being innocent a while ago, Pretty."

Dick laughed with him, hand on his belly. "You and Rock saw to that."

"It's a calling."

Dick giggled, snuggling close, pizza forgotten. Then he was given a soft kiss. "You can't sleep by yourself and you'll always miss Texas."

"Always. Texas isn't a place, it's a way of life." He twined their fingers together.

Dick kissed him again, so sweet. "You do it proud, Cowboy."

"Thank you, sir." He reached back, unpinned the bunny tail.

Dick chuckled. "Big pink fluffy bunny tails not Texas enough?"

"It's just stopping me from getting comfortable. You see any neat costumes at the gym?"

"Yep. *Lots* of skin." Dick waggled his eyebrows.

"Oh, shit, I bet. I tell you, Pretty. You and Rock ought to do a calendar. Something beefcakey."

Dick laughed. "Oh yeah, I can so see Rock going for that."

"It would be hot as hell." He nodded, this was a good plan. "Moneymaker for the gym."

Dick shook his head. "If you can talk the big guy into it? I'm in."

"My studs." He grinned. Of course, he wanted to watch the photo shoot. And he wanted the negatives. Dick ducked his head, face warm as it pressed against his neck. He kissed Dick's ear, whispering low. "You have to do a picture in a hat and jeans. For me."

Dick shivered and pressed close. "Anything you want."

"I want one of you in those soft, old white pajama pants, too." He started rubbing. "For my office, when I need in the middle of the day..."

"Oh, fuck... I'm starting to see the potential in this idea." Dick rubbed back, his Pretty's breath starting to grow short.

"Mm-hmm. I could lock my door and settle on my sofa and look and touch..." His hips were rocking, nice and slow.

"Rock wearing leather pants." Dick's hand slid down to his cock, rubbing, pressing.

"Oh, fuck, yes." He nodded, arched. "Rock in BDU pants, that nipple ring shining."

"I don't know about that one," Dick murmured, hand squeezing. "You might be tempted to lean in and lick it. You'd get the picture all wet."

"I'll need copies."

Dick laughed softly, hand sliding beneath his ass and encouraging him to keep rubbing. "If you can keep Rock from burning the negatives."

"Hell, yeah. Those are mine."

Dick grinned and kissed him. "You still have to talk him into doing it in the first place.

"It's a great idea." He hummed a little, starting to get really distracted. "And I'm convincing."

"You are," Dick agreed, tongue sliding along his neck.

"I... mmmmm..." He arched, fingers tangling in Dick's hair. Dick's hand stayed on his ass, reminding him to rub against his Pretty, while the other hand slid up his shirt, stroking his skin.

"Oh." He rubbed harder, moaning low.

"Fuck, you're sexy." Dick's fingers slid up to find the ringless nipple, teasing it, tugging on it.

"Want you..." He arched up, nipple going tight as fuck, electricity shooting through him.

"Got me." Dick's mouth met his again, tongue pushing between his lips as his Pretty's warm fingers slid across to his other nipple. His cry pushed into Dick's mouth, chest pushing into the touch. Dick fed him a sound back, fingers wrapping around the ring and tugging on it, gently and then not so gently and then twisting and then gently again.

Oh. Oh, he was gonna... "Pretty."

"Right here," murmured Dick, licking at his lips, fingers continuing to play with the ring.

"Uh-huh. Please. Fuck." He arched, groaned. Dick pressed down against him, rubbing a solid thigh against his cock. That was all it took for him to come, shooting hard, body rocking.

Dick made a happy noise, still rubbing against him, kisses filling his mouth. He shivered, lips open, entire body lit up as Dick kept moving. He brought one of his hands down to his Pretty's jeans, working the button open, zipper down.

Dick laughed breathless, cock pushing out into his hand. "Thanks."

"Anytime." He pumped, wriggling a little. "Fucking hot, Pretty."

Dick moaned. "Yeah. Fuck."

"Anytime. Any place."

"Uh-huh." Dick's eyes were focussed on his face, the long cock pushing into his hand over and over as Dick's soft noises filled the air.

The front door slammed closed. "Shh... the big scary marine's going to beat us."

Dick giggled and moved harder, faster. "Promise?"

"Uh-huh..."

Dick licked his neck, eyes rolling. "Rig."

"What?" He pumped harder. "We go in the hallway, you can fuck me."

Dick's giggles were starting to sound breathless. "That might... scar the kids more than. Rock."

"We'd have to go deep and..." He started chuckling himself. "Long."

"Rig." Dick's forehead banged against his chest, but those hips kept pushing, thrusting into his hand.

He grinned, thumb working the slit, pressing. "Come on, Pretty. Give it up." Dick's shout was muffled in his chest, heat pouring over his hand. He nodded, still chuckling. "Such a good boy."

Dick nuzzled into him, all warm and limp.

The front door opened and closed and Rock's growl sounded. "The least you could have done was made your screams sound tortured."

He started laughing, hard enough it hurt. The bell rang again and Dick called out as Rock went back for the door, "We promise to go for tortured this time."

"Shit, you go for a three-fer this fast and your balls will be tortured."

"Save some for me," Rock shouted at them just before the door closed behind him.

He grinned, licking at Dick's lips. "Happy Halloween, Pretty."

Dick chased his tongue, sucking on it lazily. "Yeah, Rig. It is, isn't it?"

He nodded, fingers sliding against that warm cheek. "Yeah. Hell, yeah."

Dick turned and kissed his palm, tongue sliding. "You know, we could just make out until Rock's done playing with the kids. Keep things revved up for him."

"Oh, I can't think of anything I'd like more." He smiled into those eyes.

Dick beamed back at him and shimmied out of his jeans, getting them all caught up in the boots. "Damn. This is why they say cowboys do it with their boots on, isn't it?"

He chuckled, nodded, then slid down to help. "You got it, Pretty."

Dick maoned softly as he pulled the boots off, hand coming down to slide through his curls. He leaned in, nuzzled one velvet soft inner thigh. Another soft sound and Dick's legs spread for him, those pretty eyes just watching him, hot. He licked, humming at the salt, the musk.

"Love you, too," whispered Dick, hand gentle in his curls.

He looked up, smiling. "I know. Count on it."

Dick nodded, smile easy and deep in those riverstone eyes. He dropped a soft kiss on Dick's sac, on the tip of the long cock.

"Sweet fuck." Dick moaned, legs spreading further.

"Yeah, Pretty." He nuzzled that pretty cock, licking Dick's shaft. Despite having just come twice, his Pretty's prick got nice and hard for him, long and hot against the fine belly. "Remember, slow and easy. Waiting for Blue..."

"Tell that to my cock, Rig. Damn, your mouth is something else."

"Mmm... and you've got a long, pretty prick..." He licked from base to tip. Dick moaned again, whimpered, sweet cock jerking beneath his tongue.

The door opened and slammed shut, the sound of the bolt driving home loud. Rock turned the light off and came over. "A man can only listen to those noises so long before he leaves the damned bowl of candy on the steps and comes in to fuck the scared right out of his men."

"Oh... Oh, yeah." He grinned, nodding, hips rocking, tempting.

Rock groaned. "Let me lose the blood."

"'kay. I'll keep Dick warm..." Rig took one ball into his lips, sucking, humming.

Dick made a squeaky noise. "Take your time, Rock."

Rock chuckled. "With that ass winking at me? Not going to happen, kid."

Fuck, they made him feel so fucking good.

It wasn't long at all before Dick's eyes were looking past him, his Pretty whistling. "You do clean up good, Rock."

He turned, wanting his own look. Rock had stripped down, and wiped most of whatever he'd used for blood away, but he still had a streak of it here and there on the hard body. Those blue eyes were looking at him like he was the most edible thing on the planet.

"Sweet fuck." He let it all show -- the need, the want, the love, the whole package. "Beautiful son of a bitch."

Rock purred for him, cock twitching. "And all yours, Rig."

He let his eyes drag, lips parting as he groaned. "Fuck, yes. C'mere."

"You gonna get me good and wet so I can fuck that sweet ass?"

Dick moaned softly. "No one sweet talks the way you do, Rock."

He nodded, licked his lips. "Any time, any place."

"Right here, right now, Rabbit." That growl was intoxicating.

"Yes." He shifted, reached out and pulled Rock close, lips sliding right over the head of that fat cock. Rock moaned for him, hands sliding through his curls. Dick's heat pushed up against his back, a slick finger teasing along his crack.

"Mmm..." He closed his eyes and hummed, happy and home and right where he needed to be.

Chapter Sixteen

Two fucking days until the start of their holiday and Rock couldn't fucking wait. It had been full on bore at the gym since their big first year anniversary push. He wasn't used to vacations putting him behind, but theirs had because he and the kid weren't just more cogs in the wheel, they were the wheel.

He'd insisted on flying out to Texas instead of driving, rumbling any time Rig so much as mentioned maybe taking a car. He could fucking afford to fly his Rabbit home for Christmas and that's what he was going to do. He got home from work well after midnight. But he was going to be able to work regular hours the next two days, so it was worth it.

As long as someone was up for some good hard fucking.

Rig was sitting in the armchair, paperwork in his lap, pen in his hand, concentrated frown on his face, sound asleep. He rumbled, wondering where the kid was, letting Rig fall asleep like that.

Just then Dick came rushing out of the kitchen. "Sh. Sh. He's asleep."

He snorted. "He's gonna get a crick in his neck."

That earned him a grin. "I figured you'd want to carry him to bed."

Fuck, the kid knew him well. He followed Dick as the kid went over and started taking the paperwork out of Rig's hands. Rig murmured, shifted a little, almost waking up. He picked Rig up, purring as Rig nuzzled close. Not that he wasn't going to wake Rig up once he got his Rabbit to bed, but that didn't mean he couldn't let Rig get a couple more winks in.

The kid trailed them, turning off lights as he went. Rig was relaxed, easy in his arms, lips soft on his neck. He chuckled. You couldn't get much past his Rabbit. Not because of sleep, that was for sure.

He laid Rig out on the bed, following the lean body down. Rig frowned a little, murmured. "Blue? Skin..."

He chuckled. "Give the kid a second or two."

"Mmm... 'kay." Those lips started sliding along his jaw.

Sure enough, Dick's fingers worked his shirt out of his pants, not bothering with the buttons in favour of pulling it over his head. Rig rumbled as the shirt got in the way of the kisses, then dived back into them. The kid was kinder with Rig's shirt, opening it and tugging it off Rig before starting to work on their jeans. It was seamless and good and not long at all before they were all naked, Dick sliding in with them. Rig hummed, smiling, hand reaching for Dick and holding on.

The kid pushed into their kisses, bringing that sweet eagerness and good taste that was their Dick. They settled together, rubbing and relaxed, Rig's hands sliding over them both. Dick was rubbing against his and Rig's thighs and he nodded and pulled them all together so he could wrap a hand around all their pricks.

They didn't need acrobatics tonight, just a good threeway orgasm.

"Mmm... Yeah. Nice and slow."

"I can do nice and slow."

Dick moaned and nudged him to the side just a touch, tongue lapping first at his and then at Rig's nipples.

"Oh..." Rig arched, heels digging into the mattress.

He couldn't help teasing Rig with those super sensitive little titties. "Thought you wanted it nice and slow, Rig."

"Huh?" Rig moaned against his shoulder, hips jerking.

"His brain's left the building, Rock." Dick kept licking, making his own toes curl as the kid's tongue slid into his nipple ring and tugged.

"Mmm. Good. So good." Rig stretched, pushing faster, harder.

"Kid leaned from the fucking master." His words were hoarse, and damn, he was close, wanting. He tugged harder on the pricks in his hand.

Rig pinked, arched. "Yeah? Close. Gonna. Fuck."

"Yeah, we're fucking, Rig." He pulled faster and the kid, just knowing, tugged on his nipple ring and he cried out, coming hard, shuddering against Rig. Rig whimpered, hips jerking, following right along behind. The kid's need was as strong as theirs, his cry good and solid as more heat splashed over his hand.

"Mmm... 's good." Rig hummed, licking, snuggling in.

"Fuck yes, it's good." He let Rig's octopus arms keep him close. "It's just never enough."

"Hmm?" Rig nuzzled him.

"Just hate working late."

Dick nodded, hand petting.

Rig stroked his head. "Vacation now, Blue. Christmas and kids and Deuce in from Camp LeJeune."

"Yeah. Yeah." He nodded, relaxing against Rig, letting their hands soothe away the last of his growls.

***

They let Rock drive to Momma's while he and Dick wrapped the presents in the car, tape and paper going everywhere. There wasn't as much as some years -- the older kids all got gift cards in fancy envelopes and Sissy got a good sized check to put away for visiting in the summer. So there were dolls for the twins and books for everybody and an art set for Maddie and that was all. Momma's recliner was being delivered.

His guys' presents were already at Momma's -- two little laptops with fitness software for the business, since he'd damn near absconded with the family one.

The shopping had been no stress this morning, they'd had a huge, decadent breakfast after a long session of fucking and sucking and the radio was calling for a cold front Christmas Eve. All good.

The presents were piled up in the front seat by the time they turned into Momma's lane and he was curled up in Dick's arms, his Pretty asleep for the last hour or so.

"Wake up, sleeping beauty!" Rock called from the front seat, making Dick jerk.

"Huh?"

"We're here." He slid out, heading up the stairs to the door. Eighteen months since he'd gotten to hug his momma.

She met him at the door, eyes full of tears and just held on tight. "Oh, baby. Baby, it's been too long."

Christ. Christ she was looking rode hard and put away wet. "Hey, now. I'm here, Momma." He looked across the front room, Sissy giving him a sad smile.

Rock and Dick came up behind him, his Blue wrapping him and Momma in a hug together. "How's my favorite lady?" Rock asked, bending to kiss her cheek.

She smiled up, a little tremulous. "Fine, now. I needed my boys home with me." Oh, she was going to break his heart.

"You telling me all those girls aren't keeping you too busy to miss us?" Rock asked. He gave her cheek another kiss. "We're here for over a week, Momma. You'll be sick of us before it's time for us to go."

Then it was Dick's turn, his Pretty taking his cue from Rock and hugging him and Momma together. "It's so good to see you, Momma."

She patted Dick's cheek. "Oh, I've missed that smile, Richard. It's good to have you home."

"Good to be here, Momma."

"We in the usual place?" Rock asked. "The kid and I'll unpack our gear, so we can spend the rest of the day visiting. We picked you up that fried chicken, too."

"Thanks, boys. Yeah, you're in the garage and there's a brisket for supper." Momma nodded, drawing him in. "Bobby took the two boys to their other granny's, but Deuce is here. Still sleeping, but here."

"Bobby should be proud of that boy, the way he's making his way through the Corps," Rock noted before heading back to the car.

"We gonna get a chance to see Jake and Louis?" Dick asked.

Momma nodded. "They'll be home the day after Christmas and I'll fetch them..." Momma's words trailed off as squeals sounded outside. "The girls found Jim, Sissy."

Dick chuckled. "I'd better go rescue him, I mean help him with our stuff or I'll never hear the end of it."

Dick gave Momma's cheek a quick kiss and his arm a soft caress.

He walked them over to the sofa, looking at her. "You feeling okay, Momma? You look awful tired."

Sissy came to give him his kiss. "I'm trying to take care of her, Bubba."

"So much fuss over an old woman. I'm just feeling my age is all." She let him sit her down though, not insisting there was something she needed to be making for the boys in the kitchen.

He held her hands. "You're not old, now. Hell, you're a spring chicken."

She squeezed his hands, looking pleased as punch. "I've just been missing my baby, now that you're here I already feel like a girl again."

Sissy rolled her eyes, winked. "Spoiled brat."

He grinned over. "Bitch."

"Queer."

"Don't make me beat you both."

"Yes, Momma." He and Sissy had that down, in stereo.

Rock and Dick came in with the bags of chicken, Rock chuckling. "How long have we been here, kid?"

"Five minutes. Maybe."

Rock nodded. "And he's already in trouble. That must be some kind of record."

"Sissy started it." He grinned over, unrepentant.

Sissy bounced up and into Rock's arms. "So? Did my girls find you?"

Rock gave her a hug and swatted her good-naturedly on the ass. "Nope. But we were met by this band of hooligans outside, bunch of older girls -- who do they belong to?"

"Hell if I know, Jim. Shit the boob fairy came and took my Rachel away."

Rock chuckled and Dick shook his head. "You've got to see them to believe them, Rig. Little Maddie is... " Dick's hand started measuring the air. "Huge."

"My Maddie?" He winked up, hollering. "Maddie? Did you grow up on your Uncle Alex?"

She came barelling in, arms still full of woodchips. "Uncle Alex! Uncle Alex!"

"We told them they had to take care of the wood before they could come in," Rock pointed out.

"You throw them in the fireplace and get your butt over here, child." He grinned, held out his arms for the littlest of his favorite girls in the world. She did and then launched herself at him, little arms going around his neck and squeezing hard. He held on, hugging the strong little body tight. "Oh girl, I've been missing this."

"Well I've been right here, 'Lex."

Rig chuckled, nodded. "I know it. Y'all like your new house?"

"Yeah. I miss the horses, though." When Hank and Sissy'd decided to leave the ranch in Arkansas, they'd left behind working on a huge spread for a little one that was theirs.

"I bet."

The rest of the girls came in, each wanting a hug, even Rachel who was at that age where such things weren't always appreciated. The twins looked as alike as two peas in a pod, and couldn't have acted more different -- Tammy was outgoing and chatty, Presley shy and silent, just watching with big eyes.

Dick had sat on the floor, Lisa settling in his lap like she owned it.

It was Rock who reminded them of lunch. "Well I'm for chicken. Anyone going to help me eat?"

Rachel grinned, hands playing with her hair, looking just like her momma. "I'll go set out plates and cups, Ma-maw."

"Did somebody say chicken?" Deuce walked into the room, a big old boy with a high-and-tight, looking as military as a man could. "Uncle Alex. Richard. Uncle Jimmy. Mornin', Ma-maw."

"Robert." Rock gave the boy a manly hug with lots of back slapping. "You do the corps proud, son."

Dick got up to give the boy a hug as well, rubbing his head. "I remember these."

Duece laughed, "Yeah. No brushing required. Y'all have a good trip in?"

Momma leaned in, whispered. "They're shipping him out to the Pakistani border, baby. For a whole year."

Ah, shit. "He'll be fine, Momma."

She nodded, tears in her eyes again.

"We did," Rock answered before Dick could. "And now we're going to eat because driving makes me hungry."

Dick chuckled and swung Lisa up onto his back, leading a procession out into the kitchen.

"Come on, Momma. Food, coffee, relax. You can fret after Christmas." He stood, held out a hand. "I need to get you to the beach, get you in the sun."

"Oh, I'd like that, baby. I want to see my baby the doctor at work." She took his hand, letting him pull her up.

"You need to meet my pup, too. Suzie's a wee thing, but she's a charmer."

"Sounds really different from your old boy. And I've seen a picture. Jim's made sure I've had pictures of all the new pups, he's so proud of those two boys of his. Mutt and Trouble."

He chuckled, nodded. "Those two hooligans, I tell you what. They're something special."

"I got that impression. More from what Jim's notes didn't say than from what they did."

The kitchen was in chaos, Rock and Dick passing out plates and cups and utensils and food, the kids putting everything on the table. He chuckled, shook his head. "Merry Christmas, Momma. Damn."

She grinned. "I hope y'all got extra legs."

"We got plenty, Momma," Rock told her, winking.

Dick walked by, whispering in his ear. "The two of them did *not* just say what I heard them say. Nope. Not. I didn't hear it."

He snorted, chuckled. "Perv."

Presley walked over to Rock, eyes wide, whispering. "Can I have some chicken please, sir?"

Rock went down onto his haunches. "Well now, do you think you can call me Uncle Jimmy?"

She backed up a step, but nodded. "U...u...uh-huh."

He looked over at Sissy, who shrugged. "Damn stutter keeps getting worse, she keeps getting quieter. Lisa says some of the kids down the road were mean to her, Tammy knocked the shit out of them."

He saw Rock's fingers start to curl into fists, but otherwise, his Blue didn't show he'd heard Sissy at all. "Well then, I guess I can give you some chicken. Can you tell me what your favorite piece is?" Rock looked around and leaned in a little. "I won't tell a soul, it'll be our secret."

Presley nodded, leaned close, whispering to Rock. He smiled, heart just aching with love. Such a good man.

Momma nodded, patting his arm. "I want a thigh, baby, and a biscuit."

"I got it," murmured Dick. His Pretty piled two plates with food. A thigh and bicuit for Momma, along with some coleslaw and beans and another plate with two breasts, a biscuit and a whole bunch of coleslaw and pinto beans. "There you go, one for each of you. Milk, beer, or coffee?"

"Tea, please." Their voices sounded together and they looked over, laughing hard, Momma looking younger already. Dick shook his head and grinned, finding the tea in the fridge and pouring them each a tall glassful. He poured out milk for all the kids and himself and a got out a beer for Rock, who was dishing out chicken, having each child's favorite piece whispered into his ear, just like Presley got to.

Maddie scooted beside him, Tammy and Presley huddled and whispering together at the end of the table as Rock and Deuce talked and ate, Dick and Lisa chattering.

Sissy sat and looked. "Rachel Denise! Get your ass in here and eat."

Rachel peeked in. "Not hungry."

"Don't care. Eat something and you can go mope about that boy after. It'll keep."

Rock's ears perked up. "Boy? Come in here and tell your Uncle Jimmy all about him. Is this boy good enough for you?"

"Not even close." Sissy wrinkled her nose. "I swear I'm locking her in a closet."

Rig chuckled. "'Cause God knows that worked for you."

Rachel wandered in, blushing. "Name's Michael David and he's real smart. He's going with my best friend 'cause she's got red curly hair, but Momma won't let me dye mine."

"You're mooning over another girl's boyfriend?" Rock asked. He shook his head. "That's a good way to lose a friend, Rachel."

"Sarah knew I liked him way before she said yes and you and Uncle Richard are still friends, even though he looks after Uncle Alex."

Oh, sweet Jesus. Rig thought he might just swallow his tongue. The table got really quiet for a long moment, his Pretty's color high.

Rock though, he looked Rachel right in the eye and spoke quietly, evenly like he wasn't phased at all. There was something to be said for marine training. "The situation with your Uncle Alex, Uncle Richard and me is different, Rachel."

"But why? Why is everything always different for everybody else and just normal for me?"

Sissy leaned in. "Should I?"

Rig shook his head. "No. Rock's got it. Don't make him look a fool, now."

"Because our situation is different, Rachel. Now, I understand that Sarah is your best friend, but you aren't looking after her the way you're looking after this boy and there's nothing wrong with that. It's good in fact, makes things easier to be just normal. The three of us, we all care for each other and care for each other enough to be different.

"If your Uncle Richard didn't look after me the same way he looks after Uncle Alex, well then there might be a problem. Now it's different. A lot of people say it's strange and there's even a lot who say it's wrong, but we aren't hurting anyone and we look after each other and make sure no one of the three of us is getting hurt. Do you understand?"

"No. No, I just want to be pretty and cute like Sarah and not be stupid when the boys talk to me." She gave Rock a sad little look. "You got two boys and I can't get even one to smile at me and that's not very fair."

Rock nodded. "No, I don't suppose it's fair at all. But I'm still not giving up my boys and the truth still is that if you go after your best friend's boy, you're going to lose your best friend. And I tell you what Rachel, you are one of the prettiest girls I know."

"You're my uncle, you have to think that. It's like a law."

Rig chuckled, covering his mouth with his hand, shoulders shaking.

Deuce saved the day by reaching out, pulling her hair. "You're just a stinky old cousin. Now will you *eat* so we can go get the Christmas stuff?"

She stuck her tongue out at Deuce. "Big honkin' marine."

"Pimply dork."

"Bottomless pit."

"Layabed."

She looked over at Rig. "Uncle Alex? Help!" He mouthed a word and her eyes lit up. "Jarhead!"

"I thought the idea was to be insulting," said Dick, "not complimentary."

Rock meanwhile looked about as relieved as a man could and had downed his beer in one go. He met Rock's eyes, nodded, gave him a thumbs up. Rock gave him a bit of a grin and went over to the fridge to get himself another beer and then dug into his food like a man who had no intention whatsoever of being interupted before his stomach was full.

Momma chuckled. "Welcome home, baby."

He nodded, chuckled as he dug in. "Yeah. Yeah, Momma."

***

Rock got ahold of Momma's list of stuff that needed doing and set to work with Dick. "Your Momma wants to visit with you, Rig. Let her spend time with her baby, the kid and I have this covered."

Not letting Rig anywhere near the list finally convinced his Rabbit he was serious.

By the time the brisket was done he was tired and dirty and growling at Dick, but they had ninety percent of the list done which meant everyone could just relax for Christmas Day. He and the kid washed their hands in the kitchen sink and took their place at the table. "I could probably use a shower. Sorry, Momma."

"Thank you for your help, Jim. There's brisket, potatoes, the whole shebang."

"I would work for a month of Sundays for your home cooking, Momma."

Dick whispered "suck up" against his neck before going to sit between Maddie and Lisa, piling his plate high. Yep, he was. But he liked Momma and liked to put that happy look in her eyes, whether it was by doing work around the place, complimenting her cooking, or being good to her baby.

Rig was picking idly at his brisket, feeding it to Maddie. Quiet. He frowned, watching his Rabbit as he dug into his own food, hungry enough to eat for himself, Rig and the kid as well. Dick was being entertained by the kids, keeping the conversation going.

Momma smiled over at him. "Are y'all missing your gym already?"

"Hell, no. It's a damn lot of work. Pardon my French, Momma." He gave her a smile, putting aside his worry over Rig until he could catch him alone.

"Building your own business always is, but Alexander says y'all are making a real go of it." She smiled at Deuce as the boy went to get another plate.

He nodded. "Yeah, it's doing well. It's a lot more challenging than I thought it would be, too. I have to admit I was worried I'd get bored, but so far there hasn't been any days where I've got nothing to do but work out." He grinned as Deuce came back with his second plateful loaded. "Now there's a boy after my own heart."

"I figure I've got a year of MREs to look forward to. I *need* Ma-Maw's cooking."

Rock nodded. "You get hungry enough you'll eat anything, but the better the food you're used to, the harder MREs are to stomach." He ate up the last of his brisket and took a sip of his beer. "So when are they shipping you out?"

"January third." Deuce sighed. "Never done anything like this before. Was sorta hoping you and I could go have coffee. Sit. Talk."

"Well nothing says we can't still do that Deuce." He'd like that. Give the kid some tips, remind him to keep his head low, to look out for himself first and his buddies second, that a marine never left a man behind.

Deuce nodded, dug in. "Thanks, Uncle Jimmy."

The twins came over, sat close. Tammy patted his arm. "Presley says thanks for the chicken this afternoon."

He smiled at Presley. "You're very welcome. I know it wasn't as good as your Ma-Maw's, but she's got a huge bunch of people to feed and it was nice to give her a break, wasn't it?"

Presley nodded. "M...momma? M...m...momma makes ch...chicken."

"Yeah? You like your Momma's chicken best?" He liked this little girl with her quiet and her stutter. Funnily enough she reminded him of Dick. Presley had a whole lot going on inside her head; she just kept it to herself.

She nodded and Tammy laughed. "Momma puts cheese on it, Uncle Jimmy. It's so good."

"Cheese? On chicken? Oh, you two are putting me on, making a joke on your old Uncle Jimmy."

They were damned cute. All the girls were, even Rachel with her teenaged attitude. Still, he was glad they weren't *his* -- he liked them just fine seeing them on holidays.

Presley giggled. "Uh-huh. W...w...with rice."

"Oh, now that makes sense, but cheese." He shook his head and winked at her.

The girls giggled and Rachel looked over. "Uncle Jimmy wouldn't like it. It has brocolli."

"Ah..." He nodded and touched his finger to his nose. "Rachel knows my weakness."

Presley's eyes shone. "I...I...I... pick around."

"Well now, why didn't I ever think of that?" He smiled at Presley. "I'm going to remember that one."

Momma's chuckle was soft. "Now, Jim. Vegetables keep you healthy, regular."

Rig stood up, headed for the kitchen door.

"Now I know where Rig gets it," he told her with a wink. "Girls, can you do me a favor? Would you clear the table for your Ma-maw and help Uncle Richard to do the dishes?"

At their nods he got up and gave Momma a kiss on the cheek. "That was a mighty fine brisket, Momma, thank you."

Then he headed off after his Rabbit. He didn't find Rig in the house, in the garage, nowhere. He was about to get worried when he saw the light of a cherry, out in the pasture, just walking. That cold front had come in and Rig was out here smoking. Something was definitely up. He made his way out, catching up with Rig, putting his arm around Rig's shoulders. "Bit cold for a walk, isn't it?"

Rig nodded, leaned toward him. "It is."

"Then why are we out here?" He didn't need to beat around the bush. He knew there was something wrong and Rig knew he knew.

"Momma's sick." Rig sighed, took a deep draw of his smoke.

His arm tightened around Rig's shoulders, pulling his Rabbit close. "You mean something specific sick."

"I mean she's got..." Rig's head dipped. "It's her liver. There's cancer. She's had cryosurgery already. That... that's why Sissy came down."

He stopped walking and pulled Rig around, his other arm looping over Rig's shoulder. "Aw, fuck, Rig. I'm sorry."

Rig nodded, leaning into him, shaking hard. "She's known for weeks, Blue. She didn't want to worry me." He just held on, hand stroking down along Rig's back. He didn't know what to say, so he didn't say anything, just gave Rig his strength. "She asked me not to tell anybody. I... She starts chemo the day we leave. Christ, Blue."

"What do you want me to do, Rig? You want to stay?" He'd move hell or high water if it helped Rig deal with this.

"No. No, she's got Sissy. I. She just wants a normal Christmas. So that's what she'll have. I just couldn't sit there and eat."

"Is this her last one?" he asked quietly.

"Her last healthy one, yeah. The doctors say she's got a couple years, if she's lucky." Rig lit another cigarette, the lighter showing the wet on his cheeks. "Liver cancer's a bitch. It's all about how much good time they can give her."

He nodded. "I'm sorry, Rig. I wish it was different." He wished he could do something. Well, there was something he could do. He could make Rig forget, if only for a short while. "You think they'll miss us if we're gone a little longer?"

Rig shook his head. "Momma knows I've gone walking and I'm not up to telling Dick right now."

"You gonna tell the kid before we go?" he asked, turning them and heading back toward the garage, giving the house a wide berth so they wouldn't run into anyone.

"I don't know. Momma didn't want me to tell either of you, but..." Rig shrugged. "That's not my way."

"I knew something was wrong, Rabbit." He chuckled. "Well and if I figured that out, you know the kid has. He just doesn't hide his feelings nearly as well as he thinks is all I'm saying."

Rig nodded. "And we're assuming Sissy doesn't go to him and fall apart. I'm surprised she hasn't gone to you yet."

"She's got Hank. And I imagine she didn't figure she's who I should find it out from." He guided Rig up the stairs. "She's got that same strength in her you got from your Momma."

Rig followed his hands, Rock didn't even think the man was paying attention, just trusting his lead. He got Rig undressed and pulled the covers off the bed, laying his rabbit out before stripping himself and covering the long, skinny body. He brought their mouths together and his hands started stroking, touching Rig just everywhere, intent on driving out everything but his touch. Let Rig have a few moments where nothing else mattered.

It took a while, but it happened, Rig going loose and warm under him, pushing into his hands, crying into his lips. He growled softly, hands sliding, finding the places that were guaranteed to drive Rig wild.

Rig was murmuring, groaning, rubbing against him and holding on tight. He reached up under the pillows for the tube of lube they'd brought, slicking his fingers up before pushing them into Rig's body, one at first, then two, then the third in quick succession.

"Yes. Need you. Please." Rig moaned, face buried in the curve of his shoulder.

"You got me." He let his fingers slide away and slicked up his prick, sliding it in just like that. No teasing, no taking his time, just taking his Rabbit. Hot and tight and made for him -- it was as right now as it had been the first time. He let out a long, low groan. "Tight. Fucking good, Rig."

Then he started fucking.

Rig took everything and then more, losing himself in their bodies. Made him feel like a fucking god, like he could do anything, would do anything for those needy little sounds. He kept it up for as long as he could, just plowing into Rig, making it last for fucking ever if he could. When he felt Rig start to get close, he wrapped a hand around Rig's prick, tugging as he slammed home over and over again.

"Blue..." Rig arched, fingers sliding on his back, ass going tight.

"Fuck yeah." He jerked, pushing past Rig's gland one more time. Rig cried out, coming hard, spunk spraying between them. He let himself go, filling Rig up as his balls emptied. He kept moving, dragging aftershocks out of Rig, keeping his Rabbit floating just a bit longer, and then collapsed down.

Rig curled in, holding him, hiding in him. He just purred and stroked the long back, ready to be Rig's Rock.

***

Dick watched Rig go. He watched Rock follow. He played and talked with the kids as they finished up their meal and then made a game out of clearing the table and doing the dishes. He wanted to follow them so fucking badly. Wanted to know why Rig was so upset, wanted to make it better. Instead he helped the kids all get dessert and glasses of milk. "Momma, Julie? You want dessert?"

Julie shook her head. "Hell, no. I ate enough of it in the making."

"I'll take some, Richard." Momma smiled over at him. "So, tell us the truth, do you like California?"

He dished her up a helping of cobbler, giving the plate to Lisa to bring to her as he filled coffee cups for the two ladies and himself.

"Oh, yeah. It's beautiful. It's warm. We don't have to pretend." He brought the cups over and sat. "Did I mention it was beautiful? We've got the ocean right out our back door. You should come and see, Momma. You too, Sissy, bring the girls."

"We will, in the summer. I already talked to Alexander. I'm coming out for a long visit, Julia will drive out with the girls, stay a bit and bring me home."

He grinned. "That's great. Say, you know it's Rock's 45th this year. You should come and help us throw a big party." He lowered his voice. "We've got everyone from the gym and Rig's clinic on board for the day, gonna really party it up."

"I wouldn't miss it for the world." Momma grinned wide. "Y'all inviting any of his military friends?"

"He hasn't kept in touch with most of them. And most of them never knew about us. I don't know; Rig and I didn't talk about it yet." He bit his bottom lip, worry coming back as he thought of Rig. But he pasted a smile on his face and ate a bite. "I always think this stuff can't get any better than Rig makes it, but you usually manage it."

Momma smiled. "He does a damn fine job on his own. I just have more practice."

He nodded. "I can see where he gets his skills."

"So're we playing poker all night tonight? Because I've been saving my pennies in a jar so I'd have plenty to lose." It was tradition for him to lose his shirt, metaphorically speaking, at poker whenever they came down to visit.

"Hell, yes. Duece is old enough to play this year." Momma grinned, winked. "Besides I need my pin money. You going to go get my wayward son and Jim?"

"If you don't mind, Momma -- I didn't want us all to abandon you."

Something made Momma smile, the look sweet and a little sad. "Oh, Richard, nobody abandoned me. Go on. Fetch 'em up."

He leaned over and kissed her cheek, walking until he hit the door and then hustling over to the little apartment above the garage. It was cold, but more than that he was worried. It wasn't like Rig to be this upset at Christmas. Especially Christmas spent in Texas.

They were in bed, just like he'd expected and he went and sat next to them, meeting Rock's eyes. "Well?"

Rock looked at Rig. Rig sighed, cuddled into Rock without a word. Dick slid his hand along Rig's back, trying not to be hurt. It wasn't like Rig not to talk to him.

"Momma's expecting me to fetch you," he said softly. "I imagine that gives you another twenty minutes, maybe a half hour before she's expecting us back for the evening."

Rig nodded, grabbed his arm and hauled him close. He wrapped around Rig, holding on tight and meeting Rock's eyes over Rig's shoulders. He needed to know what the hell was going on. Rig relaxed again, breathing deep, fingers twining with his.

"Momma's sick," Rock said quietly. "She told Rig, but wanted a normal Christmas. Didn't want us knowing."

His eyes widened and he whimpered a little, holding Rig tighter. It had to be bad if Rig was this upset.

"Just needed a few minutes away, Pretty. Wasn't trying to cut you out."

He nodded. "It's okay. How bad is it?"

"Liver cancer. Rig says it's just a matter of how much good time they can give her."

"Oh. Oh, Rig." He buried his head in Rig's neck.

"Yeah." Rig nodded, leaned into Rock, squeezing his fingers.

"What are you going to do?" Well that was a stupid question. But he didn't know what to say.

"Go down and play cards. Open presents. Cook. Laugh." Rig sighed. "Drink a lot. Smoke."

He nodded and kissed Rig's neck. "Yeah. Don't waste the time you've got left with her, Rig. Love her as hard as you can."

Rig nodded, resting against Rock, taking a shaky breath. "Yeah."

"We made her happy coming up. She's perked right up. And she said you'd already invited her down for the summer. You're doing the right thing. You're going to get time to love on her. More time than a lot of people get."

Rig just nodded again, cheek sliding along Rock's chest.

"I-"

"Need to fucking shut it. He knows all that. You want to help, suck his cock."

Dick glared at Rock. "Sex doesn't fix everything, Rock."

"No, but what it doesn't fix it makes tolerable."

Rig chuckled, shoulders shaking with the sudden laughter. "Oh, thank God I have y'all. You rock my fucking world."

"You hear that, kid, I'm his fucking world."

That had him laughing too and he whacked Rock and then let his hands roam a little. Rock was right, nothing was so bad that a little loving couldn't help and he didn't want to know anything that wasn't true for. He started sucking on Rig's spine, slowly moving down along it.

"Mmm..." Rig stretched up, kissed Rock.

He kept moving down, hands stroking Rig's hips as he followed the line of spine all the way to the small of Rig's back. He rubbed his cheek in the slight hollow there. That got him a hum, a chuckle. Sexy cowboy.

He licked his way over to Rig's hip and encouraged him to roll onto his back. Rock seemed to be reluctant in letting go of his armful, but finally he had access to that sweet cock. Rig's tattoo was dark, the skin bare and smooth, cock half-hard for him. He traced the black lines with his tongue and rubbed his cheek along cock and balls and the smooth skin around them.

Rock purred and kept Rig's mouth busy while their cowboy arched a little, rocking nice and slow. It smelled good, Rig's musk and his need, he could smell Rock, too, knew his lovers had just fucked. He licked his way up Rig's cock and then took the tip in his mouth, slowly taking it down.

"Mmm..." Rig's legs moved restlessly, sliding against Rock's. He hummed, sucking, head bobbing up and down on Rig's cock. Rig's fingers tangled in his hair, stroking, petting. He purred, going slowly down and then drawing up again, tongue teasing the head of Rig's cock every time he came up. "Oh..." Rig arched. "More."

He moved a little faster, spent less time lingering at the tip, fingers going to cup Rig's balls. Rig pushed against him, all need and want and heat. He bobbed his head faster, fingers sliding behind Rig's balls now to tease the stretched little hole. His finger slid in easily, Rig still wet from getting fucked.

"Yes..." Rig's legs spread, cock throbbing.

He pushed two fingers in, sucking as hard as he could. He heard the little cry before seed filled his lips, sweet and salty. Rig's ass tightened around his fingers as he swallowed, not missing a drop. Humming, he eased his fingers out, head still bobbing.

Rig moaned, relaxing back into Rock's arms, breathing hard.

He came off Rig's cock, kissing the tip and then slowly making his way back up the long body, dropping soft kisses and wet licks as he went. He mouthed I love you over Rig's heart. Those long fingers held him tight, shaking for just a minute. He repeated the words and then moved up to kiss Rig, pushing into the kiss he and Rock were sharing. Rig just held on, the kiss slow and sweet, easy.

When it was finally over, he settled against Rig, hand on Rig's hip, right above Rock's.

"I guess we should go down, huh? Let the kid lose his money?" Rig didn't sound eager.

"Why don't you and Rock stay here? I'll say you're tired from all that travel yesterday. Rock's getting older, they'll buy it." He ducked the swat from Rock.

"No. No, because if." Rig swallowed hard. "If this is last one, I don't want to miss it."

"All right then, we'd better be going." He gave Rig a hard kiss and got up to get dressed and give Rock and Rig a few minutes alone. Rig turned right back into Rock's body, curling in, almost like he was soaking in that unbelievable strength.

Rock purred, hands stroking Rig's back. "Tell them we'll be along in awhile, kid."

He nodded. "No problem."

He headed down the stairs, ready to spin a story about how old man Rock needed another half hour's nap to keep up with the rest of them for all night poker.

***

They'd played poker for hours, then Momma went to bed, Dick and Rock wandering in the kitchen, him and Sissy at the table. He was so pissed he was shaking. His momma -- sick, hurting, alone and nobody called him, nobody. He'd expected that shit from Bobby, the man hated him, but Julie?

He'd thought...

Rig rubbed the back of his neck, sighing.

"You okay, Bubba?"

He looked over at her, wide-eyed. "What?"

"Are you okay?" She reached out for him and he leaned back, frowning.

"Don't you fucking go there with me. Of course I'm not okay."

"Alex..." Her eyes were hurt and that just made him madder, made him get all het up and tense and shaky.

"Don't, Julie. Don't *even*. How many fucking times could you have told me? How many times have we talked? How fucking long have you *known* and not said a fucking word to me?"

Rock came over, hand warm and solid on his back. "Rig..."

He leaned back against the touch, shaking his head, biting the words out. "I can't believe you'd let me walk into this blind. I can't fucking believe you didn't warn me."

"She told me not to tell you." Julie was crying and he was too fucking close to it.

"Oh, bullshit. You've gone against her every day of your life so long as it didn't suit you. You didn't *want* to tell me."

Dick sat down next to Julie, patting her hand. "Can you blame her?"

"Fuck, yes." He glared over at Dick, then back at Julie, fucking vibrating. "Bobby knows?" She nodded, eyes hitting the floor. "Why? Why didn't you call me?"

"Momma wanted to tell you. Momma didn't want you to hear it on the phone."

"And if the procedure had gone bad? What? You'd have rather explained then? Sorry, Alex, but you didn't fucking move back home so you get to lose your Momma and never say goodbye. Too fucking bad." He stood, slamming his hand on the table. "Fuck you. I deserved to know."

Rock's hand stayed on his back, solid and steady.

Dick leaned across the table, eyes sad, intent. "Come on, Rig. This isn't going to make it go away. It's just spreading the hurt."

Julie met his eyes, stubborn as him. "You can be as pissed as you want, Alex. You're feeling fucking guilty because you get to go in a week and leave me here alone to cope."

His lips opened and closed and opened and his spine went stiff as steel, temper flaring dangerously. "Jim." Help me. Don't let me say something I'll regret in the morning.

"Okay, I'm taking you to bed. Kid, get Julie calmed down and help her make sure Santa comes." Rock's arm went around his shoulders, directing him out. "And you can wait until we get to our room before you say another word. And then you can yell and scream at me until the sun comes up."

He nodded, teeth grinding.

Rock didn't say anything, just led him back to the little room over the garage. He stood and shook his head, fixin' to just shake apart.

"You want to yell at me, feel free, but it seems to me all that energy would be better served fucking." Rock pushed him up against the wall, mouth decending on his. He pushed back against Rock hard, so pissed, so hurt, so fucking mad and needing to do something to let it loose. Rock pushed him back. "Come on, Rig. What's it going to be? Fight or fuck? Take what you need. Give it to me."

He hit the wall and pushed back, their mouths clicking together hard enough he tasted blood, hands fisting into Rock's shirt. Rock's growl filled his mouth, the powerful body slamming him against the wall again.

He needed this, needed the pressure and the release so fucking bad. He damn near crawled up Rock, pulling hard at the cotton shirt. Rock's hands fisting in his shirt, tearing it off his body, that mouth hard on his.

"Liked that fucking shirt." He bit Rock's shoulder, leaving a mark.

"You like these jeans, too?" Rock asked, hands fisting again.

"Bastard." He gasped as the denim tore, eyes rolling. "Jesus Christ, you're strong."

"Your bastard." Rock nipped at his neck, his jaw.

"Fuck, yes. Yours. God, Rock, I'm so pissed off it hurts." He held Rock close, throat bared.

"So scream, yell, hit, bite." Rock took his own suggestion, biting down on his skin.

"Fuck!" His body pushed again, their skin slapping together, nails dragging up Rock's back. Rock growled, pushing down his own jeans and then shoving back, making him hit the wall again. He used the wall to push himself forward, their bodies slapping together, hard and sharp.

Rock's hands were hard on his skin, sliding along his sides, his back, grabbing his ass. His skin tingled, burned in the wake of that touch and he responded in kind, tugging, pulling, touching. He was breathing hard, drenched in sweat, working out his fury. "That's it, Rabbit. Give it all to me."

He let out a low cry, the sound torn from him, raw and leaving him shivering. Rock's mouth found his neck again, the other side this time, teeth snapping. He arched, leg wrapping around Rock's hip, curling in. Rock started thrusting, sliding their cocks together, banging his ass against the wall with every push.

Pushing back, his bones rattling, he met every bit of it. Those big hands dug into his ass, bruising him. His orgasm surprised him, pulled out of him by Rock's body, Rock's strength. Rock roared, thrusting hard against him several more times before heat splashed along his skin.

He slumped, damn near falling, wore out, exhausted. Rock picked him up and carried him over to the bed. "Stay with me."

"I'm not going anywhere, Rabbit." Rock wrapped around him, pulling the covers up high.

"I need you. I can't do this alone." It hurt to admit it, but it was the truth. A man could only be so strong.

"You haven't had to do anything alone for close on to fifteen years, Rig. You don't have to start now."

He nodded, wrapped himself around the center of his world. "I know."

Rock just held him tight, stroking, keeping him warm, loving on him. He was asleep in heartbeats, safe and warm and, if he was hiding? Rock didn't mind.

***

The kid pulled morning wake up call duty, waking him up too fucking early. Of course it was Christmas and at 7:30 the kids were probably already going nuts because their Uncles Alex, Richard and Jimmy weren't there yet to open presents. Rig was still asleep, curled up against his side.

Dick's kiss tasted like him, eyes worried. "Should we wake him?"

He nodded. "She wants a normal Christmas and he'll kick himself if he doesn't give it to her." Dick nodded and headed back under the covers. "What're you doing?"

"Waking him up the best way I know how. It always works with you."

Rig murmured, hand reaching out, petting his belly, legs shifting. He purred, fingers headed for those sweet little titties as the kid's head started moving up and down.

"Mmm... Good..." Rig stretched, eyes blinked open, bruise dark on the gold skin. He leaned in and kissed each eye and then that sweet mouth. Rig opened to him easily, tongue warm, sweet. He purred, licking into Rig's mouth, feeling Rig's body start to push up into Dick.

"Oh. Oh, damn." Those eyes held onto his, wide, wanting.

"Kid's good at that," he murmured, licking at Rig's lips, tasting his Rabbit.

"Uh-huh." Rig's hand slid around his neck. Chuckling, he pressed their lips together again, taking Rig's mouth.

Rig arched, tongue pushing deep, body going stiff and still. Dick made a happy noise as Rig relaxed, coming up to push into their kiss, mouth tasting like him and Rig.

Rig moaned, low and deep, cuddling right in. Dick stayed where he was for awhile, kissing and cuddling with them. Then Dick got up. "Merry Christmas, lovers."

"Merry Christmas." Rig smiled, stretched. "Did Santa come?"

"He'd better have or I hauled all those presents down for nothing." Dick winked. "I'm gonna go get some coffee. I'll warm up a cup for you guys."

Rock grunted. "We're coming, we're coming."

"No Rock, you came." The kid hightailed it out, missing the pillow aimed at his ass.

Rock turned to Rig and gave him a hug. "Well? Ready to go down?"

Rig met his eyes, nodded. "Yeah, Blue. I'm ready."

"All right then. Merry Christmas, Rabbit."

"Merry Christmas, Blue." Rig twined their fingers together, held on.

He kissed Rig, letting his Rabbit know exactly how he felt. Rig leaned into him, tongues sliding slow and sweet and together. He rolled Rig beneath him.

"Oh. Yeah." Rig moaned, cuddling up against him, rubbing up.

"You wanting again already?"

"More just enjoying you." Rig smiled up at him. "I get to needing your touch."

"Anytime, Rabbit." He smiled down at Rig. "Anytime."

Rig's fingers traced over his face, petting. "Yeah." He nuzzled into the touch. "I'm sorry for yesterday. I sort of shorted out."

"You're allowed a short out day or two."

"Yeah? Good." Rig smiled for him, eyes warm, happy. "That means I'm safe today."

He chuckled. "You're gonna be safe until the day I die."

"You're going to be with me until the end of time. You wouldn't trust anyone else with me."

"Damn straight." He gave Rig another kiss, slow and sweet and then backed off. "Come on. Let's go have Christmas."

***

Everyone was already up and sitting in the front room, kids playing with their stocking gifts, by the time Dick got there. He made Rig and Rock's excuses, saying they'd be down real soon. "You know what a bear Rock is to wake up in the mornings."

Then he made a beeline for the coffee, partly to caffeinate, partly to have a cup to hide behind. Lisa and Maddie insisted Uncle Richard sit between them, so he did, threatening to steal the candy the kids had found in their stockings.

Julie was sitting on the windowseat, window wide open, smoking, not looking at anybody. When Rig and Rock came in, Rig kissed Momma and then went to Julie, took a long hit from her cigarette and then sat next to her, arm around her waist. Dick sighed, relieved as the tension eased a half notch.

Julie leaned against Rig, two white blond heads, two sets of grey eyes watching the kids. Two children losing their mom to a long, slow illness. Damn. He blinked back the sudden tears and focussed on the drawing Lisa was making with her new markers.

Rig's eyes got caught by Rock and their cowboy smiled. "You playing Santa, Rocketman?"

"If that's where the consensus is."

"Uncle Richard, what's a consensus?"

"Well, Lisa, it's a five dollar word and your uncle Jimmy usually doesn't use those."

Rock whacked his arm, making him chuckle. "It means if everyone agrees."

"Oh, look at that, he did know what it means." He ducked the next swat.

"Momma's first." The recliner was on the front porch, big red bow on top.

Rock nodded at Rig and poked him. "I need an elf, kid."

"I'll be back in a minute Lisa, Maddie -- I have to help Uncle Jimmy be Santa." He got up and they headed out front, Momma eyeing them warily.

The chair was bulky and blue and Momma squeaked when they muscled it in. "Oh, boys!"

"Where do you want it?" Rock asked, the two of them holding it.

Momma looked around. "Oh, over by the sofa and the TV. I'll just lounge."

They moved the chair over there and Rock patted the back of it. "Merry Christmas! Come on and try it out, Momma."

Momma stood, hurrying over and settling in. "Oh. Oh, it's perfect. Oh, boys, I love it."

Rock grinned. "I tested this one myself, Momma. Let me show you how everything works."

Dick grinned, going back to sit with the kids, watching as Rock showed her how to bring up the footrest and sit back at various angles.

Rig handed Sissy her envelope, whispering softly, their heads together, neither of them willing to hold a grudge or willing to fight each other long. Rock passed out all the gifts for the kids, demanding kisses and hugs before he'd hand them over.

The boxes for him and Rock were huge, identical, wrapped in camo paper. He gave Rig a look and opened his up, mouth dropping open. "Is this what the box says it is?"

Rig looked over, tilted his head. "Open it."

The box said it was a laptop and so did Rock's, but no way. No way. Hell, yes way.

"Damn, Rig. It's." He grinned and bounced up and went and gave Rig a hug. "Thank you."

Those eyes smiled up at him. "They come fully loaded -- I bought a package with gym-type software."

"So cool!"

Rock came over and kissed Rig hard. "You're the best."

Rig blinked, a little dazed. Julie's eyes were wide, shocked. "Good lord."

Rock raised an eyebrow. "You telling me you've never seen two men kiss before, Miss Julie?"

"I don't think I have seen you two kiss, not like that."

"And here Rig said you were curiosier than the proverbial cat and nosy to boot. I'm disappointed." Rock gave her a wink and went back to get Rig's gift.

Dick bit his lip. He and Rock had gone in together and it wasn't anything nearly as cool as a laptop, but the leather binder for Rig's datebook was hand tooled and made specifically to order with images fit for a cowboy and a doctor. The rest of his gift was back in their room over the garage, a dozen pictures each of him and Rock. They'd taken them themselves, half naked and dressed up and they weren't arty, but he was pretty sure Rig would like them. Of course, Rig just beamed, showing it off like it was the neatest thing ever, going to sit on the arm of Momma's chair so she could see.

He and Rock exchanged gifts, his for Rock the loudest Christmas socks he could find, complete with light up reindeer noses and a little tune that played tinnily, the kids loved it. The tie Rock got him was almost a perfect match, making them all laugh.

Presley and Tammy settled in Rock's lap, playing with their dolls, Deuce sound asleep on the sofa, snoring. Rig settled at Momma's feet, just watching.

There were sweaters and videos from Momma and homemade gifts from the girls and all in all it was a nice, regular Christmas. If there was an underlying sadness there, he did his best, along with the rest of the adults to ignore it.

Maddie found her way to Rig, distracting, chattering, making Rig smile. He helped Lisa color in one Barbie picture after another, listening to Rock spin tales for the kiddies.

Eventually Rig stood up, just sort of wandered out, quiet and still, Momma looking after him. Dick extricated himself from the kids and wandered after Rig. It was cold, the sky steel and cloudy, wind blowing hard. Rig was leaning on the porch rail, smoking.

He bumped Rig's hip. Biting back his 'smoking'll kill you' comment.

"Hey, Pretty." Rig gave him a smile. "Plumb chilly out here."

"Yeah." He put his arm around Rig, pressing close. "You okay?"

"No, but I'll manage."

"You don't have to manage alone."

"I know. I don't think I can." He squeezed Rig, leaning, pressing a kiss against his lover's forehead. Rig leaned into him, eyes closing. "Tell me I'm doing a good job."

"Are you kidding? Your Momma looks younger since you got here. Did you see her smiling this morning? You're doing an awesome job."

"Yeah?" He got a smile, a real smile.

"Yeah, Rig. Awesome." He smiled back, rubbed their noses together.

Those eyes lit up, shone for him. "Thank you."

"Anytime you need a little truth. I'm your man."

"And when I need a little fantasy?"

"I've still got that gladiator costume..." He grinned and winked.

There was the laugh, low and happy and sexy. "Hoo-boy!"

He laughed right along, bending to steal the laughter right out of Rig's mouth. Rig's arm slid around his neck, holding on, keeping him warm.

"Love you," he whispered as their lips parted.

"I know. You'll just have to keep doing it, okay?"

"You kidding? There's nothing going to stop me. Nothing ever." He'd love Rig from beyond the grave if he could.

"Good." Rig grinned. "You like your present?"

"Oh yeah. I can't wait to load up Diablo 3 and see how it plays."

Rig chuckled. "Not hunting for 'net porn?"

"Not until we get home."

Those eyes met his, suddenly serious. "Can I tell you something? Just between you and me and the bedpost?"

He nodded. "Of course."

"I want to go home. I don't want to stay here and watch her die." Rig's cheeks heated, the look ashamed. "I don't want to have to do that."

"Oh, Rig." He wrapped his arms around his lover. "I don't think anyone wants to watch someone they love die."

Rig nodded, leaned. Just breathed.

"Makes you human, Rig." He stroked Rig's back, holding on.

"Yeah. Makes me ashamed of myself."

He hugged Rig tighter. "Don't, Rig. Don't beat yourself up for this."

Rig nodded. "I'm trying, Pretty. I am."

"Well, you don't have to try alone."

"I know." Rig squeezed his hand. "That? I know."

"Good. Don't forget it." He gave Rig another kiss. "Come on. No more cigarettes. Let's go see if it's time for breakfast yet."

"No more?" Rig followed him into the house. "But, Pretty..."

Dick chuckled. "Rock's gonna start growling at you if you keep it up."

"You think? I keep thinking he'll give it up."

"Rock? Give up growling? Then what would you do for that extra thrill?" He knew as well as Rig, maybe even better, how much that growling turned Rig on.

Rig leaned close. "Let you talk to me."

"Oh." Warmth flooded his belly and he buried his head in Rig's neck, holding on tight.

Rig relaxed into him, quiet and easy. "Yeah."

"You know I love visiting your family, but there's something to be said for being able to just fuck whenever we want to."

"No shit, Pretty." Rig leaned. "Especially now. I'm used to having whenever."

He nodded. "Yeah, it was a really good choice, moving out to California. The weather's right, attitudes are a less harsh." He kissed Rig, putting his heart into it and then took a step back. "Come on. They'll be wondering where we are if we're too long."

"Yeah. Let's go make breakfast."

He chuckled. "You mean eat. I'm pretty sure Rock was organizing the kids to help with breakfast when I followed you out."

"Oh. Wow. Yeah. Eat. Duh." Rig pinked.

He kissed Rig's nose. "Come on now, Rock's gonna expect us to praise whatever he puts in front of us."

"You know it." Rig nodded, took his hand and headed toward the smell of bacon and pancakes.

***

Christmas dinner went fine and things were easier. Hank came in from driving truck and was chatting up Dick and Deuce took Rock off to the other room to talk. He was just pottering. Cleaning and washing and fixing and moving.

He didn't stop to think, just made lists of the things he was going to do when he got home and hugged kids and cleaned out the fridge and every so often watched his momma sit and enjoy her grandkids. Of course, then he started thinking again and would find other stuff to do.

Sissy was sleeping, Momma dozing in her chair and pretending not to. Eventually he made his way up to the attic, to look and make sure things were whole and right. No bugs. No mice. No bird nests. No one to bitch if he had a smoke and a sit.

He was on his third when heavy steps sounded on the stairs, Rock joining him a moment later. "Tomorrow I start bitching about the smoking, Rig."

"So that gives me how long before you start throwing them away?"

"Until tomorrow." Rock's hands settled on his shoulders, big and warm and soothing.

"That's fair enough, I guess." His head fell forward, letting Rock touch him. "I'll have to see if it ups my chances of lung cancer, Momma being sick."

Rock's hands stuttered a moment and then the butt he was smoking was taken out of his hand and Rock put it out without a word.

"It..." He just let it go. He couldn't win this argument with Rock, not even a little. Rock went back to rubbing his shoulders, fingers working his muscles.

"Oh..." Okay, this was better than smoking. Way better.

"So what were you doing up here anyway, aside from sneaking a smoke or three?"

"Looking to see if Momma needed mousetraps."

Rock snorted. "And does she?"

"Nope." He shook his head. "How's Duece?"

"Scared. He's gonna be fine. He's a real good kid, and a better Marine." Rock's hands stilled a moment. "Did you know he's got someone he's gonna miss a hell of a lot more'n his family?"

"You mean..."

"Yep. I warned him that he's young yet and that kind of long distance, especially when you can't tell anyone, is hell, but he's pretty adamant about having someone to come home to."

"Oh, man. That... Is he another marine?"

Rock shrugged, arms coming around his waist, head resting on his shoulder. "Didn't say, but I imagine we'll find out -- he wants us to have this guy's address and phone number and stuff in case anything happens. So someone calls him."

Rig nodded, hands sliding over Rock's and holding on. "It's a hard row, but I wouldn't have given for you, Blue."

Rock turned his hands twining their fingers together. "I know, Rabbit. You know how I feel."

"I do." He leaned back, snuggling in. He did. He never questioned it.

Rock purred, just a little. "You think anyone would notice if we were up here awhile, Rig?" Rock chuckled. "Hell, do you care?"

"No." He grinned. "And no."

"Good." That sexy purring got louder, Rock tilting his head back, taking his mouth.

Oh. He arched, opening right up, moaning low. Rock's tongue owned him, that muscled body pressing up against his back. He could feel Rock's prick, hard and hot against his ass, even through layers of clothes. Oh, fuck yes. There was nowhere he was safer, was held closer. One of Rock's hands slid down into the front of his jeans, wrapping around his prick.

"Oh... Blue." He licked those lips, shivering. Rock's other hand popped open the button and got the zip down, giving the working hand more room. Rock caught his tongue and began to suck in time to each pull on his cock. His eyes went wide, rolling before fastening onto those blue-blue eyes. Yeah. Oh, sweet fuck, yeah.

Rock rubbed against his ass, hand and lips just working him, tugging him toward orgasm just like that. He didn't fight it either, just went along, whimpering into Rock's lips, cock jerking. And when Rock purred around his tongue and slid that thick thumb across the top of his prick, he gave it up.

He relaxed, moaning low, world sweet and blue. Rock gave up his tongue with reluctance, pressing warm kisses across his face.

"Merry Christmas." He reached up, stroked one cheek.

Rock purred, nuzzled his hand. "Merry Christmas, Rabbit."

***

The day after Christmas, Rig and Dick and Sissy piled the kids into the cars and headed into town to check out the sales. Rock offered to stay home to keep Momma company when she'd hesitated going and frankly, he was more than pleased to have an excuse to get out of shopping. In fact, if he hadn't known she was sick, he might have thought she'd done it to give him that excuse. As it was, he teased her about it after the dust on the road settled. "I appreciate the out on the shopping excursion, Momma."

Momma nodded and settled in the big new chair. "I didn't figure you as the mall type."

"You got that right. Especially when all the sales are on. You'd think people'd never seen wrapping paper before." He sat in the old recliner, finding the perfect spot for his ass and sighing happily.

Charlene laughed, shook her head. "I tell you what, sometimes you just put me right in the mind of my Jeremy."

"I take that as a high compliment, Charlene." Jeremy'd been a good man. He saw a lot of him in Rig. Well and Momma, too. Both Rig's parents had a hand in making the man who he was today. He imagined the bull-headed stubborness was a curse from both sides.

"I'm guessing Rig talked to you?"

He nodded. "Yes, ma'am. I know you didn't want him to say anything, but Dick and I knew something was wrong."

She snorted. "That boy's never kept a decent secret from you, has he?"

"As it should be."

She nodded to him. "Is he okay?"

"You should have told him sooner, Charlene."

She shook her head. "I couldn't. He takes things to heart. I wasn't even going to tell him now, but Julie got pissy about it."

He shook his own head. "Charlene... he was upset enough to know you hadn't told him before now, the longer you waited, the harder it would have been on him." Damn stubborn redneck Momma. Rig would have done the same thing if the situation had been reversed.

"I just worry about him." She shook her head, sighed. "It's funny. Bobby and Julia? They've always lived close enough, but they'll be fine. My boy who left me? Him I worry about leaving."

He reached out and patted her hand. "He's got your strength, Momma. It's not going to be easy, but we'll see him through it." And wasn't this fucked up.

"You promise me? You'll take care of him?" She twined their fingers together. "He'll work himself to death, if you let him."

"Charlene. You think I'm going to let him get away from me? I know a good thing when I've got one." He squeezed her hand. No way was he giving up his morning blow jobs.

She grinned, nodded. "I just have to say so, Jim. I talked to Hank and that bitch Bobby's married to."

"You know it's your kids who are the strong ones though, right? You're a tough lady, Charlene."

"Yeah. I know. I'm trying not to be scared, but..." She shook her head, then met his eyes. "I don't want to do the chemo, Jim. I don't want to be sick and ugly."

He sighed and squeezed her hand, wishing Rig were here. Rig would know what to say. "It's supposed to make you better though, isn't it? Give you more time?"

"Yeah. Yeah -- a couple years as opposed to six months."

"Tell you what, you come on out after the chemo is done and I will personally escort you to the finest wig shop the kid can find." He didn't know what made him make the offer, but he didn't like that defeated look in her eyes.

"Alexander says I can come for your birthday and spend the summer. Relax. Heal."

"Oh, you can buy me a steak when I hit forty-five."

"I will. I'll cook and visit and see the ocean Alexander's always going on about."

He chuckled. "I have to admit, it's worth going on about. I've never been one to care where I got stationed, but I have to tell you, I can't think of a better place to spend my days." Not to mention it made Rig just light up, being out there.

"Good." He got a smile. "I want you to know, I asked Alexander if he'd consider coming home and he said no, that y'all were home now."

He nodded. "We're not conventional, Momma, but I challenge you to find a family that's stronger."

"Yeah. I used to cry, wanting Alexander to be a daddy, but I don't think he misses it. Y'all make him happy."

"Oh, he's a daddy. You should see him with the kids at the clinic. None of the pregnant ladies look for a pediatrician. They all want Doc Rig."

"Yeah? He told me his nurse is expecting. He sounded excited."

"Yeah, you'd think he was the dad." He chuckled. His Rabbit cared a lot. Too much.

"Y'all are great uncles. The best."

"The kids make it easy," he told her, voice gruff.

Charlene nodded. "I... They do. They sure do."

"You've got some time yet, Charlene. You'll get to watch 'em grow." He petted her hand awkwardly.

"I hope so. I'm not ready. I thought... I thought when Jeremy went, I'd be happy to go, but... I'm not ready yet."

"Good for you. No reason to give up." He nodded. He'd always said Charlene'd have made a great marine.

"Yeah." She gave him a look. "Go get your mother-in-law a beer, Jim, and let's find something good on. This thinking shit's tough on an old woman."

"Yes, ma'am." Even tougher on an ex-marine like him and he was grateful for the reprieve. He got her her beer and one for himself, settling back in.

Stallone was on the TV, Momma grinning over. "I vote, if they're not home for lunch, we finish the chocolate pie."

"I vote we have it now." He got up, giving her a wink.

Her laughter followed him into the kitchen, warm and happy. Right. Right enough that Rig'd be proud.

Chapter Seventeen

It had worked out nicely -- Dick was working the evening shift at the gym so he could take Rock out to supper without feeling bad about his Pretty being alone on Valentine's Day.

Still, thirteen years of being a... them -- that deserved a dinner out, a bit of celebrating.

He pulled up to the gym at three; he'd cancelled his afternoon appointments, got himself dressed in a nice shirt, his best jeans and boots, grabbed his hat and was ready for his Blue.

Dick came out and leaned against the door of the gym, giving a low whistle. "Don't you look sexy."

He grinned and hopped out, giving a twirl so Dick could see it all. "I pass muster?"

"Fuck yeah." Dick wrapped his arms around him and gave him a long kiss, blushing just a bit as a passerby whistled. He got a wide grin from his Pretty though. "Rock's not going to be able to keep his hands off you."

"I'll have you know *I* have self-control, kid." His Blue came out, wearing tight jeans and a light blue shirt, hair newly cut, face newly shaved.

Dick was gonna give himself a hernia, laughing like that. He wasn't laughing, though. Not at all. Not with that beautiful son of a bitch looking at him. "Hey, Blue Eyes."

"Hey, Cowboy. You're looking pretty good today. People are gonna think you've got a special date or something." Rock gave him a wink.

"Hey, a man's got to keep his marines' eyes on him."

"You don't have to worry about that. It's a good thing you're driving because I'm too distracted."

Dick's laughter had faded and now he was grinning, leaning in to give them each a quick kiss. "Happy anniversary guys. There's a little surprise waiting for you when you get home."

"Oh, now, Pretty -- you're not little." He winked and patted Dick's ass.

Dick laughed at him, eyes going warm. "Go on, you'd better go before I decide I'm coming with you."

"Oh, can't have that -- fuck knows, three's a crowd." Rock popped Dick on the ass, making his Pretty jump and laugh and then Rock walked around to the passenger side of the jeep.

"See you after work, Pretty." he started the Jeep up and pulled out. "I was thinking steak at Rick's; that work for you?"

"Works just fine." Rock stretched and relaxed back in his seat. "You have a good day?"

He nodded, headed towards the restaurant. "Hannah Barre came in today. She was working out at that scary damned gym downtown and tore up her shoulder real bad. I sent her to see an orthopedic surgeon and gave her one of y'all's cards."

Rock shook his head. "We get a lot of business flow from them. Anyone who isn't pumped and ripped to start with. They need to stop letting people in who aren't profesional body builders or someone's gonna get hurt worse. The kid's interviewing physiotherapy students, looking for a couple of people to be on hand with advice for folks with injuries." Rock chuckled. "He's real good at this, you know? Took to it like a fish to water."

"Yeah. It's weird, isn't it? He just fit right in, right from the start."

"Yep. Of course I know someone else who just fit right in, don't I?" Rock gave him a look that was all heat. "Someone who eventually just turned up on my doorstep..."

Rig pinked and grinned. "Pizza in hand and fucking scared to death that you wouldn't remember who the hell I was."

Rock snorted. "You sucked my brains out of my prick, Rig. I remembered."

"Yeah, well, I was a kid and crazy in lust and praying you'd let me in." He shook his head, grinned. Funny, because he'd never do something so stupid now, but then? Hell, yeah.

Rock chuckled, hand coming to slide along his thigh. "You still crazy in lust, Rabbit?"

"You know it." He spread a little bit, nodded. "Then I was just hoping. Now I need."

Rock growled softly for him, hand wandering along his inner thigh, little finger brushing against his balls.

"Mmm..." He pulled into the restaurant parking lot, the place mostly empty. "You're going to make me hard, now."

"What me?" Rock winked, hand shifting to rub against his cock, squeezing. Then it was gone and Rock was getting out. "Come on, you promised me steak."

"I did." He hopped out, dipping his hat against the sun. Rock's arm went around his shoulders, casual, but pulling him close enough their hips bumped together.

They got a quiet table in the back, Sally and Rick both coming out to sit a second, say congratulations and hi before getting back to work. Rock grunted and nodded, said thank you in that gruff voice of his and ordered them both beer, steak with baked potato and a salad on the side for him.

"Oh, and the fried mushrooms." He leaned his leg against Rock a little as the waitress left. "Thirteen years, old man."

"Yep. And you still giving me my morning wake-up call. I must have done something right."

"A couple three things over the years, yeah." They laughed together, knees rubbing.

"You know what the kid's got planned back home?"

"Nope. You?"

Rock shook his head. "Nope. And that's just a little scary." He was given a wink, Rock's eyes warm. "Might be awhile before we get there though. I hear tell there's a point out on the old beach road where the kids go to watch the sunset, make out. Thought I might just be feeling young enough to pretend to be a kid for awhile."

Oh. Rig felt his cheeks heat up, belly all warm and tight. "I think there's not much on earth that could make me miss that."

Rock nodded, smiling at the waitress as their beers were brought, even as those blue eyes stayed on his, making all those same promises that his Blue had never broken.

It made him hard, made him happy. Made him proud.

"So no regrets?" Rock asked after a mouthful of beer. "You'd follow this old bag of bones out of Texas all over again?"

Rig nodded. "Anywhere. I made my choice and it was the right one." To the ends of the earth and back.

"Yep."

Their steak came and Rock got down to the serious business of enjoying his food. He caught his Blue looking up every now and then though, those blue eyes just shining at him. He ended up giving Rock half of his steak and eating the lion's share of the mushrooms, and damn, it was good. Damned good.

Rock finished before he did, sitting back with a satisfied groan. One foot slid along his leg, Rock watching him outright now. It made him flush, made him fucking hard, just like always. Those eyes. They just... Yeah.

"We gonna share something sweet together, Rig? Whet our appetites?"

He licked his lips, nodded. Yeah. Yeah, they would. Rock called the waitress over and ordered the white chocolate cheesecake with fresh berries on top. His Blue was too good to him; the chocolate pie here was almost as good as his own.

He reached over, stroked one muscled thigh for that, petting, enjoying the heat under his fingers. Rock's eyes narrowed, a low growl sounding like a purr in Rock's chest.

Oh... He wanted. He met Rock's eyes, losing himself in blue, in that heat. If someone had asked how long they sat there before their dessert came, he couln't have told them, Rock's eyes just holding his until they were disturbed.

"Two forks, right?"

Rock nodded at the waitress and then turned his attention back to Rig.

His heart was pounding hard, just beating. "You still do it for me. That hasn't changed a bit."

"Ditto, Cowboy." Rock stared at him a moment longer and then reached for a fork, helped himself to a nice big bite of cheesecake. He snagged a bite himself, moaning over the raspberries. Rock chuckled. "Fruit freak."

"Just a fruit. You're the freak." He winked.

Rock laughed, eyes crinkling. "In that case, I don't want to hear anymore how I don't eat fruit."

"You like peaches well enough." He grinned. "And apple pie."

"There you go. Peaches, apple pie and your ass."

His laughter felt good, filling the air, warm and rich. They finished the cheesecake, sharing smiles and bites and by the time they were done and ready to leave, Rock looked relaxed but eager to get him the hell out of the restaurant.

He tossed over the keys, winking. "I haven't been parking in twenty-five years."

"Fuck, Rig, I don't think I ever have been." That arm went around his shoulders again, Rock walking him back to the jeep.

"No? Shit, that's a shame. I'll have to fix that right now." He bumped their hips together.

Rock chuckled and bumped back, opening the passenger door for for him before getting behind the wheel and heading for the old beach road. Alan Jackson was on the radio, the air was cool and crisp, the sun just starting to set. God, it was fine. Rock got them to a pretty little spot where you were meant to park and enjoy the view. It was deserted and the road behind them without traffic.

He looked over, unbuckling his seatbelt and turning. "Hey, Blue Eyes."

Rock's belt was undone, too, those arms open for him. "Hey. Now tell me how we do this? There some trick I should know about that makes it different from sitting on the couch and getting busy?"

"It's less comfortable and a bigger chance of being caught and used to convince someone that they're your next big thing."

Rock chuckled. "You're not exactly selling me on this, Rabbit."

"Just kiss me like you mean it, Blue. That's what I need."

"Oh, I can do that." Rock leaned in, lips finding his, tongue pressing into his mouth, making him the center of his Blue's world. He reached up, fingers curling around Rock's nape, sliding over to press close. Yeah.

Rock purred into his mouth, hands sliding on his back, one finding his ass and squeezing. Oh. Oh, yeah. Yeah, Blue. Yours. He'd needed this for so many years; he didn't know how to do without anymore. Rock broke away from the kiss long enough to shift the steering wheel up as far as it would go and the seat back, and then he was being pulled back into those arms, tugged right onto those hard thighs.

"Mmm... Hey." He rubbed their bellies together. "Fine son of a bitch."

"For my Rabbit." Rock's hands were wandering, rubbing his back, his ass, the tops of his thighs.

"Yours. Oh, your hands." He moaned low, nuzzling in.

"These old things?" asked Rock, sliding one under his shirt, the other into the back of his jeans.

"Fuck yes." He grinned against Rock's lips, moaning low. Rock chuckled and captured his tongue, sucking it into Rock's mouth. He dove into the kiss, rubbing and rocking, hands framing Rock's face. Rock's hands moved on him, slow and easy, warming up his blood.

The sun went down, the sky going purple and pink.

One of Rock's hands slid between them and popped the button on his jeans, fingers teasing the tip of his cock.

"Mm..." He groaned, pushing a little, diving into the kiss, eyes on Rock's. Yeah. Yeah, Blue.

Rock opened his own pants next and then tugged out both their pricks, fingers wrapping them together. That pulled a moan from him, his fingers twining with Rock's, holding on, stroking. Rock's free hand slid through his hair, tilting his face and deepening the kiss.

He opened right up, caught in those eyes. Love. So much. My Blue. Rock growled into his mouth, those blue eyes giving it all back to him. Oh, the world could just spin forever, he'd stay right here.

Rock just kept on stroking, kept on kissing, those blue eyes solid on his. Holding him, bringing him home.

***

Rock pulled the jeep into the driveway. The kid wasn't back yet, would probably roll in in the next hour or less. He went around and opened Rig's door, winking. He could be a gentleman for their anniversary. Rig slid out, right up against him, all warm and humming. He purred, leaning down for a kiss. He wasn't a big special day guy, but it usually got him a cuddly, affectionate Rig and there wasn't a thing wrong with that.

Those long hands wrapped around his neck, the kiss lingering, slow and sweet. He broke it with reluctance, sliding his hand into Rig's back pocket and walking them up into the house. "Let's see if we can find this surprise of the kid's."

Rig leaned against him, moving slow and easy, laughing as the dogs barrelled out of the door, Rig's tiny little Suzie along with Lucy and the beasts. Rock stopped and gave the boys some attention, leaving the calmer girls to Rig. He grumbled for show and then got up and looked in the living room, the kitchen. The bedrooms and bathroom proved equally devoid of any kind of surprise.

"I think the kid put us on," he muttered, heading for the back door to let the dogs out. There on the deck, out of the way in one corner was a hot tub. "Holy fuck."

"What?" Rig stepped out and squeaked -- fucking squeaked.

He chuckled and headed over. "Holy fuck," he repeated. "Damn, this thing's got lights and a control panel for the fucking jets, different speeds, different combinations -- top of the line -- we considered them for the club, but decided there were too many things that could go wrong, too many different people playing with all these buttons. Damn."

"Oh. Oh, too fucking *cool...*" Rig was bouncing, grinning ear to ear. "Oh, man. Blue. Can we try it?"

"I don't see why not -- it's our anniversary, right?" He put his hand in, grinning. "Water's already warm -- kid made sure it was ready for us."

"Oh. Oh, Blue, this is something else. The kid might get blowjobs for months."

"Hey, it's our anniversary, what do I get?"

"Oh!" Rig grinned and grabbed an envelope from his pocket. "This."

He gave Rig a look and chuckled, taking the envelope. "I more meant in the line of blow jobs."

Rig rolled his eyes and grinned. "I imagine I'll still manage to get to yours."

"Oh, good." He grinned at Rig and turned his attention back to the envelope, turning it over in his hand. Then he opened it, finding a membership to a local shooting range and a gift certificate for a competition rifle. "Oh. Fuck, Rig, this is sweet."

Rig nodded, grinned. "They've got some contests, some competitions. Thought you might show them what marines were made of."

"Yeah. Yeah, this is fantastic." He was grinning to beat the band, looking forward to getting out to the range, sprucing up his skills. "I suppose you think I didn't get you anything."

Rig looked over at him, arching one eyebrow. "Rock, you've never missed a single birthday or anniversary in thirteen years. Isn't it about time we stop pretending you're going to?"

He chuckled. "One of these years I will forget, so maybe we should just keep that tradition going."

He got a laugh and Rig pushed into his arms. "Then you'll fuck me into goo and I won't care anyway."

"Well it's a deal then and I'll call the landscaper back and tell him his services aren't needed after all."

"Landscaper? Oh, you *tease*. Tell!"

He chuckled. "I thought I was going to fuck you into goo and make you not care?" Rig reached for him, tickling and pinching, laughing, those eyes dancing for him. They ended with Rig's back snug against his chest, his hands holding Rig's in front of him. "I've hired a landscaper to come in. You can tell him what you want and he'll put it in for you."

"Oh, Blue..." Rig tilted back, almost bouncing. "A yard? You're too good to me."

He grinned down into grey eyes. "I know you're missing your mower."

Rigger nodded, not even realizing how deeply odd the fascination with green grass was. "And my weed-whacker's depressed, too."

His laughter was echoed by the kid's, Dick coming out onto the deck, shaking his head. "I buy you guys a hot tub and not only are you not in it, but you're talking about weed-whackers?"

Rig crowed, launching into Dick's arms. "Pretty! Thank you!"

Dick grinned and kissed Rig long and hard. "So you like it?"

"Oh. Oh, yeah. You know how I missed ours at the other house and this one? Damn."

Dick looked over at him. "What about you?"

"I can't wait to get naked and get in it. Specially if I'm having company."

That was all the invitation Dick needed, the kid starting to strip down. Rig followed right along, sitting to tug off the ostrich boots. Well he saw no reason not to join them. He imagined a good long fuck in the hot water would take care of the twitch in his back from fucking Rig in the jeep.

"So did you guys have a good date?" Dick asked, already naked and waiting beside the hot tub.

"Wasn't a date, kid."

"No? What would you call it then?"

"Supper."

Dick snorted. "Rig looks like he got more than steak and salad..."

Rig stood up, unbuttoning. "I got white chocolate cheesecake and he took me parking."

"Parking? Rock, you dog!"

He rolled his eyes at them and climbed into the hot tub, moaning at the heat. He grabbed the controls and started playing.

Rig, though? He was just beaming. "I got the whole Rocketman treatment."

"Lucky man. Maybe I'll be lucky enough to get some of that action tonight in the hot tub."

"I do owe you a thank you, kid. This thing is a slice of fucking heaven." He found a setting that had the bubbles going just right. "Can't do it alone in here though."

Dick nodded, waiting for Rig to join him before climbing in.

"Did you get some food, Pretty?" Rig settled in his lap, floating and moaning. "I can fix you something."

"No, I'm fine, Rig. Grabbed a burger on my way home." Dick sat close beside him, hands stroking over him and Rig randomly. "So thirteen years, right?" At his nod the kid continued. "Which means almost seven since you brought me home. Man, I can't believe it's been that long. And yet, fuck, I don't even want to remember what it was like before I was yours."

He rolled his eyes again and closed them, just soaking and holding Rig, feeling the kid's body pressed close. Rig drew Dick in for a kiss, lazy, relaxed. "You belong here."

The kid nodded. "I know."

"Oh, good, so we don't have to get all mushy over it."

Dick's laughter had him opening his eyes, the kid leaning in to kiss him. "You're all hearts and flowers, Rock, a real stand-up romantic."

"Hey, I fed Rig cheesecake and took him parking."

"You did." Rig leaned and kissed him. "And a lawn. A real lawn."

"A lawn?" Dick asked.

Rig nodded, grinning like a kid. "He hired me a landscaper. I'm going to have a lawn."

Dick laughed. "Nice one, Mr. I'm so not mushy."

"I'm not," he growled. It was kind of spoiled as a complaint though, given the happy tone in it. He fucking liked seeing Rig all lit up like a tree at Christmas.

"No," agreed Dick. "You're just right."

He snorted. "Now who's being mushy?"

"Me."

"That's right and don't you forget it."

Dick grinned, obviously unrepentant. "So are we gonna christen the tub?"

"Hooboy!" Rig nodded happily, wriggling into him.

He chuckled. "You expecting any answer but yes from me or Rig, kid?"

Dick grinned and rubbed against him, matching Rig's movements. "Nope."

Rig leaned in, licking and nibbling his jaw. "You going to fuck your men into oblivion, Blue?"

"You know it."

Dick moaned softly. "A fucking stud, Rock. That's what you are."

"Yes. My two studs. My men." Rig grinned, shifted. "I'll let Pretty go first, since I got mine off already."

He grinned. Rig always let the kid go first, liked to finish him off nice and hard and long. Dick was grinning, too, bringing all their mouths together.

Rig's hand worked his cock, tongue pressing into their kiss. He growled, letting his lovers make him hard. Rig moaned, arched, rubbing against him. The kid was equally enthusiastic, pushing aginst him, moaning and whimpering, making those great fucking noises. He let one hand drift down Dick's ass, sliding along his crease, making the kid's noises get louder. The water bubbled, heated them up. Rig was panting, eyes shining.

"Help me get him ready, Rig."

Dick moaned at that and nodded. "Yeah."

"There lube out here, Blue?"

"Hell if I know."

Dick grinned. "That flat corner over there has a lid and there's lube and stuff in there."

Rock laughed. "I should have known, kid."

"Oh, fucking cool." Rig dug, hooting as he pulled out a silver tube, slicking those long fingers. Dick shifted, arms on his shoulders, ass coming up out of the water for Rig.

"Sluts." Both of them. Not that he would have it any other way.

"Yep." Rig shifted and Dick's eyes rolled, lips parting.

Rock pushed his tongue into the kid's mouth, pulling those fucking sounds right into himself. Rig's eyes met his over the kid's shoulder, just shining. He smiled, fingers finding Dick's cock, fondling it. "You just about ready, kid?"

"Oh yeah. Fuck."

"That's the idea."

Rig helped, one hand around his cock, guiding him to the kid's hole. Dick lowered himself and he pushed up into that heat and all three of them moaned as he and Dick came together.

"So fucking hot. My men." Rig's fingers stroked where they joined. Dick shuddered and moaned and he gave a little shout himself. Shit, Rig was something else.

So was the kid, Dick dancing on his cock like there was nothing better on earth. It wasn't so far from the truth. Rig groaned low, cupping his balls, stroking Dick's, right there, happy and watching.

Dick leaned in, head on his shoulder, body moving up and down, riding him nice and hard. Rock slid his hand between them to tug on the kid's nipple ring, found Rig's and played it, too.

Rig smiled at him, sucking a mark up on Dick's shoulder. He purred as that made Dick's ass ripple around his cock. "Close, kid?"

Dick nodded, pushing a hand between them, but Rock batted it away and took care of that long prick himself, pulling on it. Dick cried out, bucking, jerking, heat spurting against his hand, trying to compete with the water in the hot tub for a second before washing away.

"Mmm... Pretty." Rig rubbed against the kid, moving slow and easy.

Dick's moans faded to gasps, sweet shivers sending ripples around his cock. Rock gave his prick a stern talking to -- he still needed to fuck his Rabbit, he could come then. Dick pulled up and off, moaning at the loss of his cock, and settled next to him.

Rig's hands wrapped around his prick, rubbing, stroking. "Gonna let me have my turn?"

"Fuck, yes." He would always have enough left over for his Rabbit. No matter fucking what.

Dick grinned against his arm and slicked up a couple fingers, reaching around Rig to slide them in. Rig moaned and leaned in, lips covering his own, tongue sliding in to taste him. He opened right up, hands sliding along Rig's spine, moving down to meet Dick's fingers as they slid into Rig's hole. Sexy fuckers.

Rig arched, little slut begging for it, for more, skin hot and wet and slick and he let one of his own fingers slide in with Dick's two, opening Rig up for his prick.

"Oh." Rig shivered, moving, rocking on their fingers. "Fuck."

"That's the idea, Rig." He chuckled, smiling into those passion drunk grey eyes.

"Yeah? So fine when we're on the same page..." Rig grinned wide.

He laughed, the sound turning to a moan as the kid's free hand wrapped around his prick and pumped a few times, making sure he was ready to fuck Rig. And he was. He always fucking was.

"Want to ride now, Blue." Rig was glowing, sheened with sweat, the hottub fighting the chill air.

"Fuck, yeah."

Their fingers slid away and Dick helped him get lined up, guided Rig's ass down onto him. Easy as anything, Rig took him, rode him, his slut hot and eager. He met Rig's body each time it came down, hands finding Rig's hips, getting some force behind it. Dick's hands slid around Rig's body, stroking the sensitive titties, moving down to tug on Rig's prick.

"Oh." Rig's head fell back, throat working. "More."

He pushed up harder, shifting slightly and finding Rig's gland, pegging it hard. "Slut."

"Yours. Again." Demanding slut.

Still he gave Rig exactly what he wanted, what they both needed, fucking his Rabbit hard and fast. Rig's cry split the air, body bucking, flushed and tight and close. He kept nailing Rig's gland, just fucking riding the waves of pleasure that shot through him every time Rig's ass squeezed around his cock. The kid's hands kept working Rig's nipples and cock, occasionally sliding to stroke his skin as well.

"Soon." Rig gasped, lips open wide. "Blue Eyes."

"Yeah, Rig. Come for me. Let me feel you on my cock." His voice was rough, need sharp along his spine, in his balls.

Rig pressed close, shaking, lips brushing his ear. "Love you. My Blue."

He roared as he came, hips pushing hard, filling his Rabbit with heat even as that body milked him. Rig slumped against him, breathing hard, panting.

The kid cuddled up behind Rig, hands sliding to hold his sides, stroking idly. His own arms stretched to include the kid in his embrace. Rig sighed, snuggled in, lips on his jaw.

"Thirteen years and we've still got it." Not bad, if he did say so himself.

"Uh-huh. Still."

He nodded, relaxed and feeling fucking fine. "Happy fucking anniversary to us."

"Yeah, Blue. Happy anniversary fucking to us." Rig's grin tickled his jaw.

Dick laughed. "Here's to the next thirteen."

"Hell, the next thirty." Rig kissed him hard.

He grinned. "Oh, that's a lot of blow jobs. I think I can handle that."

"Eventually I'll get too old for them and the crown will pass to the kid."

"Too old? My Rabbit? I don't believe it."

Rigger's laughter bubbled out, mixing with the sounds of the water.

Chapter Eighteen

They were all out on the deck enjoying the sun, Rig with a blanket pulled up around his shoulders. It made Dick smile because compared to Bragg? It was damn hot for March, but they'd all adapted to the warmer weather, even Rock wearing a sweater. He let his gaze linger on the big guy -- no one filled out a sweater the way Rock did.

Which reminded him of the conversation he and Rig had at Halloween about dressing Rock up and talking pictures for a calender to advertize the gym. Flyers from a company that did that kind of thing had actually come in the gym mail a couple of weeks ago. Apparently now was the time to do it, rather than closer to the New Year.

"Hey Rock." The big guy grunted at him. "We had some flyers come in. For calendars to promote the gym. I thought they'd maybe be a good idea."

"It's fucking March, kid."

"Yeah, and apparently now's the time to get that sort of thing set up. I guess you give them away or sell them or whatever starting late summer or early fall."

"Calendars, kid?" Rock sounded skeptical.

"Yeah, you know, the things made out of paper with the dates on them?"

"I fucking know what a calendar is, dickhead."

He chuckled. "You didn't sound like you did." Sometimes it paid off, sitting on the other side of Rig instead of right next to Rock himself.

"So we'd what? Have the gym's name and hours on it or something?"

"They've got everything from those little triangle desk calendars with just the company's name and phone number on it to great big glossy wall calendars with a large range of photos and options for the business to privide their own." There, he'd broached the subject. The rest was up to Rig.

Those grey eyes glanced at him and Rig grinned. "Oooh! Beefcake calendars! Too cool!"

Rock snorted. "You have any idea how much models cost? I'll bet you it's a fucking fortune."

"Why on God's green earth would y'all need models?" Rig looked at Rock, the look honestly confused. "You and Pretty are fucking stunning."

"Pictures of us?" Rock snorted again. "Why?"

He rolled his eyes. "To show what working out at our gym can do for you."

Rig nodded. "Here's how to be a stud."

Rock shook his head. "You're not serious."

"I sure as shit am." Rig held Rock's gaze. "We hire a professional, let you two be studly."

"I know I'm a stud, Rig - you don't need to be stroking my ego." Rock winked. "I've got other things you can stroke."

Dick stayed quiet, letting Rig work his magic, he was pretty sure Rig almost had the big guy.

"Mmm... stroking." Rig grinned over. "I want to be there for the photo shoot, though. I want to see."

Rock chuckled and gave Rig a shrewd look. "You just want dirty pictures to jack off to, you perv."

"Yes." Rig nodded, completely unrepentant.

Dick laughed and gave Rock a look. "So we take some pictures for the gym calendar and a few for Rig's personal enjoyment. I've got to admit, you'd make a stunning calendar model, give all the kids a real run for their money. We give those away with new memberships and let existing members buy them for ten bucks? We'd make a mint."

Rock shook his head again. "I can't believe I'm even considering it."

"Oh, Blue, it would be hot." Rig shifted, settling in Rock's lap.

"And what do I get out of it?"

Dick bit back his laughter, knowing Rock was in. The minute Rig started offering blow jobs it was a done deal.

"A desperately turned-on cock-hound?" Rig leaned in, offering Rock a long, slow kiss.

When the kiss ended, Rock was purring. "I've already got me one of those."

Rig chuckled, nodded. "My fucking fine men."

Rock just grinned and took himself another kiss. Dick let his hand slide to his groin, rubbing his cock through his jeans. There was no show on earth like the one he was privy to on a regular basis. Rig cuddled in, diving into the kiss, hands framing Rock's face.

He'd consider getting a video camera and filming them so he could have something himself to jack off to, but he figured he had the real thing as often as not, it would just be a waste of money.

Rock's hands were on Rig's back, one pushing down into the back of those tight jeans. He could hear Rig's moan, see the way those hips tilted.

"Sexy," he murmured, hand pushing into his pants.

Rig was mouthing soft words against Rock's lips, eyes fastening on Rock's, the big guy's cheeks heated. He just watched, not needing to go and push into them -- he was included right where he was. Rock's hands pulled Rig's sweater up and off along with the black t-shirt, baring the fine skin for the big hands.

Rig shivered, pressing close, Rock's sweater next. Fuck, they looked fine together. Rock's fingers went for Rig's nipples, tugging on the ring. Dick pushed his free hand under his sweater, tweaking his own.

"Oh. Blue." Rig arched, hips rubbing, sliding them together.

Dick's breath caught and then he started to moan, pushing his cock through his hand as Rock opened first Rig's jeans and then his own. Rig's hands explored Rock, thighs spreading. A warm flush crawled up along his spine.

Dick stroked his prick, fingers sliding across the tip and pressing in as Rock's hand circled Rig's cock. They moved together, the motions practiced and familiar and sexy as fuck. His own hand copied the movement of Rock's and he moaned loudly when Rock grabbed that fat prick and joined it with Rig's.

"Yeah..." Rock got another kiss, Rig moving faster, fingers sliding with Rock's.

Dick just kept echoing the movements, knowing he was probably going to come first, the sight of them so fucking good.

Rock purred. "Gonna let us smell you, kid?"

That was all he need and Dick cried out, spunk spraying over his hand.

"Oh. Oh, you're good." Rig chuckled, arching as they moved faster.

"You know it." Rock looked smug, happy.

Dick just laughed. "He's the best."

Oh, that earned him a hot look from Rock.

"Yes. And he's ours." Rig nuzzled beneath Rock's ear, lips moving.

"Yeah. Our stud."

Rock chuckled, moaned, hand working harder.

"My marines." Rig gasped, ass going tight.

"Ex-marines," growled Rock. "We're just yours now."

"Yeah." Rig cried out, lips fastening on Rock's.

His own prick throbbed, the declaration huge by Rock standards. He licked his lips, watching them as Rock's hand sped, as Rock's free hand slid to Rig's ass, finger pushing in. That's all it took, Rig jerking and coming hard, eyes wide and needy.

Rock growled, cock spraying. Dick made a small noise, happy and home, watching his lovers cuddle together as they came down.

Rig grinned over at him, one eyelid dropping in a wink. He grinned back, blowing Rig a kiss.

Oh yeah, this was the fucking life.

***

Rig looked over at Peter, the boudoir photographer. Then he looked at Rock. Then Peter. Rock.

Oh, man, Peter didn't stand a chance.

"Pretty, I think you should pose next." Rock was looking at the costume in his hands, growling low.

Dick chuckled, softly enough Rock probably couldn't hear. "You think?"

"I think. Peter's not that much bigger than me..."

"Which outfit you want me to wear, Rig?" His Pretty was getting into this.

"The chaps, Pretty." His cock jerked a little. "With the hat."

"With or without underwear, Rig?"

He groaned, leaned in. "With for the calendar and without for me?"

Dick moaned softly and nodded. "Anything you want."

"So good to me, Pretty..." He went to kiss Dick and then Rock growled again, Peter's voice rising. "Gonna save the photographer's ass."

Dick chuckled and swatted his ass as he headed for Rock.

"Hey, Rocketman. What's up?" He patted Peter's arm. "Dick's going to go next, yeah?"

"Oh, thank God. Tell me he's not some musclebound ex-marine who's going to bite my head off?"

Rock growled again, glaring at Peter, at him. "Have you seen this fucking gauzy crap he expects me to wear?"

"Dick's getting dressed, Peter." He looked at Rock, head tilting. "Gauzy?"

Rock held up something that looked like it belonged on the set of an Arabian Nights movie. "What the fuck has this got to do with the gym?"

"Well..." He took the pants, looking. "Peter? Harem boy pants? Let the man have his pride. Leather, cammo, denim -- he's fucking studly."

"It's sexy."

Rock snorted. "If you're a fucking chick."

"Peter. Trust me. Let's put him in tight jeans. In leather. In BDU's and cammo. Oooh... in those sweet little PT shorts..."

Peter shrugged. "Hey, it's your dime. Oh, now that's sexy."

Dick walked over, wearing the chaps and the hat and nothing else, half-hard and all fucking stud. "You sure about this, Rig?"

He purred, eyes trailing. "Oh. Oh, sweet Lord in Heaven."

"Oh. I'll take that as a yes." Dick grinned at him, blush high as the sweet cock headed up toward Dick's belly. "These ones are private, right?"

"I'll uh... make sure. Yes." Peter cleared his throat and nodded.

"Fuck, kid, you look good." Rock sounded impressed.

"You do." Rig nodded. "Better than any cowboy I've ever seen."

Dick beamed at him, standing tall and proud.

"How come the kid gets to wear sexy stuff and I'm stuck with the gauzy curtain things?"

"You don't have to wear the gauzy curtain things, Rocketman. Let's find you something sexy." Rock grunted and followed him to the pile of clothes, arms folded across the wide chest. He dug, humming and looking until he found a pair of faded jeans and a faded flannel shirt. "You'd look comfy and fine as fuck in these, Blue. And I need one of you in BDUs."

Rock gave him a look. "These are normal clothes."

Rig grinned, pinked a little. "There's a pair of leather pants..."

"So these are just warm ups then." Rock held out the jeans and shirt.

"I'd like one of you in the bed, with the sheet strategically placed. You'd look so fine." God, he was hard.

And Rock was noticing. "Yeah? What else you want?" That voice was low, rough.

He pressed close, whispering. "I want you. I want your cock. I want that bastard with the camera to get busy so you can fuck my mouth."

"He looks pretty busy to me. You need to be down on your knees."

"Oh..." He stole a look into the other room. "You sure?" Fuck, he wanted.

"I get a blow job and I will let that nutcase take my picture wearing any outfit you want. As long as it isn't fucking gauze or lace."

"I wouldn't ask you to do that, Blue. You know better." He slid down to his knees, damn near panting. Rock just purred, fingers slowly opening his jeans, letting that fat prick out.

"Oh... Fuck, yes." He moaned, nuzzling right on in. Rock's hands slid into his hair, fingers moving through the curls. He opened up, lips wrapping around the fat tip of Rock's prick. That fucking sexy purr just got louder, Rock's hands tightening. Whimpering, he started sucking, head bobbing, cock throbbing in his jeans. Rock's hips started moving, working with him, not too hard, not out of control. Not yet.

His hands worked Rock's balls, fingers pushing and rolling. Rock groaned, moved faster. "Shit, Rig..."

He sucked harder, pulling. Fuck, he needed. Moaning, Rock held his head in place and started to fuck his face. Rig opened up, relaxed, let Rock have him, let Rock take him.

"Fuck." The word was more groan and Rock's hot spunk was spraying down his throat.

He swallowed it all down, hips jerking, damn near creaming his jeans. Rock slid out of his mouth, hands sliding on his face, thumb stroking across his bottom lip. "You're fucking something else, Rabbit. Always have been."

He sucked that thumb in, moaning low. "Just know what I need."

Rock purred, thumb moving in and out of his mouth just like that fat prick had. Those blue eyes were shining down at him. He was given a wink. "Find me the outfit you were sure I'd balk at and I'll go get my picture taken."

He nipped the ball of Rock's thumb. "I want you in the chaps, too."

One of Rock's eyebrows went up. "I'm not putting my cock on a calendar, Rabbit."

"I wouldn't ask you to. A pair of cutoffs and a hat and you're set."

"All right. I'll play cowboy for you once the kid is done wiggling his ass for the camera."

He blushed, grinned, leaned forward to nuzzle that fat prick, kiss the tip. "You're good to me."

"There isn't another person in the world I'd do it for." Rock stroked his curls, his face.

"I know." He grinned up, so in love in hurt. "I want to watch."

"Anything you want, Rabbit." The words were soft and then Dick interupted them, jeans on now under the chaps.

"What next, Rig?"

"Now the other half of my own personal wet dream's going to wear the chaps. And a hat. He needs a hat."

"You going commando, Rock?"

"Fuck, no, kid."

"Not even for one shot for Rig's own personal collection?" Dick leaned against Rock's side. "It's a fucking beautiful body, Rock, with the world's most perfect prick. Just one picture and as soon as it's taken I'll distract Peter so you can put something on."

Rock growled.

"I'll owe you one."

"One picture."

Dick nodded. "Just one."

"Give me the fucking chaps."

Dick took them off and handed them over without another word.

Rig went to find a seat with a view. He? Was the luckiest motherfucker on Earth.

Chapter Nineteen

Fucking splinters.

Rock had a dozen in his fucking right hand and they were annoying the fuck out of him. He'd tried getting them out, but the fucking tweezers were like little sticks snapping in his left hand. Growling, he stalked into the kitchen. "I need your fucking help."

Rig looked up, one eyebrow raised. "Okay. What can I do you for?"

He thrust his hand out, trying hard as fuck not to pout. He wasn't very successful.

"What on Earth got you, Blue?" Rig looked at his hand, taking the tweezers and gently going to work,

"I shifted the crap from the old deck. Could only find the one glove. Ow! That's my skin you're ripping to shreds." Some thanks, from the man who wanted the new deck.

"The gloves are in the garage or were." Rig shook his head, tongue clucking. "I told you I'd come help with that. Thanks for doing it, though."

"Didn't think I'd wind up with a handful of splinters." He grunted. "You're welcome."

Rig looked up and gave him a smile, another splinter sliding out. "You're good to me."

"Ditto."

Rig finished up and drew him to the sink, rinsing his hand off and checking it carefully under the light.

"Gonna kiss it and make it better?" He tried on his pout again -- now was the time to use it.

"It still hurting you, Blue?" Rig leaned in, lips brushing his palm, his wrist.

"Aches. I imagine I'll live." He curled his fingers, stroking Rig's cheek.

"Mmm... Feels nice." Rig hummed, resting against him. "God, you're a fine man, Rock. Smell so fucking good."

He rumbled happily. "For you."

"Yeah." Rig snuggled close, one hand working open his shirt, fingers slipping in to touch. "For me."

He purred. "Sexy fucker."

"For you." Those lips were traveling, moving against his skin, fingers fucking petting him.

"For fucking me," he murmured, tilting Rig's chin and taking a deep kiss. Rig opened easily, tongue sliding against his, hot and wet, so fucking right. He wrapped his hands around Rig's head, tilting it to deepen the kiss even more.

Warm arms wrapped around his neck, Rig pushing close, moaning into his mouth. So hot and horny and hungry -- even after so fucking long. He let one hand slide down along Rig's back, cupping the sweetest fucking ass he'd ever seen.

"Mmm... Good. Blue..." Grey eyes blinked up at him, lazy. "Want you."

"Fuck, yeah." There was no question there -- he wanted Rig. "Bed," he growled, pulling their hips together, letting Rig feel his want.

"Yeah." He got another long, slow kiss, then Rig took a few steps back, drawing him along. The trip down the hall took a good long time, drawn out with one breathless kiss after another. By the time they were naked and hit the bed, he was hard enough to cut glass.

Rig's tongue was sliding over his belly, up over his ribs, lips hot over his nipple. He groaned, shuddering. So fucking hot. Hands were petting his cock, cupping his balls, Rig sliding against him, humming and happy.

"Want you," he murmured. "Want to feel you hot and tight around my cock."

Rig shivered, a needy little moan just pushing over his skin. "Yes."

He reached for the lube, slicking Rig's fingers and his own. Taking Rig's hand, he guided it down to that sweet ass. "Together."

Those eyes flashed, his lips taken in a heated kiss as Rig's body took them both in, squeezing and tight, holding their fingers. He groaned, hips pushing his cock along Rig's skin. So fucking good.

"Blue... " Rig licked at his lips, ass riding their fingers. "Make me feel so fucking good."

He nodded, tongue moving against Rig's. "'s what I do."

"Yeah." Rig's moan was sweet, heavy, those white eyelashes brushing his skin.

He took another kiss, fingers slowing and pulling away. "Now. No more waiting."

"Mmm..." Rig whimpered, moving to slide onto his cock, that sweet ass pulling him in, holding him.

"Oh fuck." He rested his forehead on Rig's shoulder, just feeling Rig's ass holding him, rippling around him. "So fucking good."

"God, yes. Made for this, right here." Rig's hands stroked over him, soft needy sounds making him ache.

He nodded, kissed Rig's shoulder and started to move. Long. Hard. Slow. Deep. Each thrust was better than that last. Their bodies knew this, knew each other's needs and wants, knew where to push and where to linger.

It was fucking perfect and it went on forever.

Then just like that it was gone, replaced by urgent need and he started to fuck Rig, pounding into his Rabbit like a man possessed.

Rig arched, fingers bruising against his shoulders. "Blue! Blue, please!"

He wrapped a hand around Rig's prick, tugging just as hard as he was thrusting. "Come for me, Rabbit. Come on my cock."

Rig's hips snapped, body gripping hard as spunk sprayed, that tight fucking ass milking him. He let go, soaring as he shot deep into Rig's ass.

Rig held him as they relaxed, floated down. "My sexy old man."

He purred, happy as a fucking clam. His hand was taken, licked clean, Rig's tongue touching each spot. Oh, yeah, kissing it better.

And it didn't get much better than this.

Chapter Twenty

Rock had put the fear of death into Peter and was confident that the thick envelope in his hand contained the negatives and only copies of the pictures of him and the kid that they didn't want circulated. He had a second, slimmer envelope that had twenty-four pictures for them to narrow to twelve for the calendar. Or sixteen, depending on whether they were going to run it from September of this year instead of just the twelve months. He'd leave that particular decision to the kid. Dick had a savvy business mind when it came to people.

He went around to the back when the dogs didn't meet him on the porch -- they had to be out back with Rig and Dick. Sure enough, his men were playing frisbee, the dogs running back and forth between them, barking and trying to catch the flying disk. And it was the damned mutts that caught site of him first, Mutt and Trouble barelling toward him like a slobbery, demented welcome wagon.

Rig's laugh just filled the air. "Oh, look! Daddy's home!"

He gave Rig a glare. Maybe the thick envelope would get temporarily lost. He gave the dogs some loving and then headed for Rig and Dick who'd stopped playing and were heading toward him together.

"Hey, you. How's it hanging?" Rig pushed up against him, all warmth and grins.

"Hey, Cowboy." He wrapped one arm around Rig, the other around the kid and pulled them into a three way, envelopes behind their backs. Rig licked his lips, warm and close, humming. Oh, yeah, that was more like it. He kept the kiss long and deep.

"Mmm..." Rig was blinky and grinning as the kiss faded. "Wow."

He grinned, there was nothing like his own personal slut to make him feel like the biggest fucking stud going. Dick licked his lips and grinned.

"So, what are you holding against my ass, Rocketman? You gonna share?"

"Well." He handed out the thinner envelope. "Here's the final pictures for the calendar. We have to narrow them down to twelve or sixteen."

"Oh, cool." Rig grinned and nodded. "Let's take them in and spread them out."

He winked at the kid as he slid him the other envelope. Dick played along, sliding it onto the counter in the kitchen as they gathered around the table. Rig spread the photos out, oohing and ahhing, damn near bouncing.

"So what do you think, kid? Twelve or sixteen?"

Dick looked at the pictures. "Well the price difference isn't that much. What does the average gym goer think, Rig?"

"If the money isn't a big deal, go with sixteen." Rig was happily organizing -- him in a pair of PT shorts there, the kid in a pulled up sweater here. He chuckled. Rig was having this much fun with the public pictures; he was going to be over the moon with the others.

"Sixteen then. You can choose -- I look like a stud in all of them and the kid ain't half bad either."

"Gee thanks, Rock."

"You're welcome, Dick." He ducked the kid's swat.

"Y'all are hot. I want copies for my office." Rig was happy as hell, shifting and sorting.

"I like that one of the kid and I in the worn jeans -- looks natural. Be even better if you were in with us." The one he was talking about he and the kid were arm in arm, smiling, at something Rig had said if he remembered correctly.

Rig snorted. "Like anyone wants to see my skinny ass when they could have y'all."

"I meant for here," he murmured. Stubborn redneck. Rig was plenty sexy to him and the kid. Plenty fucking sexy.

Rig looked up, grinned. "Y'all do take some pretty pictures. Now, where are the rest?"

"There's more?" he asked. It'd been a fucking long time since he was innocent, but he put on his best look.

Rig gave him a long look, eyebrow raised. "Now, that? Is a great expression. It doesn't work, but it's cute. Give me my beefcake shots."

He chuckled and nodded to the counter where the other envelope was. "Negatives and two copies of each picture. There isn't another copy in existance and it's going to stay that way."

"Oooh..." Rig's eyes lit right up, dumping the pictures out. "Oh. Oh, fucking hell. These are... Oh."

He chuckled, enjoying the way Rig's cheeks had gone hot and if he wasn't mistaken, those jeans were straining to bursting over Rig's prick. "You find something you like?"

"Uh-huh." Rig nodded, fingers sliding over the pictures, tongue sliding out to wet those lips. There were a batch that were sexy, a bunch that were risque and another few that were downright obscene, his and the kid's cocks hanging out. Well, and standing hard and proud. They both looked pretty fucking good. "Fuck, y 'all are two fine men."

Rig looked hot as hell.

He held out his arms. "And we're standing right here. Kid -- you think the trick is we're half naked in the pictures?"

"I can do half naked." Dick started stripping.

He grinned. "Hell, yeah."

He took off his t-shirt and undid his jeans, letting his prick poke out.

Rig hummed, eyes just hot on them. "Take it off, studs."

"All the way?" He turned around and shimmied his ass, tugging his jeans down, feeling a bit of a fool. Then hot hands landed on his ass, Rig's mouth on the top of his crease and suddenly he was feeling a lot less foolish.

He groaned, kicked his jeans off the rest of the way and leaned his hands against the back wall, legs spreading. Rig's thumbs spread him, tongue licking at his crease, heading for his hole. He let his head drop, a low, rough sound coming from his throat. Fuck. Those pictures were so fucking worth it.

From the groan when Rig's tongue pressed into him? Rig agreed. One hundred and ten percent.

***

It was his turn to be on call and wasn't it just his luck to pull it during flu season, too. He'd worked for sixty-eight of the last seventy-two hours and there was no fucking way he was driving home. Not now.

He called and left a message on the machine saying he'd be home tomorrow, don't fret, order pizza, Dick, feed the dogs and Rock, get the recyclables out to the curb by eight am. Rig turned off all the clinic's lights, stumbling down the hallway towards his office. Thank God he had a sofa in there.

Eight at night and he was fixin' to crash out for the night -- Christ, he was getting old.

When he opened the door he was assailed by candlelight and the scent of barbeque. There was a blanket spread out on the floor, a feast of barbeque chicken, coleslaw, fries and rolls on the blanket. A second feast was at his desk, Rock and Dick arguing quietly over several bottles of beer and an opener.

"Oh..." He slumped against the doorframe, heart beating hard. "Y'all... Oh..."

His men stopped arguing about when to open the beer, turning to him with twin smiles.

"You think you can get away from us that easy?" Rock asked.

"Away from you?" Rig shook his head, afraid to grin in case he couldn't stop. Fuck, he was a lucky man; they were so good to him. "How'd y'all get in? I thought it was just me in here."

"We've got our ways," mumured Rock, managing to look innocent. Dick almost managed the look himself, but the kid must have known he was blowing it because he opened a beer and thrust it at him.

He took it with a smile, continuing until he was wrapped in a warm pair of arms. "Fuck, y'all are a sight for sore eyes."

"I'm betting that's not what's sore," Rock rumbled, moving to stand behind him, sandwiching him up between the two of them. Rock's hands slid over his shoulders, Dick's moving into the small of his back, fingertips rubbing.

"Oh..." He slumped, holding onto Dick as they worked knots that were screaming for release. He rested his head on his Pretty's shoulder, moaning. "Oh, fuck. Don't stop. Feels so good."

"You thinking of stopping?" Rock asked.

"No, sir." Dick answered.

"Good boy."

Dick chuckled, the sound vibrating against him. "He still thinks I'm a kid."

Rock snorted.

He chuckled. "Feeling young to me, Pretty." He nestled closer, groaning as Rock stepped forward too, held him up, kept him warm.

"No, Rig, I'm feeling you."

Rock groaned, but it was good-natured and the two of them started to move, almost as if they were slow-dancing together.

"You want to eat first?" Rock asked.

"Want you first. Y'all can make sure I eat after."

"You owe me a ten, kid."

He lifted his chin, stealing a kiss from Dick's smiling lips. "That was a sucker bet, Pretty."

Dick chuckled. "I actually bet Rock wouldn't even have to ask."

He started laughing, happy and tickled down to his bones, holding onto Dick to keep his balance as his too-tired body just lost it. Dick grinned past him at Rock and then the two of them were pulling him to the couch, working off his scrubs. In moments, without any effort on his part, they had him naked as the day he was born, their skin warm and slick against him.

He reached up, pulling Rock down for a kiss, hands sliding over those amazing abs. Rock rumbled happily into his mouth, the sound vibrating against his body.

"Mmm..." He wrapped his arm around Dick's neck, tugged them all together. "Greedy. Need you both."

"Just tell us what you want, Rabbit."

Dick nodded, mouth fastening around the sweet spot on his neck. "We're yours."

"Oh... touch me. So tired, Blue. Want to come and float and rest." He licked at Rock's lips, hips rocking. God, this was good, so sweet, so fucking right.

"We can do that. We can send you to the moon and hold you while you sleep."

Dick nodded his agreement, the kid slowly sinking, body sliding against him, mouth licking and nibbling and working its way to his cock. Rock's hands were solid, moving slowly over his skin. Rig moaned, utterly overwhelmed and warm, held. He captured Rock's tongue between his lips, sucking with a gentle, steady rhythm, pulling Blue's taste deep.

As Dick started to love on his cock, taking his sweet time to explore and taste, Rock started to work on his nipples, large fingers teasing and tugging.

"Oh... Oh, fuck. Good." He was babbling, whispering encouragements against Rock's skin, body moving in slow waves, tremors shaking him.

Dick's hands slid over his ass as he was swallowed whole. One of Rock's fingers slid into his nipple ring, tugging, while Rock's other hand slid over his belly, playing in his navel and in the hollows by his hips. He was caught in the sensations they were creating as they loved him. He arched, sobbing softly, sparkles glittering behind his eyes. One of Dick's hands slid to cup his balls, the suction around his prick increasing.

Shattering, he came with a cry, sinking into Rock's arms, cock pulsing and throbbing on his Pretty's tongue. Dick swallowed him down as Rock held him, the two of them still stroking and touching, keeping him floating on pleasure, just like he'd asked.

He just rested, melted and hot and happy, tongue sliding along Rock's saltsweet skin. "Y'all staying here? Couldn't make the drive, Blue."

Rock nipped at his lips. "Better you staying than trying and missing," rumbled his lover.

Dick nodded, coming back up to cuddle up on his other side. "Rest and food and then we'll take you home, Rig."

"Mm... sounds perfect." His eyelids were drooping, fine tremors shaking him every now and again. "Need a vacation, Blue."

"The kid and I have flexible schedules now, Rig. You just say the word."

"Want to." He nodded, humming as his Pretty stroked his belly, drawing him down and down into sleep.

"Whatever you want."

The soft whispers followed him into his dreams.

Chapter Twenty One

Dick slipped into the booth at Jay's bar and ordered a beer. It was Saturday, which meant Rock was covering at the gym and he was having his weekly date with Rig. They'd kept up the tradition after moving here and it was still good, still serving its purpose, letting them talk stuff out if they needed to, giving them an opportunity to just focus on each other without any distractions if they didn't.

Rig was a little late today; Dick figured he got held up at the grocery store or something, so he ordered himself the loaded potato skins to munch on until they could order. He'd just started eating them when Rig came in.

Rig looked good, tanned and healthy, blinking against the dim light in the bar. He waved, though he was sitting at their usual table, smiling as Rig caught sight of him and headed on over. "Hey Pretty. Sorry I'm late, I was getting shit ready for Momma. How're you?"

"Good. You should have split your errand list and let me help."

He pushed the potato skins toward Rig. "Help yourself. I haven't ordered lunch yet."

"Thanks." Rig took one, nibbling. "I think I have most everything done. I put that old recliner in the front room, cleaned up the bathroom and emptied the dresser and closet. Sissy says she just sleeps, mostly. Just wants to rest."

He reached out and stroked Rig's hand. "We could get her one of those really comfy deck chairs so she could sit out and watch the ocean, the fresh air would probably do her good." He grinned. "I bet Rock would be real pleased to have it around once she went back home."

"Yeah, that would work out real nice." Rig gave him a quiet smile. "Sissy says the oncologist is real pleased."

"Yeah? I was worried she might not be well enough to come out."

"Sissy said that... well, the chances of Momma being able to come here next summer aren't great, you know?"

He nodded, fingers twining with Rig's. "She'll be with us a few months, Rig. We'll make sure she has a great time, relaxes, k?"

"Yep." Rig nodded, eyes closing for a second. "So, how's the gym?"

"Gym's great. How are you?" He didn't want to push too hard, but if Rig needed to talk, he was right here.

"Okay. Went to see Helen's little baby this morning. She looks like her Daddy."

"Oh, I bet she was adorable despite that."

Rig laughed, eyes warm and shining. "She's a sweetie, you know it. Helen's about ready to come back to work though, I think. She's feeling house-bound."

Dick grinned. "And you're not missing her one little bit."

"Hell, yes. That harridan the service sent is mean and worthless to boot. She made little Joey Gregory cry just looking at him."

"I knew there was a reason Rock wouldn't go in to pick you up the last few weeks!"

He chuckled, smiling at the waitress as she came up. "What do you want, Rig?"

"Glass of iced tea and... do I want a salad or a burger, Pretty?"

"We're having pizza for supper, so I imagine you want a salad. And I'll let you steal my fries." He smiled over, feeling good and easy in his bones.

"Grilled chicken salad, then."

The waitress giggled and nodded, looking at him. "And what would you like with your large fries?"

"I'll have the Texas burger and a large coke, please." All this talk of Momma had Texas on his mind.

"So, have you decided where we're having the party? I got hold of Sarge and Jack, they're coming down, and I got that caterer that did y'all's one year anniversary."

"Oh, that's great! Rock is going to be blown away. And I talked to the rec center -- the one that backs onto the beach? -- they'll let us have the place for a hundred bucks and a deposit. It's available the night of his birthday, too." So far they'd managed to keep Rock's forty-fifth birthday party a surprise. It wasn't really a birthday that you went to a lot of trouble making a big deal out of, but Rock's fortieth had kind of been, well, ruined.

Wow. That made it five years since Rig's bashing. He hardly ever thought about it anymore, wondered if Rig did, but wasn't going to bring it up by asking.

"Excellent. If you'll take care of arranging the booze and band, I'll get the invites out. What're we getting our old man? Any thoughts?"

"You mean besides blow jobs until he passes out?" He shook his head. He had no idea what to get Rock. The man wasn't wanting for anything.

"Well, I was thinking we could plan a camping trip in the fall, around our birthdays. If we got him a gift certificate from one of those huge stores, he could get what all he wanted."

"Oh, he'd like that. He could mess around with the brochures and all that." He nodded. "Great idea."

Rig nodded, winked. "And the girls can camp out on the beach in July."

"Sounds perfect."

Their food came and he smiled across at Rig, digging in hungrily. Rig stole his fries, one or two at a time, nibbling at his salad. "I'm scared to see her."

Dick nodded. He'd been practicing keeping his face the same, worried she'd look really bad and he'd let it show. "Did Sissy say how she was looking?"

"She's bald, tired, real skinny, for Momma." Rig shook his head. "Sissy says she's aged fifteen years in the last few months, but that she's looking better."

He reached out and took Rig's hand again, squeezing. "We'll be here to hold you, yeah?"

"Yeah. I just... I'm glad she's coming, I just wish it was happier."

Dick nodded. "Yeah, I hear you. It'll be good though. You'll be able to talk and visit and love her."

"Yep." He got a look, a quick wink. "Gonna miss fucking on the deck, though."

Dick nearly choked on his food. "Damn, warn me next time before you say something like that."

Rigger's laugh was bright enough to make the other people in the restaurant smile. Fuck, he loved the man. He ate the rest of his burger, watching without staring as Rig picked at his salad and stole french fries.

Finally Rig looked up, smiled at him. "You want to go catch a movie before Blue gets out of work?"

"Sure. Or we could rent one and watch it on the couch at home." And snuggle and make out during and after.

"Oooh. Good plan."

He nodded. "I thought so. We could even put on a CD or two and I'll take you dancing. We've got the whole afternoon."

"Sounds perfect, Pretty." Rig pulled out some money, put it on the table.

"Can I have you for dessert?" he asked.

"You know it." Rig's shoulder bumped against his as they walked.

"Then it does indeed sound perfect." He smiled at Rig, bumping back.

He got another of those laughs, low and deep and sexy, and he grinned, followed Rig into the sunshine.

***

Momma was coming today. At noon. Nine hours. Nine hours and it might be the last time she got to see him and he knew -- he knew that was always the case.

Knew.

But this time? He really knew.

The house wasn't getting any cleaner, so he headed out back, grabbing a pack of smokes as he went. The best thing about their new place? Walking along the shore. Barefoot and quiet and smoking and thinking and just right.

He was headed back when he saw Dick, the kid strolling, looking casual as all fuck except it was three fucking am. He shook his head. Rock would shit a brick. Sweet bastard. "You're supposed to be in bed, Pretty."

"I'm not the only one." Dick took the package of cigarettes out of his hand and put an arm around his shoulders. "You okay?"

"Yeah. No. You know. Nervous. Thinking. Smoking." He nodded at the pack. "That's a new pack, Pretty."

"Shame. This shit's getting expensive too, isn't it?" Dick squeezed his shoulders. "I've got something better for your nerves anyway."

He pursed his lips. Damn it. Six bucks a pack was pricey.

"If you didn't buy them the money wouldn't be wasted," Dick pointed out, leading him back up to their back deck.

"I need them sometimes, Pretty."

"You should have woken me up."

"I..." He sighed, nodded. "Yeah. I should have."

Dick pulled him around and licked at his lips. "You can always wake me, Rig. No matter what."

"You keep saying that. One day you'll regret it."

Dick laughed softly. "I never have yet and I don't imagine I ever will."

He leaned in, cuddled close. "You don't think?"

"I don't think?" Dick's eyes were focussed on his mouth, his Pretty leaning their faces together and taking a kiss.

"Oh..." He pressed against Dick, lips parting eagerly. Dick moaned, tongue sliding into his mouth, hands warm on his back and tugging him even closer. Fuck, he loved that, loved the way Dick touched him.

"You wanna test out the new deck chair?" They'd wound up getting one for Momma and one for Rock to sit in and keep her company.

"Oh, I think we should." He backed Dick up into it, hips rocking. Dick sat and pulled him down, their mouths never having to part. He straddled those thighs, settling easily. The sweet noises started, Dick's hands sliding down to cup his ass, to squeeze, tease.

The chair held up well, creaking just a little as they moved. Dick's fingers pushed his t-shirt up and over his head, dragging along his skin.

"Must be naked-time." He chuckled as their lips parted, the scent of sea and sand mixing with Dick's skin.

Dick grinned, a soft blush covering his cheeks. "Love touching your skin."

Rig licked at Dick's lips, humming. "Fuck, you make me feel fine, Pretty."

"You are fine, Rig." Dick's fingers slid along his sides and down his spine, teasing across the top of his waistband.

"Nothing like my men." He was a skinny-assed old cowboy. His men were... special.

Dick laughed softly. "No, nothing like me and Rock. Thank god. But you're still fine. I love touching you. Love fucking you. Love being with you."

"Love me." He met Dick's eyes. "I know. I count on it."

Dick smiled at him and nodded, rubbing their noses together and then taking his lips.

"Oh." Heat filled him, slow and easy, one wave after another. Dick moaned, fingers sliding around to open his jeans. He sucked in his belly, leaving plenty of room for Dick's fingers.

"Love the way you do that. Like you can't wait to be touched." Dick's fingertips slid across the tip of his prick.

"Just... oh... Just need it." He leaned in to nip Dick's jaw.

Dick whimpered, neck going back. "Need you."

"Got me." He nuzzled in, licking and moaning, losing himself in the taste of his lover.

"Good." Dick's mouth opened wide to him, fingers pushing off his jeans. He reached down, untied Dick's sweats, freed that hard cock. "Gonna ride me?" Dick asked.

"You know it." He let his fingers trail up along that long cock, petting. Dick cried out, bucking a little. Two sweet fingers slid along his crease.

"Oh. Yeah. Want you. Fuck." Their tongues tangled together, his thighs parting farther. Dick's fingers teased in and out and then slid in deep. His head fell back, body clenching, eyes flashing open. "Fuck. Again." Dick's fingers slid in deep, again and again, other hand sliding around his cock and pumping slowly. He was panting, jerking, moving into Dick's touch. "Oh. Good. Good, Pretty."

Dick nodded, nailing his gland a few more times. Then Dick's fingers slid away and Dick drew him forward, tugging his ass toward that sweet prick.

He crawled up, straddling Dick, shivering at the wind from the ocean. "Need."

"Take." Dick pushed up into him, hands on his hips, guiding him down.

That was what he needed, just that. Just there.

Fuck.

Dick moaned, licked at his neck and then his nipples, hips working to fuck him.

"Oh. Oh, fuck." He bucked, biting his lip hard.

Dick's sweet noises continued, muted by his skin as Dick licked and sucked, tongue sliding through the ring on his nipple and tugging. The world spun, his body going tight-tight.

"Rig..." his name was whispered, Dick's cock jerking inside him, his Pretty coming deep.

He slumped down into Dick's arms, breathing hard, panting. The long arms wrapped around his back, Dick pressing kisses on his face. He hummed, eyes closing, damn near purring.

"Chair passes muster," murmured Dick.

"Mm-hmm. Didn't even creak." Fuck, he was tired. Bone tired.

"You think you can make it back to bed or do you want to sleep out here tonight?"

"Skeeters'll eat us up."

Dick kissed his forehead. "Then let's go in. My cock swells plenty all on its own."

He chuckled and nodded, swaying as he stood up. Dick's hand slid to his hip, steadying him as the kid stood as well. "You good?"

"Yeah. Just tired." He smiled, blinking. "Real tired."

"Then come sleep -- I bet Rock's kept the bed nice and warm for us."

He nodded. "Yeah. 'kay."

Dick's arm slid around his waist, his Pretty guiding his footsteps inside. He leaned against his lover, eyes closed, letting Pretty take him to bed.

Chapter Twenty Two

Rock had the day off to drive Rig out to the airport to pick Momma up. Rig had protested, Rock knew he would, but he and the kid insisted everything at the gym was up to date and covered and he could afford to take the day off to help out. Truth was, as Dick had quietly pointed out to him the other afternoon, depending on how Momma looked, the best thing for Rig would be to not have to be driving. This way the two of them could sit in the back seat and fuss over each other. Hell, Dick had even volunteered his car for the occasion.

He dropped Rig off at the arrival gates and found a parking spot then headed in himself, soon finding Rig, standing in the fucking smoking section of one of the little airport cafes. Shaking his head, he went up and relieved Rig of the rest of the pack. "We early?"

"Those are expensive, Blue." Rig's heart wasn't in it. "Yeah, her flight's running a little late."

He didn't bother to reply. He didn't care of they were fucking gold; Rig wasn't going to smoke them. Not if he had anything to say about it. "You wanna grab a donut or something?"

"I could use a cup of coffee for sure." Rig nodded, walked with him. "Damn. This place is just getting bigger and bigger."

He led the way to the donut shop, buying Rig an apple fritter and himself two chocolate with coconut donuts and some coffee. They found a seat and he put Rig's fritter in front of him with his best 'eat damnit' expression.

"Mmm... I love these." Rig's boot rubbed against his ankle and Rig tore off a corner, nibbling, grey eyes wandering.

He purred a bit at the touch and ate his first donut without comment. Then he started in on the second one, working slower this time. "You nervous?"

"Yeah." Rig nodded, looked over at him. "I shouldn't be, but I am."

"You know what I do whenever I'm nervous? I think about one of your fucking amazing blow jobs." He leaned in, voice low. "That always takes my mind off whatever's bothering me."

Oh, that look? Wide-eyed and parted lips, cheeks just flushed? That was worth the price of admission. "Oh. Yeah?"

"Yep. Seems to be working pretty well for you, too." He grinned and sat back again, foot sliding up to rub at Rig's leg right above the top of his cowboy boot.

Rig shifted, long legs spreading. "Yeah. Yeah, it does..."

"There's not much that wicked mouth of yours can't fix. Gets me up in the morning, brings me home at night." He was pretty fucking fond of Rig's mouth.

"Blue..." Rig was grinning, blushing, hiding behind the brim of his hat.

He chuckled. Oh yeah, he still had it, could still make Rig forget pretty much anything else existed. "Makes me hard just thinking of it."

"Made for that." Rig nodded, actually reached over and stole a bite of his donut. "For you."

"You know it." Fucking sexy cowboy. He kept Rig distracted and flushed until it was time to go meet Momma at the arrival gate.

Rig was still smiling when she walked up, pale and red-faced and thinner than Rock ever remembered seeing her. She had a scarf and a cowboy hat on her head, and she was walking slow. Rig squeezed his hand, holding tight for a second, but she caught sight of Rig and smiled, that look familiar and good, and Rig let go, heading straight for her. "Momma!"

"Baby. I made it."

He engulfed them both in a tight hug. "Welcome to California, Momma." He put a hand behind her back, guiding her and Rig over to the baggage claim. "You let me know which ones are yours."

"I have three. All red with big orange bows tied on the handles. Two big ones and a little one." Rig kept holding, kept looking, kept talking to her like she might up and leave. Like anyone with three pieces of luggage was going anywhere anytime soon.

He pulled the suitcases off the belt as they came down and handed the smaller one over to Rig. "Now you've got a choice. I can leave you at the doors and bring around the car or you can come with me. It's a ten minute walk though and you've got to be tired after all that travel."

"I'll walk it. I've been trying to get a half an hour of exercise a day. We'll just go slow, okay?" Charlene took Rig's arm, leaned into her son. Rig's arm slid around her waist, held her up.

"You just let me know if I get to walking too fast." He led the way, keeping the pace as slow as he could manage, not wanting her to have to tell him to slow down. It was a fucking shame what the cancer was doing to Charlene.

"How you feeling, Momma?"

"Tired, but better now that I'm here. I've been looking forward to visiting y'all for weeks."

"Us, too, Momma. Rig here's been working on his list of stuff to have ready for you every day since we got back from Christmas. And just you wait until you see the ocean."

"Oh, I plan on spending hours and hours watching it. And playing with the pups and resting." The wind was blowing, the air cool. "How's Richard?"

"Dick's fine, Momma. He's at the gym, working." Rig smiled. "He said to tell you he's sorry he couldn't pick you up too, but they've got to work."

Rock nodded. "Gym won't run itself yet. I keep hearing how it will one day, though, and then I'll be able to retire. Again. I'm not sure what all I'm supposed to do with my second retirement, but I guess I've a few years yet before I have to come up with an answer."

"The day you retire, you'll lay down and die, Jim." Momma shook her head. "You might ease up, but you'll never up and quit. You or Alex either one."

"No, ma'am I don't imagine we will. Kind of like you."

Momma nodded. "I tell you what, though. I won't mind a few weeks of no babysitting and no angst, just my boys and TV and such."

He chuckled. "I don't know, Momma, those damned pups may put you in mind of kids."

"Oh, Momma will love Miss Suzie. She's a lover. Lucy's as sweet as always. Rock's boys? Beasts. Big, drooly, bouncy beasts."

Momma laughed. "Sorta like their daddy, huh?"

He growled a little, mostly for show. "I wouldn't know as I never met him. You'll have to ask Rig."

Charlene grinned over. "You don't fool me a bit, son. My boy taking good care of you?"

"He always does, ma'am." He nodded as they came up to the car. "This is the kid's. Gotta admit, it makes for comfortable sitting."

He clicked the remote to unlock the doors and put Momma's bags in the trunk.

Rig got Momma settled in the front seat, then slid into the back. "Are you hungry? Thirsty? Tired?"

He started the car up and headed off. "We can stop at a restaurant if you like. Or do take out. Or just go home. I know Rig's got something cooking -- place smelled like heaven when we left."

"What are you cooking, baby?" Momma turned to smile back at Rig.

"Got Swiss steak going, but it'll be ready tonight. There's lunch meat and salad stuff, too. Lots of fruit." Rig grinned. "Sissy said you were needing to get some vitamins."

Rock rolled his eyes and gave her a wink. "Watch out, Momma, he's a nazi about those vitamins."

Rig reached over, rubbed the back of his neck. "Just taking care of me and mine."

He rumbled a little, letting Rig know he appreciated the touch, if not the vitamins.

"You stocked up on the beer your Momma likes, Rig? Or do we need to stop on the way?" He turned to Charlene. "You are still allowed to have beer, right?"

"I..."

"Momma is not having any beer." Rig's voice was set and Rock knew just the look he'd have. "You have liver cancer. Don't stress it."

"Son, I'm dying. If I want a be..."

"No."

"Don't you start, Jeremy Alexander. I'm still your momma." He wisely kept his own mouth shut, wishing he'd done so from the start. Then he could have picked a case up in sweet ignorance. "Son. I'm not going to fight about this. I've fought with your sister, your brother. I'm tired of being sick. I only have so long on this earth; I'm going to enjoy it." Man, that woman made Rig seem indecisive.

He glanced in the review mirror at Rig. His cowboy's lips were pressed tight. fury showing in two hot little spots on those cheeks. "You can't give up, Momma."

"Rig," he said quietly, trying to catch his Rabbit's eyes. Just leave her be for a day or two, Rig. Let the beach work its magic.

Rig's eyes met his in the rearview mirror, sick and sad and scared. They held the look through the stop light and then Rig took a deep breath, that hand moving on his nape again. "I thought we could drive down to Monterey one day, Momma. See the aquarium and Cannery Row."

"That sounds like a great idea, Rig." He nodded, turning to give Momma a smile. Meet him halfway old lady, because much as I like you, he's my priority and I'm not having you hurting him more than can be helped.

"Oh, I'd love that." Momma nodded, offered him a smile. "I want to see everything -- mostly I want to see the ocean and the beach and have Jim make me pancakes and play with the pups and enjoy you, baby."

"Well, I can manage that, Momma." Rig's hand kept touching, stroking.

"And I imagine I can manage pancakes now and then. The boys bought you a special deluxe deck chair for you to sit in. They managed to buy two and I have plans to plant my ass down and pretend to watch waves." He gave her a wink, slowing as they passed the little taco shop run by a little old mexian lady and her husband. "We getting something to go, Rig?"

"Yeah. Should we get something for Dick and drop it off or was he good?"

"He's a big boy, if he didn't bring lunch with him, he can buy something. Unless you wanted to see the gym, Momma? I kind of figured we'd save it for a day you hadn't spent in a plane." That was their Rig, always looking out for him and the kid.

"I think I'd like to get settled, Jim. Richard won't mind."

Rig nodded and opened the door. "I'll run in -- you want three steak tacos and a chicken, Blue?"

He nodded and grunted. "And some sopapillas. We've got vanilla ice cream at home."

"I can do that." Rig waved his momma's money away. "I can buy tacos for us, Momma."

"Better put your order in though, Charlene, or he'll be bringing you the vegetarian ones." He gave her a wink.

"He knows what I like."

Rig nodded. "One chicken and one pork."

"Cool." He gave Rig a wink as well and then watched that sweet ass heading toward the taco place.

"Are you having impure thoughts about my son, James South?" Momma gave him a look, a chuckle. Fuck, there wasn't another person on earth who could make him blush like Momma, except maybe her son, but that was for entirely different reasons.

"I don't believe I'm going to answer that one, Charlene." He gave her an unrepentant grin and promptly changed the subject. "How're you really feeling?"

"Tired. Old. I'm not going to do more chemo, Jim. You're going to have to help me make him understand."

"It that bad?"

She nodded. "A year, maybe. The chemo will add a few months to that, but it'll take all I have and leave me sick as a dog. That's not how I want to end it, Jim."

He nodded. He figured he could understand that. He'd seen enough men living off machines and just wanting to die. "He's a doc. He worked as a nurse a long time and he'll understand in his head, but not in his heart, Charlene."

"I know. He's a doctor and they fight until the end." Charlene shook her head. "I'm tired, Jim. Five months of this has been well... I don't want to do it. Jeremy's waiting for me, you know? I got someone on the other side."

He nodded and reached out to pat her arm. "You do what's right for you, Charlene. The kid and I will make sure he gets through it. He just loves you too much to just let you go."

She nodded, smiled. "He's always loved too much. That's why he has two of you to take care of, because God knew that."

He chuckled. "Well I don't know that I ever thought of it like that, but it makes sense. Of course the other side of the coin is true, too -- takes two of us to love him right."

She nodded. "I believe that. Y'all make him happy." Charlene patted his hand, "Have you heard from Duece?"

"Hell, yeah. Took Rig awhile to decipher his scrawl, but we've had a few long letters. He sounds like he's missing home."

"Yeah, I think he's missing someone more than somewhere, though."

He nodded. "That was my impression, too. Wears his heart on his sleeve that boy. Reminds me of someone else in your family."

He got the patented, hilarious and utterly ineffective grey-eyed Roberts innocent look. "My family?"

He snorted, still chuckling as Rig came back with their bag of take-out in hand.

"Three chicken, three beef, one pork and two bean and rice with sopapillas." Rig slid in. "I got a jar of their salsa, too."

"Salsa? Cool. Any chips?"

"No, they were greasy-looking. I have some good ones at home."

"Long as there's something to dip into the salsa." He gave Rig a grin and started the car up again.

It wasn't long at all before they were pulling up to the house. "Welcome home, Charlene."

The house was looking great -- the new lawn was tiny, but green. Huge flowers bloomed everywhere else. Rig and the kid had painted the house a blue-green with white shutters, the carport and workshop matching.

"Oh. Oh, boys, look at it!"

He grinned over at Rig, who looked proud as a peacock. And with good reason, the place looked great and Rig was largely responsible. "Wait 'til you see the deck and the beach."

"Oh, it's perfect." Charlene oohed and aahed over every bit -- each flower and the deck and the glasswork in the door. Then they got her settled outside at the glass table, Rig getting the food plated, the dogs bouncing and barking.

Rock settled in his new deck chair with a sigh. "You gotta admit, Charlene, this is the life."

"Oh, yeah. This place is perfect." She adjusted the scarf, smiling out at the ocean before scratching Mutt's ears. "Which one's which, Jim, and how do you tell."

"Trouble's the one with the excessive drool problem who likes to lie on my feet and Mutt's got floppier ears and a sharper bark." And he realised that knowing that totally took away his 'they're not my dogs' cred.

She smiled, nodded. "They're good-looking pups."

Rig came out with plates. "They all are. Suzie's the growliest of them all."

"She protects Rig better'n I do." He grinned, scratching Trouble's head with his foot and grabbing one of his tacos.

"We got beer, Rig?"

"Yeah, I'll get you one. You want tea, Momma?"

She gave him a long look. "That'll do, son. For now."

Rock chuckled as Rig went in. "You're in for a fight on that one, Charlene."

"You'll go buy my beer for me, won't you, Jim?"

"Once we've talked him into it." He'd have the kid do it; Dick knew Rig's soft spots.

"Y'all got his number, do you?"

"Sometimes." He gave her a wink and started eating.

Rig came out with a beer and two glasses of tea and the chips and they settled into eating, Charlene slipping bites to the dogs. Of course even if Rig didn't notice, he'd know, Trouble would be stinking the place up soon.

He chuckled and drank some of his beer. "You bring your pennies to lose, Charlene?"

"You know it. Brought my own cards too, in case I start losing."

He nearly choked himself laughing. Oh, she did tickle his funny bone. She might not look like the spry woman she'd been, but her mind was obviously still sharp as a tack. She winked, her and Rig settling into the normal pattern of chatter -- who was marrying who and how which kid was doing in school. Normal. Easy. He finished his food and his beer and settled back in his chair, enjoying the light breeze coming off the ocean and the idle chatter, occasional laughter.

It took a while, but Momma started fading, head bobbing. Rig stood, touched her hand. "You wanna go have a rest, Momma?"

"Huh? No. No, son, I'm fine." She blinked up, smiled. "Just dozy."

Rock chuckled. "Dozing out on the deck has huge theraputic value, Rig."

Rig nodded. "I just don't want her to burn. Let's move the big umbrella, shade her."

He nodded. "You got it." He shifted it so it shaded her and then leaned in to whisper into Rig's ear. "You know they got this new fangled stuff now called sunscreen."

Rig chuckled, leaning back into his arms. "Yeah? You sure about that?"

"Dead sure. We used it as lube, just last week."

Rig turned bright red, a strangled laugh escaping him. "Blue!"

He chuckled, hands sliding arouud to hug Rig tight. "Yeah?" Rig grinned, relaxed, let him hold on. He watched the waves a few moments before whispering. "You and the kid test out my chair last night?" Rig blushed darker and nodded, fingers twining with his. "Thought I could smell you both."

"Oh..." Rig rippled, leaning against him a little harder.

He licked Rig's ear. "She's dozed back off, Rig. She's in the shade. Needs her sleep..."

Rig took a deep breath, hips starting to rock against him. "Uh-huh."

He started slowly backing them up toward the door inside, one hand sliding down to cup Rig's cock through his jeans. His Rabbit was hard, ready for him. Wanting him. He purred, getting them inside and the door closed and then working open Rig's jeans. "Fucking sexy."

"Oh. Want you. Blue."

"Got me, Rig." For fucking ever. He wrapped his hand around Rig's prick, tugging.

One hand reached back, circled his neck, tugging him down. "Yes..."

He purred into Rig's mouth, tongue sliding in for a deep taste. Rig tasted spicy, entire body moving and rocking, that hand on his nape trembling. He slid his thumb across the head of Rig's cock, pushing into the slit for a moment and then letting his hand continue to fly, stroking hard.

"Oh. Oh, fuck. Fuck. More. Blue." Rig was rocked, shuddering. He rubbed against Rig's ass, hand working that sweet prick like it was his own. "Want your cock, Blue. Just real quick. Want to feel you."

He growled, and pulled Rig into the hall, pushing his Rabbit up against the wall and tugging down the tight jeans. Rig nodded, helping him, baring that tight, sweet ass. "Fuck, yes."

He popped two fingers into his mouth, slicking them up and then pushed them into that sweet fucking hole.

"Oh. Blue. Yes. Sweet fuck." Rig rode, just like that, pulling him in. He quickly stretched that sweet ass, fingers sliding away so he could press his cock in that tight heat. Rig took him deep, muscles rolling, pulling at him. He groaned, head resting against Rig's shoulder as he pushed in over and over again. "Made for this. Made for you."

He nodded, groaned. "Mine. My Rabbit."

"Yes. Yours. More." Rig stretched, squeezing him tight.

"Fucking sexy, Rig." He fucked Rig with everything he had, pushing his Rabbit against the wall again and again. His own personal cowboy took everything, took him deep. He reached around and took Rig's cock, stroking it in time with his thrusts. "Come on, Rig. Give it to me."

Rig jerked, head falling back, entire body bucking, milking him. He buried his roar against Rig's skin, filling Rig with spunk. "Oh, needed that."

Rig panted, nodded. "So fucking bad."

He nodded, hands sliding on Rig's skin. "I know."

"You always do." Rig hummed, relaxing. "Always have."

He nodded. "Always will." He tugged out slowly, petting.

"Mmm... yeah. Guess we better clean up, 'fore Momma wakes up."

He nodded. "Yeah."

He turned Rig and kissed him slowly. Those eyes were warm, happy, focused on him. He tugged Rig's jeans up, slowly doing them up.

Rig smiled, nuzzled the side of his mouth. "Couldn't do without you."

He snorted. "You'd manage fine, you'd just be a grumpy son of a bitch who needed a good hard fuck or twenty."

"I don't know. I'd be missing my Blue something fierce."

He chuckled, but puffed up as well, feeling like a million bucks -- Rig had that effect on him. "Well good thing you don't have to find out."

"You got that right." Rig's hand slid over his belly, petting and stroking.

He purred and hugged Rig to him. "You do something for me, Rig?"

"Anything, Rocketman. Just ask."

"Just enjoy your visit with Momma. Don't fret over her, don't nag her, don't stress yourself out over taking care of her. Enjoy it."

Rig sighed, nodded. "I'm going to do my dead level best."

"I'll beat you every time you don't." He gave Rig a wink and a kiss.

"Promises, promises." Rig chuckled, patting his ass.

He laughed and swatted Rig's ass in return. "Come on, I'm going to have a beer and munch on those chips and probably doze off right alongside your Momma."

"Sounds like a plan, Blue. You want some sour cream?" Rig's fingers stroked his wrist and they headed toward the kitchen together.

***

Dick wound up having to work late and he figured he'd missed Momma altogether when it was well past dark before he got home, but the television was playing a Stallone movie, Momma dozing in Rock's chair as Rock and Rig sat together on the couch. He gave them a smile and blew them a kiss before heading for the kitchen to rummage through the fridge for something to eat.

Rig came up behind him, hands rubbing his back. "I left a plate for you in the microwave."

"Oh, cool, thanks." He turned to give Rig a proper 'hey I'm home' kiss.

Rig smiled, scooting right in, hips settling against him. "Hey, Pretty."

He grinned, hands dropping to Rig's ass. "Hey yourself. How's it going with your Momma?"

"Going good. She loves the deck. Spent all afternoon out there. How was work?"

"It was work and I'm glad to be home." Working both shifts made for a long day. "I missed you."

"Mmm..." Rig's lips brushed against his, the kiss slow and sweet. He moaned softly, making the kiss a little harder, a little deeper. Rig gave it up, hands sliding into his hair, welcoming him home.

His stomach growled, making him chuckle. "I guess I'd better have that plate."

"Swiss steak and potatoes and beans." Rig went to start the nuker, got him a glass.

"Cool. Sounds yummy." He got out the milk and filled his glass. "What movie are you guys watching?"

"Over the Top, I think. I wasn't really paying attention. I got a new book at the grocery."

"So you don't mind keeping me company while I eat? You don't think Momma will think I'm being rude not eating in the front room, will she?"

Rig smiled over, eyes warm and shining as he started a pot of coffee. "I'd love to keep you company."

He took that to mean he wasn't being rude either and when the microwave dinged he sat and started in on the food. "Mmm, this is great."

"Thanks." A piece of strawberry pie was put on the table and then Rig settled, sipping his coffee.

"Oh, wow. Cool." He grinned at Rig, foot sliding over to rub along Rig's leg and he ate heartily. Rig chattered a little, updating him on tomorrow's plans, on this and that.

"And how are you doing?" he asked as he made short work of the pie.

"I'm okay. Enjoying visiting with Momma. Trying not to fret."

He reached out and squeezed Rig's hand. "Fretting's not going to do much for either of you, is it?"

"Oh, I don't know. I'm good at it." Rig winked, their fingers twining together.

He laughed softly and then sobered, just looking at Rig, thumb sliding across his hand. Offering his support one of the best ways he knew how. Rig blushed and held on, nodding.

He stroked Rig's face with his free hand and heard Rock's low rumbles, a lighter voice instersperced. "I'd better go say hi."

"She'd like that." Rig's lips brushed his wrist.

He moaned softly at the touch, cock starting to go hard. He took his hand back ruefully, not wanting to embarass himself or Momma. "Should we bring out coffee?"

Those grey eyes shone at him, warm and wanton. "Yeah, I reckon."

"K." Neither of them made any move to get up and put the pot on through, they just kept watching each other and his cock got a little harder. Rig was breathing hard, tongue sliding over those lips, just watching.

"Your Momma's right in the other room," he murmured, talking to himself as much as to Rig.

"Uh-huh." God, he could feel how much Rig wanted him.

"I could use a shower," he noted. "There's a lock on the bathroom door."

"I'm right behind you."

He nodded and got up, letting go of Rig's hand and hurrying out, slipping down the hall as quietly as he could. He got the water started and then the door was opening and closing, Rig right behind him. He turned and grinned, bringing their mouths together as his hands worked on their clothes.

Rig pushed right into the kiss, fingers in his hair, holding their lips together. Fuck, he loved that, the way Rig made it all about the two of them and heady desperation to taste and touch and crawl into each other.

It didn't take him long to get them naked, though he had to fight Rig to break their kiss so he could slide their t-shirts over their heads. Then they were skin-on-skin, Rig sucking on his tongue, cock rubbing against his hip.

He whimpered and moaned, filling Rig's mouth with his sounds as he filled his own hands with Rig's ass, pulling them closer together. Rig moaned low, grabbing and holding on tight.

He shifted, moving them slowly into the shower without losing contact. The water was hot, Rig's skin hotter and he moaned and rubbed, their kisses growing even deeper. One of Rig's legs slid around his hip, held him closer.

He brought one hand between them, gathering both their cocks together, his other hand stayed on Rig's ass, fingers teasing along the hot crease. They found a rhythm, moving sure and steady, both panting. The slap of flesh was intoxicating, soft and low beneath the sound of the water hitting skin, making him moan, making his cock jerk as it slid with Rig's.

All the time those eyes were watching him, loving him, needing him. A man could get lost in Rig's eyes and he let go, let himself get lost, knowing he was found, too, safe and warm and hot and loved in Rig's arms.

He cried out, spunk spraying from his cock as he came.

"Yes..." Rig hissed, arching, moving faster now, panting. "Pretty..."

He squeezed his hand around their pricks, making himself shudder, and pushed one finger into Rig's body. Rig jerked, eyes wide. "Oh. More."

He pulled harder on their pricks, pushing a second finger in with the first, sliding them in and out of Rig's heat. Rig whimpered, head falling back as spunk splashed on his fingers. He kept working both hands, slowing them, bringing Rig down as he licked at the patch of water gathered in the hollow of Rig's neck.

"Mmm... glad you're home." Rig grinned, relaxing.

He chuckled and hugged Rig tight. "Yeah, me too."

He took one last lick from Rig's skin and then bent for the soap, working up a lather and making quick work of washing them both up. Rig helped, sort of, just playing and touching, fingers sliding through the bubbles.

It was warm and good and home and he took his time before he turned the shower off and dried them both. Leaning in, Dick kissed Rig one more time and then stood back and grinned. "There, I just need a pair of sweats and I'm ready to go say hi to your Momma."

Rig nodded over to the sink. "I brought some from the dryer."

"Oh, you do take care of us, Rig." He leaned in for another hard kiss. "Thank you."

"Anytime, Pretty." His ass was patted, squeezed.

He was still grinning wide once he was dressed and headed out to give Momma a proper hello. Rock was setting up the dvd player with another movie, teasing Momma about how Arnold could take Sylvester any day of the week. "Hey, there, Momma. You know the best way to convince him he's wrong is to remind him Arnie's given it all up for politics."

"Richard! You're home!" She stood, held her arms open.

He gave her a warm hug, heart breaking for Rig as he got a good look at her face. She didn't look that different really, but there was a frailty about her that had to be beaking Rig's heart.

"How're you doing?" he asked when he finally let her go.

"Doing good, you letting that old man work you too hard?" She winked and smiled.

He laughed. "Nah, I just have to work twice as hard to keep up with him." Rock purred, hand stroking across his ass as the big guy made his way back to the couch. Sometimes it paid to stroke the big guy's ego.

"Did Alexander fix you some supper? I could make you something, if you need it."

"Oh, no, Momma, he took care of me." Oh, that was suggestive. At least it was considering what they done and Dick fought his blush.

"Oh, he's a good boy." Momma patted his arm, completely oblivious to Rock's look.

He nodded. "He is, Momma. You taught him well." He gave her a wink and another quick hug. He was going to go help Rig with coffee, but it looked like it was too late. Rig brought in a tray with four steaming cups and a plate of goodies.

"Here y'all go." Rig looked fine and lazy -- shorts and an old tshirt of Rock's, hair still wet.

Rock gave them both a knowing look, but Dick ignored it, figuring he'd blushed enough already and he didn't want Momma trying to put two and two together and coming up with him and Rig fucking in the shower.

"Oh, you brought cookies, Momma! Or did you start baking the minute your plane landed?"

"Nope. I brought them in my luggage. Figured I'd get a head-start." He chuckled and happily took some fudge and a lace-cookie, snatching his hand away when Rock would have slapped it away. They might have been Rock's favourites, but that didn't mean the big guy was going to get to eat them all. Charlene chuckled, shook her head. "I'm going to teach Alexander how to make them for you, Jim."

"Won't be the same," groused Rock.

"Well, no. But it'll do."

Dick reached out and petted her arm. "It will," he said softly, giving her a smile.

She winked and took a piece of fudge, handing half to Rig. "Eat. Tell me it's good."

Rig nodded. "Yes, Momma."

Dick laughed and finished his own fudge and cookie, going for seconds. "It's good, Momma."

"Of course it's good. I made it." She chuckled, hand taking Rig's, patting it. "I do love y'all's house."

"Rig's fixed it up really nice, hasn't he?"

Rock bopped him. "We helped."

Dick snorted. "Sure, but all we do is nod and do whatever he asks us to."

Charlene grinned. "That's usually the easiest thing with him."

"Hey! He is right here!" He and Rock and Momma started laughing and he reached out to squeeze Rig's arm. Rig winked at him, rolled his eyes. "They're abusing me, Pretty."

"You poor, poor man."

Rig nodded, giving him the innocent Rig look, which only made him laugh harder. Sometimes he thought Rig actually believed he could pull that look off.

Rock snorted. "You haven't been innocent in a long time, Rig."

"Years and years and years." Momma seemed more than willing to play along, teasing Rig right along with them.

"Maybe even decades," Dick suggested, hand still on Rig's arm, stroking.

"Watch it, kid, before I beat you." Rig winked, pouncing him playfully, tickling. He laughed, half-heartedly defending himself, fingers sliding on Rig, but not really tickling. Rig tickled him unmercifully, not even noticing Rock getting ready to tackle.

He positioned himself just right and when Rock started to go to town on Rig? He was lying right under that flailing body. And that was worth getting tickled any day. Rig laughed hard, Charlene cackling away, those eyes shining over at them.

Fuck, it felt good to laugh and Dick knew it had to be doing both Rig and Charlene a whole lot of good.

At last they were all quiet again, him and Rig catching their breath, Rock looking smug. Charlene shook her head. "You boys. Going on like teenagers. Does a heart good."

"You bring it out in us," he teased, enjoying the color in her cheeks. Momma looked pleased, relaxed, happy.

Rig smiled over, winked. "Got to give you something to lecture me on, Momma."

Rock chuckled and winked. "I probably give her plenty, Rig."

Rig pinked, chuckled. "What all are we going to do tomorrow?"

Momma grinned. "Sit, son. Sit and look at the ocean."

Rock nodded. "Excellent plan, Momma."

"I could get into a day of just playing on the beach. What about you, Rig?" Dick asked.

"I can do that." Rig nodded, "Work on my tan."

"MMmm. Yeah." He blushed as he realised where his mind was going.

Charlene cackled, clapped. "You boys be good, now. I'm fixing to go to bed."

"I'm sorry, Momma. I hope I'm not chasing you off." Oh man, he hadn't blushed this hard since he'd first come home with Rock.

"Not at all. I'm too pooped to pop." They each got a kiss. "Goodnight, boys."

Rig stood. "I'll make sure you have towels and stuff, Momma."

"Night, Momma. I'm glad you came; it's nice having you in our home."

"Sure is," agreed Rock.

"Thanks, boys." Rig helped Momma down the hall.

"Oh man," he said softly.

Rock's arms looped around him from behind. "Yeah. We'll show her a good time though, keep Rig from fretting."

He nodded. "Yeah. 'S what we're here for, right?"

"You know it." Rock grabbed him in a headlock and rubbed his head, laughing as the thick fingers got tangled in his hair. "Fuck, kid, you still need a damned haircut."

"Yeah, yeah. When I re-up I'll get it cut."

Rock snorted. "You're not re-upping, kid, not in this lifetime."

He nodded. "Yeah. I'm not going anywhere."

Not as long as Rock and Rig needed him and if he had any luck, they were going to need him for a long, long time.

***

Rig threw the balls, watching the pups run, listening to Momma and Rock chat. The sun was bright, warm, and he was leaning against Dick's knees, trying not to fidget and fret.

One of Dick's hands slid to his shoulder, squeezing gently.

"Hey, Pretty." He looked up, rolling his eyes. "Have I relaxed enough yet?"

Dick chuckled. "I don't know, you're fidgeting."

"I should go weed something or something."

"Relaxing means not going to weed. It means sitting right here and enjoying just sitting, even if it kills you."

"But..." He rolled his eyes. No weeding. No cleaning. No fucking. Blah.

"We could play Scrabble," Dick suggested.

He looked over. "Strip Scrabble?"

"Only if your Momma is really, really good at the game."

He blinked and gaped for a second, then started laughing, hard enough it hurt. Rock and Momma looked over at where he and Dick were sitting. That just made them laugh harder, both of them holding each other up.

"They're up to no good," Rock noted.

"Who? Us?" He fucking giggled. Giggled! That sent all of them laughing this time, the atmosphere comfortable and easy. Just a day on the beach.

"I got something I want to tell you, Alexander." Momma looked over, eyes serious. "I've been doing some thinking and I don't want you to have to tangle it up with Bobby after I die. So I'm giving Sissy the house and an acre and Bobby the rest of the land. You get my life insurance and the furniture that was your Granny Boulware's."

Rig sighed, shook his head, not wanting to talk about it. "Whatever you want, Momma."

Dick's hand started kneading the shoulder it was resting on, the other one rubbing his side, offering wordless strength.

"We're doing okay, Charlene," Rock told Momma. "Frankly, I think Rig's more likely to tie it up with Sissy over your photographs. Your boy knows what's important."

Rig leaned against Dick, giving Rock a smile. "You know it. I just want to make sure Daddy's tools and stuff stay in the family."

Momma nodded. "Sissy's bringing a big old trailer of stuff when she comes."

Dick chuckled. "I still can't believe Rock told Sissy to bring the kids for the summer. Not a week or two but the summer."

"Temporary insanity," Rock replied, winking.

"Well, they'll only be here a month, in total. The two oldest have band camp and cheerleading camp. So you're pretty safe through June. July, though? Lord Lord."

"We'll set the kid up as chief bodyguard and boy chaser-offer for Rachel."

"Gee, thanks, Rock. I guess that leaves dressing up the dollies and doing each other's hair with the younger ones for you."

"Hell, he'll teach them to play football and have them growling and grunting." Rig winked, chuckling at the thought. "You know, Maddie'd be good at that."

"Growling and grunting? Or tackling her sisters?" Rock asked.

"All of the above."

Momma started cackling, cheeks pink.

"A little linebacker in training, is she?" Rock grinned. "We should bring her down to the gym, Dick. Show her how to put those muscles to good use so she can grow up big and strong like her Uncle Jim."

"Oh, good Lord and butter." Rig cackled at the thought of husky little Maddie up there, pumping iron.

"Can you imagine?" Dick asked, chortling.

"I can," said Rock. "And I don't see why it's so funny. There is such a thing as women body-builders, you know."

"I think it's more that she's a little one, Jim." Momma grinned, winked.

"It's never too early," Rock insisted, shit-eating grin on his face.

"Maybe that should be our new campaign, Rock. Give a free membership to anyone who brings their under-six kids with them to work out." Dick's laughter laced his voice.

"Rug Rat Weightlifting with the Rock!" Rig cackled, head falling back, sun in his eyes.

Laughter filled the air again and Dick's mouth brushed his, a ghost of a kiss. He grinned, shifted so he was lying against Dick's legs, cheek close to that pretty cock. Dick shifted slightly, the bulge in his Pretty's jeans expanding just a little.

"When do you want to come and see the gym, Momma?" Rock asked. "We've got hot tubs -- you could sit in one for awhile, it's very relaxing."

"Hell, she could use the one here, Rock."

"Well, yeah, I guess she could."

He nodded, letting his cheek rub. "Or the sauna, at the gym. And you could get a massage."

"Oh yeah." Rock nodded. "The kid had the idea to hire up a bunch of massage therapists from the college. Work damned cheap and shit, there's this one kid with the sweetest touch. Dick, remind me and we'll make an appointment with Jason for Momma."

Dick chuckled. "You mean Joshua?"

"Yeah, whatever. The kid with the talented hands."

Rig arched an eyebrow. "You watch yourself around those talented hands, now, old man."

Rock looked just about as pleased as if he'd just given his Blue a blow-job. "I know which hands belong to who, Rig."

He nodded, settling back down. It wasn't that he was a possessive man. It was that they were his and he wasn't in the mood to share. Hadn't been for a while. Dick's hand squeezed his shoulder, his Pretty leaning in to whisper in his ear. "Joshua's straighter than an arrow and the way Rock talks about you at the gym? Everyone knows he's well and truly taken."

He pinked, nodded. "Y'all both are."

"You know it," Dick murmured, using Rock's expression.

"Yeah." He stretched out, rubbing against Dick's lap just a little.

"You don't behave Rig and I'm gonna embarass myself and your Momma." Dick's hand slid along his spine.

"I was just stretching, Pretty." He grinned, winked.

Dick laughed softly. "Is that what we're calling it now?"

He winked again, settled back down idly petting Suzie. "Are we done being lazy yet, Momma?"

"Good Lord, Alexander. You're still the busiest kid..."

Dick laughed. "You can't keep him down for long. There's always something he thinks he should be doing."

"There always is something I'm supposed to be doing."

"You and your daddy, I swear." Like Momma wasn't the busiest person he'd ever known.

"Oh, now," said Rock. "Jeremy knew when to sit back and relax. I can remember more than one evening spent sitting in front of the fire and just enjoying the quiet."

"My Jeremy enjoyed that about you, Jim. He said he could tell you knew how to work, because you knew how to rest."

"And one of the things I liked about him was that he knew a life of all work and no play wasn't much of a life." Rock looked out into the ocean. "He was a good man. Knowing you and Jeremy explains a lot about the kind of man Rig is."

He found himself a little breathless, a lot glad that he had sunglasses to slip on because soon he wouldn't have his momma anymore and that ached. It was quiet for awhile, Dick's hand hot on his back.

It was Miss Lucy who broke up the melancholy mood, dropping a dripping wet tennis ball in Dick's lap. His Pretty jumped up and chased her back down to the beach before throwing the ball into the water for her to chase down. Suzie growled low, chasing Dick and barking furiously, Mutt and Trouble damn near falling over their own ears to figure out what the trouble was.

Rock chuckled. "The dogs are gonna run him ragged."

Rig got up to join them, maybe take a swim. He'd been sitting too damn long.

"Get me a beer while you're up, Rig?" Rock asked, looking very comfortable in his new chair. "Maybe there's more of those chips left."

"Laze." He chuckled. "You want anything, Momma?"

"I'll take a beer, too."

"Don't start, Momma. You want a Coke?" He wasn't going to go there, so she'd best just stop.

"Tell you what," suggested Rock. "Bring me a Coke, too -- we'll save the beer for after the sun goes down."

He bit back his rumble and nodded. "Cokes and chips, coming up."

Rig wandered in, pouring chips in one bowl, salsa in another, grabbing two Cokes and two Dr. Peppers. Rock came in just as he was putting the salsa container in the sink. Those big hands dropped to his shoulders. "The beer thing isn't going to go away, Rig. You're both as stubborn as each other."

"She'll destroy her liver, Rock. She's got to try."

"From what I understand her liver's already destroyed and the least of her problems as the cancer spreads. Besides, I'm not the one you've got to convince."

"She's giving up." He shook his head.

"She's hurting and tired, Rabbit. Missing your Daddy." Rock sighed. "How much time is not drinking gonna buy her? How much longer is fighting gonna stretch things?"

Rig closed his eyes, bit his lips against the snarl that wanted out, against the cry that was just too close to the surface. Rock's arms went around him, just holding him.

"I'll go to the liquor store. I need to hit the grocery anyway." He needed to drive, to speed down the highway, to smoke, to go for a while.

"You need company?" Rock asked, hands working his shoulders, thumbs digging in. He damn near sobbed, trying to decide whether he needed Rock or a cigarette worse.

"Don't suppose you'll let me smoke in the Jeep?"

"No, I don't suppose I will."

He nodded. "Come with me and I'll buy you an ice cream at Twisters."

"You're on." Rock took the tray from him. "I'll take this out for Momma and Dick. Let them know we're going to make a food run."

"Cool." He turned on the cold water so he could wash his face. "Thanks, Rock."

Rock grunted. "Anytime, Rig."

He nodded. Yeah. Yeah, he knew.

Chapter Twenty Three

Rock wasn't sure why he'd gotten roped into driving Momma to a senior's event at the community center. Hell, he had a hunch Momma'd been roped into going in the first place. Charlene seemed to have learned how to just stop and sit in a way Rig still hadn't and maybe never would. He'd never even heard of senior's evenings, wasn't sure Charlene would appreciate being considered a senior, but Rig had brought it up that afternoon and Charlene had agreed to give it a try, only both Rig and the kid had been called into work and so here he was on a perfectly good Saturday night, playing chaufeur. Not that he begrudged the time to Charlene.

He pulled into a fairly busy parking lot and went around to help Charlene out and give her his arm to walk her in. His plan was to get her settled, give her the cell phone and be home in time to watch the WWF Smackdown. He opened the door for her and then followed her in.

"Surprise!" The noise was deafening, the sight of banners and balloons and tons of people -- friends, gym members, just tons, left him speechless.

"Happy birthday, Jim." Charlene's eyes were just twinkling. "Surprise."

"Well I'll be fu..." He shut his mouth before he could say it and gave her a grin and a hug. "You got me. I should have known something was up when you agreed to attend a senior's evening."

She patted his back. "I hope your next forty-five are even better."

"Well, well, if it isn't the birthday boy. How's it hanging, South?" The gravelly familiar voice made him blink again, his old Sarge standing there, big as life. He shut his mouth, figuring he had to look like a fool with it hanging open, but he was surprised. He couldn't believe Rig and the kid had pulled this off.

He gave Sarge a grin and and they hugged, pounding each other on the back. "Good to see you, Sarge. You look like life is treating you well."

"It is. Me and Jack? We've retired to Florida. Bought us a little condo on the beach, living the good life."

He chuckled. "There's something about the beach, isn't there?" He put his arm around Charlene and introduced her. "This is Rig's Momma, Charlene Roberts. Momma, this here is an old, old friend of mine, Sarge. Well, Bill, I guess."

"Good evening, Bill. We're so glad y'all could come. Have you known Jim long?"

Sarge grinned wide, the old wolf. "Yes, ma'am. Quite a while."

He chuckled. "I was still a wet behind the ears baby green when I met Sarge."

He looked around, just floored at the number of people who'd come on out for his birthday, wondering where his men had gotten to. He owed them both for this. There was a little band, table after table of food, a fucking pile of presents to the ceiling and his men, side-by-side against the back wall, watching him.

He grinned at them and pointed; I'm coming to get you. "Charlene, you don't mind if I leave you with Sarge, do you?"

"Not at all, we'll go find a place to sit." She was still talking as he started moving.

He tried to make a beeline toward his men, but he was stopped again and again by well-wishers, friends and clients. It was nice, but he couldn't help wishing he had a beer in his hand and hoping that he'd get a chance to get to the buffet tables before too long.

Helen walked up, baby in one hand, beer in another. "Doc Rigger sent me to give you this. Happy birthday."

"Bless you." He grabbed the beer, but kissed her cheek and chucked the baby's chin before taking a nice long drink. "Oh, that hits the spot."

"Good deal. You'e a popular man, Mr. Rock, and pretty well loved, it looks like."

He chuckled. "It's just Rock, Helen." He'd told her that a couple dozen times and imagined he'd have to keep telling her. "And I imagine there aren't too many people who'd say no when Dick or Rig ask them to come to a party."

"Especially when Doc does it with that look in his eyes, yeah? That 'oh, I'm fixing to do something special' look."

"Yes, ma'am." He grinned. He imagined he had a slightly different look in mind when Helen said that, but that look belonged to him and the kid.

She chuckled, "So do you feel older today than yesterday?"

Rock considered and then winked. "Not until this shindig."

Helen laughed and the baby started crying. "Oops. Feeding time. Have a fine party if I don't wander by again. Congratulations."

"Thank you, Helen." He raised his beer to her with a grin and decided to work his way toward the buffet table before he tried to find Rig or Dick again.

It seemed like dozens and dozens of people talked to him, clapping him on the back, congratulating him. After a while the lights dimmed and people were on the dance floor, the band pretty solid. That gave him a bit of a break and he heaped up a plate and held up a piece of the wall as he ate, beer on the edge of the table next to him. The food was good and he was well past hungry. He caught sight of Rig, dancing with this person and that -- hell, the bartender from Jay's, the one who'd had his eye on Rig for months, was even getting a dance.

Dick came over after he'd refilled his plate with seconds, laughing with Sarge and Jack. "Hey Rock."

He grinned at the kid. "Good one, kid."

"So you were surprised?"

"Fuck, yes."

Dick bounced. "Cool."

Sarge chuckled, grinned at Dick. "You did good, you and the Doc."

Dick grinned. "Well, we figured forty-five was a good year to celebrate and it gave us an excuse to have a great big party."

"Hell, yes. Of course, next time, you three have to come see us." Sarge winked, smiled. "My Jack? Is a chef."

He chuckled. "We just might at that. A vacation to Florida might be just the thing."

"Hell, yes. We'll go fishing. Wrestle alligators. That sort of thing."

"Sounds perfect." He and Dick laughed and he finished up his plate of food, drank down his beer. "Well I don't mean to be rude, but there's a man on the dance floor who needs a new partner."

Sarge arched an eyebrow. "You dance?"

"Hey, it's California, everybody dances. And I more sort of shuffle." He cleared his throat and took it like a man. "Yeah. I dance." He looked out onto the dance floor, finding his Rabbit. "With two men and two men alone."

"Well, go get him, then, South, before he's romanced away."

He might have bristled a bit at that, but Dick snorted. "Never happen, Rig's a one man... uh, two man man."

He grinned at the kid and winked at Sarge and moved his way through the dancers, eyes on his prize. The bartender was dancing with Rig again, making his Rabbit laugh, and a lesser man would have been jealous. Then again, a lesser man wouldn't have gotten that smile, either, full-on and happy, eyes lit up for him. "Happy birthday!"

He smiled back and gave the kid Rig was dancing with an apologetic shrug, taking Rig into his arms. "Thank you for my party."

Rig pushed right in, those grey eyes happy. "You're welcome. You were surprised?"

"Fuck yeah, I was floored." He pulled Rig in a little closer, moving slowly.

"Jack and Sarge are staying through the weekend, so y'all can visit. Thought we'd have a cookout at the house." Rig felt good, warm and close.

"That sounds great. This whole thing is great. You and the kid did an amazing job."

"Thank you. I wanted this one to be what the last one wasn't."

He rumbled a little. "Last one couldn't have compared anyway -- we couldn't have danced. I couldn't have done this." He bent and pressed his lips to Rig's. Being out had its advantages.

Rig opened to him, hand sliding around his nape, holding on, those eyes shining for him. He kissed Rig as deeply as he wanted, not caring that there'd be teasing later. Everyone knew they were together and it was his birthday. He was going to fucking kiss his lover thank you for the party.

The song ended and his Rabbit was grinning, holding him. "You rock my world." He got a playful wink.

He chuckled. "That's why they call me Rock."

Damn, this cowboy made him feel like a million bucks, like turning forty-five was just another day to celebrate instead of another year closer to fucking old.

"That's not the only reason, Blue Eyes."

He chuckled, sliding their hips together under the guise of their dancing. "No?"

"No." Rig hummed, licked his lips. "My hot fucking stud."

He purred. "You know it."

Did he say a million bucks? Fuck no, it was closer to ten million with those grey eyes looking at him like that. "So there's a private party planned for later, right? Just you me and the kid?"

"There's a hotel room rented with a big assed bed and Momma isn't expecting us home 'til late, late tomorrow."

"Oh, yeah... Would it be rude to leave now?"

"Probably, but I can be rude." Rig gave him a look. "I want to make you fly, Blue."

"Oh fuck, Rig." His cock was hard as his name, just like that. Just fucking like that. "I've said hello and thank you for coming to everyone. The only people who had to fly in we're seeing for the cook-out, right?"

"Yeah." Rig was vibrating against him, wanting.

"Then let's get the kid and get the fuck out of here."

"Momma's got Dick's keys. The guys from the gym are helping to clean up." Rig lifted his head, looking for the kid. Dick was already kissing Charlene and heading for the door.

He grinned. "Kid can read your ass from a hundred yards, Rig."

"Pretty fucking cool, isn't it? Like mind-reading but... not."

He snorted and slapped Rig's ass. "Come on, cowboy. It's time to saddle up."

"Hell yeah." Rig took his hand and practically tugged him out of the party, toward the Jeep where the kid was waiting. "We did it, Pretty. We pulled it off."

Dick laughed. "The surprise party or kidnapping Rock from his own birthday party?"

Rock snorted. "Both, kid. Now move over so I can drive."

Rig hopped into the back, laughing. "We're at the Hilton."

"No, Rig, we're at the community center -- how many drinks did you have?" He winked at his Rabbit as Dick climbed in and backed the jeep up, heading them toward the hotel.

Rig chuckled, hand rubbing his nape. He purred, driving carefully. Out or not, he didn't want to have to explain to highway patrol that he was speeding so he could get to a hotel to fuck his two lovers through the floor.

It still didn't take very long before he was pulling up to the valet parking, handing over the keys. Dick grabbed a bag, Rig pulled a card key from his wallet. "Room 848."

"Checked in and everything. Men after my own heart." He followed them, just pleased as punch that they seemed to have thought of absolutely everything.

"Hell, Blue. There's birthday cake and champagne waiting on us." The elevator closed, headed up.

He purred, gathering Rig up in his arms for a hard, happy kiss. Rig pressed close, laughing into his lips, the happiest his Rabbit had been in weeks. Fuck, it was good to hear that sound, to see those grey eyes dancing and happy. He reached out for the kid and tugged him into the kiss, making it a fucking perfect three-way.

He only let go of them when the elevator dinged, doors opening on their floor.

The room was huge -- complete with big-assed chocolate cake and champagne on ice. Of course, that was going to have to wait, as his Rabbit was kneeling in front of him, working his jeans open.

Happy fucking birthday to him.

Dick locked the door and gave him a grin, taking their bags in and then he fucking lost sight of the kid and didn't give a shit for even a second as that magic mouth wrapped around his prick. Rig gave him everything, sucking and pulling, eyes staring up at him, hands wrapped around his hips.

He slid his fingers through the almost white curls, purring, letting his Rabbit know just how fucking amazing it was. A long, sweet hum vibrated his cock, Rig leaning into his touch. Oh fuck, yeah, that was the good stuff. He started rocking his hips, nice and slow.

Everything. Rig took everything and still pulled, still sucked, still took more.

Dick's heat pressed up behind him and he purred a little louder, sharing the sound between them, his hips still working, moving faster now, harder. Rig reached back, hand sliding over Dick's hip. He pushed in deeper and deeper still, Dick's fingers pushing up beneath his shirt and tweaking his nipples, tugging on the little ring in the one.

They made him fucking roar, both of them. He came hard down Rig's throat. Rig kept up, humming around his cock, working the aftershocks. He let Dick's body support him as Rig's mouth made him shiver and shudder. Then that sweet tongue was licking him clean, Rig looking like the cat that got the cream.

"Fucking sweet," he muttered, wiping a drop of his come from the side of Rig's lips. Rig sucked his finger clean, humming, happy. He chuckled and tugged Rig on up. "Come on. Naked. Bed. Fucking. All night long."

His cock jerked with anticipation.

"Hell, yes. You have to start your year like you want to continue it." Rig started stripping.

He nodded his agreement and let the kid undress him, hindering just a bit as he tried to get the kid's clothes off, too. Rig managed to get the boots and jeans off and the sheets pulled down by the time they got naked.

Which was just about perfect because he was getting too fucking old to be tackling people unless they'd end up rolling around on the bed instead of the floor. Rig's ass was the perfect target, too. Wiggling, tight, fine as fuck. He pounced, getting Rig to go down under him, the kid right behind him.

"Oof! Neanderthal." Rig wriggled, pressing back against him.

He laughed, mouth going to Rig's neck, teasing that sweet spot. "Slut," he muttered back against Rig's skin.

Dick's laughter chased across his own skin, the kid's fingers sliding over him, over Rig.

"Yours." Rig's word was moaned, sweet slut rocking against him.

"Fucking right." He turned Rig around, wanting that mouth on his. Rig tasted like him, hot and salty and male.

"Wanna fuck you," he muttered into Rig's mouth.

"Please." Rig groaned, nodded. "Remind me, Blue. Show me why I follow your fine bod all over God's earth."

"Fuck, yes."

The kid handed him the lube and he got a couple fingers good and wet and shoved them into tight heat.

"Blue!" Rig arched, so hungry, riding his fingers.

"That's right."

Dick's fingers slid over his back, down to his ass and he pushed back into the touch, encouraging it. Rig pushed up, tongue sliding into his mouth, kissing him hard. He kissed back, pushing his fingers deep, curling them to peg that sweet little gland. Rig cried out, bucking on his fingers, eyes wide. He just kept pegging that spot, not losing it until Dick's fingers slid in and hit his, making him groan into Rig's mouth.

"Now. Deep. Hard. Please, Blue."

Purring, he split Rig's legs and settled between them, pressing his cock into the sweet, tight heat.

"Yes..." Rig arched, bore down onto him, took him deep. He sank until he was all the way in and then he stopped, waiting for the kid to catch up. He moaned, head dropping as Dick's long cock pushed slowly into him.

"So good..." Rig hummed, licking his lips.

"Fuck yes." He chased Rig's tongue with his own, groaning as that long fucking cock slid past his gland. Then they were moving, the three of them finding a rhythm together, one meant to send them to the fucking moon. Hands and lips and cocks -- they moved hard and fast, bodies slamming together. It was the best fucking thing in his life, these two men and the way they moved together and he wanted another forty-five fucking years of it.

He pushed harder, faster, driving into Rig as Dick ploughed into him and it was fucking fantastic. He came hard, pushing his breath into Rig's mouth. Rig's spunk splashed against his belly, hot and wet and just fine. Dick tumbled next, jerking hard and filling him with heat.

Fucking perfect.

Rig's hands stroked his cheek, petted him. "Happy birthday."

"Yeah," murmured Dick. "Happy, happy."

He nodded and smiled. Yep. Happy happy him.

***

Dick was playing with the dogs, keeping them occupied on the beach while Rig fussed and fiddled and did last minute jobs to get everything just so. It was actually good to see -- Rig was back to normal, smiling and dancing and fucking on Rock's birthday and then making everything clean and perfect for their guests, marinating steaks, him and his Momma in the kitchen making potato salad and pea salad and desserts out the wazoo.

Hell, Momma and Rock were sitting in the new deck chairs now, sipping on beer and Rig hadn't even blinked when Rock had brought them out, hadn't said a word to Charlene about it at all.

Dick was looking forward to getting to spend a little more time talking with Sarge and his man Jack. He figured Sarge had some great stories from when Rock was just starting out in the marines and he wanted to hear them.

The sun was shining hard, but the breeze off the ocean kept it from being oppressive. It smelled good, like salt and sweat and coconut from the sun block and a faint hint of sweet from pies.

It felt good to be alive.

The dogs suddenly veered away from him and headed for the side of the house. Sarge and Jack had to be here. Dick made his way slowly back to the deck, letting Rock and Rig greet them first. He almost laughed when he saw Sarge, dressed damned near exactly like Rock, a smaller, older version of their lover. Jack was dressed a little more colourfully, wearing bermuda shorts with a matching shirt, laughing at something Momma'd said.

Dick climbed the stairs. "Hi there."

Rock grinned and held open his arm and Dick went over to stand with him. "Sarge, Jack, you remember Dick?"

"Of course I do. You need a haircut, marine." Sarge winked as Rock laughed, hard.

He laughed. "I'm not a marine anymore."

Jack tilted his head. "I thought it went once a marine, always a marine?"

Dick nodded. "Yeah, but they can't make you shave your head once they're not actually paying you anymore."

Rig chuckled, "That explains Rock's hair. He's getting his pension."

Rock chuckled and rolled his eyes, giving Sarge a long-suffering look. "A man likes to be neat and all he gets is grief for it."

"You look fine, Rocketman. Just fine." Rig winked, admired a little. "Can I get you two a beer?"

Jack nodded and held out his bags. "I brought a few things, so if you lead the way I'll help you get them."

Rock was leading Sarge over to the new deck chairs, giving the older man his and pulling up one of the other ones. Dick sat between Sarge and Charlene, fingers sliding through Lucy's fur.

"So Florida, Sarge? You'll have to tell me all about it -- I'm afraid I got waylaid at the party so I never got back to you." Dick hid his grin. Waylaid. Well the laid part was right anyway.

Sarge chuckled. "Me and Jack threw our loads in together and bought a little condo. He works part-time at a resort cooking and I do consulting shit every now and again. It ain't fancy, but it's ours."

Momma nodded. "That's the best way to do it, Bill."

"So he's a chef, your Jack?" Rock chuckled. "I guess the way to a man's heart really is through his stomach."

Dick snorted. Oh, Rock loved Rig's cooking, but he loved the man's mouth even more.

Sarge actually pinked. "Well, I ate breakfast at his cafe every morning for damn near three years before we, uh... saw each other outside the restaurant."

"Three years?" Rock looked surprised. "Not like you not to go after what you want with both barrels blazing."

"Things change when you get older, South. Take longer."

Momma cackled, hiding her grin behind her beer. Dick bit his own lip, trying to be good in front of Rock's guest, but damn, it was hard not to rise to that bait. Rock just laughed and thumped Sarge on the back.

Jack and Rig wandered back, both holding a bunch of beer, heads together as they talked. "...if you could send me that recipe, I'd appreciate it and I'll send you the enchiladas."

Sarge smiled, "Yours cooks, too?"

"Yep. Charlene here's taught him everything she knows and we get down home cooking every night."

"Except the nights it's your turn to cook." Dick couldn't help teasing. Rock leaned past Sarge and aimed a lazy swat at him that he avoided easily.

"What about you, son? Do you cook?" Sarge took his beer from Jack with a warm smile.

Rig grinned, settled at Rock's feet. "He does."

Dick nodded as Jack settled at Sarge's feet, legs stretched out as he lay back against Sarge's leg and took a long drink. "I've learned to cook some easy favorites."

"Kid does pretty good."

Dick beamed over at Rock, pleased.

"Don't let Jim fool you, Bill. He makes the best pancakes ever." Charlene sounded dozy, a little woozy and Rig frowned, worry starting to creep in.

"You need anything, Momma?"

"I'm fine, son. Just need a little nap. I tire out so fast these days," she said apologetically.

"You want to go in or just snooze out here?"

"Maybe I'd best go in, I don't want to be rude."

"Oh, please, Mrs. Roberts, we won't mind if you drift off." Jack laughed softly. "Bill's likely to join you at some point."

Dick laughed. "Yeah, Rock, too."

Momma grinned, winked. "That's what summer cookouts are for, isn't it? Good music, beer and napping?"

He grinned and reached for the sunblock, passing it over to her before Rig could start fussing about falling asleep in the sun. Rock would no doubt put up the big umbrella over her in a bit. "Do you guys need any?" he asked Sarge and Jack. "It can feel deceptively mild with the breeze off the ocean."

Sarge held his hand out. "Jack'll need some."

Jack leaned back to smile up. "You going to put it on me? I can't reach the back..."

Man, they were a sweet couple. Dick bit back his chuckle, thinking that Sarge at least, would be a little put out at the label of sweet. He was a grade A American stud, just like Rock. Sarge rumbled softly and leaned down, whispering something to Jack that made the younger man blush. Rig chuckled, rubbed his cheek against Rock's knee.

"I figure we could go for a dip in a bit," suggested Rock. "Work up an appetite."

"Works for me. I have some new snorkels." Rig grinned. "I'm considering going to scuba school."

"You ever tried surfing?" Jack asked.

Dick nodded. "Once or twice, but I think it's a young man's game."

Rock snorted. "Says the ancient child."

"I'm not eighteen anymore."

"No, you're, god forbid, twenty-five."

He stuck his tongue out at Rock, who stuck his out back and then they were all laughing.

It wasn't long before Rock put the umbrella over Momma and Rig walked down to the water with Jack, pointing out this and that.

"So you're doing good, Sarge? Really?"

Sarge smiled. "I am. We... Well, hell, you know me. Jack is something special. Worth waiting for."

Rock grinned and smiled over at Rig and then him. "I hear you, Sarge. I certainly do." Rock sat back and rocked a bit. "What's the situation like in Florida, for a couple of old boys who are together?"

"Shit, South. Key West? The fucking gay capitol of the southeast." Sarge grinned, shook his head. "We're the conservatives."

Rock chuckled. "Must be something in the salt-water."

Dick grinned, but he was kind of facinated, too, at how Rock was less... not less Rock, but less all hard man with Sarge than with most.

"Must be. This place seems to be treating you well. The gym thing good?"

"Yeah, it's going better than we could have hoped. New businesses stand a better chance of going under than not and from everything we'd read, we knew it could be years before it started turning a profit. It's paying for itself now though, ahead of schedule." Rock nodded toward him. "Kid's got a real knack for business."

"Yeah?" Sarge gave him a nod. "That's a hell of a skill. Jack's got it in him. Me? I'm just an old dog."

Rock nodded. "I hear 'ya."

Dick snorted. "You're not old, Rock. You just like to use the card when you think it'll get you an advantage."

"Oh, ho! Someone's got your ticket, South!" The Sarge threw his head back, laughing.

Rock gave him a look, but he just grinned back, unrepentant. At least he hadn't called Rock out on his marshmallow center.

"So, Mrs. Roberts? She gonna make it?" Sarge leaned close, whispering.

Rock shook his head. "Liver cancer. She's done all the crap they wanted her to and said enough. She's got maybe a year, maybe less. Or she could go through more chemo and get a few extra pain-ridden months." Rock sighed. "Truth is, she's not willing to fight anymore and it's breaking Rig's heart."

"Oh, that's a shame." Sarge shook his head. "That cancer stuff just ain't right. Tearing people down."

Rock nodded. "Fuck yeah. Cancer, AIDS. Seems like there's a whole lot of shit that can do you in."

"No shit. I'm sorry about things. Is your cowboy's mom living here now?"

"Spending the summer. Rig's sister's coming down in July with her girls and they'll drive Charlene back with them. She wanted to spend some time with her boy, you know?"

Sarge nodded. "I hear that. Your cowboy's a good one. He and Jack have been emailing back and forth, making arrangements for the trip."

Rock chuckled and grinned over at Dick. "They sure did pull the wool over my eyes."

"Anytime you got too close, one of us... distracted you." He winked and blushed just a bit for saying something like that in front of not only Rock's Sarge but Momma as well.

Sarge and Rock laughed, Rig and Jack wandering back up to the deck. "What are y'all laughing about?"

"The kid was touting his -- what did you call it? Oh yeah -- distraction techniques as the reason the surprise party was such a surprise."

Dick groaned, cheeks heating hot hot.

Rig crowed, making Momma shift. "Oh, he's pure temptation, right enough."

Dick rode the laughter out, knowing if he let it get to him they'd just keep it up. "Of course it also proves how easily distractable Rock is." And giving what you got was the best cure to get the attention turned elsewhere.

Rock chuckled. "I will admit, I do like my distractions."

Rig chuckled. "Man, I've been downgraded to a distraction."

Rock rumbled. "Hey, I didn't make up the code."

"Nope." Rig waited until Rock was looking at him, until he had an escape path. "You'd have used smaller words."

Rock's eyes narrowed and he rumbled and then he was up and off, the two of them running along the beach.

"Should I bring out some munchies?" Dick asked as Rock tackled Rig into the water. "Or we could go swimming." Rig and Rock rolled in the surf, Rock taking Rig's mouth in a passionate kiss. Dick grinned. "Maybe munchies first and then swimming."

Jack laughed. "We'll give you a hand. Bill and I would like a tour anyway."

"Cool. Come on in."

Sarge's eyes were twinkling as they went in. "South's cowboy likes poking the bear, does he? God, I can remember him when he first got in, all muscles and temper."

"Yeah? He's mellowed a lot since we moved out here, but yeah, Rig does like to poke."

"Well, no one can be as angry as he was, son. Once he found someone..." Sarge nodded to him. "Someone to give him what he needed, he was bound to ease."

"They are made for each other," Dick noted, showing off their little beach house.

Sarge nodded at the pictures in Rig's office. Photo after photo of him, Rock. "And you're made for them, it looks like."

He nodded and smiled fondly. "Yeah. I am."

Jack slid his arm around Sarge's waist. "It's hard enough making a relationship work just one on one, you three must have something really special."

"I don't wonder about it too much, just accept it."

"Works best that way, most of the time. Thinking's bad for a man."

Dick laughed. "Is there anything you didn't teach Rock?"

Sarge grinned and winked. "Nope."

He laughed, hiding his blush by leading the way back to the kitchen and burying his face in the fridge. "Now I know Rig made all sorts of munchies for us."

"Jack brought some stuff, too. He makes this dip with green stuff in it that I like." Sarge smiled at Jack.

"Cool, you can help me figure out what's supposed to go out now then and what's supposed to go with the meal." He and Jack got stuff out onto a tray, Sarge taking charge of getting out another round of beer. By the time they got outside, Rig was sitting between Rock's legs, Rock looking smug as hell. "The dripping wet look is good on you," he teased, setting out the food on the table.

Rock just winked. Rig blushed deep, cheek rubbing Rock's knee, damp curls bobbing.

They all settled again, munching away, drinking their beer and chatting. Dick really liked Sarge and Jack -- they were easy to be with. At some point Charlene woke up and got the dominoes out, playing with Sarge while Rig and Jack got the grill started.

"Want me to do the honors tonight?" Dick asked, teasing. "Let you rest?"

Rock growled and popped him as he walked by. "I can still burn meat."

"Og burn meat. Og man." Rig thumped his chest, winking at Rock, the smile the big guy got warm and fond.

"No caveman here. It takes an expert to get it just right for everyone. Isn't that right, Charlene?"

Momma nodded. "You know it. Beef's pricey to be screwing up, too."

Rock nodded. "Yep. You can come and stand by me if you want, kid, and I'll impart some of my grilling wisdom to you."

Dick laughed. "Thanks, Rock."

Rig chuckled, but didn't say anything, letting Rock have his moment.

It didn't take long before they had the steaks cooked and everything laid out for supper. The meal went as well as the afternoon had, Rig and Jack's food both really good and Dick thought it was a shame they lived on the opposite coast, because it would have been nice to have more occasions like this one.

The wind was blowing, the pies were eaten, the mosquito candles lit and flickering. Charlene went on to bed and Rig settled in Rock's lap, easy as you please. Dick was safely seated with Sarge and Jack between him and Rig, so he ventured the question he'd been dying to ask all day. "So have you got any stories about Rock?"

Rock growled, but Sarge just chuckled. "What kind of stories? I have tons -- he's the best battle buddy I ever had and started in at the corps with a chip on his shoulder."

"How did you meet?" No sense in not going after the question that he was most curious about first. He figured Rock would put an end to this soon enough.

Sarge looked over at Rock. "You were in training, if I recall. Got an Article 15 for fighting and that put him in my sights pulling CQ duty from dusk to dawn."

"Oh, I bet he hated that."

Rock nodded. "Almost more than I hated KP duty."

Sarge chuckled. "You did fine once we got settled, South."

"Once we got settled?" Dick asked, looking from Sarge to Rock and back again.

Sarge looked at Rock, not saying a word. Rock cleared his throat. "You remember how I brought you home, kid?" Dick nodded, eyes widening as he put two and two together. "Sarge here showed this old man the ropes back when I was still wet behind the ears. Sort of a gay tradition that I continued."

Sarge nodded. "Not that you needed a whole lot of showing, South. You were eager for those ropes."

Rock chuckled. "I do like my ropes."

Dick laughed. "Oh, I'm going to remind you of that one of these days..."

Rig grinned. "Hey now, Rock's got himself a fine, fine rope."

Rock laughed. "Any way you take that it's the truth."

They all chuckled, Sarge's hand on Jack's neck.

"You have anything embarassing to share?"

"Kid..."

"Hush, Rock, I'm never going to get another chance like this."

"Now, son, what would you want South to say if I asked him the same?" Sarge gave Rock a smile, a nod.

Dick grinned. "I don't know, I don't think I'm all that different now from the baby green Rock brought home."

Rig tiled his head, looking over. "I don't know. I sure didn't think we'd come to need you like we did."

"Oh..." Damn, Rig could make him just melt. "Thanks," he said softly.

Rig nodded, smiled at him, grey eyes happy.

Rock chuckled. "Oh, with that look on his face, he wouldn't care if I started telling embarassing stories."

Rig smiled a little longer. "Y'all interested in a moonlight swim?"

"Oh, that sounds nice," answered Jack, turning to look up at Bill. "Romantic."

Sarge pinked, but nodded, holding Jack's eyes. "I could manage that."

Rock chuckled. "I guess you can teach an old dog new tricks."

"Don't make me beat you to death, South."

"I'm not sure you could, Sir." Rock winked.

"Only because I'm outnumbered."

"Yep." Rock chuckled. "I tell you what you can do though -- if you and Jack are in town a little longer you should come see the gym. Try a few things out."

"I'd like to see your set-up. You remember lifting at Gregory gym on those old rusty things?"

Rock nodded. "Fuck yes. It was better than nothing though. Our place is a little nicer."

Rig grinned and stood. "The gym's fabulous. Come on, Rocketman, Pretty. Let's go play in the water."

"We skinny dipping?" Dick asked.

Jack chuckled. "Oh, I don't think I can compete."

Sarge rumbled softly and Dick just heard the whispered assurance that Jack didn't have a thing to worry about.

"Well then, let's go." Jack stood and took Sarge's hand and they all headed down to the water.

Rig leaned into Rock's arms, hand holding his, looking out. "Wow, look at that moon."

"It's almost too bright to skinny dip," Dick noted.

Jack laughed. "Oh, no, if I'm dropping trou here you all are."

"Like you two have anything to worry about." Rig rolled his eyes, grinned.

Dick grinned right back. "Hey, this is Rock's old *Sarge*. A man's gotta keep up."

Rig looked over at Jack and winked. "They don't know how hard it is, do they? Living with the marine studs."

"I don't know, Rigger, it's us they're with -- I'd say we're doing something right." Jack looked happy, almost peaceful.

"Of course they are. Have you seen them try to cope without me?" Rig winked and ducked Rock's swat.

Dick started stripping. "You don't need help, do you Rig? Rock?"

Rock snorted and started taking off his clothes, too. Rig undid his cutoffs and tshirt, heading right into the water.

"Your cowboy modest, South?"

"Yep. Seems to think he can't compete. I keep telling him he doesn't even need to try."

Dick grinned and went splashing in after Rig, pouncing him into the water. Talk was cheap. Rig laughed, splashing him back, body brushing right up against him. He and Rig played, Jack paddling near them as Rock and Sarge went past, swimming out aways.

"Is the ocean warmer for y'all, Jack?"

"Than this? Yeah, some, but this is nice." Jack smiled.

"Yeah, I love it here." They got deep enough that Rig could rest in his arms.

Jack nodded. "I can see why. Wouldn't give up our little place, though it would be nice to have more old friends like yourselves around for Bill."

"Yeah. Rock's damned fond of him."

Jack nodded. "He keeps tabs on most of his 'boys' but I think Rock, of all of them, feels most like a friend or son. Or some weird cross between the two."

Dick just listened to the two of them chatting, holding Rig as the waves gently buffeted against them. He kept one eye out for Rock and Sarge, their skin bright in the moonlight, not because he didn't think they could swim out as far as they were, but just in case.

Rig nodded. "Rock puts a lot of store in what Sarge thinks."

"I get the feeling he doesn't listen to too many folks like that."

"He listens to more people than you'd think. He's a careful man, my Rock."

"I didn't mean that as an insult, Rigger."

"Oh, I know." Rig grinned over. "He's a strong-willed one. Learned well from yours."

Jack laughed. "Well we certainly all admire our men, don't we?" The older man gave them a wink. "Of course they aren't perfect."

"No? Are you sure?" Rig leaned up, licked his jaw. Dick nuzzled, letting his hands wander beneath the cover of the water.

"Pretty sure, yes." Jack was still laughing softly, eyes dancing.

"Mmm... I'll have to think on that one." Dick just laughed and goosed Rig. So like their cowboy not to admit that there was even one thing about Rock that drove him nuts. "Hey, my men are stunning." Rig grinned. "They take care of my skinny ass."

"This skinny ass?" he asked, whispering into Rig's ear as he slid his hands over it.

"They are stunning, Rigger. Though I bet you take care of them as much as they take care of you." Jack gave them a wink.

"I just love them." Rig turned, rubbed against him, eyes shining. "Do I take care of you?"

"Yeah. Every minute of every day." His hand slid down and cupped Rig's ass.

Rig hummed, scooted in. "Blue okay out there?"

He nodded. "Yeah. They're headed back now. Two white asses popping up every now and then like dolphins."

"Ah, they've turned back," murmured Jack. He came and put a hand on each of their shoulders, squeezing. "I'm going to head in and find the bathroom."

"Don't let us run you in, Jack." Rig smiled, slid away.

"Oh, you're not. I really do need the head."

"'kay. We'll let Sarge know." Rig floated right back into his hands.

"Thanks."

Dick wrapped his hands back around Rig, bringing their mouths together and taking a soft kiss. Rig moaned, legs wrapping around him. He glanced out, gauging how long it would take Rock and Sarge to get back. Probably a little longer than it took them to swim out, they were moving a little slower. He brought one hand up to tug at Rig's nipple ring, the other squeezing Rig's ass.

"Yes..." Rig groaned, cock hard and hot against his belly.

He moaned. "Wanted to touch you all day long."

"Uh-huh. Love having folks, but I need, Pretty."

"Yeah." He slid his hand down Rig's belly and wrapped their cocks together, tugging slowly, thumb sliding past the tips.

"Oh..." Rig dove into their kiss, tongue fucking his lips.

He whimpered into Rig's mouth, starting to suck on that moving tongue, hand pumping faster and faster. Rig's hands were hard on his shoulders, squeezing as they moved. The waves moved against them, slower than his stroking, and soft. Another whimper and he pumped harder, squeezing their cocks tightly together.

He felt Rig's cry more than heard it, heat just barely hitting his fingers before it was washed away. A shiver went down his spine and Rig's orgasm triggered his, balls emptying into the ocean.

"Oh. Oh, that was... Mmm..." Rig nuzzled, panting.

"Yeah, just right." He licked at Rig's jaw and those slightly swollen lips and tugged on Rig's lower lip with his own.

He heard Sarge's chuckle. "You're right. They are insatiable."

He was glad for the darkness to cover his blush as Rock's laughter answered Sarge's chuckles.

"My sluts," Rock murmured, voice fond.

Rig nodded, smiled over. "Jack's in the house, Sarge. He said to tell you."

Rock clapped Sarge on the back as they came to stand near him and Rig. "He's a good man, Sarge, I'm happy you found someone to settle down with."

"Yeah, he is. I think I'll keep him."

Rock chuckled. "Good. Because you can't have mine."

"No? You won't share? Damn, South. I might teach your boys a thing or two." Rock got a wink, Sarge moving toward the shore, chuckling.

Rock laughed. "I don't think you could teach the kid anything he hasn't already looked up with his computer."

Dick blushed and grinned, buried his face in Rig's neck.

Rig leaned, laughing softly. "You have a good swim, Blue?"

"I did. It's real nice to see Sarge again. I wasn't exactly out with most of the old corps buddies, you know?"

Rig nodded, holding his arms out to draw Rock closer to them. "I know."

Rock wrapped a hand around his and Rig's heads and pulled them in for a long, three way kiss. "Come on, we've still got guests and I'm turning into a fucking prune."

"Prunes can fuck?" Dick asked.

"Nope, they can't, kid, and that's why we've got to get out of the water before it's too late."

Rig was laughing, heading for the shore, long body almost glowing in the moonlight.

"You coming, kid?"

"I just did."

Rock groaned. "Leave the funny to the experts."

Laughing, Dick headed out of the water, following his lovers, like always.

Chapter Twenty Four

Rig stood in the front room, staring Momma down.

"I'm going home, Alexander."

"Like hell you are. You're not fucking flying, Momma." Four days he'd listened to her hack and cough. Four days until he gave up and dragged her kicking and screaming to the clinic where they found out she had pneumonia. Then three days in the fucking hospital on antibiotics, her bitching non-stop the entire time and now?

She wanted to fucking go home.

He was going to kill something.

The front door opened and closed, the dogs going to greet Rock and Dick, barking like crazy, unnerved by their arguing.

"Hey," said Rock.

"Hey," added Dick. "Everything okay?"

"I'm going home." Momma was all teary. "Jim, I want you to get me to the airport."

Rig slammed his hand on the sofa, just seeing red. God damn it. He could have lost her. Here. Over her fucking stubbornness. "You are not flying, damn it! You are not well."

Rock looked trapped and unhappy, but Dick came forward and gave his shoulder a squeeze and then went and knelt before Momma in her chair, taking her hand. "Momma, did we do something wrong?"

"I want to go home. He treated me like a child. I didn't want to go into the hosptial." The tears were real now and it was all he could do to keep from growling.

"But Momma you were sick. Pneumonia. You need to go to the hospital when something like that's got a hold of you."

"I didn't want to go. He didn't listen to me."

"You weren't being sensible, Momma."

"Are you calling me crazy, Alexander?"

"Not yet."

"Oh, for fuck's sake." Rock growled and strode into the room. "Quit acting like a baby, Charlene and he'll stop treating you like one. You're sick and your son the doctor says you need the hospital, then you fucking well go. And if he says you can't fucking travel, then you can't. You think he *wants* to make you miserable?"

Momma stared up at Rock, completely shocked, mouth open.

Rock just stood there with his hands on his hips. "You wouldn't put up with this from one of your own, Charlene. You know I'm right."

"I'm going to bed." She stood up, sniffling, looking pale and old but twenty times better than she had two days ago.

Rig sighed as she pushed past him. "I love you, Momma."

"Goodnight Alexander." The guest room door slammed shut.

Rock sighed and wrapped him in those strong arms. Dick just knelt where he was, looking almost as shocked as Momma had. He was vibrating and he leaned into Rock's strength, looking up into those blue eyes, holding on.

Rock held him close, big hand sliding soothingly down his back. "She's almost as stubborn as you."

"Almost." Rig nodded. "I did the right thing."

"You did."

"Yeah." Dick stood and came to hold him from the back. "She won't stay mad forever, Rig."

"I know. I'm just frustrated as fuck." He leaned, closing his eyes. "We gotta get away for a night."

"Tonight?" Rock sounded surprised.

"No. No. I can't leave her. But soon, yeah?"

Rock nodded. "I didn't think you'd go tonight, 's why you surprised me."

Dick licked at his neck. "You want to wait until Sissy and the girls get here? We could spend a whole weekend somewhere. Oh! We got some mail at the gym for this spa -- they want us to put out their flyers. I was thinking when she was feeling better, Momma might like to spend a few days."

"That works. I just... It's hard, you know? Christ, we haven't ever had company this long. I'm getting tired of not being naked."

That had Dick giggling and Rock snorted. "Don't laugh, kid. The man has a fucking point. And hell, once Sissy and the kids get here we're going to have to lock the fucking bedroom door."

"And make sure the curtains are down. Sissy's a curious old bitch." He relaxed, grinning a little.

Rock chuckled. "And here I was worried about little ones barelling in without knocking."

"That too." He sighed, grinned. "They're not so little anymore, either."

Rock nodded. "There's some questions I just don't want to answer."

Dick snorted. "Oh yeah."

Rig nodded. "I'm not even wanting to deal with the 'where do babies come from' talk."

Rock chuckled. "Oh, that one's easy, Rabbit. 'I don't know, I'm gay -- go talk to your momma'."

"You can't say that!"

"Why the hell not, kid?"

"I don't know -- you just can't."

"I could. No sweat." Rig nodded. "Cause you *know* Sissy's setting us up for it."

"You think?" Dick asked.

"Oh fuck, yes," murmured Rock. "Hell, she'll get one of them to ask just because, even if they already know the answer."

"Yep. Out of sheer meanness." Rig took a deep breath. "Can y'all imagine if we had to deal with three families?"

"Fuck that shit." Rock shook his head.

"Well they're not all like Rig's," Dick teased.

"Thank God for small favors. Good lord..." Rig shuddered.

"Okay, okay. If we're finished discussing our families and the fact they're all fucking nuts in their own way, can we go fuck our brains out?" His Blue could always be counted on to get to the heart of things.

"Fuck, yes. Bedroom. Now." He nodded, pushing.

Rock's arm went around his shoulders, Dick's around his waist and they headed down the hall to their bedroom, Rock closing the door firmly behind him, as if locking out all their problems and worries. He started unbuttoning his shirt, not even bothering to play coy. He needed. He needed now.

His men followed suit, each taking care of their own and joining on the bed by silent agreement. It felt fabulous, legs and arms twining together, his hands finding two strong necks and pulling them in for a kiss. Three tongues, three pairs of lips, there was nothing like it.

The heat built slowly, hands sliding on skin as the kisses went on and on. He needed this. He knew it, but it wasn't until now, when he was not able to have it whenever he wanted that it hit him. He was spoiled. Lucky.

Blessed.

Rock's tongue kept fucking his mouth as Dick slid down his body, working his nipples. Rig floated, touched, giving back as much as he got. Rock's big hands slid on his skin, finding the places that made him moan, made him ache. Moaning, whimpering, he twisted, body moving toward the touches, moving away, wanting the pleasure to last and last.

"What do you want, Rabbit?" Rock asked, voice low and needy.

"Y'all. Oh, fuck, I want y'all." He dove into another kiss, damn near whimpering.

Rock chuckled. "Well you've kind of got us, Rig. I was just thinking in particular."

"Thinking? I'm not doing something right if you're thinking, Blue."

Dick laughed. "His prick's not in your mouth or up your ass. Then he wouldn't be able to think."

He chuckled, slid down, until he had two hard cocks within sucking distance. "I can fix that."

Rock purred. "Gonna take us both?"

"Mm-hmm..." He helped Dick shift over, lips parting to cover the heads of their cocks. Their groans slid down along his spine, fingers tickling on his skin. Yes. He moaned, tongue sliding, tasting them both, salt and male and good.

Dick's sweet sounds started up right away, Rock's moans underlying them. He opened wide, moaning, hips rocking into the sheets as they slid over his tongue. The sounds became muffled, his men kissing each other as they moved in tandem, his Pretty pushing in as his Blue pulled out.

Fuck, they were hot. Sweet. Strong. His. Fucking hell. All his.

They started moving faster, faster, their sounds getting louder, more desperate. He moaned, sucking harder, pulling at them. Hungry.

"Oh fuck, Rig!" Dick's cry pressaged the splash of liquid down the back of his throat. He drank Dick down, panting, fingers pulling Rock in deep. Dick's prick slid away and Rock started fucking his mouth hard. He cried out, nose buried in Rock's curls.

Dick's mouth suddenly slid around his cock, his Pretty taking him deep. He jerked, so close, right fucking there. Dick sucked hard, lips sliding on his prick as his slid on Rock's. He could feel his Blue's cock swell, hitting the back of his throat as Rock roared and came.

That flavor sent him over the edge, sobbing and pumping into Dick's mouth, entire body on fucking fire. Dick sucked him down, mouth gentling same as his on Rock's prick.

Then his men were flanking him, wrapping around him like a living breathing blanket. "Good. Needed."

"Thought so," murmured Rock, hands warm and solid on his skin. He cuddled in, snuggling, the exhaustion from the last few days catching him.

Rock's snores sounded about the same time Dick's hand slid into his. His fingers twined with Pretty's. "Mmm..."

"Love you," whispered Dick, lips soft on his earlobe.

"Yes. Yes, Pretty." He cuddled into Dick, eyes already closed, already sinking.

***

Rock woke up first, something that happened very rarely. All right, practically never. He liked his sleep in the mornings and he didn't like facing his day without his morning blow. He was on a mission this morning, though, to get up before Rig did and talk to Momma, who had Rig's own habit of being up at the crack of dawn.

It had been ugly yesterday; fuck, it had been been ugly for longer than that. It was easy to see where Rig got that stubborn streak that just wouldn't quit. But stubborn or not, things were going to change. He didn't mind having Charlene here; he'd even fought for her right to have beer and not to have Rig hassle her about not going for anymore chemo, but enough was enough and if she wasn't going to let Rig take care of her when she so obviously needed it? Well, hell, he'd drive her back to Texas himself.

He pulled on a pair of jeans and a t-shirt and padded out to the kitchen, pouring himself a cup of coffee and heading onto the deck. Sure enough, Charlene was sitting and watching the waves.

"Morning," he grunted, joining her.

He got a surprised look. "You're up early."

"My house is unsettled."

"I've offered to go home, Jim. I don't want to be a bother."

"Now, Charlene, lets not play that game. You know very well I don't want you to leave, you know Rig doesn't want you to leave. And he's doing damned well with the accepting you not fighting the cancer anymore, if you ask me. You can't expect him to just sit back and let you ignore every other ailment that sets you low." He took a mouthful of coffee. He hated this kind of shit at the best of times, but first thing in the morning without his coffee in him? He was turning into a masochist in his old age. "Is that really how you wanted to go out, Charlene? With months and months of good days left, letting something like pneumonia just knock you out for the count? Because if it is, maybe you should go home -- I'm not letting you put that kind of guilt on your boy."

"I just hate that he treated me like a child, Jim. All the damned poking and prodding and..." She sighed, coughing a little bit as she got riled up. "I'm scared, Jim. Real scared."

Rock sighed and took her hand, giving her something to hold onto. "You didn't give him a chance to treat you as anything but a child, Charlene. He begged you to go into the clinic on your own. And maybe it's not me you should be telling how scared you are, but him. Because I can tell you that he's fucking scared, too. He loves the hell out of you, Charlene. He doesn't want to lose you."

"I'm his momma, Jim. I hate to see him hurting. I hate that I'm the cause of it. I should've died of something quick, like Jeremy."

Rock snorted. "I don't know, there's something to be said for having time to say the things you need to say." Like it hadn't hurt Rig like hell when his father had died.

"I suppose." She sighed and squeezed his hand. "I keep looking at the ocean and thinking how pretty it is. It suits y'all."

He chuckled and gave her a wink. "Because we're all so pretty."

"Oh, yes, just darling." He got a smile, warm and natural. "I'm sorry for disrupting your house, Jim."

"No apologies needed on that account, Charlene." He squeezed her hand. He wasn't the one hurting and upset.

"You figure Alexander would like some homemade biscuits for breakfast?"

"I thought we could drive down the coast, eat out, just take it easy, Momma." Rig's voice was husky, low, his Rabbit looking tired himself.

Rock nodded. "Oh, I wouldn't say no to a little steak and eggs special. You can make Rig those homemade biscuits next week when that cough stops dogging you."

Rig gave him a smile. "I was thinking that Magnolia House down south. The one with the good coffee?"

"Oh, you'll like Magnolia House, Charlene. It's got a real Southern feel to it -- they know how to treat their guests right."

Dick came out then, yawning. "What's everyone doing up so early?"

Rock snorted. By everyone the kid meant him. "Just enjoying the morning."

Rig gave Dick a smile, hand stroking his wrist. "We're talking about taking a drive, going for breakfast. You wanna?"

"Yeah, okay. If everyone's feeling up for it." That was their Dick -- kid hated tension and fighting.

"Jim offered steak and eggs, Richard, and a nice drive. I'd like that. Alexander? Do you have a minute?" Charlene nodded and stood, taking Rig's hand and leading him into the house, closing the door behind her.

Dick took her seat, eyes a touch worried. "Everything okay?"

He nodded. "Should be. I imagine they're just sorting things out between them. We should be good to go in a few minutes."

"Oh, good."

"Yep, except for one thing."

"What's that, Rock?"

"We're leaving in a few minutes and I still haven't had my morning blow."

Oh, the kid's laughter was almost worth being up that early.

Chapter Twenty Five

It was Dick's night to cook, but he'd gotten held up at the bank on the way home, so he grabbed a variety of subs and a big fruit salad on his way home, along with a pint of ice cream so Rock wouldn't bitch.

Everyone was out back on the deck, Rig's Momma looking better than she had in a while.

"Hey, sorry I'm late. I picked up supper on the way."

"Yeah? What did we get?" Rig was stretched out under the last of the sun, still damp from the ocean.

"Subs. I got a bunch of different ones, so hopefully there's something for everyone." He gave Lucy some loving, petted Mutt and Trouble on the head and gave Suzie a quick back scratch and then dropped kisses on Rock and Rig's heads, Momma's cheek and put the subs on the table. "Damn lines at the bank get longer every time I go in there it seems like."

Rig stood up, hands rubbing his shoulders. "Someone needs a beer, Rocketman."

Rock nodded. "Yep, I do."

Dick laughed, relaxing into Rig's touches.

"Oh, you mean I should go get it?" Rock winked and stood. "We allowed to eat off the wrappers or am I supposed to bring plates out, too?"

"Just grab some forks, we'll be fine, yeah Momma?" Rig's hands kept working, kept rubbing.

"That's fine. Can you bring me a bottle of water, Jim?"

"Sure thing, Charlene."

Dick smiled. Things had eased between Rig and his Momma since the blowout; it was obvious they were both trying to see the other's point of view.

Sissy and the girls would be out in a couple of weeks, their little house filled to bursting. Rock had bought three tents -- two little ones and a huge one, so people could sleep on their beach. "Oh, there's ice cream in there -- it ought to get into the freezer before it melts."

"I've got it," grunted Rock, handing out their drinks and dumping the forks on the table. "Fruit salad? What the fuck is this?"

Dick laughed. "That's why there's ice cream, too."

"Fruit is good for you, Jim." Momma grabbed a fork and speared a piece of pineapple.

Rig? Did a good job of not laughing. Him? Not so much. Of course that meant he got the whap and Rig got away scott free, despite the twinkling eyes.

"I got two vegetarian subs, too. Thought you might like one of those, Rock."

"I'll have the steak ones. Because I know you bought me steak ones, kid."

"Maybe Momma wanted those. Or Rig."

"I want the avocado and hummus." Rig pounced, grabbed the veggie sandwich and the salt, happy as he could be.

He grinned and poked through the others. "Momma, I've got a chicken one here."

"Oh, that sounds good. Although I might just make do with the fruit. It tastes so good."

He nodded. "It's all fresh and tastes amazing here, doesn't it? You get used to it, but I remember me and Rig exclaiming an awful lot the first while."

Rock snorted, snagging two of the steak subs. "Fruit is fruit."

"So observant, our Rock. And concise, too." Rig chuckled, stole a bit of steak from the end of Rock's sandwich.

Rock groused good-naturedly and Dick settled back, eating his own chicken first, so if Rig wanted to steal more steak there'd be some left in his second sandwich. The waves were relaxing, washing the last of the annoyances of the day away. Momma was going to town on the fruit and he was glad he'd gotten the extra large. He bet it would make Rig happy, too, to see her appetite back.

Rig ate half his sandwich, then picked at the insides of the second half, sharing the bread with the dogs, little Suzie begging for the tomato.

"Gonna give her the farts you let her eat that," Rock warned.

"You think? At least she needs an excuse..."

Rock laughed, totally uninsulted, while he and Charlene chuckled.

"So have we got plans for the weekend?"

Rig nodded, grinned. "Momma's going to visit an old friend in Oakland. We're going to a fair."

"A fair? Cool!" Oh man, he hoped Momma didn't think he was all excited just because it meant a couple days just the three of them. Because it wasn't just that.

"Yeah, Rock found a hotel for Friday and Saturday night and we'll pick Momma up Sunday afternoon." Rig looked just as excited.

"Yep. I'm going to win everyone some stuffed fluffy things." Rock looked pleased.

Momma chuckled and nodded. "Oh, that reminds me, I need to give y'all some money for groceries. Those grandbabies of mine eat ten tons a day."

Dick waited two heartbeats and there was Rock, right on cue, voice gruff. "I think we can manage to buy groceries, Momma. You save your money for spoiling them."

Rig nodded. "We'll buy some hot dogs and burgers, simple stuff. Make Uncle Jimmy grill."

Rock nodded. "I grill, that means I don't have to clean."

"Aren't they old enough to pick up after themselves now?" Dick asked, laughing.

"Maybe we ought to get a couple briskets, too, baby. We can all eat on those a while."

Rig nodded to his momma. "We'll figure it out, Momma. Honest."

"You're supposed to be on vacation," Dick reminded her softly. "You know, relaxing? Letting us do the work."

Momma snorted. "I've been relaxing for weeks, Richard."

"Yeah, and it looks good on you." He winked at her.

She pinked, patting her head, the short-short stubble pure white. "I'm not going to win Miss Texas."

"I don't know, Charlene, there's something sexy about a high and tight cut." Rock waggled his eyebrows at her.

The pink went a dark red, but Momma's giggle was girlish, pleased. "James South!"

Rock just looked smug and Dick grinned. Rock liked to pretend Dick was the one with the people skills, but Rock could charm anyone, man, woman or child, no matter their age, when he set his mind to it.

Rig grinned, looking so pleased, just beaming back at them. "You want some ice cream, Momma?"

"You should, Charlene -- the kid bought me the good stuff to make up for all that fruit. Chocolate chocolate chocolate."

Dick grinned. "You've probably noticed, I mean you've known him longer than I have, that Rock's a little partial to chocolate."

"No... Jim? Never." Momma grinned. "And did you get some cherry for Alexander?"

He shook his head. "Last I looked there was still some in the freezer." Only Rock went through it like it was going out of style.

Rig grinned. "Because you know, cherry? So safe from Rock."

"You got that right." They all laughed.

Rig headed toward the kitchen, stopping to whisper in his ear. "You're the last cherry Rock hunted, Pretty."

He felt the heat spread through him and Rock's eyebrow lifted. Rig blew air, sweet and soft, then headed in. He watched that perfect ass as it walked away, biting back his moan.

Momma shook her head. "I wish he could see himself the way y'all look at him."

Dick felt his cheeks get impossibly hotter, knowing he had his heart, and probably his prick, out on his sleeve.

"He is who he is," answered Rock.

"Ain't that the truth." Momma chuckled. "That boy? Was born who he is."

He and Rock chuckled. "Yeah. He's one of a kind."

"He's ours, kid."

Dick nodded.

"No. He's mine. Y'all are late-comers."

They laughed, but Rock growled a little. "Now don't make me call you out, Charlene. I'm not giving him up."

She chuckled. "You'd fight his own momma for him?"

"You know it," Rock said softly.

"Good. That's why I let you have him." Momma's voice was serious as a heart attack.

"Yes, Ma'am." Rock was just as serious.

Momma's eyes suddenly filled and she stood. "I'm fixin' to walk the dogs down the beach a ways. Save my ice cream. I'll be just a minute."

"You want me to come with you?" he asked.

"Nope. I just need a walk." She stood and headed out, whistling up the dogs.

"S'okay, kid." Rock told him quietly. "She'll be all right."

He sighed. This was a fucked up situation. It sucked that she was dying like this, just sucked.

Rig came out with four bowls, frowning when he didn't see Momma. "She okay? Decide to take a walk to make room for dessert?"

"Yeah, she's fine, Rig." Rock took his bowl, digging in.

Rig handed him his bowl and set Momma's aside, settling between them. "Thanks for supper, Pretty.

He leaned over for a kiss. "You're welcome. Sorry it wasn't homemade."

Rock snorted. "Suck up."

Rig gave him a real kiss, deep and hot, happy and flavored with cherries. He moaned softly, grinning over at Rock when the kiss broke. "Yep. And I'm going to do it some more."

"Do what, Pretty." Rig's eyes were on his mouth, hot and needy.

"Suck..."

"Up," Rock finished for him.

"Uh-huh. You say tomay-to, I say tomah-to."

"You don't either. We all say tomato like normal people. I want y'all. Is it bedtime yet?"

He giggled and licked at Rig's lips.

"Nope," answered Rock. "Your Momma's looking pretty healthy tonight. I bet she's got a Stallone double header in her."

Rig groaned, hand sliding on his thigh. "You think? Y'all could be tired..."

Dick nodded. "It wouldn't even be a stretch, I am."

"So we're all tired all of a sudden?" Rock asked.

"Nope. Just me and Rig. You can keep her company."

"Oh, you're mean, Pretty." Rig's hands started rubbing his shoulders, their cowboy moving to straddle his lap.

"I'm being nice to your Momma, letting her have the pick of the crop to keep her company." Dick fought his smile and buried his face against Rig's chest. "Don't let him hurt me too badly."

"I'll protect you from the big bad marine, Pretty."

He giggled and Rock snorted. "Save it. I'm going to let you get away with it. But you both owe me. Big."

Rig looked over at Rock, eyes hot. "I'll suck you until you forget your own name, Blue."

Rock growled softly. "Works for me. Kid?"

"I'll suck you every night at bedtime until Sissy and the kids leave."

"Excellent. Get lost."

Rig stood, hand held back to him. "Come on, we go now? We don't have to explain."

He nodded. "For all the sucking Rock's just been promised, having to do the explaining is a small thing."

Rock grinned at them. "I'm just going to let her draw her own conclusions."

"But she's gonna think..."

"The truth, kid." Rock winked and laughed.

Dick rolled his eyes, stopped to give Rock a kiss and then grabbed Rig's hand and headed inside. Rig scooted him down the hall, hands on his ass, lips on his shoulder. Half-laughing, half-moaning, he hurried his steps and turned, closing the door, as soon as they got to the bedroom.

His lips covered Rig's, the kiss more desperate than he'd intended. How long had it been since it was just him and Rig? The three of them were fucking good together, but he was used to early morning make-out sessions with Rig and later morning fuckings alone with Rock. Both had to be sacrificed when they had guests.

Rig opened wide, hands sliding around his shoulders and holding on. With a whimper, he pushed Rig up against the door, rocking against his lover, rubbing their middles together.

"Oh. Pretty. Want." Rig worked his pants open, fingers searching for his cock. He nodded, moaned and slid his lips to Rig's neck and started sucking and nibbling. His own hands were tugging at Rig's button's, trying to open Rig's shirt.

Rig started pumping and pulling, fingers hot and right on his cock, soft little gasps filling the air. Oh, fuck, he was gonna come before they even got this party started. Of course he had great faith in Rig's abilities to get him back up, so that was just fine. Moaning and whimpering, he pumped his hips into Rig's hand, his fingers finally finding skin and sliding over it.

"Mmm... yeah. Come on. Let's get the edge off and then we'll play." Rig's tongue slid over his skin, thumb sliding over his slit. He cried out, pumping harder, fingers tugging on Rig's nipple ring.

"Fuck." Rig groaned, bucked against him, teeth just brushing his neck. He cried out again, muffling the sound on Rig's shoulder as he shot. "Oh. Bed. Fuck, Pretty, I want to touch."

He nodded, taking another kiss first and then backing up, eyes on Rig as he stripped out of his clothes, letting them drop where he stood. Rig stepped out of his swimming trunks then went to sit on the bed, arms open to him. He slid into Rig's arms, bringing their mouths together.

Rig pulled them down, bodies rocking and sliding, Rig hard on his belly. He closed his eyes and just concentrated on feeling, on the sensations of their skin sliding, their cocks bumping, fingers working. Rig's kisses left him breathless and shaking, hands holding on tight. They rocked together, so hot, so close.

"Want you to fuck me," he murmured, lips sliding along Rig's jaw.

Rig nodded, hand sliding to cup his ass. "Yeah. Need you."

"Uh-huh." He reached up under the pillows, finding the tube shoved way up out of the way and brought it down, pressing it into Rig's hand. Rig purred, spreading his thighs, bending to lick at his belly as two slick fingers pressed inside him. So different from Rock's fingers, thinner, but a little more agile, stretching him and hitting his gland. He cried out, hands going behind his knees to hold himself open.

"Mmm... my Pretty. So fucking fine." Rig nuzzled and rubbed, eyes closed.

He whimpered, hands dropping to Rig's head, sliding through the almost white curls. "So good, Rig.""

"Yeah." Rig nodded, fingers moving slow and easy, rubbing over his gland again and again.

His legs shifted restlessly, body writhing on Rig's fingers.

"Mmm... gonna take my time, Pretty. Haven't been able to linger." Rig's tongue slid over the tip of his cock. He jerked, hips trying to encourage that tongue, that mouth on his prick. Oh, he was going to die from pleasure.

Rig hummed, lips sliding just over the tip and sucking, pulling so softly. He could feel it all the way to his toes and his balls pulled up tight against his skin, need making him ache. Rig groaned, rocking sweet and slow, cock rubbing against his leg.

"You feel amazing," he muttered, words almost coming from someone else as he sank into the pleasure Rig was pulling out of him.

"Mmm... You ready for me, Pretty? I'm needin'."

"Fuck yes. I've been ready from the start." He pulled his legs apart again, tilting his hips, offering Rig his hole

Rig pushed up, groaning low as that heavy cock pushed right in, filling him. He moaned, legs sliding to lock around Rig's waist, tugging him in deeper. Rig's lips slid over his, tongue slipping in to taste, to lick, those thin hips pushing, fucking him. He met the thrusts, met Rig's tongue, hands coming up to hold onto the skinny body he loved more than anything except Rock.

"Fuck. So good."

He nodded, grunted some sort of agreement, too far gone for words. There were only the sounds he made when his men were blowing his mind, whimpers and moans and gasps as Rig pressed into him over and over again. Rig's fingers found his cock, pulling hard.

He pushed their mouths together to muffle his scream, body bucking at Rig's touch. He didn't want it to end, but he was barelling down toward the finish. Rig's eyes were dark, sharp, watching him, hips slapping against him. He watched them, watched as the world slowly turned the color of those eyes, pleasure making him shake, making him shoot.

Heat filled him, Rig cuddling down against him before the aftershocks even faded. His legs slid away, resting on the bed as he held Rig, hand stroking, petting.

"Mmm... My Pretty." Rig's lips ghosted against his jaw.

"Yeah, yours." He took a deep breath and let it out slowly, feeling lazy and sleepy and good right down to his bones. It was worth giving Rock blowjobs for the next six weeks. Hell, he was looking forward to paying off his debt.

He didn't go to sleep, didn't want to just yet, instead he just touched Rig, enjoyed being with his lover.

"Mmm... been missing you. Missing this." Rig hummed, petting him.

He nodded. "Nice as it is to have your Momma here, it kind of cramps our style a bit, doesn't it?" He chuckled. "Fuck, we're spoiled."

"We are." Rig kissed his chin. "We earned it."

He nuzzled Rig and found his lover's hand, nodding. "Yeah."

Rig slipped from him, got a towel and cleaned them both up before settling again, fingers drawing circles on his belly. He closed his eyes and let his own hand play over Rig's body, just enjoying the peace and the quiet and them while he could.

Chapter Twenty Six

"Uncle 'lex! Where's Ma-maw?"

Rig grinned and rolled his eyes, looking over at Rock and whispering. "Hiding in her room with the door locked."

Shit, Sissy and the crew had been in for two days and Momma was looking ragged. Of course, Sissy had come in looking that way -- ragged and unhappy and bitchy as hell. She was currently sleeping on the sofa in his office, hiding away herself.

"She's got the idea," Rock muttered. "Tell you what, lets bribe the kid to walk them down the beach to that ice cream stand and back and go do our bunny imitations."

"Ooh... Good plan. Uncle Richard? Could you walk your nieces down to Twisters? They need ice cream."

"Ice cream!" Maddie squealed.

"Walk them? All the way to Twisters?" Dick frowned. "Oh, you guys are going to owe me, big."

Rock dug out his wallet and handed over two twenties. "Take your time. Eat there before heading back."

"Big. Big. Big." Dick took the money. "Maddie get your sisters and the dog leashes and wait for me in the back." Once she'd gone, Dick turned back to them. "Big."

Rock grinned and grabbed his crotch. "Don't worry, kid. I'm big."

"I'm talented." Rig grinned. "And I'll make strawberry pie for supper."

"Okay, I'll take 'em." Dick took a deep breath, shook his head and went out, the sounds of the girls fighting and yelling and the dogs barking soon fading as they headed up the beach.

"You think he's pissed, Blue?" He watched them go, feeling a touch guilty.

"He'll take it out in trade -- he'll be fine." Those blue eyes were locked onto him.

He shivered, one hand sliding down Rock's belly. "Blue..."

"We've got a lock on our door, Rabbit. I suggest we get there and use it before one of the ladies comes out to see why it's gotten so quiet."

"Fuck, yes. Yes. Now." He grabbed Rock's hand and pulled. You didn't have to tell him twice.

They hustled down the hall, locking the door behind them and coming together like it had been a month of Sundays. Damn, this was getting to be a familiar scene. Rig damn near crawled up Rock's body, hips jerking, rubbing against the amazing fucking six-pack. Rock purred, hands helping him get his feet locked around Rock's back before working on their t-shirts, not even breaking the kiss to get them off.

Rock's shorts were pulled off, his ripped off and then he was pressed up against the wall, Rock humping against him, fingers finding his ass and teasing along his crack. He nodded, groaning and rocking, diving into the kiss.

Shit, he needed this, needed Blue.

Now.

As if Rock heard his thoughts, one thick finger pushed into him, opening him. Their eyes met, grey meeting blue, his cry lost in Rock's lips. Rock's tongue fucked his mouth as one finger became two, stretching him for that fat prick. He begged the best way he knew how, not holding anything back. Rock didn't take his time, those fingers splitting him open quickly and then disappearing, Rock tilting him to spear him with that hot cock.

"Yes. Blue. Fuck. I need." His eyes rolled, hips bearing down.

Rock pushed into him with a groan. "Rig..."

And then his Blue was fucking him, each thrust going deep, hitting his back against the wall. His heels dug into Rock's ass, tugging them tighter together. Rock's growls filled his mouth, that cock starting to nail his gland over and over again.

Rig shuddered, belly tight and hard. "Fuck. More."

"Always," growled Rock, pushing harder, mouth finding his again so that tongue could fuck his mouth.

He was flying, aching, needing it, needing Blue so bad, and Rock just gave it to him, over and over, pounding into him, cockhead sliding past his gland, making him shake with it. He arched, bucked, fighting his cry with all he was worth. Rock's mouth closed over his again, the thrusts getting harder.

Fuck. Fuck. Blue. Yes. He groaned, clenching down on Rock's prick, shooting hard. Rock's roar was fed into his mouth, heat pulsing into him.

Rig whimpered, panted, room spinning. Rock straightened and carried him to the bed, putting him down and following with a chuckle when he wouldn't loosen his legs and let go.

"Not yet. Stay." He wasn't ready to let go yet.

"Are you kidding? The girls are gone and the door is locked, I'm not going anywhere."

"Oh, good." He squeezed Rock's prick, moaning low.

A shudder went through his Blue. "Fuck, you make me need."

"Yeah." He knew exactly what Rock meant, the hunger, the ache. Rock purred, tongue sliding on his neck, along his collarbone and then back to tease the sweetspot. He kept squeezing and shifting, chin lifted, moans filling the air. Eventually Rock started thrusting again, long, slow pushes as that mouth explored his skin.

Oh. He moaned, rocking into the thrusts, entire focus on the pleasure inside him. Rock rumbled, moving like he was going to do this the rest of the day. His hands slid over Rock's shoulders, stroking, petting, just flying. Rock's mouth found his nipple, tongue sliding through the ring and tugging.

"Oh. Blue. Fuck." Electricity zipped through him, nipple to cock, making him arch.

"That's what we're doing, Rabbit." He got a wink and then Rock went back to playing his nipples. He almost chuckled, almost because he was real busy bucking and rubbing and holding.

On and on, Rock licked and nipped and sucked, cock moving, always moving inside him.

"My Blue. Oh. Oh, I... Blue." He was babbling, petting Rock's shoulders, damn near flying.

"Right here, Rig. Right fucking here."

"Yes..." His hissed the word, body going stiff as a board, spunk spraying. Rock made a noise that was almost a whimper, head resting on his shoulder as one more thrust filled him and then heat pushed inside him.

He took a soft, slow kiss, melted and happy down deep.

Rock rumbled, lying on him, heavy, solid, cock slowly softening inside him. He petted Rock's temple, Rock's face, just loving. He got another rumble, Rock's breathing slowing, his Blue drifting off.

He waited until Rock was well and truly asleep, then slid out to play Uncle Alex and help Dick. Nearly a month before they were just them again. Much as he loved his Momma and Sissy and the girls? It couldn't come soon enough.

***

Rock roared and chased Lisa into the water, enjoying the squeals as she ran to Uncle Richard to save her. He enjoyed this game, being the monster and chasing the girls around. It let him get a little of his aggression out. Made him wonder how they survived every year they went to visit Texas, except there they had the garage and the kids weren't there full time.

He was gonna have to talk to Rig about having a room built on top of his workshop so they had somewhere to escape to next time around. Not that it was that bad, but damn, five girls were loud and fucking curiuos and a man coudln't just tackle his lovers anytime he felt like it.

He roared and chased Rachel, grabbing her when she wouldn't run and tossing her in.

"Uncle Jimmy!" She squealed and splashed water at him. "When are we going to a beach with boys?"

Rig chuckled. "Hey, we're boys!"

"Nuh-uh! Y'all are old guys!"

Rock sputtered, but the girl was right. He was fucking old, especially when compared with these little she-devils running around. "Young guys don't buy you ice cream," he reminded her, winking at Dick.

Her eyes twinkled. "I don't want the boys to buy ice cream, Uncle Jimmy..."

"Rachel Diane! You watch your mouth right now!" Julie came over, looking tired and bitchy as anything.

Rock chuckled. "You think boys are gonna buy you anything with me and your uncle Richard standing as chaperones, Rachel?" He gave her a wink and put his arm around Rig's sister. "Lets take a walk, Julie."

She nodded, shooting a look at Rachel as they passed. "You watch your sisters."

"You enjoying our beach, Julie?" He asked after they'd walked a bit, put some space between them and the girls.

"Yeah." She nodded, eyes fastened on the sand.

He snorted. "Yeah, about as much as I enjoy my visits to the proctologist."

"I thought you liked those..." Those eyes so much like his Rabbit's flashed up at him, unhappy, scared, worried.

"Only if you're brother is the doc in question." He nudged her shoulder. "Quit stalling and start talking."

"You gotta promise not to tell, Jimmy." Her hand slid into his, shaking.

"That depends on who I'm not telling, Sissy."

"I haven't told anybody. Nobody at all." She sighed, squeezed his hand. "I... I'm pregnant, Jim."

He almost congratulated her, then remembered Momma saying Hank had gone back to Arkansas in the early spring to work. He squeezed her hand back. "I take it Hank's not..."

"No. No, I... There's a guy from when I was in school. He... me and Hank aren't... Oh, shit, Jim. I just wanted somebody to tell me I was pretty, to not be pissed off or dying or whining or wanting supper, you know?"

He shook his head, gave her a quick hug. "You weren't using condoms?"

He was so not the person she should have confessed to. The kid would know what to say, what to do.

"We did. I mean, he says we did. I was real drunk and I don't... Shit. Shit, Jim. I'm in trouble. I'm in real trouble and I don't know what to do." Tear-filled grey eyes looked up at him. "I... I don't know what I'm going to do."

"Okay, Julie. Having hysterics isn't going to help you. A lady's tears send big strong men like me running, you know that." He waited until she gave him a watery smile and then gave her a serious look. "And then we go find Rig, and we take another walk and you tell him." He held up his hand. "Look, you stick with me, my first question is do you want to keep the baby or not -- if you don't, we see Rig and he helps you find a doctor. If the answer is you do, we see Rig and he helps you find a doctor."

"He's gonna yell at me, Jim. He'll tell Momma. I... I don't want him to be ashamed of me." Julie's free hand rubbed her belly. "I... I don't think I can... I mean, it's a baby, Jim. It's not its fault that I'm a fuck up."

"Okay, first of all, he's not going to tell Momma, he's going to make you do that. And if you're going to keep the baby, you're going to have to start telling people. And we all fuck up, Julie. Even me."

"Hank's gonna leave me. I can't... what if he takes my girls? And Momma? What..." Oh, sweet fuck. He needed Rig before the real sobbing started.

Thank God for cell phones. He got Rig on the first ring. "Blue?"

"I'm about a quarter mile south of our place on the beach, Rig. Haul ass, but be casual about it."

"No sweat. Give me five." Good man. Rig knew when to follow orders.

Julie sat at the edge of the water, tears running down her face. He went over and crouched behind her, patting her shoulder. "Rig's on his way." He squeezed gently. "You know we won't turn our backs on you, Julie. Anything you need."

It didn't take any time before Rig was there, frowning, worrying. "Hey y'all. What's up?"

Julie sobbed, buried her face in her hands.

"Rocketman?"

"Julie?" He gave her the chance to be the one to tell Rig.

She shook her head, cried harder, and Rig was right there, holding her, looking to him for answers. Damn it. He growled. There was more than one reason he didn't do women. "She's pregnant."

Rig's eyes went wide and he could see it as Rig figured it out. Those grey eyes closed, but Rig just held her closer, rocked her. "Oh, Sissy. Oh, girl. It's okay. It's okay. Don't make yourself sick, now. We're here."

"Oh, Bubba... what am I gonna do?" Julie sobbed, clinging, and Rig sighed.

"Well, first? No more beer. No more smokes. And prenatal vitamins."

He chuckled. "Oh, now I see why you really didn't want him to know."

She reached out and popped him, then drew him close, too. "Oh, y'all... Tell me you don't hate me."

"Shit, Sissy. You're family. I love you." Rig patted her shoulder. "Does Hank know?"

"Not yet."

"Momma?"

"No."

"How far along?"

"Six weeks, tops. Maybe less."

Rock just held them both. Letting Rig do his thing, thanking god he didn't have to deal with this on his own.

"You... you wanting to stay with Hank, Sissy?"

Julie shook her head. "Can you imagine? My Hank? Raising another man's child?"

"Well... what about its daddy?" Rig was trying to be so careful.

"He's married, Bubba. He... He says I'll have to prove it's his."

"Lord."

Rock growled. "Give me a name Julie and I'll make sure he doesn't do this to anyone ever again." A man could still support a family without his balls.

"You know it. Rat bastard better learn not to screw over my family." Rig was just as fierce, rumbling.

Julie laughed a little, sniffling. "Y'all are good to me."

"Like Rig said, you're family."

Rig nodded, then looked at Julie. "You gotta tell Hank. He... he's a good man, Julie. I know y'all haven't been happy, but... you have to tell him."

"Would you..."

Rig shook his head. "No. No, ma'am. I'll stand by you 'til the end of time, but I won't."

Rock nodded. "It's done and you've got to take responsibility and that starts with telling the people you need to tell yourself."

"What about Momma?"

Rig winced. "Let's not say anything until you have yourself a plan, Sissy. Something solid."

Rock nodded. "Good call. And we'll tell the kid."

Rig met his eyes. "Yeah..." Julie shook her head and Rig gave her a look. "He's family, Sissy, and he'll be able to help. He's got a way about him. A way of seeing stuff."

"And he'll know something's up. He can smell a mood a mile away. The only reason he's not here right now is someone's got to watch the girls."

Rig nodded. "I won't lie to him, Julie. Not for you, not for Momma."

"Okay. Okay. I... Do I wait to tell Hank 'til I see him?"

"And when is that going to be, Julie? You want to wait until the man can tell just by looking at you? Come on, I know you're a smart woman, start using your head. This isn't the end of the fucking world. No one's dead."

"So, I'm supposed to call him? Hey, I've fucked around with Noah Swan, remember him? He's a dentist? And I'm having his baby!"

Rig handed her his phone. "Yes."

"We can give you some privacy," Rock offered, standing.

Rig nodded, "You tell him and we'll wander."

He put his arm around Rig and started walking.

Rig shook his head, sighed. "Good Lord and butter, Blue Eyes. What the fuck else is gonna happen?"

"I don't think that's the kind of question you want to be asking." He took a quick kiss.

"No. No, I don't guess." Rig shook his head. "Didn't shit used to be simpler?"

He considered a moment, remembering visiting Rig in the hospital, those grey eyes almost shut they were swollen so bad. "No. No, I don't think it was."

"No?" Rig smiled a little leaned toward him. "Well, so long as I got you next to me? I'm okay."

He chuckled and gave Rig another kiss. "I'm not going anywhere, Rabbit."

"I'm counting on that." Rig shook his head. "Hank'll leave her. It was close to that anyway and the man's got his pride."

"From what your Momma was saying he was as good as gone when he left for that spread in Arkansas." He shook his head. "I can't believe she's going to have another mouth to feed."

"I can't believe she..." Rig shook his head. "What if she's got something, Blue? What if the baby does? Christ."

"Don't start, Rig. You get her into the clinic, you get all the tests run you want, but don't start worrying on stuff you don't know about."

"Worrying is part of the job description."

"I know." He turned Rig and looped both arms over his cowboy's shoulders, looking into those grey eyes. "We're going to be there for her, Rig. But this is her baby, her responsibility. No making yourself sick over it."

Rig nodded. "I don't know, Blue. She's got a hard row to hoe."

"I'm not saying we're not going to help her out. I'm saying you aren't her husband or her keeper." He wasn't letting this take over Rig's life. Rig had a life.

"No. No, I'm not." Rig sighed. "Momma's gonna shit a pink twinkie."

"Yep, I imagine she will." He shook his head. "What a fucking mess."

"Yeah. I... How's Sissy gonna take care of Momma, now? I mean, You heard what they told us at the hospital. Six months to a year. Shit. And Sissy having to support six kids? Shit."

"Not to mention what's going to happen is your Momma's gonna wind up taking care of the kids." He shook his head again. He loved Rig's family, had taken them on as his own. He was not living with them. He couldn't. "You think she'd be willing to stay out here instead of going back? She's looked like hell ever since Sissy and the girls showed up, they take it out of her." He held up his hands. "I don't mean with us, not unless we build a little inlaws suite on the other side of your workroom or something where we have a locked door between us."

Rig sighed. "We do that and Sissy'll come. You know she won't stay in town with Bobby and them looking at her."

"I'm not having that brood in my house, Rig. I will help out as much as I can, hell, we can help with rent until she finds herself something and Hank starts paying child support. I do not want to suddenly be playing Daddy to her kids. Hell, Rig, I don't want to be playing Daddy to my *own*, which is why I don't have any." He grinned suddenly. "Well that and I fuck guys. Seriously though Rig, they are not moving in with us. It's not happening. I'm a gay man, I have to worry about AIDS and the fucking courts honoring my will when I die and wasn't married to my men. I'm forty five years old, I served my country and served it well, I'm working fucking hard on making a goddamned second career work. I won't do it. I'm sorry."

He figured he'd just screwed his morning blow jobs for at least the length of Sissy's pregnancy, but damnit, living with them all for a week had more than proved there was no way he could do it for any length of time.

Rig looked at him for a long time, eyes still and quiet. Then, to his utter shock, Rig pushed into his arms, pressing close. "Thank God."

He wrapped his arms around Rig automatically. "Really?"

"Oh, fuck, Blue. I love them, I do, but I miss us. I miss our life. I want everybody to go home."

He chuckled. "And here I thought I was about to get grumped at." Relief went through him that Rig felt the same way.

Rig shook his head. "I was scared you were gonna offer to move them in."

"Fuck, no." Not unless he had a labotomy or something. "I'm a selfish old bastard, Rig. I want my peace and my quiet, my football and my men. I want to come home and have a beer and a steak and a blow."

Rig nodded. "I love them, I do, but... this is our life. Ours." That amazing fucking mouth was offered to him.

He growled. "Fucking right. We've built it. We've fucking earned it."

He took Rig's mouth, took that offered kiss and gave one in return. Rig melted against him, tongue fucking his lips, hands holding his head. He slid his hands along Rig's back and down to that fine ass, more than a little tempted to just forget where they were.

Rig moaned, just a little, and it felt surprisingly sweet, knowing Rig wasn't pissed. He squeezed Rig's ass, letting the kiss continue but not pushing it further. Rig relaxed, resting against him, the kiss long and lazy. He purred softly, one hand coming up to slide through those curls.

"Christ, you two are like fuck-starved jackrabbits."

Rig went a little stiff, arched an eyebrow. "You're really not in a place to throw stones."

"Not to mention this is the first quiet moment we've had since you and those hooligans of yours showed up, Julie." He nodded at the phone. "How did Hank take it?"

She shook her head, rubbing her forehead. "He wants... he wants custody of the girls. He's got a lady, he says, who he's been seeing. Doesn't want them watching Momma die. Doesn't want them with me."

Rock folded his arms. "And what do you want?"

Looked like Julie hadn't been the only one stepping out on the marriage.

"I... Those are my girls. I... Christ, I haven't worked in fourteen years. How can I support them?"

"You study, get your license back. There's work in nursing homes everywhere, Sissy." Rig hugged her.

"How am I supposed to take care of Momma, then?"

Rig sighed, "Well, she's leaving you the house. The place is paid off... I... I guess I could take some time off, come and help for the last few months..."

"No." They'd work something out, but not that. "She can come out here. Hell, you all can. You sell that house and put it toward something out here it would be way cheaper than renting. We'd be close to help out. You get that fucking son of a bitch you married to pay his share for the kids and you'll manage."

"But..."

"You heard the man, Sissy." Rig's hand slid in his, held on. "I'm not crossing Rock on this."

"You've got our support, Julie, we'll do what we can to help, but we have a life of our own and there is only so far I will let you push into it. Now Rig and I were talking about an addition. An inlaw suite or something where Momma could live with us with none of us feeling cramped. There's houses in the community here that you could afford if you got a decent price for Momma's place. Nothing on the beach, but close enough to us you won't be on your own."

Hell, maybe Momma wouldn't even want to come out here, though if Julie and the girls were, he imagined she'd want to come, too. "We figure it out and then we talk to her. We should bring the kid in on this, he's good at this sort of shit."

Rig nodded. "This is his place, too. He deserves to worry with me."

"How much time you need to decide exactly what you want to do, Julie? The sooner this gets cleared up the sooner we can work toward making whatever it is happen." He fell back on his training. Problem. Solution. Implement solution.

"I... first things first. I gotta find out if he can really take my girls..."

Rig nodded. "Let me call Holly, she's a good friend of mine."

Rock nodded. "All right, that's number one. Let's get moving."

Rig nodded, got on the horn as they headed back towards the house, arranging things like a master.

Fucking shit, he knew that Sissy and the kids coming to visit was going to be disruptive, he'd had no idea just how disruptive. He put his arm around Rig's shoulders as his lover got off the phone. He wasn't letting go of his men.

***

Dick was champing at the bit, just on edge. Rock and Sissy had gone off and Rig had followed. And they'd been gone awhile. When they got back? The three of them were putting on a good show, but he knew his lovers, knew something was wrong. Maybe even something big.

He had to wait until Momma had escaped to her bedroom and the kids were in watching a movie before he had a chance to do something about it. Sissy was about to excuse herself, but he cleared his throat and shook his head. "I need to talk to Rig and Rock."

Rig and Rock shared a long look and nodded. "Bedroom or beach, Dick?"

"Lets go out to the beach." They could get a little further away out there, be sure they weren't interupted.

Rig stood, grabbed three beers from the fridge, Rock right behind, the two of them focused as hell. Frankly, it was scaring the shit out of him. He followed them, breathing in the salt air, sand cool underfoot now that the sun was going down. "So? What the fuck is going on?"

Rig's hand slid in his. "Sissy's gone and got herself knocked up, Pretty. A dentist there in Flats. A guy she went to school with. Momma doesn't know."

"Oh, fuck."

"Yep, that's about it," agreed Rock.

Rig squeezed his fingers. "We were just waiting until Momma and the kids went to bed to talk to you about it. What a mess."

"Wow, I'll say." He shook his head. Man. Thank God, he didn't ever have to worry about that kind of thing. "What's she going to do? Her and Hank were having troubles as it was."

Rig sighed. "Hank wants the girls. He's got himself a woman."

Dick snorted. "What makes him think he's going to get the girls?"

"Money, mainly. He's got a steady job, has for years, but that's not the big thing." Rig sighed. "Fact is? Rachel and Lisa? Are old enough to decide where they're going to live."

"You think they'd rather live with their Dad?" Dick shook his head. "God, your Momma's gonna have a heart attack when she finds out."

"No shit." Rig rubbed his forehead. "This whole thing's a clusterfuck of epic proportions."

"Oh man." He sat down on the sand hard, head spinning. "Well first thing we need to do is get her to talk to a lawyer. And then a doctor if she hasn't already seen one. Rachel and Lisa need to be told before the others, find out what they think about it, who they want to live with. You know they could move out here -- it wouldn't be fair to Sissy or Momma to throw them together with a baby on the way and no outside help."

Rig's hands landed on his shoulders, rubbing hard. "She's got an appointment to talk to Holly Grayson at nine tomorrow morning and Dr. Allison at noon."

"Oh, that feels nice. So you're on top of this. Good. Man." Shit, he hoped they weren't all going to stay 'til Sissy had the baby. "Are they... are we?" Damn, he was a selfish prick, worried about how it was going to affect him.

"No, Pretty. No. I can't. This is our house. If Momma wants to come out here, I'll find her a little apartment. If Momma and Sissy stay in Texas I... Well, I don't know what I'll do."

Relief went through him. "Oh, good. I mean." He gave them a wry smile. "I mean good."

Rock nodded. "Yeah, kid. We all kind of feel that way."

Rig squeezed his shoulders. "Yeah. It's not our bed to lie in. I'll help but... Well, you know."

"You okay?" he asked Rig, figuring Rig was probably stressing it almost as much as Julie had to be.

"No, but I'll live." Rig's chin settled on the top of his head.

He leaned into Rig, smiling as Rock sat behing Rig, arms coming around them both. "When is she gonna tell Momma?"

"I don't know. When she's got a plan, I guess?" Rig shrugged. "And she's forty, there's a chance that there'll be problems..."

"Man, this is messed up."

"Yeah." Rig sighed, leaning against him. "I don't know what we're going to do."

"We're going to help her as much as we can and pray."

Rock nodded. "I keep telling him this isn't our responsibility and we can't take it from her."

Rig nodded. "Right. We have our own shit to deal with."

"We've got shit?" There was more?

"Well, the gym, the clinic, the fact that I'm not getting my daily recommended dose of man."

"Oh. Normal shit." He grinned. "I thought you meant other shit."

"Normal shit is enough, Pretty." Rig chuckled. "More than enough."

"I kind of like the normal shit," he admitted.

"Yeah, kid. Me too." A soft sigh sounded. "I'm tired of the chaos."

He turned and wrapped himself around Rig. "Yeah. And it just seems to keep building, doesn't it?"

Rock's arms wrapped around them both. "Just a few weeks more, men. And then we can walk naked in the hall and belch to our fucking hearts' content."

"Amen, Rocketman. A-fucking-men."

"Speaking of fucking... God, I want you guys. I want to fuck and suck and play strip poker and truth or dare and just... screw our brains out."

Rig nodded. "I'm sorry. I shouldn't have brought them all here. I just... She's my momma and I wanted to spend some time before the end."

He squeezed Rig. "Of course you did. You don't need to apologize!"

Rock grunted. "Kid's right."

Rig leaned against him, cheek hot against his jaw. He rubbed his hands on Rig, stroking, glad of the growing shadows. They rested together, the three of them, staring out at the ocean together.

"This is nice," he murmured.

Rock chuckled. "A little quiet before the storm."

"Yeah. Just a little." Rig grinned against his shoulder.

"We could just stay out here until they all go to bed," Dick suggested, hand sliding on Rig's thigh.

"Works for me. Or we could sneak around the side of the house, go right to the bedroom."

"I feel guilty," he admitted.

"Yeah. Look, why don't y'all go to bed, I'll deal with kids and Sissy. It's only fair."

"How is that fair?"

"Well, they all belong to me, yeah?"

"Yeah, but we're in this with you."

"Kid's right. We're a team."

"Team Rocketman?" Rig's chuckle was low, sexy, honest.

He giggled, leaned into them.

"Who gets to be quarterback?" Rig licked his ear, humming happily.

"I do." Rock sounded very sure.

"I'll warm the bench. Among other things."

"Oh, Pretty..." Rig nuzzled, licked. "Nobody'd leave you on the bench."

"I was kind of hoping you'd join me," he murmured.

"Mmm..." One of Rig's hands found his belly, started petting. His muscles jumped under Rig's touches.

"Feels good," he whispered, realising he missed this as well, maybe even more, the random touches and cuddling, holding.

"Yeah. Yeah. I'm spoiled." Rig rubbed between them, humming and happy.

They didn't take it further than that, just rubbed and touched, shared kisses between them as they enjoyed the breeze off the ocean and the sound of the waves.

***

Rig sat on the floor, staring at Momma. "What?"

"I'm not moving here. Not under any scenario. I've lived in that house for forty years. I'm going to die there."

After Sissy had gone to the lawyers and the doctors, they'd all sat down together and told Momma. Momma hadn't reacted well -- at all, taking to the guest room for three days without talking or screaming or anything. Then tonight, after the kids were all out camping outside the back door? She'd come to sit, explaining that she was going home.

"But Momma..." Sissy reached out one hand and Momma glared.

"Don't you but Momma me. You're forty years old, Julia Dawn. You know what causes babies."

Rock snorted, but otherwise kept silent and Dick was just sitting there, staring back and forth between them like he was at a tennis match.

"So, what? We go back to Flats and?" Sissy was growling a little, cheeks red.

"And you find a goddamn job. You sell that little house you got and move into the house and talk to your Aunt Patty about babysitting after school while you're working and pray to God I don't up and die before you get your shit together."

Rig sighed, reached out for Momma's hand. "Momma, I'd build you your own place. I would."

"I have my own place, baby." Those unhappy eyes caught his. "Jeremy Alexander, you listen to me. Y'all have worked and sacrificed and given up and you've made a home here. It's a good place, but it's not mine."

"But it is ours," Rock said quietly. "And we're not coming to Texas. None of us. Not for more than visits."

Momma's eyes met Rock's, dead-on. "I wouldn't ask and Julia won't either, if she knows what's good for her. Y'all didn't sign up to help raise babies. This isn't your cross to bear."

"God damn it, Momma! Quit acting all holier than thou! I fucked up. It happens. Hell, I came home to take care of you, didn't I?"

"Did you? Or did you come home to give you and Hank the excuses you needed to split up and neither one of you feel bad about it?"

Dick made a soft noise, his Pretty looking distressed as fuck. "Is this helping? It's a shitty situation from any angle and we just need to figure out what everyone needs and what's the best way of making sure everyone gets what they need and what they want."

"I'm going home. Julia can do what she wants, but I'm going back home."

He shook his head. "Momma, you're going to need help, in the end."

Rock reached out and took her hand. "I wish you'd reconsider, Charlene."

Momma squeezed Rock's hand. "You know I love you like you were my own, Jim. You take care of my boy; he takes things hard."

Rig dropped his head into his hands, just torn up. It was hell on earth, because, as much as he wanted to take care of her, part of him was happy that they weren't staying, were giving them their lives back and damn, didn't that make him an asshole of epic proportions? Rock's hand dropped onto his shoulders, squeezing and massaging. Dick's hand landed on his spine, caressing his lower back.

"Well I can't say I'm happy that's the decision you've made, Charlene, but it's your decision."

"It's the right one. Y'all are dear, but you'd regret losing your privacy and resent it."

"I wouldn't resent you, Momma. What are you going to do when it gets close? When Sissy's as big as a house?"

Momma smiled, winked at him. "Cope, that's what the good Lord put us on Earth to do."

Rock chuckled. "You're a woman after my own heart, Charlene, I'll give you that."

"I just want to die in my own house. Now, boys, can you keep an eye on the girls? Julia and I are going to take a drive."

Sissy blinked up. "But Momma..."

"Now."

Rock nodded. "I imagine we can keep an ear and eye out for anyone out of bed."

Rig nodded. "We'll open the back door and listen, Momma. You... you want me to come with?"

Momma shook her head. "No. This is between me and Julia right now."

Rock and Dick's hands stayed on him, touching and soothing.

"I'm not a little girl, Momma. You're going to have to stop giving orders sometime." Still, Sissy got her purse, her keys.

"Now, Julia. We need to talk." Momma stood, pointed toward the door and suddenly he was eight years old again.

"Wow," whispered Dick. "She's good at that."

"Yeah. She's all momma." Rig nodded, eyes filling with tears. "I need a good stiff drink."

"I'll get it." His Pretty got up and got three tumblers, filling two with a couple fingers of whiskey and one with coke. Two beers were pulled out of the fridge and opened, set in front of him and Rock along with the whiskey. He nodded his thanks and tossed the whiskey back, wincing at the burn before he chased it away with the beer.

He'd wanted a simple, peaceful visit.

He'd wanted.

Oh, fuck. He wanted another whiskey.

Rock had his own whiskey and a growl and then gave the kid a look. "I'm going to take Rig into the bedroom and fuck him through the mattress. You got a problem with that?"

Dick smiled and shook his head. "My only problem is I can't join you."

He reached out, fingers brushing Dick's. "Soon, yeah?"

Dick nodded and bent to kiss him. "I'm sorry, Rig."

"Yeah. Me too and the weird thing is? I can't figure out why."

"Well I'm sorry it's not the visit we were all hoping for. You especially. This was supposed to be us showing off our new home, not... soap opera central."

Rock snorted. "Drama keeps Rig from being bored."

He reached out and popped Rock's butt. "I was getting used to being bored."

Rock chuckled and stood, taking his hand. "Come on, Rabbit. I want that ass."

"Romantic." He stood up, just a little wobbly. God, he was getting to be a lightweight.

"You want romance, you hitched your wagon to the wrong man."

"I know what I need, Blue." They headed down the hall. "I do."

"I got what you need right here." Rock's eyes were hot, making him promises.

"Always." They hit the bedroom, shut the door. "Shit, Blue. This is all a mess."

"It'll sort itself out, Rig." Rock's fingers worked off his clothes.

"Yeah? You think?" He helped shrug his shirt off, unbuckled his belt.

"It always does." Fingertips slid across the top of his prick as Rock undid the button on his jeans and worked his zipper down. He smiled, reaching out to touch his Blue. Sometimes? The man just saw things right.

Rock purred for him, the sound low and wanton. "Get me naked, Rig.'

Rig nodded, working Rock's shirt loose and off and then undoing the worn denim shorts. When they were both naked Rock picked him up and carried him over to the bed. They started touching, those thick fingers sliding on him. He closed his eyes, mouth moving on Rock's skin, letting himself get lost in flavors and textures and smells.

Rock growled softly, the sound pleased. Thick fingers plucked at his nipples and stroked his belly, tugged on his cock. Oh. Yeah. He'd needed. He moaned low, lips tracing Rock's jaw.

"Want you," Rock told him, hands spreading his legs wide.

"I'm yours." He nodded, pulled his legs back.

"Yes." Rock reached under the pillows at his head, lips pressing against his, the kiss heated, good. It was easy as pie, just opening right up, letting Rock ease him.

Rock's tongue slid into his mouth, taking everything he offered, fingers sliding down his body to find his hole. Thick and hot and slick, one teased its way into him and then out, another pushing in and out and then Rock's thumb sliding all the way in.

He sighed, pleasure filling him down deep. He rode Rock's fingers, moving nice and slow, moaning and gasping. Rock kept switching them out, thumb, index finger, middle finger, middle and index, thumb, middle and index, stretching and playing, hitting his gland randomly. Groaning, he spread wider, trying to get more, find a rhythm, find something he could settle into.

Rock played a little longer, had him just about ready to tell him to just fucking do it already before three fingers slid in deep and started a solid, easy rhythm.

"Oh. Yeah." He wrapped his hands around Rock's shoulders and held on, hips moving sure and steady.

Rock growled softly, teeth nipping at his bottom lip, tongue sliding along it to soothe any hurt.

"My Blue..." His eyes rolled, so hot, so right.

"Yeah, Rabbit."

Rock's voice was all growl and need, his fingers moving harder, faster.

"Oh. Oh, Rock. I... Oh, sweet fuck, I need you." His body was on fire, fucking burning.

Rock's fingers slid away, the heat of that fat prick pushing against him a moment later. Oh, yeah. There. Right there. He groaned and arched, pushing down onto that thick heat, taking Rock in.

"Fucking perfect," groaned Rock, pushing until he was deeply seated. "Could stay right here for fucking ever."

Rig nodded, focusing on touching that hot skin, on feeling Rock inside him. Rock stayed still, right where he was until they were both panting with need and then he started to move, long, slow strokes that seemed to last forever. He got lost in them, just sort of let the world go and let Rock have him. Time faded away with everything else and Rock kept it going and going, just taking him over and over again like he really was never going to stop.

He reached up, cupped Rock's jaw, heart and soul in his eyes. Rock purred, those blue eyes dark, his own face reflected back at him in the pupils. He couldn't have stopped the smile if he'd tried, so he didn't, he just smiled and brought their lips together, still holding Rock's gaze.

Rock's sweet purr filled his mouth, his Blue moving faster, starting the drive to bring them home. Fucking magic and, God forgive him, he'd give anything to keep this. Rig arched, his cock rubbing Rock's belly.

Rock's hand slid around his prick, pumping in time with the hard thrusts. "Gonna give it to me, Rig? Gonna come on my cock?"

"Forever. Oh, fuck. Blue. Fucking *made* for this."

"You know it." Rock growled again and thrust harder, faster, sending him fucking flying.

His world spun a little and he jerked, tightening as he came, balls just aching. Rock roared, pushing hard and fast and then shooting deep inside him. He held on tight, just sort of clinging as he came back to earth. Rock was pressing kisses to his skin, lips on his cheeks, his eyelids, his neck, more touches than anything else.

"You ease my soul, Blue Eyes." He stroked Rock's nape, humming and happy.

Rock purred for him, weight coming off those amazing arms to rest against him. "It's what I do."

"Yeah. Thank the good Lord. I can't do without." He rubbed their noses together, grinned.

"You don't have to." Rock nibble at his nose, grinned back.

"I know." They laughed together, soft and intimate.

Rock purred. "That's a good sound, Rabbit. 's been too long."

"It has. It's time for everybody to go home, Jim. It's been good, but it's time." It hurt a little to say it, but it was *so* true.

Rock nodded. "Under the circumstances it'll probably be better to cut this visit a little short. A month was a long fucking time to start with."

"Yes. I want our lives back."

Rock nodded. "Fuck yes."

He took another kiss, enjoying the quiet, the peace, the heavy weight of Rock above him. Rock's breath got slower, that weight a little heavier as his Blue drifted off, holding him, not rolling over and sprawling out.

He just hummed and cuddled in, hands petting and holding, waiting for his Pretty to join them so he could sleep.

Chapter Twenty Seven

The kids were out on the beach with their Uncle Richard and Rig was off at the grocery store. Again. Between Sissy eating the house and Rachel and Lisa's Hoover imitations, they were doing a grocery run every second day. Rock was sitting on the deck with Charlene and Julie, thinking again how they needed to buy a third one of these chairs, because damn they were comfortable.

It was a couple days since Charlene had announced that she was going to go home to finish out her days, effectively making Julie's decision on where to have her baby for her. That was just fine with him, he was looking forward to peace and quiet and life back to fucking normal with his men.

And it was time for that to happen. Now. He'd waited as long as he could, but Rig wasn't relaxing, the kid was looking a little haunted around the eyes and he was starting to growl at the kids.

He cleared his throat. "Well, I'm thinking you're probably wanting to get on home, Charlene."

Momma looked over, one eyebrow raising. "I was telling Julie that this morning. Alexander's looking drawn."

He nodded. "I'm getting to be an old man. I'm not used to the noise and chatter." He chuckled, watching the girls take Dick down in the water. "Hell, even the kid's having trouble keeping up."

He smiled at Charlene, putting as much charm as he could muster into the look. "We've enjoyed having you, Charlene, but it's time I got to be a gumpy old bastard again."

Julie looked like she was going to say something, but Momma just gave her a look. "I was thinking Julie and I could take the girls sightseeing, take the long way home."

"That sounds fun." Well, to be fucking honest it sounded like hell on earth, stuck in the van with all those kids, but he figured Julie and Charlene were used to it. "I don't mean to be kicking you out, but I think the stress level's been a lot higher than any of us bargained on."

Momma nodded. "It's been a good visit, but y'all need your little house back, you need to feed my son and make him sleep."

"I didn't mean to make things hard, Jim." Julie sighed. "I just wanted to come relax a bit."

"And you did, Julia, but we're on a bit of a timeline and you need a job."

Rock bit back his chuckle. Damn if he didn't always think at least once in a visit that Charlene was tougher than any drill sargeant he'd ever known.

"It has been good having you and the girls here, Julie. I mean that honestly. But it's been hard, too, even without the... situation, having all the girls here day after day's been a lot harder than we expected."

Charlene nodded. "Y'all'd need four more bedrooms to make that easy."

Rock chuckled, making a mental note to *not* add on four bedrooms. Maybe they could try one of the closer motels next time they did this. Just to have the place to themselves for a bit every day.

"I thought we could have a big cookout tonight and then in the morning I'll treat everyone to a nice brunch at the IHOP."

"Oh, that sounds perfect. Steaks or brisket or burgers?" Momma grinned, stretched. "I need to know what kind of potatoes I'm making."

"Steaks for the grown-ups, burgers for the kids and the large of appetite. If you were making dessert, too, I might be talked into doing dishes or something."

"Did Alexander say he'd pick up the fixin's for chocolate pie?"

"I think those are always on the list, ma'am." He gave her a wink.

Julie chuckled. "And what does Richard eat?"

"Anything you stick in front of him." And it wasn't like he was picky, he just had the good sense not to enjoy fruits and vegetables when there was good red meat around and lovely things like potatoes to go with them.

"Yes, he was raised right, Alexander said." Momma winked. "So does Alexander still refuse to eat green peas?"

"I'm not sure, Charlene, you'll have to remind me which ones those are..."

"Little green ones in a can. And there's not a can one in the pantry, Momma." Sissy winked. "You ought to make split pea soup for him."

"You've got a mean streak in you, Julie." He gave her a wink, too, grateful for a few minutes that almost felt normal between the three of them.

"Who? Me?" Julie's eyes twinkled, laughing. "You know it. If I can't abuse my baby brother, who can?"

He nodded. "Good point."

Dick was coming up the beach with six girls in various stages of hanging off him, only Rachel too much of a lady now he supposed, walking along behind them, looking as if she just couldn't believe what they were getting up to.

"We're about to be invaded."

Maddie was frowning. "Where's 'Lex?"

Rachel shook her head. "You still can't go into the deep water. Uncle Alex won..."

"'Lex *said* me an' him would go in the big water!"

Presley and Tammy rolled their eyes in unison.

Rock frowned. "Are you sure that's what he said, Maddie?" Maybe Rig had meant him and Rig and Maddie.

Maddie nodded. "'Lex said that I could go in the big water with him and that Uncle Jimmy and Uncle Richard would help hold the ra...rapt?"

"Raft, Maddie-love. And we'll all go together, but we have to be safe in the ocean, yeah? Buddy-system." Rig came around, hauling groceries. "You big girls go unload for me?"

"Does that mean Rache and Lisa or your Momma and Sissy?" Rock asked, winking at his lover. Damn, Rig looked good. Tired and stressed, but good. The man always did.

Rig laughed, Presley and Tammy taking the bags he already had. "Uncle Jimmy says we're having a cookout!"

Rig nodded. "Yep. Mindy and Jerry are bringing homemade ice cream and their boys and I called Helen and she's bringing husband, baby and watermelon."

"Long as we don't mix up the one for the other." He winked and Dick threw a towel at him.

"Did y'all want me to call anybody from the gym? I bought burgers and dogs enough for everybody and some chicken breasts and some steak." Rig watched the kids drag in bags. "Oh, and stuff for chocolate, strawberry and apple pie. And chips. And I stopped at WalMart and bought a volleyball net and dog food and beer."

Rock chuckled. "If you want a party, call a redneck."

Dick was chuckling, heading in. "I'll call the people who aren't working today, see if they want to drop in."

Rig nodded. "And call up to the gym. We'll be around after closing. Julie, I bought stuff for dip and queso, too. You want to dig out the crockpot?"

Dick nodded and headed in. "I'll get it out for you, Rig."

Rock purred happily. Oh, he did like it when Rig went all out in the food department.

Rig leaned down, nuzzled his ear. "There's a six-pack of the good beer in the back of the fridge."

He rumbled happily. "Do I have to share with your Momma?"

"Nope. She has a few of her own left."

"Excellent. You're good to me." He kissed Rig's cheek, earning himself some 'ewws' from the short set. He fixed them a look and growled, sending them laughing and scattering.

"I'm going to get to cooking. You want to come marinate the steaks?" Rig looked at the girls. "Y'all stay out of the water while we're busy, you hear?"

Did he want to go marinate steaks. Hell, yes. Especially if he could cop himself a feel while he was doing it. Or talk someone into a quick blow. That tight little cowboy butt shimmied and shook, leading him right into the house.

Dick was on the phone, pulling down bowls for chips and glasses for drinks, grouping the groceries by things that needed to go together. Rock thought all he needed was an apron and they'd have a picture. As if hearing his thoughts, the kid stuck his tongue out at him.

Rock chuckled. "Good thing he's on the phone or I'd make him use that."

Rig's eyes warmed. "Isn't that, 'it's a shame he's on the phone,' Blue?"

He grinned and nodded, stuck his own tongue out. Oh, that got him an armful of happy, wriggling redneck.

"Good lord and butter don't the three of you ever stop?" Julie was rolling her eyes at them, Momma right behind.

"Not if I get a choice." Rig took a kiss, defiant and feeling his temper. He dove in, hands sliding to grab Rig's ass, figuring if Rig didn't care if they put on a show, he wasn't going to either.

"Don't make me get the hose," Julie sassed.

"I'm going to play with the children. Julia, help me."

"Momma, I'm watching."

"Julia Dawn!"

Rock let the kiss end. "It's okay, Charlene, we didn't mean to chase you off. We'll be good." He shot a glare at Julie. Girl was lucky his mouth had been occupied while she'd been sassing or he'd have had a few choice words for her.

Dick got off the phone. "Okay, Julie from the front desk is coming with her boyfriend Trevor. And Paul and Simon are coming and some of the guys working now might drop in after hours. And no more pawing at each other unless I can join in."

"I wasn't pawing. I was snuggling." Rig was unrepentant, maybe even a little belligerent. Oh, yeah. Time to lose the company.

Dick came over and kissed Rig's neck. "Sorry, Rig. I guess I can't tell the difference anymore."

"Come on, we've got a party to put together and your Momma needs help getting it arranged. And I need a fucking beer, pardon my french, Charlene."

They all laughed and got busy, the cowboy music coming on the stereo and the Roberts' clan singing along.

He looked over at the kid, rolling his eyes at one particularly twangy song and the two of them started doing their hound dog impressions, howling in time to the music.

It was little Rachel, not Charlene, that gave them a raised eyebrow and a look. "Y'all are just jealous you aren't from Texas."

Rock laughed so hard he nearly snorted up his beer and he rubbed her head. "I might just be at that, 'cause I do have to admit, while the music sucks? I sure do appreciate some of the stuff y'all send out." He drawled the y'all out exaggeratedly and winked at Rig.

Rigger chuckled, rolled those grey eyes. "Wolf brand chili?"

He snorted. "As if you didn't know."

The laughter started up again, tension eased as they worked.

He started getting grumpy after his fifth potato and Rig chased him and Dick out to set up the volleyball net and break up the fight between Presley and Tammie and Maddie. He grabbed another beer on his way out, tossing the kid a new coke and pinching a handful of Rig's ass, just so his cowboy had something to remember.

Maddie was crying, clinging to the kid and Tammy stomping her feet and Presley standing between them frowning. "Uncle Jimmy? I think Maddie needs a nap."

"Yeah? Maddie? You want to come inside and nap on the sofa with the King of Naps?"

"Will Uncle Lex nap too?" Those tired eyes blinked up at him, arms lifting for him.

He picked her up and gave the rest of them a good glare. "You behave for your Uncle Richard and I mean it now."

He carried her back through to the living room, mouthing "nap" at whoever chose to look. "Well now, your Uncle Alex is busy making good food. 'sides, he's not a very good napper at all."

"He's not? Why?" She curled up with him, cheek on his chest, thumb in her mouth.

"I guess he's just happier being busy doing stuff. Some people are like that. Me though? I believe there's nothing like a good nap to make your evening more pleasant."

"Oh. Can I help you cook hot dogs tonight?" The words were interrupted by a yawn.

"Sure thing. But only if you nap with me now." He tapped her cheek gently with one finger. "No more talking."

Maddie giggled and nodded, hand sliding into his and holding on. He didn't know if she fell asleep before he did, but she was quiet as he dozed off.

***

They'd partied hearty well into the late evening before everyone had wandered home. Now the kids were sleeping in the tents and he and Rig and Rock and Sissy and Momma were out on the deck with a last beer and the leftover munchies and were relaxing.

He'd grabbed the hammock as soon as the girls were settled, feeling like he was Rock's age instead of his own. He had no clue how Sissy dealt with them all the time and all by herself -- they just tired him the fuck out.

He was just swinging idly with one leg on the ground, listening to the others talk. He had to admit, he wasn't sorry it was their last night. And he didn't feel too guilty about that because he knew Rock and Rig felt the same way.

It was just hard work being Uncle Richard. He liked being Dick, the kid, hey stud, much better.

He took another sip of his Bailey's which someone had brought and sent the hammock swinging again. The sky sure was pretty.

Rig was stretched out underneath him, long and lazy, head on Rock's lap. "Y'all gonna leave after IHOP tomorrow, Momma?"

"Yeah, we want to hit LA and spend some time sight seeing."

"The girls are likely have more fun playing tourist in LA than being stuck with their old boring uncles out here." Rock's voice was all low rumble.

Dick smiled as it went through him, made him want. This time tomorrow when that happened? He could just dump out of the hammock and do something about it.

"I don't know, Jim. Maddie's in love with y'all. You sure you don't want to keep her?" Julie's voice was teasing, all laughter.

Rock chuckled. "Well of all of them, she's the one I'd take if we were in the market for little girls. But we're not." Oh, that growl sounded very, very sure.

He chuckled.

"You got something to say, kid?"

"Nope. Just remembering the way she followed you around tonight at the party. The way she pretended her lemonade was a beer and the belching? I thought I was going to die laughing."

"I'm telling you, that girl? Is her Uncle Jimmy's through and through. Did y'all see her power-napping this afternoon?" Rig chuckled. "Happy as a clam."

"She just knows a good thing when she finds it and indulges as often as possible. Makes her smart." Rock sounded smug, hand stroking Rig's curls.

Rig hummed, looking happy in his skin. "That's a Roberts trait."

"It's a Rocketman trait, too."

"I don't know, Rock... smart isn't the first adjective I'd use for you." Dick dared to tease the bear.

"And what is?" growled Rock.

"Big." Sissy grinned.

"Strong." Momma added in.

Rig's hand reached up, brushed Rock's jaw. "Mine."

Dick grinned and nodded. "I was gonna stay stud, but any of those work."

Rock purred at Rig's touch. "You're lucky, kid."

"I know it." Luckiest damned guy he knew, in fact.

Rig grinned over at him, winked. He chuckled, smiling back, thinking that they both looked fucking edible. Fuck, he wanted a taste of those cocks, wanted to feel them losing control and fucking his mouth... He shifted, letting his hand with the glass cover his crotch.

Rig's eyes slid down his body, hot and hungry. He bit back his groan. Maybe he should go for a swim. The cold would help with his little swelling problem.

Rig smiled, head moving in Rock's lap. Rock shifted, legs spreading just a little. Looked like he wasn't the only one with that swelling problem.

"So did you like our beach?" he asked, trying to distract himself.

Momma nodded. "I did. It's lovely."

Julie grinned. "Next time I come, I'm renting a hotel room for the girls. On the other side of town."

Rock chuckled. "I could live with that."

Rig grinned. "I don't know. I kind of enjoy them. We just need more quiet time."

"Which the hotel thing would give us," Rock pointed out, reasonably.

Dick chuckled. "You need to send them out a couple at a time next time."

Momma nodded. "Send the two oldest one year, the twins the next. Then Maddie and the baby."

"Yeah, exactly. You could come with Maddie and the baby -- the others would be old enough by then to stay on their own." And they wouldn't be overwhelmed by kids.

"Well, and they'll spend some time with their daddy in the summer, I imagine." Rig's words were gentle.

Julie nodded. "He wants to share custody. Maybe move south so they can live with him half time."

"He changed his tune after you spoke to the lawyer, huh?"

Rock rumbled. "He changed his tune after he found out you were here, I bet. Knew we'd go kick his ass if he tried to take your babies away from you."

Julie nodded. "And... and I think he was real hurt, too. We've talked some and, well, we have five girls, we can't be evil."

"Good for you, Julie. Kids can pick up on all kinds of tension, the less of it there is, the better." Dick shivered a little. His folks had never divorced, but they'd had tension enough.

"Ain't that the truth." Momma nodded, then sighed. "I wanted to tell you, Jim, Richard. Y'all and Duece and my friend Thomas McCardle are named as my pall-bearers. I've paid for the stuff I need to, I'm going to be put beside Jeremy and I want to wear my purple dress and I want 'In the Garden' played at my service." She held her hand up as Rig and Julie started to talk. "Hush now, and listen. I won't ever be back here and I don't know that I'll see these boys again. This is stuff they need to know."

Dick reached out and slid his hand along Rig's arm as Rock answered. "Yes, ma'am."

He couldn't quite believe they were just sitting here, calmly talking about her being dead. Actually, he couldn't believe she'd ever be gone. She was so... strong and present. He could remember the first week he was there and her wanting to speak to him, to say hi to the kid her son had taken in.

"Alexander, I don't want you and Bobby fighting after I'm gone. He's your brother, you can be polite for one funeral."

Julie snorted. "Can I fight with him?"

"If anyone gets to fight with him, it's me," rumbled Rock, bristling a little. "That man makes me itch for a good, hard fight."

"He's just got a big chip on his shoulder." Momma sighed. "Sometimes I wonder if I hadn't married, if maybe he'd have been different."

"From what I hear Jeremy took him on as one of his own," Rock pointed out. "And look at how Rig turned out, and Julie. Meantime you've got guys like Dick who's folks didn't give a shit and he turned out good. You can only blame so much on a man's upbringing. Sooner or later he has to take responsibility for himself."

Momma chuckled. "And what about you, Jim?"

Rig made a soft noise. "My Rocketman made himself, Momma."

Rock purred, hands sliding on Rig. "Marines might have had a little to do with it. They really get to the core of a man. It might be a fancy slogan, but you really do discover what the best you can be is."

"Best or worst," Dick murmured. "It's your fellow marines and the friends you keep that guide you in the right direction."

Rock snorted.

"No, I'm serious. The marines might have made a man out of me, but it was you and Rig who made me a good man." And Rock might have been rolling his eyes, but Dick knew it was the truth.

Momma nodded. "You took up with good folk, Richard. I'm proud of y'all."

He felt himself blushing. "Thanks, Momma."

Momma nodded, eyes on him. "You going to take care of Jim and Alexander for me?"

"Yes, ma'am." He very nearly got up and saluted, she just had that kind of effect on him when she got that serious look on her face, it made him want to show her he was just as serious. Which is why he didn't actualy do it, because people would think it was a joke, when it wasn't, not at all.

"Good. They'll need you and you'll need them, which is what being a family's for, I reckon."

He nodded, reached out to touch them again. "Yeah." Rig's fingers twined with his, face turning to hide in Rock's belly.

"Well," said Rock. "I think it's time these good ole boys got to bed. Your girls get up at an ungodly hour in the morning."

Momma nodded. "And we've got a date with packing and IHOP."

"Yep. Best pancakes in the country, next to mine." Rock got up and helped him and Rig up, making it clear he was expecting them to go with him. "Good night, Charlene, Julie. Sleep well."

"'Night," Dick added, giving them hugs.

Rig kissed Momma, hugged Julie, Rock herding them into the house and down the hall.

He opened his mouth to say something, but Rock got there first. "It's plenty late, kid. We're going to fucking bed."

Rig just nodded, forehead on Rock's shoulder, hand in his.

He nodded, too, closing the door behind them and locking it. They could brush their teeth in the morning.

Chapter Thirty Eight

Rock drove them home from the IHOP and Rig started cleaning when he hit the door. Laundry. Bathrooms. Kitchen. Floors. Dusting. He kept moving and working, making the house theirs again. He did real good too, until he got to the guest room where Momma and Daddy's bedroom suite was now. Part of his inheiritance, come early.

Rig dusted it, touched it, fingers trailing over the smooth wood. Shit.

Dick's fingers were suddenly there, sliding over his, warm and solid. Somehow his Pretty always knew. He turned and pushed close, letting Dick hold him.

"It's okay, you know," Dick whispered.

"What?" He couldn't quite breathe.

"To cry. I'll just hold you forever and you do what you need to."

He nodded, swallowing hard, hurting and so tired. So tired. The sobs started, making him shake, making him shudder.

Dick sat them on the bed and was good to his word, just holding him, rocking a little, not saying a word. Those warm hands slid along his back, never let him forget he wasn't alone, he was held, loved.

Finally it just stopped, all the hurt and guilt and shit just fading away, leaving him bare and aching and empty.

Dick turned his face up, kissing him, softly at first, but with growing heat. He nodded, letting the passion and pleasure fill up the empty places inside him. Yes. Please.

Dick stood and tugged him up, guiding him back out and across to their own bedroom, fingers working on tugging off his clothes. He went easy, gasping, the sound almost like a sob.

Once he was naked, Dick pushed him onto the bed, following him down and his Pretty started to lick him, cleaning the salt from his skin.

"Yes." He arched, rubbing, swallowing his cry.

Dick licked him from head to toe, slowly working his way down, taking extra time at his nipples, his hips, his balls, the backs of his knees.

"Pretty. Oh, sweet fuck." His voice was harsh, hoarse.

"Uh-huh." Dick's voice was soft, slightly distracted as his Pretty made the return trip, lingering at his cock and then ducking, spreading him wide and licking at his hole.

He gasped, bucked, entire body lit right up. "Dick. Oh. Oh. I need. Need you."

"I'm getting there." That hot tongue speared him, pushing into him.

He wrapped his hands around the headboard, rocking, riding the pleasure.

"Thought I saw you come in here," murmured Rock, the bed shifting with his weight. Rock kissed him and then set to work licking at his nipples, hands sliding on his belly.

"Oh. Oh, fuck. Y'all. *Please.*" Rig's eyes went wide, cock spraying spunk over his chest, hot and wet.

Rock rumbled and Dick moaned, two hot tongues sliding over the tip of his cock, his belly, licking him clean, fighting over his spunk. He moaned, still hard, still wanting, caught between his men.

They kissed each other for a moment, fierce, passionate, and then Dick pushed up, cock nudging at his hole. "Want you."

"Yes. Yes." He tugged at Rock, hungry for both of them, now. Needing both of them.

Rock straddled his head, mouth at his cock, taking him down into that hot mouth even as Rock's prick nudged at his lips. Dick cried out, pushing into him as Rock started sucking.

Yes.

Fuck, yes.

He sucked hard, hips riding Dick's cock, world spinning.

Rock started fucking his mouth, head bobbing on him. Dick was thrusting, the three of them moving together in an obscene, wonderful dance.

His eyes rolled, hands tugging Rock's ass closer. Rock's knees spread and his hips moved faster, harder, taking his mouth. Dick was moving hard and faster, too, hips snapping that long cock deep inside him over and over again. Rock's groans and moans were muffled, but Dick's sweet noises were loud and unfettered, filling the room with the sounds that meant them and love and fucking.

He was close again, already, needing, burning. He swallowed around Rock's prick, sucking hard. Dick got them started, crying out, shoving deep as heat filled him. He tumbled right after, jerking and pushing into Rock's mouth. Rock was right with them, cock hitting the back of his throat, pouring seed into him.

They stayed like that for a moment, him and Rock swallowing, shivering, his ass squeezing Dick's cock tight.

Then they all moaned and slid away, regrouping, his men lying curled up on either side of him.

He cuddled in, hands sliding over their skin. "Need a nap."

Rock rumbled happily. "Now you're talking my language."

Dick chuckled. "Yeah, the language of cleaning you were talking earlier just had him confused."

"Fuck off, kid."

"I just did."

Rock chuckled. "Yeah, I guess you did at that."

"Done cleaning. Nap. Then pizza and beer. Then naked in the hot tub."

"Fuck yes."

Dick nodded, hand sliding in to hold his. "Yeah. Sounds just right."

He nodded, held on tight. Yeah. Yeah, just right.

***

Rig had gone to bed when he got home, his head pounding. He'd cracked one eye open at midnight when the boys got home and damned near hurled it hurt so bad. Somebody called in for him at five am and somebody put a cold rag on his forehead at seven. There was somebody right there keeping him dozing and cool and settled all day and when he finally managed to get both eyes open without his head exploding, it was dinner-time again. Migraines were a real stone-cold bitch.

He managed to sit up, taking a few deep, long breaths before convincing his legs to hold him and get him to the pot. He had to piss like a racehorse. Dick hauled himself out of the big chair by the bed and hovered, but didn't help. His Pretty gave him his privacy in the pisser, too, waiting quietly outside.

He stuck his head out of the door when he was done, giving Dick a wan smile. "I'm needing a shower, Pretty. I'm sticky." He hated being sticky.

"You gonna let me come in and wash your back?" Dick asked. "Rock's 'making supper." Which he translated as out buying take-out.

"That'd be real nice." He nodded. Yeah. Real nice. Rig turned the water on, swaying a little as he bent over. "Fuck, I hate not feeling good."

Dick's hands slid along his sides, steadying him. "Yeah, it sucks. Me 'n Rock at least have you taking care of us -- that always makes me feel a hundred percent better than I did right off the bat."

"Y'all do right by me, no question." They managed to get into the tub, Rig moaning softly as the mixture of hot water and warm skin touched him.

"You sure you're okay with the shower? I could run you a bath instead," murmured Dick, mouth on his skin.

"Whatever. Just stay." He snuggled in, relaxing against Dick's strength, trusting it completely.

"Okay." Dick's hands slid over his skin, helping wash away the sticky. Dick's touches were light and sweet, warming him inside.

Rig hummed, cheek on Dick's shoulder, lips just brushing the smooth skin. "Feels so good, Pretty."

"Yeah? Good." Those hands kept moving, sliding across his belly and down along his thighs.

God, for the first time in two days, he was feeling human -- a little slow and clingy and blinky, but alive. Dick's fingers tickled the insides of his thighs and then slid around to rub at his ass, leaving his cock and balls untouched, teasing gently.

He could feel his Pretty's prick nudging at his ass, but there was nothing in Dick's movements to give away the fact that Dick wanted anything aside from just touching him. He closed his eyes, humming, just letting Dick have anything, everything.

"Missed you. Missed this," murmured Dick, as if he'd been gone for a week.

"So good to me. Love your hands, Pretty." So warm, so quiet. Happy. Home.

"Yeah? You love my mouth, too? 'Cause I've a hankering to have a little creme de Rigger."

He chuckled, cock twitching. "You know it, Pretty. In bed? My knees are shivery." Besides, if Dick managed to get him off, he'd probably pass out from sheer bliss.

"Sounds perfect." Dick got the water off and him dry and in bed in what had to be record time. "Want my taste before Rock comes back and realises you're back in play." Dick winked at him and started licking and kissing down his body.

He chuckled, stretching out under Dick's tongue. The sheets felt good, his lover felt better -- warm and steady and right. Dick explored him thoroughly, belying his earlier words by taking his time and licking him absolutely everywhere before settling at his hip. He was moaning, hard but not desperate, hot but not burning. Melted.

Dick took each testicle into his mouth, rolling them gently. Then his Pretty began to lick at his cock.

"Oh, God. Dick." He shifted, moaning, just whimpering. "Hot."

"Love this," murmured Dick against the skin of his prick. "Love the taste and feel of you."

"Mm... love you, Dick." He reached down, stroking the silk-soft hair as he whispered.

Those riverstone eyes turned up to him and Dick smiled and took his cock into that hot, tight mouth. He just moaned and spread wide, pushing deep. Dick took him in happy and easy, sucking and licking the entire time.

In and out, in and out, slow and easy and hot and sweet and fuck, this was perfect. No wonder Rock was so fond.

Dick pulled his prick right into that throat, humming around his flesh.

"Oh..." He arched and came, simple and easy as that. No argument, no question. Just heat. Dick swallowed it all down and then kept sucking, gently now, cleaning him and loving on him, fingers sliding along his balls and inner thighs. He petted and hummed, trembling fingers stroking Dick's hair. His eyelids were heavy -- not sleepy as much as tired -- and his bones gone. Dick slowly licked and kissed, moving back up his body and finally coming to a stop at his lips.

"Thank you, Pretty. Felt so good." He whispered against those warm, swollen lips, lost in riverstone eyes.

"Anytime," murmured Dick, settling next to him and pulling him close. "I bet you could get a nap in before Rock gets back -- he wanted to check in at the gym first, just making sure things are running as smoothly as Jesse claims."

"You'll stay?" He snuggled close, could hear Rock's laugh and accusation of being an octopus in his head. He was asleep before his cheek hit Dick's shoulder, never any doubt in his mind that the answer was yes.

***

Their Saturday nights had gone by the wayside with Charlene and Julie and the girls down and once they'd gone Rig threw himself into his work like a man possessed. Rock figured maybe he was.

Still. He put his foot down and insisted that this week they were starting their Saturday nights up again. He made sure the kid picked up the beer and cleaned the house, called Rig himself to remind his Rabbit it was happening and he'd come and drag that sorry ass home if he had to.

On his way home he picked up a meal of steak, potatoes and salad from their favourite steakhouse and thank fuck that was Rig's jeep in the driveway, because he really didn't want to have to make good on his threat.

"Okay, boys, line up for it -- your stud is home." He laughed as the dogs came running to slobber all over him. "Not exactly the boys I had in mind."

Rig came out of the kitchen, chuckling, shaking his head. "Look at those tails a waggin'."

"What's your tail doing?" he asked. Damn, his Rabbit looked good.

"Waiting on my stud to be home." Rig smiled, the look warm and happy, horny.

Dick followed up right behind Rig. "Oh, it's Rock and he brought the meat." The kid winked, pushing Rig right up against him.

He purred, arms going around both of them.

Rig's lips slid along his jaw, heading for his mouth. "Blue."

"Got it in one," he muttered, taking Rig's mouth hard.

Dick gave them a moment together and then licked at their lips, asking in for a threeway. Fucking sweet kisses, those threeways. They swayed together, the kiss going deep and then easing and getting hard again.

Finally he realised Trouble was trying to get ahold of his bag of food and he growled at the beast. "Let me get this in the oven. If it wasn't fucking steak, I'd let the beasts have it."

"Mmm... steak." Rig smiled. "I brought home brownies and vanilla ice cream."

Dick grinned. "I brought home me."

Chuckling, he goosed the kid on his way to the kitchen. "That makes you the starters, kid."

"Mm-hmm. And you brought beer. Good beer." Rig's words were muffled and when he got back, Rig was on his knees, working that long cock.

He purred, his own prick going fucking hard, just like that. "Fucking sexy."

Rig moaned, hands sliding up Dick's belly. He purred and moved around to stand behind Dick, tugging off the kid's shirt. Rig's hands reached, stroked Dick's tight nipples, head just bobbing. The kid was moaning and carrying on like he did, one hand on Rig's shoulder, the other moving through the blond curls.

Fucking sexy indeed.

He tugged Dick's jeans off the rest of the way, helped him step out of them.

Rig's groan was audible, their redneck's eyes hot, hungry.

He purred, stroked Rig's cheek. "Save some for me -- I'm next."

Rig nodded, nuzzled into his touch, throat working as he swallowed. Dick cried out, hips moving, driving that long cock into Rig's mouth over and over. Bending, he licked at the kid's cock as it slid into Rig's mouth.

"Fuck!" Dick shouted, jerking, his Rig swallowing hard.

Rig's eyes went hot, hand sliding out over his belly. He purred, licking at a drop of the kid's spunk from the corner of Rig's mouth. Rig groaned, swallowing convulsively. He licked his way in, the kid's cock like a brand against his tongue.

Rig kissed him over Dick's cock, licking and sucking. He purred, grinning as Dick sank down, cock disappearing, the kid joining their kiss again. Rig's hands were on his head, on the kid's, holdng them together.

"Fuck, this is good," he muttered, hand roaming. "Fuck, you've got too many clothes on, Rig."

"I'll take care of that."

He nodded. He'd had a hunch the kid would.

Rig chuckled, smiling and licking at his lips, those grey eyes shining for him. In no time at all Rig was naked and then the kid's capable hands were sliding his own clothes away and they were all fucking naked. Rig pressed into his arms, rubbing against him, warm skin sliding on his own.

"Let's get you guys to the couch so I can have those cocks." Dick was encouraging them to stand, tugging on his arm.

Grinning, he stood, bringing Rig up with him. "You gonna take us both, kid?"

"Fuck, yes. Best fucking appetizer ever."

Rig chuckled, cuddled right into him, and they settled together on the couch, long thigh pressed against him. Dick kissed their lips and moved slowly down, hitting his nipples, Rig's, lingering over the nipple rings. Fuck, the kid could play them anytime he wanted.

Rig's fingers twined with his, a soft whimper sounding. "Fuck, that goes straight to my cock."

"That's the idea." He could hear the smile in the kid's voice, but could only groan as another tug to his ring, coupled with a little twist, went straight to his own cock.

"Fuck, kid, you're getting too good at that."

"Uh-huh." Rig panted, cock leaking, the scent of need making him rumble.

Dick moaned, moving down his body until his cock was pressed against Rig's, the kid's mouth opening wide to take both heads in.

"So fucking hot." Rig's hand slid behind him, holding him close, just staring down.

He took a look himself, moaning at the sight of both their cocks sliding into the kid's mouth. "Fuck, yeah."

Rig reached out, traced Dick's lips, petting their cocks at the same time. Dick moaned around their cocks, making him jerk and he took Rig's mouth, the kiss hard. Rig groaned, opening wide, tongue sliding against his own. He let one hand slide into the kid's hair, stroking as he kissed Rig, his tongue imitating the rhythm Dick was sucking them with.

Rig's eyes were dark, happy, watching him, damn near holding him. He was a lucky fucker and he damned well knew it. And that was the last coherent thought he had as Dick's suction increased, head bobbing like crazy over their cocks. The heat of Rig's prick was like a brand against his. So fucking good.

Rig bucked, crying out over and over, fingers sliding on his skin. "Pretty!"

The sucking got harder, Dick taking them deeper and he reached out to tweak Rig's nipple ring, not wanting to shoot all by himself. A single, sharp cry and Rig's heat poured over his cock, right into the kid's mouth. His own joined in and Dick just swallowed and swallowed, taking everything they had.

Rumbling, he settled against the couch, feeling fucking fine.

Rig leaned against his shoulder, fingers petting his belly, Dick's hair. "Happy Saturday, y'all."

"Yeah," he grunted, nodded. Fucking. Steak and potatoes. More fucking. Sounded pretty damned happy to him.

Dick pulled off their cocks slowly and kissed their bellies before sliding up and lying on them. It made him chuckle, remembering the look on the salesman's face when they'd all laid out on the couch, their main criteria being it was comfortable enough for three to lie on.

Rig's fingers slid over Dick's lips, the touch light, a happy noise sounding when Dick kissed them.

He just purred and held his men, sated and content. Life was fucking good.

Chapter Twenty Nine

Fall cleaning.

You'd've thought it was a plague, his announcement every September that he was taking a few days off, doing the fall cleaning, renting a steam cleaner, turning mattresses.

It was a stunning thing -- how quick his boys got busy at the gym, how people called in and classes got scheduled and he'd thought this shit would stop once they were all civilians. Well, okay. He'd hoped.

His Momma hadn't raised a friggin' moron, after all.

Still after cleaning out all the kitchen cabinets and scrubbing them down, regrouting both bathrooms, washing the linens, and hauling a huge amount of random shit up into the attic -- not to mention washing fucking windows, scrubbing walls and doing the rest of his list -- without help from the ungrateful bastards he lived with? Rig sighed. He was going out for a beer or three.

He showered, quick as a bunny, then wriggled into his good, starched jeans, put on his grey ostrich boots and his dove-colored button down the boys had given him for his birthday. Brushed his hair, slapped on his fancy watch, and grabbed his good hat and his wallet and headed out.

Travis Tritt blaring on the stereo, Rig zipped down the highway towards his favorite little watering hole, Rig let his frustration go. He wasn't ever going to change them and it didn't do a damned bit of good to get all twisted and pissy over things and damnit, Momma! If she didn't quit lecturing from the back of his head he was going to...

By the time he'd reached the parking lot, he was laughing. Goddamn, he was a looney old queer cowboy.

Definitely time for a few longnecks. It didn't take him anytime to finish off his first two, laughing and flirting idly with the Jay behind the bar. The place was slow, just the regulars, George Strait on the jukebox. Sammy came to sit with him -- good looking boy, too... shit, if he were twenty-five years younger and not taken, hoo-boy -- and started buying shots for the bar. After his second hit of tequila -- and his fourth beer, but who was counting -- Sammy asked him to dance and he nodded. He needed a break from the booze, that was for fucking sure.

He was halfway through a second slow dance when there was a tap on his shoulder. He turned and there was his Pretty, looking fine in a pair of jeans and a tight t-shirt. "I thought you saved all your belt-buckle polishing dances for me and the old man."

"Hey, Pretty." He moved into Dick's arms, Sammy already forgotten. "I was more trying to sober up than dancing, you know? How're y'all this evening?"

Dick chuckled and pulled him in close, winking past his shoulder. "I've got him now, thanks, Sammy." Dick danced nice and slow with him, definitely polishing *something*. "House looks nice, Rig. Real nice."

"Yeah? Thanks." He smiled, leaning to rest one cheek against Dick's. "I was glad to get it finished. Seems to get longer every year."

"You know you don't have to do it, right?" Dick said softly, one hand stroking along his back. "Hell, you let Rock call in a weekly maid service back in Bragg when you were studying. Why not do that now? It's not like we can't afford it."

He snorted, even as he melted into his Pretty's arms, his world all put to right by those touches. Christ, he was easy. "The day I can't take care of my men is the day y'all ought to have me put down."

"Oh, I'm not suggesting you hire someone to do me and Rock -- just the house." There was laughter in Dick's voice, sweet and happy. One hand slid down and settled firmly on his ass.

"Mmm... Feels good." George Strait had become Alison Krause which became Doug Stone and damn, laughing with his lovers was a good thing. "Maybe we can talk about it, when I'm sober and not feeling so easy. Y'all had supper yet?"

"Nope. Figured you'd have cooked on top of all that cleaning and neither of us were brave enough to come home already fed."

"I was too tired to do the shopping. Needed some liquid fortification." Damn, he should get a friggin' medal for saying fortification without fucking it up. Dick laughed and gave him a kiss right then and there and then dragged his ass off the dance floor to where Rock was sitting at the bar, nursing a beer and eating peanuts.

"Eat out or order in?" Dick asked. "You know, before Rock here eats them out of peanuts."

Jay laughed, low and easy. "Christ, Rigger, make a decision. I can't afford that. Your Rock's a big boy."

Rig grinned, nodded, one hand just brushing Rock's in a quiet hello. "I'm a fucking lucky redneck."

Jay handed Dick Rig's keys. "He's had a bit. I figured to call him a cab if y'all didn't show."

Rock grunted and took out one of his business cards, writing something down on the back and handing it to Jay. "You call the kid's cell before you call a cab."

Dick nodded. "Come on then -- I'm thinking order in." Dick winked and waggled his eyebrows.

Rig chuckled. "You go, I'll follow. I'm easy."

"We know that," Rock told him, Dick laughing, leading the way.

"You want to ride in the jeep with me or in the truck with your old man?" Dick asked him.

Sammy looked over with a wink. "I'll drive him home, if you want. Save him the choosing."

Rock put an arm around him, growl low, warning. "We've got it covered."

"Mm... Sorry, young'un. Told you earlier, they don't get more taken than I am." He leaned into Rock's strength and let his men lead him out.

"You pick something up on your way home," Rock suggested to Dick. "I'll get our tipsy cowboy home."

Dick nodded. "Works for me. I'll stop at that little tamale place that opened up just off the interstate turn-off, 'k?"

"Mm... get some chips and salsa, Pretty. We're out at the house." He looked up at Rock, blinking a little. "'m not that tipsy, Blue. Just being safe, is all. I could drive if I had to."

"Ri-i-ight," said Rock and Dick coughed and Rock continued, "Good thing you don't have to."

He nodded. "Glad y'all came down. Thank you." Rig dropped a kiss on Rock's jaw, giving the good love where it was due.

Rock's arm tightened around him and then the door to Rock's truck was being held open for him and Dick gave him a quick kiss before heading off to the jeep. He hopped up, Rock's hand scooting his ass over when he misjudged the distance. Yeah, well... He'd have been ready to drive before the night was out. Rock didn't say a word though, just got in around on the other side and started up the truck.

They drove in companionable silence for awhile and then Rock glanced at him and asked casually, "You gonna quit being so stubborn about the housework any time soon?"

"I'm not stubborn. It's got to get done, Blue. The house would be nasty otherwise." He turned a little, cheek on the seat, looking at his old man. "It's not like I'm cleaning to piss you off."

"I know the cleaning needs to be done, Rig. I just wish you'd let me hire a fucking service. You've got better things to do with your time."

Rigger snorted. "Like what, Blue?"

Rock gave him a look, one eyebrow raised. "You're more drunk than I thought if you can't come up with stuff to do instead of clean."

He started chuckling, shaking his head. "Like I told Dick, the day I can't take care of my men is the day y'all should take me out back and shoot me." Yep. There was Momma's voice again. Weird.

Rock snorted. "That's a load of crap."

"You say that, but you sure like clean sheets and the bathtubs scrubbed." He was laughing now, completely in fucking love. Oh, yeah. There was nobody like his men. Nobody.

"Sure I do -- doesn't mean you have to be the one to do it." Rock shook his head. "You'd rather be sucking floor than sucking cock, that's your problem, but you don't have to do it."

"Sucking floor?" Oh, now that was just too much. "Blue, how many orgasms do you really think you could manage in a day? I mean... I've cleaned for the last four days."

"'s not just the blow-jobs, Rig. I know you and the kid get off on walking along the beach and spoiling those dammed dogs."

Rig tilted his head. "You're fucking serious."

"I've been fucking serious every single damn time I've made the suggestion, Rig. There isn't a reason on earth why you should have to do any of that stuff yourself. Aside from your own stubborn ass."

"Okay. I'll try for a month. If I don't like it, we'll stop."

Rock gave him a shocked look. "You serious?"

Rig nodded. If he was sober, he'd argue his way out of it, but his rule was to let Rock win if the man appeared to be making any sense. It had worked for damn near twenty fucking years, no reason to stop now. "You got my word, Blue. I'll give it my best for a month."

"All right -- kid's going to be over the fucking moon."

"Y'all getting tired of making up shit to do while I'm cleaning?"

Rock shook his head as he pulled into their driveway and then turned. "We're getting tired of doing shit without you when we could be doing it with you, Rig. Between the gym and your practice, there's a whole shitload of time we don't get to see your skinny ass."

Rock leaned past him to open the door for him and then got out of the truck with a growl, heading in.

"Oh, shit. Blue! I didn't mean to piss you off! Hold up!" He hurried out of the truck, or sure as shit tried to, bootheel catching on the sidestep and sending him flatdab onto the fucking pavement.

God fucking damn!

He stayed there for half a second, blinking at an oil stain and trying to decide if he was going to hurl or not. When it looked like he was going to hold his liquor, he turned over and sat up, shaking his head as Trouble came up to lick at his face.

The jeep pulled up a moment later, Dick peeling out of the cab. "What the fuck!"

"I fell. No big deal. My fucking bootheel caught is all. I'll be inside in a minute." If he could get Dick in, he could walk around back and clean off his hands, wash out his mouth. His knee was aching some, but the jeans had saved it. He was good.

"You fell." Dick shook his head and a hand was held out to him. "Come on, let's get you up and in and something in your belly besides all that beer."

Rig sighed, took Dick's hand, hauled himself upright, refusing Dick's offer to steady him. He wasn't anywhere near tipsy anymore. "Watch yourself, I got a scrape or two."

Dick gave him a look, eyebrow arched just like Rock's. "And what? You're going to bleed on my shirt or something? Get your ass inside before Rock comes looking for you and realises you were face first on the ground."

As Dick went back for the food, he heard his Pretty mutter "stubborn asshole" under his breath. That sort of stiffened his back right on up and he just headed in, making a beeline for the bathroom to do some damage control.

He locked the door behind him and pulled out the bactine and peroxide along with the pack of smokes safely hidden in the box of leftover tampax that Sissy's girls had left behind. He cleaned his mouth out with peroxide, spitting 'til the blood stopped, then cleaned his hands up as he smoked. The shirt was salvagable -- thank god for dry cleaners -- and the jeans were fine.

Hell, the knee was just going to bruise and his cheek might escape that altogether.

He started some bathwater, tossing his butt in the pot and lighting another. His pride was going to need at least a pack of cigarettes and a bath, possibly a little more, he'd just have to play it by ear. At least the tub was clean.

The doornob turned and then there was a knock. "Come on, Rig. Put out the cigarette and let me in."

He sighed, shaking his head. He held the cigarette away from the door when he opened it partway. "I'm cleaning up, Pretty. I'll be out in two shakes of a lamb's tail."

Dick gave him another look. "You're smoking and probably being an ass over something or other. I can't believe you and Rock managed to have a fight between the bar and here."

His temper flared, bright and hot as fuck. He was being an ass? For cleaning. For not fucking nagging for help. For agreeing to try to do what they'd asked. What a great, big, fucking asshole you're being, Rigger. He turned and put the cigarette out and turned off the bathwater, breathing slow and deep. He was not going to lose it. Not. "We didn't have a fight, Dick. Ask Rock. There wasn't any fighting at all."

"Then what's with you all upset on the pavement and in here smoking and Rock growling about stubborn fucking assholes?"

"Look. Rock asked about the fucking maid service, I said yes, let's try it for a month. He made some comment about you being pleased, I made a joke about it being nice for y'all not to scramble to avoid the work. He got all het up and I fell over my own fucking feet trying to apologize for pissing him off. That's the story. I'm smoking because I'm tired and grouchy, because I've worked my fucking ass off for four days and I need one and they make me feel better." He sighed, rubbing the bridge of his nose.

"I don't know why Rock's pissed. Maybe he's pissed because I flipped the mattress. Maybe he's pissed because I went for a beer. Maybe he's pissed because some kid half my age thinks I got something to offer. Maybe he's pissed because he's Rock and he's really good at it. For that? You'll have to ask him."

"You really think we want you to get a maid service so we won't have to worry about avoiding the work?" Dick asked quietly.

"Yeah. Exactly. I think you're both lazy fuckers who'd rather spend a hundred dollars a month than listen to me bitch." He looked at Dick, sarcasm thick, shaking his head. Please. He wasn't a fucking masochist. His lips were tight as he tugged his jeans back on. He fucking hated fighting naked. "Give me a little credit, would you? Last time I checked I was not a stupid man. Y'all don't find it important. I do. Y'all think someone else can do it to where I'm satisfied with it. I have my doubts."

He headed down the hall to grab a t-shirt. Hated arguing naked. "Hell, I've given you both what you're fucking asking for. I've agreed to give it a fair chance. What else do you need?"

"I don't know, Rig. Maybe it would be nice if you didn't act as if having more time to spend with us was a bigger fucking chore than the housework." Dick turned and headed down the hall in the opposite direction, back stiff.

"Give me my fucking car keys." Jesus fuck, he was tired.

Dick sniffed hard and half turned to fling them in his general direction on the floor before continuing down the hall, turning at the kitchen. He grabbed his sandals in one hand, keys in the other and headed out the front door.

The keys were snatched out of his hand, Rock spinning him on the front porch. "Where the hell are you going?"

"Give me the motherfucking keys."

"You've had too fucking much to drink to be driving."

He wasn't going over it again. Not until he could figure out the connection in their brains that added him and keeping them clean, fed and their bills paid and equalled out 'you don't care.' "Jim. I don't get more sober than I am. Give me my keys."

"Call yourself a fucking taxi, I'm not letting you behind the wheel with all that beer and tequila in your system." Rock turned on his heel and went back inside, keys still in that big hand.

He put on his shoes, grabbed a jacket and his ball cap out of the backend of the jeep and started walking, tears hot on his cheeks. Rig's cheeks were dry when he made it to the convenience store, dry enough to head in, buy a Coke and a Snickers bar, and make a couple decisions.

He called a cab, sitting on the curb as he went over her options -- he could hop a bus to San Fran and drink himself stupid until Monday. Highly unlikely. He could go back to the club. Hell, Sammy'd probably take him home. Again, unlikely and he wouldn't fuck with his boys. Not like that. Course there was heading home. Right.

That left heading to the office, catching up on paperwork, and sleeping there for a while. Rig sighed, rolling the coke bottle between his throbbing hands to ease them.

Dick's car went by, stopped ten yards up, pulled a U and came back. The passenger door opened. "Get in, Rig. Please."

Rig sighed, stood, walked over to the car, sliding into the soft seat. Hell, maybe he'd just sleep here. "I've already called a cab to take me to the office."

"So we'll wait and give the man a twenty for his troubles. Let me take you home, Rig, okay? We don't have to talk or nothing, just... don't go."

"You know that's cheating, right?" God, he was miserable and hurting and... miserable. He closed his eyes for two seconds, remembering how good dancing had felt earlier this evening. He should just keep his fucking mouth shut. Permanently.

"All's fair in love, Rig." Dick's fingers were warm and soft on his cheek.

He nodded, still trying to decide what to or not to say when the cab pulled up. "Let me pay the driver."

"Okay. I'll be waiting."

He slipped the cabbie a twenty and then headed back to Dick's car, sliding into the passenger seat. Dick drove him home without a word, just touching him every now and then.

In no time at all they were pulling back up at the house.

He took a deep breath, eyes roaming over the windows, looking for a sign of Blue. "Thanks for the ride."

"He wanted to come with me. I figured you'd be happier with just one of us." Dick gave him a small smile. "I won the toss."

"Yeah?" He looked over, eyebrow arched. Fuck, but it was hard to stay mad when Dick was so close. "You won?"

Dick smiled at him. "Yeah, Rig. I won."

Rig gave Dick a small smile, taking his lover's hand. "I never once suggested I liked cleaning more than I liked being with you, you know?

Hell, I do it all because I love you both, because you're my family, because taking care of y'all is what I do." He looked at Dick, tears in his eyes. "I didn't try to piss y'all off. Hell, I was doing my dead-level best to not piss y'all off."

"Oh, fuck Rig -- please don't..." Dick's fingers slid across his cheeks, collecting the tears that slid from his eyes. "You'll get me started and Rock'll come out here and growl again." Dick sniffed and shook his head. "Wanting to have someone come in and clean isn't about thinking you can't do it right or anything like that -- you know that, right? It just... I want to be with you, Rig, more than I need for it to be you who washes my underwear."

Rig nodded. "I know, Pretty. I said we'll try it, didn't I, see if it works for us."

Dick gave him a warm smile, squeezing his hand. "Thanks, Rig. I sure do appreciate it."

"Does that mean we can go in now? Stop this garbage? I just wanted to be home with my men."

"Fuck, yes, please."

He nodded, opened the passenger door and headed toward the stairs, one ache eased, one left. Rig opened the door, searching out those blue-blue eyes. Rock was in the big chair in the front room, right where he had a good view of anyone coming in the front door without it looking like he was looking. The stiff posture eased when Rig walked in.

"We gonna fight or we gonna kiss and make up?" Rig figured he was better off just getting shit out in the open with Blue.

"You know where I stand on kissing."

"I do." He toed off his shoes, meeting Rock's eyes dead on. Yep. Loved this man. No question. "There room for me on that chair?"

"Always," rumbled Rock, patting his lap.

"Good." Rig didn't wait, just moved onto that lap, into those arms. "Hey."

"Hey," growled Rock, taking his mouth in a hard kiss, arms coming around him tight.

Oh. Right. Why hadn't they all just done this from the start? He settled in, one hand draped around Rock's neck, the other petting the tense belly.

"There room for one more to this party?" asked Dick. Not waiting for an answer, Dick's mouth joined theirs, licking at their lips before pushing his tongue in. Rig groaned, humming as the heat and touches eased him, warmed him.

Brought him home.

The rest would come out in the wash.

***

Okay, so the housekeeping thing wasn't bad. It wasn't perfect, but it wasn't bad. Especially on days like this one -- bright and shiny and starting to get crisp and on the road headed for a cabin in the woods for a long weekend because they had the time.

Rig stretched out, head on Rock's lap, reading some mystery novel out loud to amuse them while his Pretty drove this leg. Every so often he'd reach out and snag a grape or a strawberry out of the ziploc bag of fruit and snack on it, feeling decadent as fuck.

Rock was half snoring, warm hands on him, moving randomly whenever Rock was awake.

"You doing okay, Pretty? Need a Coke? A snack?" He reached out and stroked Dick's side, fingers playing lightly, caressing.

Dick looked back at him, giving him a smile. "I'm fine."

Rock grunted and those hands started moving again. He hummed, shifting so that those strong fingers touched right where he wanted them. Oh, yeah. Nice.

"Slut," murmured Rock.

"Yours." He turned his head and nuzzled Rock's belly.

Rock purred for him. "You know the kid's back seat's got a lot more room in it than the truck."

Up front Dick chuckled. "Now who's the slut?"

Rig grinned, nuzzled again, warm and happy all through. "You wanting, Blue?"

"Always." One of those hands slid through his hair. His lips parted, head relaxing in Blue's hand. One hand started working Blue's jeans open, tugging the buttons on the fly.

Rock's legs parted slightly, shifting under him, that purr growing louder. His tongue played as the fabric parted, licking idly as he breathed in the musk that was one of the defining parts of each fucking day.

"Rig..." He looked up into the bluest blue eyes he'd ever seen. Rock just stared at him, everything right there.

He smiled, cheek rubbing that sweet fucking cock as he nodded. Yeah. "My Blue."

Rock nodded, free hand nudging the fat prick against his lips. He took Rock in with a moan, fingers moving to cup the heavy balls as he started sucking, slow and steady. Oh, fuck. Yeah. So hot. He could feel Rock's rumble through the hot flesh in his mouth, vibrations sweet. Humming, Rig started bobbing his head, taking Rock deep. His own prick was hard and throbbing, wanting.

Dick groaned. "Oh, not fair. Not fair at all."

He would have lifted his head, told Pretty to pull the fuck over for the next turn, but he was fucking busy, so he just moaned, long and loud. Rock liked that, hand tightening in his hair, the other one sliding blunt fingertips over his face, his neck. So fucking right. He groaned, moving faster, harder, hips shifting in time with his mouth. Oh, yeah.

Fuck, yes.

Rock leaned over, hand sliding oh so fucking slowly down along his body until it was covering the bulge in his jeans. He whimpered, humping into Rock's touch, lips pulling harder, faster.

"Fuck!" That was from the front seat and suddenly the engine stopped and Dick's noises got louder.

He deep-throated Rock with a sharp cry, burying his nose in those soft curls and filling himself with his Blue. Rock groaned and pushed up into his mouth, hand popping open his top jeans button and working its way in to grab his prick.

He could hear the sound of flesh slapping, knew that Dick was pulling himself off in the front. Probably watching them through the rear view mirror. It was what he'd be doing if he were in the front and they were in the back. Moaning, he rocked between cock and hand, hips pushing as hard as his mouth. Fuck, he needed.

"Nothing like your mouth, Rig."

That made Dick moan and cry out up front, his Pretty coming. He could smell it. He swallowed hard, pulling as his balls tightened, threatened to spill. Rock growled for him, hand tightening on his head and then his mouth and throat were flooded with the pure taste of Blue.

His own orgasm followed right behind as he drank his Blue down, not missing a drop.

Rock was petting him, both hands moving softly, soothingly, one in his hair, the other still down his pants.

"Warn a guy next time," Dick complained. The engine came back to life and the car started moving again.

Rig kept sucking in time with the touches, cleaning and tasting, loving Rock in the best way he knew. His old man was purring, those blue eyes still gazing down at him.

Finally, he let that soft flesh go, kissing the tip as he tucked Blue away, then nuzzled that warm belly, whispering 'love you" against the skin. Rock's hand tightened in his hair, just for a heartbeat, and then the idle stroking began again.

Rig settled, eyes closing for a minute, the sound of Dick singing with the radio mixing with the road under the tires mixing with the sweet touch of Rock's fingers.

Sweet. Fucking sweet.

Chapter Thirty

Rig got home at midnight from the police station and headed straight for the bathroom, not saying a single frigging word. Goddamnit all to hell and back anyway. He stripped down and turned on the water, wincing at the scrapes on his knuckles.

Goddamn Sammy, too.

The stupid kid *knew* he was taken, knew he wasn't interested, knew he wasn't playing.

But Sammy had had four or five too many and followed him into the bathroom and wouldn't take no for an answer and then...

Shit.

He hadn't been in a bar fight in damn near ten years. Hadn't ever been in one where the asshole wanted to press charges.

Lucky for him, Jay took his side on it, said Rig had been telling Sammy no all along. Even luckier that Sammy was drunk enough to admit to throwing the first punch or he'd be the one locked up waiting to post bail and not the one fixin' to hide in the shower for a week.

Rock was going to shit a pink twinkie.

Dick wandered in, pulling off his pants and stepping in behind him. "What's up, you didn't even stop to say – whoa, are you hurt?"

"Don't, okay? Not now, Pretty." He turned his face up into the spray, wincing as the water slammed into a bruise. Damn the stupid kid anyway, cornering him in a bathroom like a rat, like an animal. Like he had been once before and never fucking again, thank you.

Dick's arms came around him from behind, fingers stroking gently. "I won't tell Rock, long as I know you're okay I'll just leave him sleeping in his easy chair. Gotta know you're okay though, Rig."

"He's going to know. I'm gonna bruise like a son of a bitch." Rig sighed. "You know that kid at the club, Sam Mason? He got drunk and decided he was going to take what wasn't his. He jumped me in the men's room and we got into it. Cops came and everything. I damned near spent the night in jail."

"Jesus fuck!" Dick's arms tightened aroung him, his Pretty pressing up close. "Rock's gonna kill him if he finds out who it was."

"Yeah. Don't know what to tell you, Pretty. The whole fucking bar saw them take us out in cuffs. He's going to hear." He gave a chuckle that was too close to a sob. "Maybe we can move. Tonight."

"Both in cuffs? If he jumped you why were you in cuffs?"

"'Cause I lost it, Dick." He turned, looking Dick in the eye, refusing to be ashamed. "I swore I'd never let... That I'd never go down like I did before. He threw the first punch, but after that we were both fighting."

"Then we tell Rock you beat the shit out of him first and he doesn't need to get involved." Dick shook his head. "Asshole."

Rig nodded. "The cops know the truth of it. Sammy admitted to starting it and all. He'll be out tomorrow morning. He decides to press charges against me and I could get arrested, at least brought back in."

"Rock'll kill him for sure then. You want me to go tell him to back the hell off?" Dick sounded a cross between angry and worried and relieved.

"No, Pretty. We just keep on like normal and hope to hell he sobers up and figures out what he did." He rested his forehead against Dick's shoulder. "Rock's gonna be pissed no matter what."

"What was he thinking? I mean he's seen Rock." Dick held him close, dropping kisses on his head. "Thank God you're all right."

"He's been coming on pretty strong for a while now. I just figured he'd get the hint. I mean, Christ, Dick, he's half my age. Half." Rig shook his head, groaning as his cheek throbbed. "I'm damned near forty, too old for a youngster to come hunting."

"You're sex on a stick, Rig. Always have been, always will be. What do you need, Rig? Want me to wash you? Love you? Anything -- long as it's not leave you alone."

"Just... Just stay here for a minute with me." He didn't move, just held on to Dick, letting the warmth and strength settle him.

"I can do that, Rig. I can do that forever." Dick's fingers slid up and down his back, soothing and petting.

They stood that way until the water started to cool. Then he lifted his head and took a soft, slow kiss. "Thanks, Pretty. I needed that."

"Anytime, Rig." Dick reached past him and turned off the water and then got him a towel, riverstone eyes warm, following his every move.

He looked in the mirror, wincing. He'd have a shiner tomorrow, already had a sweet little blood blister on his chin where Sammy's ring caught him. That was the worst of it, though, couple of bruises on his arms from being shook, his bruised knee and a raw spot on one wrist from being cuffed the only other marks.

"What do you think about me heading to the clinic for a nice, long, avoiding Rock sabbatical?" He offered Dick a wry grin, grabbing his toothbrush. "I'm thinking two weeks, tops."

Dick's smile answered his, just as wry and gentle fingers ghosted over his face. "He'll think he did something to piss you off." Dick shrugged. "He's mellowed out lots since coming out here, maybe he won't take it so hard."

"Take what so hard?" came the growl from the doorway, his Blue blinking at the light.

"Hey, Rock." He sighed, eyes flashing to Dick."There was a bit of a tussle at the club, is all. I gave better than I got, no worries." He'd eat his hat if Rock was satisfied with that, but it was worth a try.

"A tussle?" Rock growled and came in, looking at his face carefully. "Been awhile since you felt the need to mix it up, cowboy."

"No shit. Guess I'm losing my edge, either that or just slowly getting smarter." He winked and started brushing his teeth, telling himself he wasn't lying.

Rock gave him a long look, watching him closely. He could feel the tension rolling off of Dick. "And if I ask the kid, he'll tell me the same story?"

"Hey, I wasn't there, Rock."

Another long look and then Rock nodded. "If you're going to start fighting I want you in the gym and beeffing up."

He nodded, tense as a spring as he rinsed out his mouth and grabbed the bottle of aspirin. "I hear you."

Rock took the bottle out of his hand and shook out a couple of pills, handing them to him along with a glass of water. "You need a massage?"

"Yeah." He met Rock's eyes dead on. He was too old to play games and lie to his old man. "It's been a shit day, Blue."

"Yeah, it looks like it has. Come on, let's get that fine ass of yours to bed. Dick, quit dripping all over the floor and go find the oil."

Rig nodded and let Rock lead him to the bedroom, head hanging low by the time they got there. Rock pushed him onto the bed on his front, straddling his ass, hands already soothing as they stroked his back.

He rested his not bruised cheek on his hands. "I'm getting too old for this shit, Blue."

"Yeah, I'd have thought you were."

"I didn't start it, Rock. I didn't have a choice."

Dick came in with the oil and climbed up onto the bed, lying next to him, giving him a soft kiss. "Don't hassle him, Rock, he's taken enough shit today."

Rock just growled. "Something going on here you're not telling me?"

He looked into Dick's worried eyes and nodded. "Yeah, Blue. I spent the evening talking to the police and the guy who jumped me's still locked up and he's a friend of ours. You want to know more? Start rubbing and don't get pissy. I hurt and I need you."

Rock growled, but his hands started moving, slick and easy on his back, easing tight muscles. "Talk."

He told the story, all of it, starting with the wandering hands and ending with Sammy going ass over teakettle out the bathroom door and the indignity of being cuffed and arrested in front of their friends. He didn't exaggerate, didn't lie, just 'fessed up and let Rock and Dick touch him.

"You kicked his punk ass?" growled Rock. His Blue was angry, he could hear it in Rock's voice, but the hands that worked his muscles never touched too hard.

"Yeah. Kid's got a busted nose for sure. I'm betting he's going to be damned embarrassed when he sobers up, fighting with a skinny old cowboy about getting a piece of ass." It felt good, those hands, felt damned good.

"You know I want to go down there and beat the shit out of him, right?"

"I do." Rig nodded. "You know that I want you with me next time I go to the bar, right?"

"You gonna let me growl?"

"Blue, that kid touches me again, I'm gonna let you tear his arms off. I could lose my license for going to jail for assault." He was forgiving, not stupid.

"I'm holding you to that," growled Rock. A soft kiss was pressed against his neck and Rock slid off him to lie beside him. "Somebody better tell that kid he even looks at you wrong and I am going to end his career in looking."

Dick nodded. "I'll make sure he gets the message that he'd better not hang out there anymore. Without breaking any legs."

Rig nodded, giving them both a kiss. Dick would fix it and Rock would be at his side and things would be just fine. "Thank you."

"Can we fuck now?" Rock asked, voice plaintive. Dick bit his lower lip.

Rig looked over at Dick and winked, then turned to push into Rock's arms. He couldn't let Rock kill for him, but he could let his old man know how much he needed. "God, yes, Blue. Please."

He lifted his chin for a kiss, pressing into solid heat with the practice of years. Rock's mouth closed over his, his Blue rumbling for him. Dick pushed up behind him, his Pretty warm and hard. He moaned and snuggled in close. God, yes. How could that kid think for a second he'd give heaven up?

Rock's kiss grew hard, possessive, like his Blue was staking claim. Rig opened wide, one leg sliding up Rock's thigh. That's right, Blue. Yours. Yours and his and nobody else's. Touch me. Rock's hands slid between him and Dick, moving over his oil slicked skin and down to his ass, coming around to grab the leg that was overtop of Rock and pull him in closer. Dick's fingers were teasing his crease.

It was what they needed, it erased the anger and the fear and the bullshit and left truth. Fuck the idiots who said sex didn't solve problems. It was sure as shit solving theirs.

Dick slid a finger into him, mouth working the back of his neck. Rock pulled him even closer, opening his body to his Pretty. He rocked slow and easy, watching his Blue, taking one deep kiss after another. The anger faded quickly, soon replaced by pure need.

"Blue... Pretty..." His moans were low, long sounds that vibrated between them. Rock rumbled, the sound sliding along his chest. Dick pushed a second finger in alongside the first, his Pretty making those sweet porno noises. The kisses got deeper, the touches more insistent, driving him mad, making him ache.

"Oh fuck, I can't wait anymore," murmured Dick, fingers sliding out of him. As the heat of Dick's prick slid against his hole, Rock's hand circled his and his Blue's cocks, pulling with long strokes.

He cried out, the sound coming from deep down inside him, pure need, pure fucking joy.

They worked together, pushing and pulling, grunting and groaning, kissing and fucking and sending him to the god damned moon. His fingers twined with Rock's, soft gasping sobs pouring over Rock's jaw. Dick shifted, nailing his gland and at his cry, his Pretty stayed there, getting it every single time.

He blinked up at Rock as he came, shaking hard, ass clenching Dick's cock for all he was worth. His Pretty called out, something that might have been his name, or Rock's, filling him with spunk. Blue eyes gazed down at him, hot, solid hand still working his and Rock's pricks.

"Yours." He whispered the word into Rock's lips, serious as shit. "Love you."

"I know and you are," murmured Rock, the words ending on a groan as more heat flowed over Rock's fingers, his Blue coming for him.

He cuddled right into Rock's arms, reaching back to keep Dick close, exhaustion taking him. "Stay."

"Fuck yeah, it's after midnight."

Covers were drawn up over them all and two sets of lips pressed against his, kissing and loving on him.

Before he could sleep, he made sure his cheek was resting against Rock's heartbeat and his fingers were twined around Dick's, holding tight.

***

They took the car, Dick driving, having promised to be the designated driver. He was nervous. They were going back to Jay's. Just two short weeks after Sammy'd cornered Rig in the bathrooms and refused to take no for an answer.

Rig's injuries had cleared up, they'd gotten word that Sammy wasn't going to press charges and he himself had found the kid and talked to him. Put the fear of Rock into him. Sammy'd been petulant at first about losing his watering hole, but Dick figured that was Sammy's own fault. Not to mention Jay'd mentioned that he was banning the kid from the bar.

Still, this was the first time Rig was going to be back there since it had happened and he knew their cowboy was more than a little embarassed at having been arrested right there in front of God and everyone.

If they were going to do this though, they had to do it. It was their favorite place to hang out. They could have munchies, booze, play pool, darts, dance, touch each other without worrying they were going to offend anyone. None of them wanted to have to find another place.

The question was whether or not Rig would be able to be comfortable there again.

He pulled into the parking lot and grinned back at his lovers, who were necking in the back seat. "We're here."

It looked like Rock was doing a stellar job of distracting Rig, the thin cheeks flushed, lips just swollen.

He put the car in park and got out, went around to open the door. "Let's go get some grub and a couple beers."

"Yeah. I could use a cold one or four." Rig stood, pulled his hat down a little, hiding his eyes.

He and Rock flanked Rig and he realised how they probably looked and forced himself to step ahead of them, giving Rock a look that made the big guy visibly try to look less grim. That possessive hand around Rig's waist stayed right where it was though.

It wasn't busy, the lights dim, the Eagles on the jukebox. There was a little silence when they walked in and then Jay's eyes lit right up. "Hey strangers! I thought I'd lost my favorite customers!"

Dick gave Jay a big grin, pleased with the welcome, knowing it would help put Rig at ease. "Hey, Jay. You think you can set us up with some longnecks and a couple combo plates?"

"You know it. You want some potato skins, Doc?"

Rig grinned, nodded. "I think I do, thanks. How's things?"

"Same old, same old. Glad to see you back." They got another big smile and three beers were put down in front of them. "The booths you like in back are free and the pool table's going wanting."

Rock nodded and grabbed his beer. "Have the food sent back. Thanks, Jay."

"Yeah. Thank you, sir." Rig stayed with Rock -- not leaning or anything, just stayed close and let Rock shield him. Dick wasn't sure either of them paid attention to it even.

He gave Jay another smile and followed them back, nodding at the other regulars before settling in across from them.

"Gonna shoot some pool, Rock?"

"Yep. After we eat, I'm munchie."

Rig settled in the corner, hat still on, but tipped back a little as he pulled on the longneck bottle. He nodded and smiled at Rig, foot finding Rig's leg and rubbing it.

"I invited Jack and Sarge out for Thanksgiving, Rock, but that's their anniversary and they're heading to a little cabin in the woods to celebrate."

Rock chuckled. "They're going to fuck like bunnies. Jack's a lucky man."

"Oh, I imagine Sarge is, too."

Rock nodded. "I imagine so, but I don't have direct experience in the fucking department with the man."

Rig chuckled. "Man, what I wouldn't give to have known you then, Blue."

Rock shook his head. "Sarge was right -- I had a chip on my shoulder a mile wide. I was a little growly."

Dick chuckled, wondering just how bad Rock had been considering the man was growlier than just about anyone he knew.

"Something funny, kid?"

He shook his head, but couldn't lose his smile.

Rig's hand slid along Rock's arm. "I bet you were fine as fuck."

Rock purred. "Sarge saw something he liked. The confidence was all false bravado back then though. I knew I was a stud when we met."

Rig laughed, the sound welcome, relaxing Dick inside. "Oh, Lord yes. I swear, my heart stopped."

Rock chuckled. "Well you sure didn't let on. Oh, I knew you were interested. And once you put that mouth into play? Damn."

Dick just sucked it all up, hoping they'd go on. They didn't reminisce much and he enjoyed hearing about it.

"Shit, Blue. I damn near delivered my ass into your hands at the pool table." Rig chuckled. "You should have seen it, Pretty. I had this wee pickup and watching Rock trying to fold into it? Something else. Looked fucking fine on my little bed, though."

"He looks fucking fine pretty much everywhere -- that much hasn't changed at all."

Rock was looking pleased and smug and extremely studly. "I bet you haven't changed much."

"Got older, kid."

Dick shook his head. "You don't look it."

"Flattery will get you laid."

He nodded. "Yep, counting on it." He gave Rock a wink and turned back to Rig. "So did he look pretty much the same?"

Rig nodded. "Little less grey, little less bulked up. He's changed less than you have, Pretty."

Dick nodded. "I grew up, he was already grown when you met him."

Rock nodded. "I was. And like I said -- just as well. Sarge taught me to work within the system and still take what I wanted."

"Yeah." Rig chuckled. "I was better looking then and fucking fearless, flirting with Rock like he couldn't have turned me into a greasespot on the carpet."

"I can think of better things to do with you on the carpet than turn you into a greasespot." Rock winked.

"You look pretty good to me, Rig." Dick assured.

Rig grinned and blew him a kiss, then nudged Rock's shoulder. "I tell you what, those were two amazing fucking weeks."

"Fuck yes." Rock chuckled. "I spent the next few months trying to find someone who could suck like you did. Never have, though the kid comes close."

"I learned everything I know from Rig."

"You learned well." Rig grinned over at him. "You know, as much as we played? You were the only one we ever needed."

He blushed and reached out to touch them both briefly.

That was when their food turned up along with another round. "This'll be my last one," he told Jay. "I'm driving home."

"Gotcha. Coke for the rest of the night?"

"Thanks." He nodded and waited for Jay to head back to the bar. "It's funny to think of what might have happened if Rock hadn't found me. Or if you'd sent me on my way after a few weeks or months."

Rig nodded. "I've thought on that. Where I'd be if I hadn't followed a certain fine marine across country."

"I guess we're all lucky it turned out the way it did." He grabbed a chicken finger, munching on it.

Rock nodded. "I like things the way they are."

"I got all I need." Rig stole one of his french fries, humming along with the jukebox. Rock dug into the other combo, dipping things liberally in the various sauces.

"You and Rock gonna play pool?" he asked. "Do a little reminiscing?"

Rig chuckled. "I don't know. You still thinking my ass is worth chasing, Blue Eyes?"

Rock gave Rig a look. "I chased it out to here, didn't I?"

"You did. Thank God for favors large and small."

Rock snorted. "Like there was ever any doubt. You might have chased me down all those years ago, but I know a good thing when it finds me."

Rig nodded. "One of the best things I ever did, buying that pizza."

Rock chuckled and nodded and Dick looked from one to the other. "Pizza?"

Rig nodded. "I didn't know what else to do. I'd moved, got a job, an apartment, looked Rock up, everything. I'm sitting out in the old truck one Friday night, freaking out and this delivery guy pulls up. I bought the pizza and knocked."

"And what did you think when you opened the door?" he asked Rock.

"I thought I was gonna get lucky and get me another of those amazing blow jobs I'd been pining over."

"It was a good welcome, yes sir." Rig chuckled. "Man, I was walking bowlegged going into work that Monday."

"You got used to that."

Rig nodded, a shit-eating grin on his face. "I did."

Dick wriggled, cock taking a definite interest. He knew that feeling himself. He stole one of Rig's potato skins, dipping it in the sour cream, watching as Rock did the same now that his own plate was empty but for the carrot and celery sticks. Of course, Rig grabbed a stalk of celery, dipping it in the bleu cheese sauce, toe of one boot brushing his leg.

It was just a normal Thursday evening out at their favourite watering hole and it felt good, being able to come back and do the things they used to, knowing this incident hadn't hurt any of them the way the last one had.

Rock went in for another potato skin and his last chicken wing and he slapped that hand away. "Time to go play pool."

"We all playing?" Rig finished his beer, ate another carrot.

"Sure. You can show me your pick up moves."

"That's all in the wiggling and accidental rubbing."

"'Accidental' rubbing?" He grinned, suddenly very eager to learn these moves first hand.

Rock nodded. "Not that you'll have any need to use them."

"Oh, I'm thinking they'll be fun to try out on the two of you." He wasn't looking to pick anyone else up.

"Just us, Pretty. I've decided Rock can kill anyone who messes with us from now on." The words were a joke, but the tone wasn't.

"You got that right," muttered Rock, taking a drink of his beer.

Dick nodded and squeezed Rig's hand before getting out. "Well let's play some pool and you can show me the right way to accidentally rub."

Rig nodded and slid out. "I'll get us more beer and Coke. Y'all rack up."

He bit back the offer to go himself, watched as Rock visibly forced himself to step toward the pool table instead of off with Rig. "Okay."

Rig moseyed, chatting with Jay and making their order, every so often looking back at them. He and Rock did their best not to look like they were watching Rig like hawks, but Dick wasn't sure they were entirely successful. Of course he wasn't sure that was a bad thing, either. Let everyone know Rig was theirs and they weren't going to let anything else happen to him.

Rig brought the beers and soda, visibly relaxing when he got to them, even hanging the cowboy hat on the little hook. He bumped their hips together, smiling.

Rock handed a cue over to Rig. "You can have the honors."

"Thank you, sir." Rig gave Rock a flirtatious, wicked grin, then bent over, ass snuggling right into Rock's body. "Oh, oops."

Somehow Rig managed to rub against Rock and stand all at the same time. Impressive.

"Oh, oops." He giggled, the sounds increasing as Rock's hands dropped to Rig's hips, wrapping around them and rubbing that ass against his cock again.

"Yeah. Oops."

"Mmm..." Rig almost purred, rocking and rubbing, thighs parting.

"You think anyone'll notice if we duck into the bathroom?" Rock asked Rig.

"I will!"

Rig chuckled, took his shot and looked pleased as punch.

"My turn. Let me see if I've got this right." He went over and bent, snuggling his ass up against Rig. "Oops."

"You forgot the 'Oh!' It's important to sound surprised." Rig's hands found his ass, squeezed.

"Oh!" He looked back and grinned, wriggling.

"Sluts," muttered Rock.

"You wouldn't be saying that if I was rubbing up against you."

"You know it."

Rig swatted his butt. "Take your shot, now. Then we get to do it again."

"Cool!" He took his shot and wriggled as he stood, enjoying this game.

"That was well done." Rig kissed the back of his neck, lips warm and soft. "Well done."

He moaned softly. "I'm a fast learner."

"Always have been." Rig's drawl slid right up his spine.

"Oh... Hey, you think anyone'll notice if we duck into the bathroom for a quickie?"

Rock snorted. "I will."

He grinned and nodded. "Yeah. Your shot, Rock. Who're you gonna rub up against?"

Rock gave him a cocky grin. "I don't rub up against people, kid. I wait for them to rub up against me."

Rig nodded happily. "Like this."

When Rock bent for his shot, Rig draped himself against Rock's hip, hands sliding over the strong arms. "You might want to take this shot instead."

"I'll take any fucking shot you suggest, Rig..." Dick grinned, watching those blue eyes go dark. Rig smiled, moaning low, helping Rock take his shot, one long thigh sliding between Rock's. Rock might have said something in reply to that, Dick didn't hear though, he was too busy moaning. Fuck, they were sexy together.

Rig backed off, getting ready to take his shot, cock full and heavy in the tight jeans.

He moved right in, copying Rig's movements and bending over the lean body, hand sliding along the long arms. "You might want to take this shot instead."

Rig blushed, body hot and fine beneath him. Then Rig turned to brush those soft lips against his jaw. "Yeah? Show me."

He let his leg slide in between Rig's, the shot going hopelessly wide. "Oh. Sorry. I'm a little. Distracted."

"There's nothing little about you, Pretty." That was enough to have his cheeks grow hot and he rubbed against Rig's ass. He certainly didn't feel little just now...

Rig's eyes met his. "We done flirting yet? I need y'all."

He nodded. "We could pay our tab and go."

"Already taken care of," said Rock, coming back -- he hadn't even noticed the big guy going.

"Oh, good. Take me home." Rig's eyes were warm, needy. "I want."

"Me, too."

"Then let's go," said Rock. "Give me the keys, I'll drive while you two get busy."

"I thought I was the designated driver."

"I've only had the two and had plenty of food. I'm fine."

"Cool." Rig waved as they headed out. "Have a good one, Jay."

"You too, Doc."

"I'm having two good ones, sir."

Jay laughed. "I can see that."

Dick walked out, cheeks hot, but proud as fuck to be walking out next to Rig and Rock.

Rock purred a little. "You make a man feel a hundred feet tall, Rig."

Rig's smile lit up the parking lot. "I just know what I need, Blue."

Rock purred and Dick helped Rig into the back seat, eager to touch and rub and kiss. Rig let him get settled and then pushed into his arms, lips searching for him. He moaned as their lips met, hands sliding on Rig's back. Rig just pushed into the kiss, groaning, tongue pushing right into his lips. He sucked on Rig's tongue, tugging Rig so his leg was insinuted between Rig's. Rig rubbed, cock hard and hot, pressed against him.

He hardly noticed the car starting up and them moving, just focused on Rig and the hot body in his arms. Those eyes were fastened on him, hot, happy. In love. He gazed back, hands sliding beneath Rig's shirt, stroking warm skin, sucking hard on Rig's tongue.

Rig was riding his thigh, moaning low, soft cries pushing into his lips. Rock moaned from the front seat and he felt it in his balls. Fuck he hoped it never stopped being this good. Whimpering, he tugged on Rig's ass, encouraging the movements. Rig groaned, hands stuttering over his shoulders, fingers holding him tight.

He pushed his hands down the back of Rig's jeans, grabbing that sweet ass. Rig cried out, the scent of spunk strong, sweet, the wide-eyed stare sweeter. Oh. Oh, fuck that was sweet. He squeezed again, moaning softly. Rig panted, holding his gaze, eyes rolling just a little.

He just beamed at Rig, licking the red, swollen lips. "I'm glad you agreed to come home with me."

"Never could resist your offer."

"Thank god." He rubbed up against Rig, wanting, wanton.

"Mmm... Yeah. Hell of an offer, Pretty." Rig reached down, cupped his cock, rubbed. He rippled and pushed up into that hand. "Yeah. Oh, yeah." Rig pushed into his kisses, hand driving him harder, higher.

"Uh-huh." He whimpered and let Rig send him flying. His eyes rolled as he came, body shuddering.

"Mmm... fucking sweet. My men..." Rig's tongue slid over his lips.

He moaned, trying to catch Rig's tongue, chuckling as the back door opened. "We've been here for the last five minutes, you know."

He laughed at Rock. "No, I didn't know."

"Sluts."

He nodded and grinned, waiting for Rig's familiar answer.

Rig smiled up at Rock, looking fucking tickled. "Y'all's."

Rock nodded. "You know it."

"Yep. Let's go in and play, Pretty!"

"I'm right behind you."

"Checking out your ass," put in Rock.

He nodded and grinned again. "Best view in California."

Rig blushed dark, tipped that hat, and grinned. "Y'all..."

"Don't go all modest on us -- you're one sexy fucker -- look at the men you've caught." Rock put an arm around Rig's shoulder.

Rig grinned, licked his lips. "I have good bait."

He laughed, but his prick perked up again at the sight of that pink tongue.

"Here Pretty, Pretty, Pretty." Rig chuckled and took off running.

Rock snorted, but Dick took the bait, heading off after Rig as fast as he could. And if he wasn't mistaken, that was Rock's bootsteps following.

Rig was laughing, running, holding onto that hat with one hand. Rock caught up to him as he caught up to Rig in the bedroom, grabbing them both around the waist and tossing them on the bed. They bounced, making a united 'oof' before they tangled together, lips meeting.

He moaned into their mouths, Rig's tongue sliding, Rock's more insistent. Rig's hands pushed between them, working at Rock's jeans, fishing for that fat prick. He did his level best to get the rest of their clothes off, insisting when Rock didn't want to break their kisses. Of course it only worked because Rig had found Rock's prick at that point, distracting the big guy from their mouths. Rig wriggled down, lips parted, eyes on the prize, so to speak.

Dick got Rig's shirt off just before he lost the chance to suction and, grinning, he kissed Rock. The big guy kissed back, mouth hard on his own. Rig was going to town, devouring Rock's prick, head just bobbing.

He broke the kiss and licked his way down Rock's neck, finding first one nipple and then the other, tugging on the little ring, making Rock moan for them. One of Rig's hands reached back, circled his leg, held on. His hand met Rock's in Rig's curls and he moaned around the metal in his mouth, the sound making Rock push against his mouth.

He was hard again, eager for every sensation. Rig was making low, happy little sounds, rocking and rippling against them.

He slid his hand down, touched where Rock's prick went into Rig's mouth and then below, cupping the heavy balls, feeling them draw up. Rig's fingers slid against his, rolling Rock's balls, jostling them. Rock moaned loudly and jerked, cock going deep into Rig's mouth as the big guy came.

Rig hummed, sucking Rock dry, making their old man shake and shiver.

Rock groaned, petting him, petting Rig. "That was worth the fucking wait."

Dick heard Rig's soft, happy little sound, that mouth sliding up Rock's body. They met in a kiss that tasted like each of them and most like Rock's spunk. It made him moan and rub against them, wanting.

Rig turned, legs sliding around his thighs, making him a blatant offer. Moaning, he slid his fingers around Rig's ass, teased that waiting hole.

"Yeah." Rig nodded, pulling him close. "Yeah."

He buried his face in Rig's neck, licking at his lover's sweet spot. One of Rock's fingers slid along his, spreading slickness around and then sliding in along with his.

"Oh... Fuck, that's sweet." Rig groaned, rubbing against him, ass taking him right in.

He pushed in another finger and so did Rock, the two of them fingerfucking Rig, making that long body move, his cock sliding with Rig's. He loved the look on Rig's face, amazed, hungry, wanton -- pure need.

"Okay, kid," murmured Rock, fingers sliding away. "You better pony up before I decide to take him."

Rig groaned. "'m a lucky fucking redneck."

"You know it," Rock growled, tilting Rig just right for him.

Dick pushed in and then rolled to his back, bringing Rig with him.

Rock chuckled. "Ride 'em, cowboy."

Rig's head fell back, nodding, moving on his cock, just like that. He moaned, bringing his legs up, pushing his heels into the mattress to give himself leverage to thrust into Rig. Rock grunted and moved in to lick at Rig's skin, fingers working the sensitive titties.

"Fuck, yeah." Rig's hands found his knees, bowing that long body.

He whimpered and thrust harder, cock jerking as he watched Rock's thick fingers slide on Rig's skin. Rig groaned, hips bouncing, lean muscles working as Rig rode him. Fuck it felt good, amazing really. The only thing missing was Rock's cock either in his mouth or Rig's, and given that Rig had just had Rock, Dick figured it was his turn.

"Could suck you," he told Rock.

Rock groaned and shifted, his answer to straddle Dick's face, push his cock right on in.

Rig's ass went tight around him, squeezing. "Fuck. Y'all... So fucking fine."

"You know it," muttered Rock as Dick wrapped his hands around the thick thighs, encouraging Rock's movements. He whimpered and thrust harder, trusting Rock to work Rig's prick and complete the circle. Things got dizzying, the three of them moving and groaning, rocking together faster and harder.

Rock's cock stole his breath, the sensation of Rig's ass around his cock finishing the job and he just moved, sucked, held, searched out his pleasure and found it in his lover's cock and ass. He cried out around Rock's prick, coming hard. Rock and Rig moaned together, both of them following him, tumbling after him. He swallowed around Rock's cock, drinking him down as Rig's ass squeezed him tight.

Fuck. Damn. Good.

The air was filled with groans and pants, all of them slowly coming down.

Rock pulled out and shifted over, stretching out next to him. "Fuck, that was sweet."

He nodded.

Rig just settled down against him, sighing softly. "Yeah."

He nodded again.

Yeah.

Sweet.

He let his eyes close and just lay there with them. There was nowhere else he wanted to be.

Chapter Thirty One

Rig pulled up to the house, unloading the couple three bags of groceries he'd picked up, along with the leftovers from the cake Helen'd made him. It had been a quiet day; he'd talked to Momma, to Sissy -- who was talking about getting back together with Hank, for chrissake -- even Jack had emailed from Florida. Now, though? He just wanted to be home and not think about getting older.

Dick met him at the door, blowing one of those noisemakers and throwing confetti. Rock came along right after Dick, popping a bottle of champagne, cork aimed out the door behind him. "Happy Birthday!"

He chuckled, shaking his head at his boys and grinning. "Look at y'all."

"Nah, we've been looking at each other all day, rather look at you." Rock gave him a wink and wrapped him in a hug, gave him a kiss.

Dick took the bags from his hands and let him melt into Rock's warmth, lips opening right up. His Pretty must have taken the champagne out of Rock's hands, too, because they slid down his back to cup his ass, tugging him closer, rubbing their cocks together.

"Mmm..." He smiled, arching a little, hands settling on Rock's shoulder.

"Champagne's gonna lose its bubbles," Rock warned.

"Yeah?" He reached for the bottle, Dick handing it over and he took a deep swig, bubbles tickling his lips.

Rock purred and bent, licking the bubbly right from his mouth. Dick moaned softly, pressing against them. He opened right up, taking another drink when the tingle of the bubbles faded, letting them both drink from his mouth. Again and again he drank and fed them, their tongues all tangling together as they shared the champagne between them.

His head was swimming, cock hard as fuck, the room moving around them. Oh, too fucking sweet. Before he knew it the bottle was empty and he was naked and so were his Blue and Pretty, the three of them lying on the couch, touching and kissing and petting.

"Mmm... " He was rippling, lips sliding over Dick's skin, tongue licking.

One of Rock's hands slid around his prick, pumping easily. Dick's sounds filled the air, getting louder anytime his tongue slid over his Pretty's skin. Floating, he just moved, rocking and touching, needing this, loving it. Rock's prick was hard and hot against his ass, just rubbing, sliding on his skin. Dick's was just as hot, just as hard against his belly.

"My men." Rig groaned, face lifting for someone's kiss.

It was Rock's mouth that landed on his, tongue invading, filling his mouth. Dick's mouth fastened on his neck, pulling up a hickey with strong suction. His cry pushed right into his Blue's lips, shaking hard, cock hard enough to cut glass.

Rock's rumble filled his mouth as Dick's lips slid over to his collarbone, his Pretty pulling up another mark. He was fucking going to come, just from this, just from being fucking *theirs.*

Dick's mouth slid again, down to pull up another mark right above his heart. Rock's hand was still working his prick with long, lazy strokes, both his lovers' cocks hot as they slid on his skin. It was just easy as pie to just give it up, moan and come and melt. Dick whimpered and moved to suck up yet another mark, this one over his ringed nipple, making him ripple with aftershocks.

"Y'all's... Oh, fuck it feels good..."

Dick nodded and moved to leave yet another mark, this one on the top of his belly.

"What the fuck are you doing?" Rock asked.

Dick licked at the last mark and looked up at them, grinning. "It's his birthday."

"Yeah, I fucking know that."

"So I'm leaving a mark for each year and one for luck."

"Th...that's a shitload of marks, Pretty."

"Too much?" Dick asked, looking crestfallen.

He chuckled, touched Dick's face. "No, sir. You just keep counting."

Dick nuzzled into his touch. "To be honest, I've lost track."

His Pretty worked backwards, tongue sliding over each mark as he counted. "One. Two. Three. Four. Five."

"We're going to be here all night at this rate," muttered Rock.

"You got somewhere else to be?"

"Well, no."

Rig giggled, looking up at Blue. God, he loved them. Rock winked at him. "But I want to fuck, not watch you turn him into a giant polka dot."

Dick stuck his tongue out and then went back to sucking, lips wrapping around his hip.

"Mmm... can't we have both? Fucking and sucking."

"Oh, now there's an idea." Rock's prick slid along his ass as Dick moved to take one of his balls into his Pretty's hot mouth.

"Yes..." He nodded, one leg resting on Dick, spreading himself for Rock.

Dick purred around his ball, sucking just hard enough not to hurt, but he bet it would leave his ball nice and red, marked. One of Rock's fingers pushed into his hole, burning slightly. He tilted his head back, searching for a kiss. Rock gave it to him, tongue sliding into his mouth, just like that finger was sliding into his body, sure and insistent. He rocked, moaning low, right where he wanted to be.

Dick moved along his skin, leaving marks here and there and everywhere as Rock's fingers opened him up, one after the other. He floated, panted, rocking between Rock's hand and Dick's mouth. Eventually Rock's fingers became Rock's prick, solid and hot, pushing into him over and over as Dick started counting again. Shit, this was fun. Damn near worth getting older for.

"Thirty-three. Three more."

Rock chuckled, shifting to slide past his gland. "Let's hope he doesn't need to get naked for the next little while, kid."

"I'm going to look well-fucked."

Rock snorted. "That's one way to put it."

"Oh hush," Dick told Rock crossly. "You're just upset you didn't come up with the idea yourself."

"No, I'm just fine where I am, kid. Fucking this sweet ass." Dick stuck his tongue out again. "And don't be sticking that out if you aren't going to use it."

"Oh, I'm using it." Dick bent and licked at his prick.

He chuckled. "I'm... oh, that's nice, Pretty... I'm not doing my job if y'all can nag each other."

"You're not supposed to be doing anything," Dick murmured between licks. "It's your birthday."

"Yeah. Yeah. Happy fucking birthday..." He nodded, happy all through, fucking flying.

"Uh-huh." Dick's mouth slipped over his cock, taking him all the way in as Rock's thrusts got harder, more intense.

"Oh, fuck yeah." He arched, hips rocking furiously, eyes wide.

They worked him together, sucking and fucking, sending him to the moon. Yeah. Yeah. Fuck, he loved this. His whole body went hot, come pouring from him into Dick's mouth. Rock roared in his ear, filling him with heat even as Dick swallowed him down and heat splashed against his legs, the three of them so in tune that was all it took. He shivered, settling into Rock's arms with a happy hum.

Dick left a kiss on his cock. "Three more. Any requests for where?"

"Let Blue decide." He grinned, stroked Dick's hair.

Dick looked up at Rock. His Blue chuckled. "Well... his back is pretty fucking bare of marks."

"That's because you're hogging it."

"I do believe the technical term is fucking."

Dick laughed, his Pretty happy and relaxed.

He got tickled, started giggling again. "Y'all are nuts."

"Yep, there's six here between us," noted Rock, hand sliding to cup his balls. Dick managed to fall off the couch from laughing.

Rig looked up, giggling at Rock. "You? Are a funny, funny man."

Rock nodded sagely. "I know. It's why you keep me around."

"One of the reasons, yeah."

Rock laughed, prick sliding out. "Roll over, Rabbit, the kid wants to give you the rest of your hickeys and your back really is wanting them."

"It is?" He chuckled, nodded, turning to give Dick his back.

"Oh yeah, look at all this bare skin! I should have saved more than three..."

Rock purred, licking at his lips. "Well he could probably use more than just one for luck, kid."

"Oh, I do like the way you think, Rock."

Rock gave him a wink before answering Dick. "I know. It's why you keep me around."

God, he was stupid in love. "What's for supper? Besides me?"

"Ask the kid, he was in charge of food. Made him promise there'd not be lots of vegetables."

Dick just hummed against his spine, mouth closing over his skin.

"Oh..." He shivered, eyes wide, unexpectedly aroused.

"You like that," purred Rock. "Keep it coming, kid."

Dick laughed softly and moved to the small of his back, licking first before sucking.

"Oh. Oh, fuck." He bit into his bottom lip, groaning low. The top of his right ass cheek was next, Rock rubbing against him, sliding their pricks together.

Then his Blue's hands slid down to hold his ass cheeks open. "Give him one right in the pucker, kid."

"P...perv." He groaned, lips finding Rock's nipple. Rock snorted, the sound turning into a moan. Dick's mouth closed over his hole, licking and scraping with his teeth. He whimpered, sucking on Rock's flesh, needing something fierce.

Dick bit the top of his thigh. "Want you."

"Uh-huh. Y'all's. Fuck, Pretty."

"Yeah, that's what I'm going to do." Dick slid back up his body, cock nudging at his stretched hole. He arched, hips just begging for it, begging for his lover. Dick pushed in, long cock going so deep.

"Pretty!" He tugged Rock's nipple ring with his lips, thighs parting wide. Dick and Rock's moans merged together into a single sound of want. Rig nodded, moving faster, harder. Rock's hand circled his and Rock's cocks, squeezing and tugging as Dick fucked him. God, was he thinking he was old? Because he was hard again. Wanting again. Their mouths met over his head, the kiss noisy.

"Fucking love you both." He moaned the words over Rock's heart. Rock's hand squeezed their cocks hard and Dick whimpered, pushing hard into him, coming. He grunted, body shaking as he shot, pushing right into Rock's hand. Rock purred, jerking and coming a few moments later. Rig just slumped, panting, eyes closed. Damn.

Dick's mouth closed over one shoulder, Rock's over the other, both of them sucking and purring. Theirs. Hell, yeah. Lock, stock and barrell.

Chapter Thirty Two

Rock flipped another pancake out of the frying pan and onto the plate destined for the oven to stay warm. Day three of their visit and already he was working on his second day of making breakfast. Rig and the kid had done the bulk of the Christmas cooking, which was why they'd come down as early as they had. A good thing, too, because Momma was looking haggard. Between having a houseful of six girls all under the age of fifteen and the cancer, Rock figured all her energy was being sucked right out.

Tomorrow was Christmas and then on Boxing Day the girls were going to spend a week with their dad and Rock was torn between them going with the plan and sticking around for the week or going home early so Charlene could have the peace she so obviously needed.

He flipped another set of pancakes into the oven and had a good gulp of his coffee.

Rig came in, eyes quiet, unlocking the cabinet full of pills and searching for some. "Momma's only going to eat one, Rock and she just wants syrup, no butter."

"You want me to make her up a plate for you to take up with her pills?" He fucking hated seeing his Rabbit looking like that. And it was worse when there wasn't a single fucking thing he could do about it.

"Yeah. Julie's coming in late from work -- she's going to pull another girl's shift until noon and get off at two in the morning tomorrow." Rig crushed the pills up, mixed them with some applesauce.

Rock shook his head. It was a damned good thing a couple of those girls were old enough to take care of the little ones, because Charlene sure couldn't anymore. Jesus it was messed up. He'd managed to forget about it after Charlene, Sissy and all headed back off to Texas and their life had gone back to normal.

He put together Charlene's plate, throwing on a couple of slices of peaches out of the preserves. "Should I cut the pancake up?"

"No, I'll help her if she needs it. She's trying hard to come off normal."

"She got a mirror?" He winced. "Sorry, Rig, that was uncalled for."

Rig's lips just twisted and he took Momma's plate. "Save me a couple, yeah?"

He nodded. "I'll save back some batter and make them for you when you come back down." He handed over the plate. "We going to town to pick up the last minute stuff?"

"Once Julie gets here, yeah. Dick's pulling the tree down now..."

"Alexander! I need my pills!" Rig winced, the line between those eyebrows deepening. He growled a little, kissed that line and then Rig's lips and put a cup of water on the tray.

Rachel came in, wearing a t-shirt and sweats, hair touseled. "Uncle Alex, Ma-maw's crying. You want me to call Momma?"

"No, honey. I got it. You help in here."

He shook his head and managed a smile for Rachel. He could see how this was going to go and if he could see any way around it, he'd have brought it up already, but Charlene needed Rig. "You can set the table, the pancakes are almost ready."

"'kay. How long are y'all staying? Will you be here when we get back from Daddy's?"

"We're staying 'til just after New Years and yeah, we should be here when you get back. You looking forward to spending time with him?" He knew they didn't see that much of Hank during the school year, not with Hank still working that spread in Arkansas.

It had been a visit home that had prompted the short-lived try to make the marriage work again.

"Yeah, sorta. I mean, I'm gonna miss Stephen something fierce, but it's just a week, I'll live."

"Stephen?" He'd thought the boyfriend's name was Johnny. Or Billy Bob or was that the first one?

Rachel blushed. "Captain of the football team. We've been going together since Halloween. He... uh... He really liked my costume."

He bit back his snort and the urge to go all primal. Rachel wasn't his daughter. "And what were you dressed as?"

"A slutty cat." Lisa wandered in, all tomboy, rolling her eyes. "Momma damn near died."

"Lisa!"

"Well, it's true."

Rachel rolled her eyes. "The other drill team girls and me were different cats -- I was a lioness."

He'd just bet this Stephen liked her outfit. "You talked to your Momma about boys and stuff lately?"

Rachel snorted. "Momma's busy with work and Ma-maw and getting ready for the baby. I know what I need to, Uncle Jimmy. Don't listen to Lisa. She's just pissed because Daddy's buying me a car."

"You know about STDs and stuff, Rachel? You know about getting pregnant?" With Julie and Hank both MIA, sounded like the perfect chance for things to happen to her. He'd been fifteen. Once. Of course he hadn't been interested in girls...

"Hell, living with Momma? Who doesn't know about getting pregnant?" Rachel rolled her eyes. "The entire *town* figures we know how."

"Rachel Diane, you show your mother respect or I will fill in for your father and put you over my knee. And I have big hands, child."

He got a look and then the plates slammed on the table, rattling, and Rachel stalked off. Lisa shook her head, grabbed forks. "Don't worry about her, Uncle Jimmy. She's been a bitch and Momma's riding her hard. I think she's gonna just stay at Daddy's this time."

"I just don't want to see her get hurt, Lisa. You kids think you're fucking invincible." He knew. He'd been there, too. And if Sarge hadn't taken him under that wing, who knew where he'd be now.

Lisa nodded. "She's just Rachel. She hates it here."

"She's a teenager, I think it's a prerequisite. I'll bet you any odds you like she'll be just as miserable at her Daddy's."

"Yeah? I'm not a teenager yet. Not 'til May. Of course, I haven't, you know, started yet, which is what Momma says Rache's problem is."

Rock closed his mouth quickly on his urk and grabbed a bunch of forks, pushing them into her hands. That was way fucking more than he'd needed to know. "Dick? Round the kids up, it's time to eat."

Maddie came in right away. "Where's Momma?"

"Working. I think your Uncle Alex said she'd be home at two."

Dick came along a moment or two later with the twins. "Rachel said something about not being hungry and stomped up the stairs."

He nodded. "Apparently she's started, you know, and that's what her problem is." Oh yeah, that had been worth it for the twelve shades of red the kid turned.

Lisa chuckled, gave Maddie two pancakes. "Thanks for breakfast."

"You're welcome. It's the kid's turn tomorrow."

Dick nodded. "I figure we'll do oatmeal -- it's quick and easy and nobody really cares about breakfast when there's presents to be had." The kid was subdued, picking up on all the fucking undercurrents and letting them get to him. It was how he was.

"We like oats, but Momma promised to bring donuts home from work, so no one has to cook." Tammy chuckled, grabbed the juice from the fridge and poured everyone some.

"Donuts for breakfast? Damn, I can handle that." He nodded. And Rig was too busy to complain.

Dick chuckled. "I'll still make a small pot. For those that want it."

"Spoilsport," he accused.

The kid shrugged. "Rig'll make something if I don't."

He nodded. Dick had a point.

"Why do y'all call Uncle Alex Rig?" Lisa tilted her head. "Isn't that a bad thing? Like rigging a contest?"

He shook his head and had to think a moment on the origin of the nickname. It was all they used; "Alex" seemed like a different person. "If that's what it was for it would be a bad thing, but your Uncle Alex can jury rig just about any injury until you can get to a doctor or hospital."

"Really? He must be a really good doctor."

Maddie nodded. "Lex is gonna fix Ma-maw."

He sighed and looked at Dick. What the fuck did he say to that? Dick just shook his head and pushed at his half-eaten pancakes.

It was Lisa that patted Maddie's hand, shook her head. "No, Mad. Ma-maw's going to see Jesus and live in Heaven and be our guardian angel with Pa-paw. Uncle Alex wouldn't argue with God, remember?"

"All right, everyone finish up and then we'll get the dishwasher loaded and go decorate the tree."

"Yeah, and I do believe there are letters to be left for Santa. I'll volunteer my services, as usual." The kid dumped out the rest of his pancakes and put his plate in the dishwasher.

"And we need to make cookies, too!" Tammy put hers and Presley's plate in the dishwasher, bouncing. "We want to make cut-out cookies."

"You'll have to talk to your Uncle Alex about that -- I'm strictly a pancake and grill man, myself."

Lisa nodded, got her plate and Maddie's. "I'll make cookies. I can follow a recipe okay."

"Santa might like that -- that you made them yourselves." He hoped that was okay. Cookies involved all sorts of measuring and the oven and timing and he didn't want to have to eat burnt cookies or rock hard cookies just to help clear "Santa's plate.

The girls headed out to the front room, leaving him and Dick alone in blessed silence for a minute. Dick came over and rubbed his shoulders some. He grunted his thanks.

"I wish there was something we could do," murmured Dick.

"Like what? Leave the gym and everything and come stay here full time?" He shook his head, because short of that? There wasn't much they could do.

"I don't know. Maybe have a nurse come in and help or something?"

He nodded. "She starts the morning we leave. Comes in every day to get Charlene her pills and give her a couple hours peaceful rest." He saw the look on the kid's face and shook his head. "You were busy looking after the kids when Rig and I talked about it and there just hasn't been a fucking chance to bring it up."

Rig wandered in with dishes, cleaning them and putting them in the dishwasher before pouring another cup of coffee. The kid went over and hugged his back, hands sliding around Rig's waist. "You okay?"

"I'll live, I guess. How're y'all?"

Dick shrugged. "Okay."

"I'm guessing we'll all live," he noted. "Julie gets in at two? You're coming out with us. We'll have supper out."

"She'll be here at noon, I think. Off at two in the morning." Rig leaned into Dick for a second, nodded. "Supper sounds good. I need..."

"Alexander! Julia! I need some help!"

Rig sighed, stood. "Coming Momma."

Dick shook his head as Rig hurried off. "He's going to stay, isn't he?"

Rock nodded. "I imagine so."

"Do you think one of us can stay with him?"

He shrugged. "You work out the math kid, but without his salary and putting in for a nurse here in the mornings I don't see how we can swing it."

Dick nodded and sighed. "I've got the laptop, I'll go over the numbers when I get a chance, but you're probably right. You think he'll be okay?"

"Nope. But he'll have us to come home to." Dick nodded, the kid's eyes soft with worry. "Come on. We let those girls decorate that tree without us and it'll be done entirely in pink."

The kid found him a smile and they headed off to make like they were full of Christmas cheer.

***

Dick sat in the back seat of the car, holding Rig as Rock drove them back to Momma's place. By tacit agreement they'd left the issue of Momma and Sissy and the girls and birth and death behind, focussing on picking up stocking stuffers and last minute gifts, some groceries, and then spending a long, leisurely supper at Cattleman's. He'd even danced a few slow songs with Rig, Rock nursing his one beer, watching.

Soon as they'd gotten in the car to go back though, the tension had returned to Rig's shoulders and Dick had just pulled him close, held and patted.

Rig cuddled close, eyes closed. "I don't think we're going to need the nurse. I don't think she's going to be out of the hospital that much longer. She's hurting pretty bad."

"You sure?" Rock asked from the front.

"Not one hunded percent, no, but... I'm pretty sure. She won't meet Sissy's baby."

Dick squeezed Rig. "I'm sorry."

"I know. I... Oh, God. I'm not. She's not all there anymore. She's hurting and she's ready."

Dick nodded. It was a horrible way to die. And it was hurting Rig so badly. He didn't know what to say, what to do. So he just kept holding on. If his shirt collar got a little wet, he didn't mention it and neither did Rig.

All the lights were on when they got home and he sighed, not sure he was ready yet to play Uncle Richard again, to pretend that it was another Christmas, just like all the others. But the kids deserved a good day so he squeezed Rig and got out.

Julie came down the stairs as they pulled up, belly huge in her scrubs, "I need to talk to you, Bubba."

Rig nodded, climbed out without a word. He didn't know whether to follow them or just go in, but Rock's hand landed on his shoulder and guided him toward the living room where the kids were going nuts.

"All right, everyone front and center." Oh, there was still more than a little gunnery sargeant in their Rocketman. Four little girls and one pouty teenager appeared, right on cue. "We're going to clean up this mess and then it's bedtime."

"But... What about cookies and milk and..." Tammy looked shocked.

"We'll do all that at Daddy's, Tammy." Rachel's voice was flat.

Maddie frowned. "Santa's not coming here?"

"Of course Santa's coming here." Rig came through the front door. "But he can't come if it's so messy he can't see the tree! Clean up, now, and we'll all sit and watch the Grinch after."

"And then you've got to go to sleep," added Rock. "He knows if you're sleeping and he won't come if you aren't."

Dick grinned, remembering how many nights that had sent him straight to bed, eyes closed tight.

Rig came over. "Sissy called the doctor. We're taking Momma to the hospital once the girls leave for Hank's. He stopped by and left morphine."

"Oh." He wrapped his arms around Rig, feeling Rock engulf them in a hard hug, the two of them offering what support they could.

"I'm going to check on her. I'll be out for the Grinch and a coffee."

"Okay."

"I'll make sure the kids behave," growled Rock. It felt surreal, cleaning up the room with the kids, Momma's big chair next to the fireplace, but her not there, Sissy and Hank not there. It was almost like someone had stolen the Roberts' Christmas and replaced it with a Main one.

Lisa came over, hand sliding into his, squeezing hard, just holding on for a minute. He went down onto his haunches and gave her a hug, holding on for a minute, letting it soak in that it wasn't his family, it was Rig's and even in the midst of chaos and pain, they loved each other and him, too. He was welcome here.

"Almost done?" he asked, looking around.

Lisa nodded. "The twins are getting cookies, Rachel's helping Maddie with her nightgown."

"What about you?" he asked.

"I'm waiting for you to sit so I can sit next to you."

He smiled at her. "Oh, okay."

He found a spot on the couch and got comfortable and then held out his arms to her. She settled right in, the twins pouncing Rock as the big guy sat. Rachel sat between all of them and little Maddie looked around, frowning. "Lex!"

"He's coming," Rock told her. "Someone has to put the movie in for us."

Sure enough, Rig came in, turning the lights off, putting the cartoon on the television before settling in Momma's chair, Maddie in his arms.

They settled altogether, quiet and relaxed, watching the Grinch. He soaked it up, the normality of it. Rig and Maddie fell asleep, the little cheek on Rig's shoulder, Rig looked older than Rock. It broke his heart to see Rig like this. Rig hadn't looked drawn and aged like this since the bashing. And he was even more helpless to do anything about it now than he'd been then. Maddie wiggled and Rig petted her back, hand gentle, not even waking up.

When the Grinch was over, he and Rock helped the girls put out the milk and cookies and got them to bed, Rock picking Maddie up from Rig's arms and getting her down without waking her.

He peeked in on Rig's Momma, who was sleeping sound, a thin, pale husk of the woman they knew. He wasn't a very religious guy, but he said a small prayer, asking God to stop her pain and take care of her, and of her family. Then he went to find Rig and help take care of some of her family himself.

Rock was on the sofa, Rig curled in his lap, covered in a blanket. He joined them, hand sliding along Rig's back. Rig hummed, settled. Rock looked fierce, miserable, like he wanted to just pick Rig up and go. He understood that, felt it himself, the need to do *something* to help, to keep Rig from this pain.

"I don't want to come here next Christmas. I want to stay home, Blue."

Rock nodded. "Anything you want, Rabbit."

"Yeah," Dick agreed. "We'll stay home next year."

"Good." Rig took a deep, shuddering breath, holding on tight.

"If there's anything we can do to make this easier, you'll tell us right? Anything at all, Rig."

Rock nodded his head. "Yeah. Kid's right."

"You just take me home after and give me my life back."

"You know we will," growled Rock, pulling Rig closer, holding him tight.

Rig nodded. "I know."

"Good." Rock grunted. "Julie's here, right? We can go sleep over the garage?"

Rig nodded. "She's in her room. She can hear Momma."

"Come on then. It might not be for long, but I know how to make you feel good for awhile."

Dick smiled and nodded. They could do that for Rig, make him forget anything else existed outside the three of them.

"You always make me feel good."

"That's what we're here for," Dick murmured.

"Kid's right, it's why you keep me around after all."

"One of the reasons. One of them."

Rock stood, bringing Rig up with him, carrying their cowboy out. Dick followed, like he always would.

***

Rig nodded to Alyson and Courtney, "Mornin' ladies. She have a good night?"

He'd been spending the nights here with her, but his men were heading home this morning and he'd needed one more night. One more.

"She's resting, Doc. Quiet. She missed you some." The tall nurse smiled at him, at his men.

They had admitted her the day after Christmas and Momma was going to die here, it was just a matter of time. Rock's hand was at his elbow, gave him a little squeeze as they headed down to her room. He looked up, found a smile, nodded. He wanted to go home.

"I wish you were coming with us," murmured Dick, echoing his thoughts. "I'm sorry, I know it's selfish, but I don't want to leave you here alone with the hurt."

Rig nodded, "I do too. I do too."

Dick's hand slid into his and squeezed and then they were knocking on the door and going in to see Momma, his boys needing to say their goodbyes.

Momma's eyes were open, tired. "Baby. I missed you last night."

He nodded. "Jim and Richard are going home today, Momma. I wanted to spend the night with them."

Dick and Rock went and stood beside her, Rock taking her hand. "We'd stay if we could, Charlene, but the kid and I have to go."

Momma nodded, patted his hand. "You know I love you like one of my own, Jim."

"I know you do. The feeling is mutual and you know I would take this from you if I could."

Rig moved to sit on the windowsill, the parking lot wavering.

"You take care of my boy."

"You know I will, Charlene. There's nothing more important to me than that."

Dick made a soft noise and gave her a hug. "I love you, Momma."

"I love you, Richard. You don't worry on me. My Jeremy's going to come for me."

"You were more a mother to me than my own," Dick said softly, stroking what was left of her hair off her face.

"You're a good boy, Richard. You remember that. A good boy."

"Yes, Momma." Dick was crying softly, wipping his eyes with the back of his hand. "I'm sorry."

Momma nodded, holding him. "It's okay, son. It's okay."

His heart was breaking and he didn't know if he could do this. He patted his pockets, looking for his smokes.

Dick held her for another long moment and then kissed her cheek and whispered "I love you."

Then his Pretty came over and hugged him, held him, while Rock sat on the edge of the bed and just held Momma's hand. Rig just breathed, just leaned into Dick and tried to keep his shit together.

"We have to go," Rock finally murmured. He stood and looked down at Momma. "I guess there really isn't anything else to say. I'm proud to know you, Charlene Roberts. And I won't forget you."

"Goodbye, Jim. I'll be waiting for y'all when you're called home."

"Yes, Ma'am." Rock gave her an awkward hug and then came over. "Walk us out, Rig?"

He nodded, staring into those blue eyes. He didn't want them to go. "Be right back, Momma."

They walked out to the hall and Rock just folded him in those strong arms, Dick wrapped around his back.

"We're just a call away," rumbled Rock, voice low.

He nodded. "I know."

"Gonna miss you," murmured Dick. "Gonna worry about you."

"I know. I'll be here until the end and then y'all come for me, bring me home."

Dick's eyes filled again but he cleared his throat and didn't start crying. "We will."

Rock nodded and echoed the words. "We fucking will."

He was given one last hug, one last look into those blue blue eyes and then Rock's face closed. "We've got to go."

"'kay. Don't forget to feed the dogs." He didn't wait to see them go; he couldn't. He just went in and sat and held his momma's hand.

Chapter Thirty Three

The phone woke Rock from a deep sleep, the sun not quite lighting the sky yet. It was fucking deja vu, too, with Rig not in the bed, the kid's worried eyes blinking at him, a woman's voice on the phone, asking to speak to him. Fuck.

"What?" He growled.

"Jim? It's Julie. Mornin'."

"The fuck it's morning." He cleared his throat a couple times, relaxing just a little. Rig wasn't the one they were expecting a call about.

"Yeah, well, I'm just getting off my shift, so it's my night." She sighed, turned the car radio down. "I need to talk to you, Jim. About Alex."

He tightened up again. "About Rig? I thought you were calling about your Momma."

"No. No. She's dying. She hasn't been awake in days, but... Jim, you gotta come get him. You *gotta.* He's not eating, he's not sleeping. He's scaring me."

He growled. "I knew this was going to happen. I fucking knew it." Fuck.

"I would have called earlier, but I've been busy and didn't see him for a week. I didn't know how bad it was. Momma's as good as gone, she'll never know y'all took him."

"The problem is going to be convincing him of that." He peered at the clock. Just after four fucking am. "At least one of us will be there today, Julie. Both if we can swing it."

"Okay. You need me to do anything? You need me to find y'all a hotel room up in Greenville?" Sissy sounded relieved, almost in tears.

"Yeah. Close to the hospital. I'll call you when I get in." The kid's eyes were huge and he put his arm around the broad shoulders. "Is there anything else I need to know, Julie?"

"He needs y'all. He looks... worn. He's smoking. He's slept at the hospital since the week after you left."

"I'm gonna kick that skinny fucking ass."

"Yeah. You do that. Just come, Jim. Y'all just come."

"We will. Thanks for calling, Julie." He hung up the phone. He was going to kill Rig. After he fucked him through the mattress a few times.

"Well?"

"Seems Rig is set on dying right along with his Momma."

Dick shook his head. "I was worried this would happen. He's really hurting over this and there's no one there to support him."

"Well that's about to change. I'm taking the first flight I can get and you're coming on the first one you can get after clearing our desks."

Dick nodded. "They're cleared." He raised an eyebrow and the kid shrugged. "I knew we'd have to go sooner or later when she passed on and I've been keeping things take off ready."

"Smart, kid, real smart."

Dick ducked his head and got up, pulled on sweatpants.

"Where are you going, the travel agents won't be open yet."

"Nope, but the internet is."

He shook his head. Not just smart, damned smart. Which was a damned good thing, because his Rabbit needed.

***

She'd passed quiet -- no words, no last looks. She just breathed out once and sort of forgot to breathe back in. He'd been in there -- he had been most of the time, Sissy had the job and the kids and Bobby had his car lot. Momma'd been gone for almost a week, really, never came back from where she'd gone one late, dark night. In his soul he believed Daddy'd come for her and she couldn't bear to leave her other half again, not even long enough to say goodbye.

He made the calls he was supposed to -- Sissy, Bobby, the preacher, the funeral home. He signed papers and made the arrangements she'd already started and Sissy'd finalized. He stayed until Sissy got there to say her goodbyes, Bobby on his way. Then he wandered out to the little hospital courtyard to have a smoke and make the call he needed to.

One ring. Two. "Rig."

"It's over, Blue. She's gone." He took a long drag, sat down on a hard concrete bench. The pansies were blooming, looked awful pretty in the February sunshine. He probably needed to order some flowers for the service, something purple and sweet-smelling and not too uppity.

"You okay?" Growly and low, that was his Blue and fuck, he'd give his left ball to see them right now, to know they weren't all the way in California holding down the fort.

"Yeah. Can you... would y'all do me a favor?" He watched the cherry burn on his smoke -- his hands looked more and more like Daddy's every day, thin and wrinkled and callused and old. Real fucking old, with tears catching in the wrinkles, sparkling with the sun.

She loved the springtime, should be home now with her grandbabies, planting leaf lettuce and globe radishes and watching for the bluebonnets to bloom in the west pasture.

"You know it. Just say the word."

"Can y'all come? Please. I need." He took a deep breath, pinched the bridge of his nose hard as the phone line got real quiet and still. He needed to eat. He needed to sleep. He needed to go home. He needed his men, his lovers, his family. "Please, Blue."

Hands fell on either one of his shoulders, one heavy and hard, the other warmer and holding tight. "Yes, Rabbit. We can. Come on."

Rigger looked up to see Rock putting his cell phone away, his Pretty and those riverstone eyes right there helping him find his feet. "Come on, Rig. Let's go."

He nodded and put out his cigarette, standing and following without another word -- if it was a dream, he was too fucking tired to wake up and if it wasn't, then wherever they took him was right where he needed to be.

***

They'd checked into the hotel and then gone to get Rig, their timing perfect as Momma'd gone and Rig had made all his calls and was needing them by the time they got to the hospital. So they were able to take Rig right on up to their room. Dick worked on his clothes and Rock pushed him down onto the bed and then they flanked him, touching and kissing, learning him again. Rig was shaking, holding onto them both like he wasn't sure they wouldn't disappear.

"It's okay," Dick murmured. "We've got you."

"You fucking know it," Rock agreed, hands mapping Rig's body.

"I want to go home." Rig's mouth searched for his, then Rock's. "Please."

"We'll take you home," Rock murmured as their mouths all met together, three on three, tongues tangling and fuck, it had been too long. He moaned, rubbing against Rig. The sound Rig gave was low, needy, broken and happy all at once. He took one last lick from Rig's mouth and then started moving his way down the long body. Rig wasn't hard yet, but he was getting there, filling, remembering how to need.

Dick spent some time with those little titties, relearning how they tasted, how they felt pebbling up under his tongue.

"Oh, fuck. I've missed y'all." Rig shuddered, shifting for him.

"Fuck, yes. We're not doing it again." Rock sounded emphatic and Dick nodded. Yeah. They couldn't do without Rig.

"No. Not again. Need." Rig took Rock's mouth, almost sobbing.

Dick's mouth slid over the skinny belly, a soft whimper leaving him at how much weight Rig had lost, ribs prominent along with hip bones. He got to Rig's cock and sucked it in, whimpering as he tasted

Rig for the first time in weeks. Rig's cry was rich, low, sweet and muffled by Rock. Perfect.

He sucked, head bobbing, nose burying in Rig's pubes on the down stroke. That long hand slid in his hair, petting him, holding him. He nuzzled against the touch and worked harder to draw Rig's pleasure up through his cock. It didn't take long, not long at all before Rig was shifting, shaking, rocking into his mouth.

"That's it," rumbled Rock. "Give it to him."

"Pretty." He heard the soft cry, the heat of Rig's spunk salty on his tongue. He swallowed it down greedily, moaning at the taste so long missed. Rig leaned into Rock, settling back with a moan.

Rock purred. "Gonna let me fuck you, Rabbit? While the kid takes your mouth?"

Dick whimpered, rubbing his cheek against Rig's prick. It was all that was missing to make it really real.

"Fuck, yes. I need y'all." Rig nodded, groaned.

He nodded and moved back up Rig's body, finding that mouth again, cock just as hard as anything at the thought of being sucked. Those grey eyes were already less haunted, more normal. Theirs. He gazed into them, telling Rig without words how much he cared, how much he loved. Rig nodded, tongue sliding alongside his, slow and sweet. Rock disappeared for a moment and then came back with a familiar tube, fingers disappearing behind Rig.

"Oh... my Blue..." Rig groaned, leaned towards him. "My Pretty."

"Yeah, yours."

Rock just purred, the sound deep and satisfying.

"Yeah." Rig smiled, tears dotting those long, white lashes.

He moaned, licking the salt from Rig's face. Rig started shifting, sliding, rubbing against him. He brought their mouths together again, licking and tasting, a deep, necessary thing being satisfied inside him. Rig's arms circled his shoulders, holding on, smiling against his lips.

"Love you," he breathed into Rig's mouth.

Rig nodded. "Yeah. Yeah, Pretty."

"Gonna take you now," murmured Rock.

"Want my cock, too?" he asked, rubbing against Rig's belly.

"Want both of you. Please." Rig moaned. "Need y'all."

He nodded, eager to take Rig's mouth, to feel those lips tight around him. They shifted, Rig settling on hands and knees, lips sliding down his belly. He moaned, meeting Rock's eyes, seeing his own need and passion echoed there. Rig whimpered as those lips dropped over his cock, taking him in deep. "Oh fuck. Fuck."

"Yeah, that's what we're doing, kid."

Rig's chuckle around his prick? Fucking magic. With a whimper he started to move, hips matching Rock's. Rig just took them in, took them both and loved them, brought them together. He met Rock's mouth over

Rig's back, the kiss hard, good, better than anything had been since they'd left Rig here. Rig's back was warm under his hands, mouth fiery, the three of them creating a circle. Whimpering, he moved faster, harder, balls drawing up as he got close. Rig kept pulling, sucking, demanding.

He cried out, hips snapping as he came, pouring himself into Rig. Rock was right with him, roar loud and good. Rig nuzzled against his belly, panting, eyes closed. He and Rock settled back onto the bed, putting Rig between them. His hand slid into Rig's, holding on.

Rig wrapped around them, holding on tight. "What do I have to do? For the funeral. What do I have to do?"

"Not a thing, Rig. Charlene had it all set up. Remember?"

"Oh. Yeah." Rig took a shuddering breath. "I need a nap."

Rock snorted. "You need to sleep until noon tomorrow and the kid and I are here to make sure that happens."

Dick nodded and cuddled close, holding on tight to Rig's hand.

"'kay." Rig nodded, settled right in, asleep almost before his head hit Rock's shoulder.

He met Rock's eyes over Rig's head, the big guy purring, looking more at ease than he had in days, weeks.

Dick let his own eyes close, let sleep have him now that they were all together again.

Chapter Thirty Four

They walked into the house, and fuck, Rock had never been so happy to get home, no matter how shut up and stuffy it seemed, the damned dogs not there to greet them. It had been a hell of a few days, Rig so fucking thin and not eating and sneaking smokes and drawn. He looked better now though than he had when they'd first gotten to the hospital. Fuck, his Rabbit had looked like a ghost and it had scared the crap out of him.

They were home now though and the no eating, no sleeping, only being half fucking alive crap was going to stop right now.

"You want to go over to Rick's for steaks or just order something in?" he asked as he set down their bags.

"I don't want to go out, Blue. I just got home." Rig looked around, took a deep breath.

He nodded. "I just wanted you to have the choice."

"There's a pot of stew in the freezer," Dick put in. " I can have it heated up and ready to serve in the time it would take to get something delivered."

"Whatever's easiest, Dick. Nothing sounds good right now." Rig headed out to the back, looking out at the ocean.

"Just fucking call for something so no one's stuck in the fucking kitchen or with dishes and then get your ass outside, this ghost shit is stopping."

"Hey, his Momma just died, Rock."

"Yeah, and he's killing himself right along with her -- he's got a fucking reason to live, two of them and we're going to remind him of that."

"Just don't growl and yell at him." Dick glared at him and went to the phone, picking up the flyers they kept there for food.

He went outside and stood behind Rig, wrapping himself around his Rabbit.

Rig hummed and leaned back into him, snuggled right in. "Hey, Blue Eyes. I been missing this."

He purred, head resting against Rig's. "Yeah, me too."

Rig's fingers stroked and petted his hands, his wrists, his Rabbit close and warm and relaxed, eyes on the water.

Dick joined them a moment later. "I've got subs on their way and a big salad. There's still beer in the fridge. It'll be a half hour."

The kid leaned against his and Rig's sides, arms coming around both of them. "This feels good. Right. It's nice to be home."

Rig nodded. "It is. I feel like I've been sleeping for weeks and just got to wake up."

Sleepwalking was more like it. Rock squeezed Rig tight, but kept his mouth shut. Dick nodded and turned Rig's face, taking a kiss. Growling, he pushed into it, tongue sweeping through both their mouths. Fuck it was good. Necessary. Like fucking breathing. Rig groaned, turning to cuddle into them, hand sliding around his waist, holding on. Yeah, that was fucking it. He left the kid and Rig to kiss, mouth finding that sweet spot on Rig's neck and working up a mark, loving it with his teeth and tongue and lips.

Rig laughed, the sound a little ragged, a little rough. "Oh, fuck. So good."

"Yeah, you better fucking believe it." He growled and pulled open Rig's shirt, mouth going for that little ring, the metal that meant his and Dick's and he tongued it.

"I do. Fuck, Blue. I believe it." Rig's fingers wrapped around his head, Dick holding Rig up.

He growled again, dropping to his knees, mouth dragging over Rig's skin. He left another mark on Rig's belly, realising how much of his tan Rig had lost. His fingers were impatient, strugging to undo Rig's belt, to open the blue jeans. Rig sucked in and he snorted. Like there wasn't room. He bit that too skinny belly and finally got the fucking zipper down along with Rig's tighty whities. And there was his Rabbit's scent, strong and male and all fucking his. He took Rig's cock into his mouth, sucking hard.

"Oh. Oh, fuck. Blue. I..." Rig's cry echoed before Dick's mouth muffled it, so fucking sweet.

He wrapped his hand around the base of Rig's prick, hand sliding as his mouth worked the top half. It didn't take any time at all, his Rabbit needing and eager, shooting into his lips. He swallowed down the bitter liquid and kept sucking a moment longer before placing a kiss on the tip of Rig's prick and standing again.

He grunted as his knees protested. He was getting too fucking old for this shit. Not the fucking and sucking and kissing, but the on his knees crap.

Rig's eyes went concerned, lips covering his in a long, slow kiss. "You've been missing your glucosamine haven't you? You need your vitamins, Blue."

Dick laughed as he groaned. "Oh man, it's good to be home."

Rig nodded. "It is. I was gone too long. When is Jay bringing the dogs back?"

"I suppose when I call him and tell him we're back."

"Tomorrow," suggested Dick. "He'll want to sit and talk and have a beer and tonight's just for us."

Rig nodded. "I don't want to visit."

"Fuck no. We're going to eat and then we're going to fuck in the shower. And then we're going to fuck in bed. And then we're going to sleep." And possibly not even in that fucking order.

"And then morning blowjobs and pancakes and fucking again." Rig nodded.

"Yeah, that sounds about right."

The doorbell rang and Dick grinned. "Just in time to start off the plan." The kid dropped a quick kiss on each of their mouths and took off to get the door.

He gave Rig a squeeze. "You good, Rabbit?"

"Not yet, but I'm heading there." Rig met his eyes. "I don't do real good on my own, Blue."

"I know. And it won't happen again. I'd rather lose the fucking business than you."

"How 'bout I just spend a few dozen months home with y'all?"

"How about the rest of your fucking life, Rabbit."

"Okay, you got a deal." He got a grin, one that actually reached those grey eyes. "Let's go eat, Blue."

"Yeah." He smiled back and looped his arm around Rig, guiding his Rabbit in.

Epilogue

He had been standing at the pantry, looking in when it hit him. He didn't have any Wolf brand chili, no pecans from the farm, none of Momma's lace cookies packed away careful in a box. None of it. None of Texas left. Or Momma. Or home.

It hit like a blow to the pit of his stomach and he walked into the front room, hands on his hips, damned near furious at he didn't know what.

"I want to move back home." Rig looked right at his men. "I don't have any good chili or those nuts I like."

"You already are fucking home," growled Rock, going back to his paper. Dick just looked at him, eyes concerned.

"I... I miss the farm and the kids and good chili that I didn't have to cook." He wanted to grab Rock's paper and tear it up. He wanted to get well-and-truly drunk. He wanted a cigarette. He wanted to talk to Momma. Just one more time.

Dick's eyes softened, his lover getting up and coming to him, wrapping long, warm arms around him. "Oh, Rig."

Rock sighed, folding the paper down carefully, setting it aside. Those bluer than blue eyes looked over at him. "You can't go home again, Rig." Rock's voice was soft. "It's not your home anymore. You live here. With us."

To his utter horror, his eyes began to fill and he backed away from Dick with a groan. God, he was a fucking basketcase, fixin' to fucking cry. Over goddamned chili. "I'm going for a drive. I'll be back."

"Come on, Rig -- don't go." Dick got hold of his hand and tugged him back to the couch, putting him between his men.

Rock's arm came around him with a grunt, clamping onto him. He stayed stiff for a minute, but he was caught -- they weren't going to let him go and he was tired and hurting and they loved him -- so he let himself relax, let them hold him.

"Tell us what's really wrong?" Dick asked softly.

"And don't give me any bullshit about chili -- I'm the only one who gets het up about crap like that," growled Rock.

"It's not bullshit. There's no good chili or Momma's lacy cookies or phone calls on Sunday. I've been gone so long that people are going to think I belong here and I've always thought leaving Texas was a temporary thing and now I'm getting fucking old and I'm happy here and it's not where I thought I'd be and..." He shook his head, blinking hard,. "I miss her. I know she's in a better place and I know it's for the best and I know she's with Daddy now and happy... I miss her."

Rock's mouth closed over his for a single quick, hard kiss and then his Blue pulled him in for a hug, just holding him.

Dick's fingers slid over his back, petting. "Of course you miss her, she's your Momma. There's no shame in that, Rig."

He shook his head, aching deep, letting the solid heat on either side of him ease him, hold him up.

"You just tell us what you need and it's yours," murmured Dick. Rock grunted an agreement.

"I don't suppose a fifth of tequila and a pack of cigarettes is the right answer?" He let himself grin against Rock's chest, let himself wrap his arms around Rock and hold on.

Rock snorted. "How about a fifth of marines and a pack of dogs?"

He chuckled. "I can live with that."

He rested his cheek against Rock's chest, eyes closing, enjoying Dick's warmth behind him. Rock rumbled, chest vibrating beneath his ear. The sound eased him and he just curled in, dozing, happy. Home.

When he woke up he was stretched out on the sofa with Rock and there was hot chocolate on the table next to two old photo albums and a plate of brownies. Dick gave him a soft smile. "I thought maybe we could go through the photo albums when you were done napping."

He blinked, stomach rumbling at the good smells. "Smell fabulous. 'd I sleep long?" Rig settled himself, sitting up and yawning, feeling a little more settled in his soul.

"Not long -- the brownies are only just out of the oven."

Rock grunted and stopped snoring, blue eyes blinking. "Do I smell chocolate?"

He chuckled, grinning over at Dick. "Yep. Kid's spoiling us again. Guess we'll have to keep him."

Dick smiled at him and came over to the couch, pushing at Rock until his Blue sat up and he was sitting between them again.

"Have a brownie, Rock." Dick shoved one into Rock's mouth as his Blue opened up to complain.

"Nicely done." Rig nodded and opened his mouth. "My turn."

Laughing, Dick gave him a soft kiss first and then fed him a still-warm brownie.

He chewed, moaning as the sweet dissolved for him. "Oh... Good. Damn. Thanks Pretty. I'm sorry about earlier."

"Hey that's what we're here for, yeah?" Dick licked at the corner of his mouth and then nudged him. "Show me the pictures, Rig. Tell me the stories."

"Yeah? You sure?" He reached for the book as Dick nodded. "This? This here's Momma's sister, Kristina. She robbed a bank back in the fifties, her husband was shot to death right there in front of her..."

Rock's arm slid around his belly and the brownies were good and they laughed and chattered and maybe cried a little until it was time for the news, the sun setting on them.

On him and his men and their home.

End

Breinigsville, PA USA
31 May 2010
238970BV00001B/108/A

9 781933 389417